Renée

THE ARRANGEMENTS OF LOVE

Timeri N. Murari has written novels, non-fiction, as well as screenplays and stage plays. His film, *The Square Circle*, made *Time* magazine's top ten best films. He later adapted it for the stage and directed it at the Leicester Haymarket Theatre. His novels include the international best-seller *Taj* (reissued by Penguin India in 2003) and *Steps from Paradise*. His new non-fiction work, *My Temporary Son*, will be published by Penguin India.

After many years away Timeri N. Murari returned to live in India. Visit the author at http://www.timerimurari.com

Praise for *Taj*

'An exotic, passionate novel, sensual and violent by turns, always compelling.'

—*The Guardian*

'Only a masterly historical novelist like Timeri Murari could skate so teasingly near the lip of a volcano. The structure of this novel is as fascinating as the building it describes.'

—Bill Aitken, *Sunday Observer*

'An expertly crafted novel with richly textured details, especially of violence and eroticism.'

—*The Telegraph*

'A book of powerful simplicity.'

—*Gloucestershire Echo*

'One can read into the symbolic undertones, and find this a complex and disturbing novel.'

—*Asia Magazine*

Also by the same author

Fiction

The Marriage
The Oblivion Tapes
Lovers Are Not People
Field of Honour
The Shooter
Taj
The Imperial Agent
The Last Victory
Enduring Affairs
Steps from Paradise

Non-fiction

The New Savages: Children of the Liverpool Streets
Goin' Home: A Black Family Returns South

Plays

The Square Circle
Chicanery
Lovers Are Not People
Hey, Hero
Killing Time

Films

The Square Circle
The Only Thing

timeri n. murari

the arrangements of love

PENGUIN BOOKS

PENGUIN BOOKS
Published by the Penguin Group
Penguin Books India Pvt. Ltd, 11 Community Centre, Panchsheel Park, New Delhi 110 017, India
Penguin Group (USA) Inc., 375 Hudson Street, New York, New York 10014, USA
Penguin Group (Canada), 90 Eglinton Avenue East, Suite 700, Toronto, Ontario, M4P 2Y3, Canada (a division of Pearson Penguin Canada Inc.)
Penguin Books Ltd, 80 Strand, London WC2R 0RL, England
Penguin Ireland, 25 St Stephen's Green, Dublin 2, Ireland (a division of Penguin Books Ltd)
Penguin Group (Australia), 250 Camberwell Road, Camberwell, Victoria 3124, Australia (a division of Pearson Australia Group Pty Ltd)
Penguin Group (NZ), 67 Apollo Drive, Rosedale, North Shore 0632, New Zealand (a division of Pearson New Zealand Ltd)
Penguin Group (South Africa) (Pty) Ltd, 24 Sturdee Avenue, Rosebank, Johannesburg 2196, South Africa

Penguin Books Ltd, Registered Offices: 80 Strand, London WC2R 0RL, England

First published by Penguin Books India 2004

10 9 8 7 6 5 4 3 2

ISBN 9780143031499

This is a work of fiction. Names, characters, places and incidents are either the product of the author's imagination or are used fictitiously, and any resemblance to actual persons, living or dead, events or locales is entirely coincidental.

Typeset in Perpetua by InoSoft Systems, Noida
Printed at Repro India Ltd., Navi Mumbai

For my good and dear friends
Chrissie and Roger,
who have always been my safe harbour

acknowledgements

I must thank David, Ravi and Poulomi for all their help, hard work and encouragement in bringing out this novel, with the usual rider that all mistakes are entirely my own.

I would also like to thank my friend Bill Shapter for his belief in the story.

susie/sushima

I do love America. You know that. When I fell in love with your father and stepped foot on American soil, I was doubly enchanted with love. No woman could have been as fortunate as I was. I love it that everyone calls me Susie, not Sue-shee-maa. Susie is so much more me. America dissolves our original identities. Mohan becomes Mike, Ashok becomes Ash, Bharati, Barbara. We're freed from the albatross of our past. It's because I'm an American that I don't wear ethnic clothes, as you want me to. Yes, yes, I see those exotic Indian women hurrying along the streets in their saris but that's not me any more. I don't know why you can't understand that. I'm not ethnic, as you like to keep saying, I'm an American. I would prefer wearing Donna Karan or jeans to a sari. It typecasts me, the sari, I mean, while even a pair of jeans lends me an air of mystery and people have to ask where I'm from and I tell them, 'Why, New York, of course.' That always shuts them up.

That's why I'm telling you darling, you won't like India at all. Not one bit. You'll hate it. Why? Because you're American, like me, and you're always so fastidious. India certainly is not that, not in the least. It can be a very deceitful place, and most confusing too. You have absolutely no idea how miserably hot it can get there. You won't just be blackened, you'll be burned to a crisp. Yes, like the burnt offerings I sometimes make for your dinner, if you have to joke about my opinion. I'm only telling you this for your own sake. If you love me—and you do, I know it—you won't even think of going there. Put them out of your mind, for my sake darling. There's nothing there for you.

I just don't know where you got your persistence. Certainly not from me. I was never persistent; I've always been carried along by the currents of my destiny. I used to call it karma when you were younger but now everyone's using that word—it's become fashionable in New York, like yoga and gurus—so I prefer destiny.

There's little I can tell you about Madras. It's been so many, many years since I left that I can't remember much about the city. It had wide streets and narrow streets. No, certainly not anything as organized as Manhattan. They ran higgledy-piggledy. Stop laughing. Isn't that an American expression? I'm sure it is . . . Then what would you call something disorganized? 'Outasight'? Are you sure? It means something unpleasant? I must write that down immediately. Well, the city's 'outasight' then, nothing running in a straight line in any direction. No, that's a lie. Where I was born and grew up, the streets ran in straight lines, east-west, north-south. Oh, all right, if you insist, like Manhattan, but that was only a tiny part of the city. It was called Georgetown, after one British king or another. I can never remember the numbers after their names. I prefer the American way—George Junior. And the streets were always so crowded with everything that you had to edge down them sideways because there was never enough room to walk properly. I think that's where I learned to dance so well: hopping over excrement, dodging cows and rickshaws, gliding past carts, jumping over heaps of garbage. Yes, I did learn some of its history when I was in school. It was lust that had conceived Madras, so now you know how that city was born. An East India Company employee, Francis Day, a scoundrel from all accounts, was having an affair with a Portuguese woman in San Thome colony. For his own convenience he decided that this spot on the Coromandel shore was ideal for his company's trading post, and so the city was begot from the loins of a foreign man and a foreign woman. Well, that's about all I can remember because I was so embarrassed when I learned how it all came about.

It doesn't say anything about your going to India in your horoscope. One minute, I'll get it and read it out. See if you find one line which says you'll be going there. I know I've read it out to you before but you always stop up your ears. There's nothing Indian about believing in horoscopes, so don't lay that trip on me. There are tarot card readers, horoscope casters, coffee grind readers, tea leaf readers here too, so India doesn't have a monopoly on such things. Nearly all my friends read their horoscopes in magazines and newspapers; they're not all Indians. I believe in pre-destination and that our life is written on our foreheads and in the stars. That's why I was watching the clock in the delivery room of the hospital so I would know the exact time you were born. Yes—don't keep laughing—down to the second. Now you're making fun of me. How can anyone tell the future from someone's garbage? Garbage is yesterday and it only records that person's past, especially what he's been eating and drinking. See, I had your horoscope cast when a purohit was visiting the Queen's temple two months after you were born. I used to read it to you when you were a baby so that it would subconsciously inspire you to greatness. I hoped the predictions of success and good fortune in your horoscope would guide your footsteps through life and you would sidestep the mines of misfortune. The purohit predicted all that. If only you'd sit down and listen to it or else read it, just for my sake, it could inspire you. Well, I went to the purohit only because I heard he was very good. I could have gone to Simon Lucas on Bleecker Street, who also casts horoscopes and reads palms, but I believe he's a bit of a fake. Besides, it's the angle of the moon that's important.

nicky/nikhil

My many names merely reveal the ambiguous nature of my soul. I am neither one—Nick, Nicky—nor the other. I hover in between, uncertain of who I am. Gabriel Garcia Marquez wrote that he always chose the name of a character according to the nature of the person. What would he make of me and my nature? Schizophrenic?

My mom drove me nuts. I love her, but she still drove me nuts. All mothers drive their kids nuts at some stage in their lives. My pals in school thought the same way about their moms. Our fathers didn't drive us nuts, mostly because we never saw them long enough. Mornings, evenings and little league was the most we saw of them. I should be thankful for that. What drove me nuts about Mom, more than anything else, was that she refused to acknowledge her past. For her, it didn't exist, it had vanished into the ether. She never wore a sari, though I would've loved to see her in one. I think she'd look real cool. When I saw Indian women on the streets in their saris I'd always turn to look, imagining my mom in one. When I was eight or nine, I caught the Lex subway south to 23rd Street. Around there, for a few blocks east and west of 23rd, it's ethnic Indian. There are cafeteria type places where you get all kinds of curries and Indian candies. We never ate Indian food at home because my mom said it would smell out the apartment. I wandered around for an hour—into Prasad's eat-and-takeaway which also sold candies of many colours, Govind's Groceries, which like the Uptown Korean all-night stores sold fresh vegetables but was also musty with the smell of cardamom, pepper, cloves, ginger, garlic and pickles that tickled my nostrils and made me dream that this was how India smelt in the streets and in the villages, and finally into Lalchand's sari emporium. In each store they spoke a soothing musical language and when I asked which one, they gave me different answers—Gujarati, Marathi, Punjabi, Hindi, Tamil, Bengali—contradicting each other. My billfold was bulging with cash, all of eighty dollars of saved pocket money. I was going to buy Mom a sari. I had spent weeks weighing up a sari against Nintendo games, CDs, software I could do with, but my yearning to see her in a sari outweighed my own selfish needs. In Lalchand's sari emporium I found a pale, seductive, yellow sari, my mom's favourite colour, patterned with green silk mangoes and bordered green and gold. It cost me the whole eighty dollars. I didn't want to seem a cheapskate for my mom's present. I gift-wrapped it and presented it to her on her birthday. She blushed and gushed and enveloped me in warm smothering kisses, then splashed it out across her bed. The dull pastel-shaded bedroom shrank away from the bold colours, and we both agreed she'd look wonderful in it. My mom was so exotically beautiful that no one could mistake her for an Anglo-Saxon. Her eyes were mesmeric like Saturn's rings and cut men off at their knees. I waited to see her in my gift, but as the days and months passed I realized I never would. It remained in her closet, gift-wrapped, just as it had been when I gave it to her. It was only years later that I discovered she did own a sari, hidden away in an old suitcase.

The man my mom called my father wasn't really my father. He was my stepfather. Gary, a tall, glossy man snipped out of a Vogue advertisement, had a nose for sin, especially the sin of narcotic possession. His pulpit was the television screen where, as an interlocutor of some reputation, he railed against drug abuse, among many other things, with the same zeal that nineteenth-century preachers displayed against masturbation. I never watched his television show and never called him dad, pop, father, only Gary. He always confirmed her tale on how they had met in Bombay and embellished it with a sun setting in the background, lighting up her face with an angel's glow, the colour of her sari, the flowers in her hair. He probably remembered the colour of her toenails too, but I never asked.

My father died in a car smash, my mom told me when I was old enough to notice the difference between her and the man she married. He was driving to Bangalore when a truck hit him head-on, wiping him off the earth. Period. I missed him although we had never met. I didn't even know what he looked like. Somewhere between Bombay, Brooklyn, SoHo and the Upper East Side, their upwardly mobile trajectory, she had lost a whole album of photographs of back home. Her physical description of him was vague. Tall, a full head of hair and ferocious eyes was the best she could do for me. And no, she hadn't fallen in love with him; it had been an arranged marriage and there hadn't been any time for love to blossom between them. 'Blossom' was her vocabulary, not mine. The moment he died she took off for America like a bat out of hell. I wish she'd stayed there.

So, instead of living in that funky Georgetown place where you moved sideways through the streets and learned to dance, I was raised on the Upper East Side in a pure white ghetto of a co-op on 73rd Street between Lex and Park. I felt like a cockroach that had fallen into a milk carton. In the elevator, the perfumed women—

and if that isn't air pollution tell me what is—in their Donna Karans, Guccis, Armanis would peer down at me with my school backpack and wonder what the super's child was doing riding in their elevator. Sometimes I would say 'Buenos Dias, senora y senoritas' and jabber away in Spanish although I didn't know another fucking word. They would give me space then so I wouldn't contaminate the air they breathed. The men, all in dark suits in the fall and winter, off-whites during summers, wouldn't even notice me among the forest of briefcases.

In the summers the Hampton's plague hit the building from the first floor up to the penthouse where the Lunds lived in their eighteen rooms. I had visited them only once. It was the equivalent of heaven for every aspirant in the co-op. My best friend in school, Mike Holding, was the first to lose his cherry to sixteen-year-old Linda Lund, a truly beautiful American princess with long blonde hair and innocent blue eyes, after he grabbed her expensive ass in the elevator one day. Mike, who was built along Nordic lines—tall, blond and a wide grin—told me it was like sinking his dick into an oil well, and we both understood what he meant as the Lunds had a whole bunch of stock, a billion dollars I'd heard, in Texaco, Gulf Oil, Exxon, Hess. The next day, with Mike's tuition, I timed my grab too and Linda obligingly led me up to the penthouse, through the expensive maze of rooms and corridors, and took my cherry in a bedroom overlooking Manhattan out of a south-facing window on the thirtieth floor on a clear winter's day. We lived on the third floor, burrowing our way like moles through perpetual ConEd light. I was the first, and probably the last, dark-skinned person Linda laid, more as an experiment than out of sexual pleasure. Thankfully, as Gary actually worked for a living and wasn't living off GE, GM, GF stockholdings, we only spent a week or two in the Hampton's. It was as exciting as moving from a highrise co-op to a horizontal co-op with exactly the same neighbours. The only relief was that Mike, who lived on the fifth floor, was also exiled to the Hampton's. Both of us agreed it was just a wealthy Gulag and a hundred times more boring than the ones in Russia. At least the Gulags produced Solzhenitsyn. Who did the Hampton's ever produce?

susie/sushima

My darling boy, you have absolutely no idea how horrible it is to be a widow in India. I mean, I would have had to shave my head, dress all in white—yes, like an angel but not to lead an angelic life—not wear any jewellery and mope around the house for the rest of my life. It's truly worse than death itself and I'm not surprised that in the old days the widows threw themselves on their husband's pyres. No, we didn't do that in the south so much; it was more a north Indian habit. They do have pretty bad habits, I must say.

I was lucky to have met Gary and fallen in love. I was visiting my cousin in Bombay; they call it Mumbai now, god-alone-knows-why. I mean, what would happen if New York suddenly became Yorkville or Newsville, just on a whim? I'm certain it's a whim, just to confuse everyone. And my city's called Chennai, don't ask me why. I don't remember which cousin in Bombay, it was so long ago. Anyway, it's not important. Your father (and I wish to god you'd call him that and not Gary, he feels it's disrespectful) was introduced to me while we were having dinner at the Taj Hotel. It's a magnificent hotel. It's probably been demolished by now. He was a friend of a friend and joined us for dinner. At that time he was working for

Newsweek and was such a dashing chap. Okay, guy, man. I think he was doing an article on Indian women and wanted to interview me. So that's how we met. And when I was widowed, he heard about that and flew down from Delhi to console me. I learned later he was coming down anyway on an assignment but at that time I was flattered to think he'd flown a thousand-odd miles just to see me. As he couldn't call at our house, we would meet in the tea room of the Connemara Hotel. It was a lovely old British hotel. It looked like a stale wedding cake, but it was *the* place to be seen in and I doubted any one of my relatives would have set foot in it. I knew my parents would never ever, ever allow me to marry this tall, handsome white American and so we flew away to New York without telling a soul. They never forgave me, that's why I'm not in touch.

nicky/nikhil

It was when I saw the beggar girl at the traffic light on Mount Road, next to a building called Spencer's Plaza, that I decided to unload the emotional baggage of my past.

I was in India, Madras/Chennai to be precise, with my heart full of hope and trepidation. The sun had slammed me as I surfaced from the cool caress of light in the plane and the arrival hall. This wasn't the tempered sun of New York on a summer's day or the warm sun of Florida where Americans baked and browned on the beaches, turning into a paler shade of my colour. This was the Indian sun, swaggering and arrogant, full of itself, hurling down its tremendous heat and light. You'll get sunburned, and then you'll get sunstroke, Mom had said. I believed this sun could do such things; there was no forgiveness in its malevolence. The sky wasn't the eggshell blue of the East Coast summer, it was white with heat.

If I wanted to be immersed in the people, the baptism began the moment I stepped out into the still, clammy soup of instant sweat. They waited in rank upon rank of uniform dark faces, glistening black hair, splashes of bright saris, white shirts, odours of coconut oil and sweat, quietly lapping at the portals of the airport, as if pressing to invade. They worried and panicked me. What did they want? What were they waiting for? Would they harm me? This was unlike any experience I'd had before. There were no milling crowds outside JFK, La Guardia, Logan, Heathrow, just neatly lined cabs waiting to whisk you away. I wanted to retreat, to change my mind. I should have listened to Mom and not come. What would I find here? Already, I was pessimistic about discovering anything of the past in such madness. Yes, I could melt into them, vanish without a trace, no one could pick me out from this sea of people. My brown would blend indistinguishably into theirs. I wouldn't be the lone brown in a classroom, on a baseball field or on a train. Since 9/11, the lone brown on a plane was being eyed suspiciously by American whites, my fellow citizens, who sidled away while security raked me and my baggage through minute inspection. I had existed always with a secret fear of rejection. Yet, I wanted to distance myself from the people I saw now and retain this difference. Could they separate me out as a foreigner? How would they? They were a small people; I was a head taller than most, looking beyond them to the taxi rank.

The taxi I approached was a square tank on wheels, with a chipped and peeling yellow roof and an equally chipped and peeling black body. Like small pox, rust speckled the lower portions of the bodywork. The driver was pleased to see me, greeting me like a long-lost companion, and bundled the case into the dusty boot. He wore a crisply ironed khaki shirt and a crumpled white dhoti. He opened the door, not with a flourish, but carefully, as though the door would fall off otherwise. He closed it gently after me. I didn't notice the black idol on the dashboard until the driver started the car. The six-inch high idol lit up in delight, tiny green and red bulbs flashed mesmerizingly up and down its outline. I leaned forward to identify the deity, the lights winking their welcome. The idol wore a rectangular crown that covered half its face like the visor of a helmet. 'That's Venketeswara.'

'Lord Balaji,' the driver contradicted and then, to confound, added, 'yes, yes, Lord Venketeswara too. Balaji from Tirupati. I can take you to Tirupati if you wish for his darshan.' A quick glance back and a calculation. 'Only ten thousand rupees.'

'Not Tirupati yet.' I was pleased. I'd passed a test with this recognition of one of Vishnu's avatars. There were a million gods, each with many names and, no doubt, I'd flunk any recognition test for the rest of them. I took out my yellow pad and showed the address to the driver, hoping he also read English.

'One thousand rupees,' the driver understood enough English. 'Before.'

In my hurry I'd forgotten to change my dollars. I remembered the rupee's worth however and countered, 'Fifteen dollars.'

'Okay. In dollars.'

He grabbed the money as the taxi, reluctant as a tired bullock, moved out of the airport onto the main road. The driver's avatar however was of a medieval knight, jousting with the dragons and beasts on the highway, daring them to knock him off his ancient charger.

'Watch that truck . . . watch that scooter . . . oh god . . . You missed that bus by your paint's breadth,' my screams only delighted the knight-driver.

'God will look after us.' He took both hands off the wheel to get his blessings from Lord Balaji, who continued to wink cheerfully.

'Steer with both hands, for god's sake, I want to remain alive.'

I sank down in my seat and a statistic flashed before my eyes. I'd read that the daily road fatalities in India equalled a Boeing 747 crashing with a full planeload of passengers. I wondered who'd made that comparison. I prayed that I wouldn't end up as an air crash statistic on this Indian road after having flown thousands of miles to get here. Once the taxi circled the roundabout with someone's statue standing aloof in the centre, it slowed, jostling for space with fuming buses, three wheelers buzzing like yellow bees in-between lanes, scooters, motorcycles, cars, bullock carts and lorries. Although I could scarcely breathe in the diesel-stained air, I could now relax and look around. The main road edged slowly past an overbridge, potted with holes, and taller buildings that inspired nothing in me. This wasn't the city I had imagined from my mom's vague descriptions. A large village, she had said with barely concealed disdain. I always thought that as her plane had left India twenty-seven years and four months ago, she had snipped off the umbilical cord of memory. I had imagined it falling away, spilling out grandparents, parents, uncles, aunts, sisters, brothers, cousins, friends, her whole history smashing onto the hard earth, leaving no trace of her. Although she had told me little about the city, apart from Georgetown, I had accumulated its topography and history off the web. I had hoped to see the old colonial buildings of Mom's past, gracious colonnades, wide verandas and sprawling gardens. But that's if they had existed at all, since, like a python, the city crushed in on the road leaving no room for its past, leaving no room even for sidewalks.

'Mount Road?' I asked the driver to confirm my recognition again.

'Anna Salai,' the driver deliberately contradicted again, then nodded vigorously. 'Mount Road.'

'Which?'

'Anna Salai, Mount Road. Same.'

I wanted to ask how a road could have two names but then stopped. If a deity had hundreds, why not a road? It only further confirmed Mom's prediction.

I searched for signposts to Georgetown. The city was bilingual, the rare signboards in Tamil and English pointed to Parrys, Marina, Nungumbakkam. *Georgetown* was also the secret Mom had hidden away. I'd discovered the book by chance. I had never told her about my discovery. But there was no signpost to Georgetown. This wasn't a city for a lost stranger. The web hadn't revealed the noise, the chaos, the crush of people, even Grand Central at rush hour couldn't match this human density. Splinters of America and Japan had embedded themselves on the passing billboards—Ford, Coke, Pepsi, Honda, Mitsubishi, GM. Europe, I had found, had been culturally colonized by America. It was creeping in here, an insidious fungus taking over the world. The billboards brooded over sidewalk temples, small and seemingly insignificant mantras to ward off any further invasion but they were puny against the might of the giant billboards which were not yet as seductive as the nightly dazzle of Times Square. The city's breath suffocated me. I had an American's sensitivity to odours—gas, diesel, bad breath, armpits, foot sweat, cigarette smoke, toilets. America was sweetly perfumed; even the magazines seduced my nostrils as gently as a woman's scented breath.

Just before 'Gemini Flyover', clustered with billboards, and the Mercedes Benz showroom at a corner, the taxi turned towards Nungumbakkam. I checked the map; I wasn't yet being taken for a ride. We were on a narrow side street which then turned onto a busy road. I took pride in knowing a city before I arrived, the street map printed off the web. Mom was to blame for this caution in my character—she could get lost between Madison and 53rd Street and 63rd Street and Lexington. She lacked any sense of direction, heading south when she should be north-bound, east instead of west. She drove me, and cab drivers, crazy. If it hadn't been for Gary she would never have found her way to America.

When the cab driver pulled up for a red light I noticed the girl urchin, holding a grubby rag, pressing her face against the darkened windows of the cars, mouthing her need for money. The windows were hermetically sealed from her intrusion into the air-conditioned chill of the cars.

I saw her glance towards my taxi, the window half-open and inviting. She moved towards it, flicking her rag, cheery and cheeky, bold as a courtesan dancing for money. Her dress hung like a shroud on her slim body. It had once been a bright red, with gold thread embroidery, but had now faded to a dull pink. Her hair was urchin-short, a fringe on her forehead, her large eyes wiser than mine. I figured she had no intention of cleaning cars as she carried the dirtiest rag possible with which to wipe the windscreens of these sparkling cars. She had guessed the drivers would pay her to keep that rag off their windows.

I patted my pockets, the quarters, nickels and dimes worthless to her. Her small, thin hand, with a red plastic bangle around the wrist, thrust triumphantly through the window. She was too small to see me but there was confident hope in her voice.

'Money, sar, money, sar . . .' Since this was a taxi, she assumed I was a tourist, a stranger in her city.

I wished I had rupees and not ten- and twenty-dollar bills. The sun's glitter on my wedding band caught my eye. It seemed an omen at the right moment. The ring was just fourteen carat gold. I'd bought it at a Macy's Valentine's Day sale. It wouldn't fetch much in a pawnshop. It had been warm and comforting once, now it seemed to constrict and tighten.

I tugged at it, even as the taxi began to move.

'Wait . . . wait.' I was desperate now to rid myself of my marital past. Cars honked deafeningly at the impatient taxi. I couldn't hold it still for long; it edged along, with the girl moving alongside, sensing this afternoon would be lucky for her. The ring came free, leaving a pale indentation on my finger. I held it for a moment, like an unlucky coin, then freed myself by letting it drop into her open palm. I spoke the magic words: 'Goodbye Renee', knowing I should have cleansed my heart long ago. The urchin's fist closed on the memory, her hand withdrew. I looked back as she accelerated away amid the fumes, a soiled jewel pressed against the central divide in the traffic's slipstream staring at another in her palm.

The battered taxi pulled up to the curb with its dying breath. It nudged past an indifferent cow, crowding out cyclists and motorbikes in its determination to reach the safe harbour. The driver was proud he'd deciphered the address correctly and, even as he slowed, pointed to the number above the doorway of the old building on Khadar Nawaz Khan Road. Except, there were two numbers.

'Old number, new number,' he said as an inadequate explanation.

The building had the pretence of looking Indo-Saracenic, misplaced in this city a thousand miles from the old Mughal empire but still possessing a faded beauty. The walls were ochre, the door was set in an ornate arch and the long balcony was railed with patterned brickwork. It lacked minarets but hinted at something Muslim in its stature. Incongruously beside it, all plate glass and painted a bright green, was an elegant restaurant, Fellini's.

I stood by the driver's door, gestured, and said, 'Wait.'

Even as I spoke, I heard the rear door slam. The taxi shuddered from the impact and a woman screamed, 'Sekrum, poh, poh.'

The driver, startled by the woman's urgency, stepped on the gas and the taxi lurched out into the traffic, barely missing a lorry crammed with men waving political flags.

'Shit,' I yelled and ran after the taxi, 'my suitcase.' But the taxi accelerated away as the traffic cleared a gap for it to squeeze through. I chased it for fifty yards, the years of tennis and jogging in Riverside Park gave me the stamina, but the foul air stopped me from going all the way.

My lungs hurt and when I caught my breath I screamed, 'Fuck.'

As if Brahma had lowered the boom, there was a second of astonished silence as buses, cars, cyclists, bullock carts, pedestrians, faltered and looked for the blasphemer. Who cared a shit? My suitcase was gone, swallowed up in the maelstrom of vehicles. I'd never see it again. Mom would have chuckled: that's what I mean by karma. You have freedom of choice until a taxi steals your suitcase with all your clean underwear in it. Not that she had ever paid much attention to my laundry requirements. She was a woman of such delightful eccentricity that the mundane needs of others, including her son, eluded her. I removed my jacket—I was soaked, as if I'd plunged into a pool—and trudged back to the address. I felt angry, exhausted and frustrated. I hadn't expected my taxi to be stolen in this city. It happened often in NYC where people would kill for a cab on a rainy night.

I checked the numbers again. Only god knew if I was at the right address and why there had to be two numbers on one doorway. It was a couple of degrees cooler inside and it took a moment for my eyes to adjust to the gloom. There was a directory board on the wall. I was at the right address. To my left was a wooden staircase and I banged my way up, still raging at the theft; it wasn't my underwear that concerned me but the manuscript tucked away in the folds. I looked up to see a woman, barefoot, descending, her toes winking with silver rings. I wasn't in the mood to give way and saw her toes curl at the heavy stamp of my shoes. She stopped and edged to a side, allowing me to pass, saving her bare feet from being crushed. I was being the rude, impatient, angry American, and I checked myself, turning to apologize but she had slipped out into the street, leaving me niggled with guilt.

There were three tiny shops on the landing, all with similar names, as if the owners had run out of imagination: Xcellent Watch Co., Xcellent Tailoring Co., Xcellent Typing Co. Three people worked industriously at their small trade. The watchmaker looked like a Cyclops, with the eyepiece peering up at me, and a pencil-thin moustache on his upper lip; the tailor, smaller and slim, already balding, stared through a flounce of fabric; the woman with sulky eyes and a pout continued to type while looking at me.

I couldn't help myself. 'Thieves,' I said out aloud, silently weeping for my lost manuscript and spewing my outrage. They barely flinched, maybe not even understanding the word. As I started up the next flight, my footsteps were lighter as if I'd spent my weight in the expletive.

I paused at the door on the next landing, suffused with guilt at my rudeness towards innocent people. I had meant to be polite, courteous, kind and understanding. Guilt was such an American trip; it ruined so many lives and made shrinks rich. I forgave myself instantly and promised I'd not lose my temper ever again. I read the lettering on the door, feeling furtive, as if about to enter a brothel. I had never stepped into a private detective's office; I'd never even been in a police precinct. The Continental Op Detective Agency boasted in bold letters beneath its name: Lovers Located, Deceit Discovered, Doubtful Deaths, Cheaters Caught, Suspects Shadowed, Lost and Found.

I read it again, as a Haiku poem.

Lovers Located
Deceit Discovered
Doubtful Deaths
Cheaters Caught
Suspects Shadowed
Lost and Found

Although Mom would have loved such a list of chicanery from India, the gloomy hallway didn't fill me with much hope. I was reminded of a late late night movie, set in the forties, with a Bogart beyond the door.

The receptionist, a young though motherly looking woman, in a pink salwar kameez disproved me by reading a glossy *Cosmopolitan* magazine. The reception was brightly lit, with pale blue, soothing walls and armchairs for its clients. A fish tank bubbled cheerfully in a corner, watched by five men and two women waiting to see the detective with a sense of dread as though he were their dentist.

The receptionist ignored me until I spoke. I couldn't quite keep the snap out my voice; after all, I'd flown ten thousand miles to keep this appointment. 'Mr Balraj. I called from New York and made the appointment.'

She glanced up and reluctantly stopped reading 'Ten tips on how to be good in bed' to pick up a ledger.

'Your good name?' She had a surprisingly deep voice.

'Nicky Figgis.'

She checked, and looked up with disapproval. 'Your appointment was for 2.30 pee. m.'

'My flight was late, I haven't even checked into my hotel.'

She chose a phone and daintily picked on a button. I barely heard her whisper but when she finished her call, she said, 'Please wait,' and returned to her ten tips.

A fan wound slowly overhead, cooling nothing. I was soaked, my shirt sticking uncomfortably to my chest and back. I stood under the fan, flapping my arms in the hope I'd dry before the meeting. Mom had mentioned heat but not sweat, she'd probably forgotten that too. The others returned to contemplating the fish tank. They had stirred at my accent but had now lost interest.

'You wouldn't have a cold beer?' I turned to the receptionist, deliberately hopeful, although I felt I was in a kosher restaurant asking for a pork sausage. I would've settled for cold water but there was no water cooler in sight. Not that I would've drunk the water.

She looked up with a steady gaze, assessing me. Was I teasing her? I guess I was, it passed the time. Quite deliberately, she marked her page and put down the magazine, not allowing me to escape her stare. She opened a drawer, searched for something, and brought out keys. Only now did she let me off, as she turned towards the cupboard behind her. It was a good piece of wood, well polished and cared for. I expected her to bring out a file. Instead, when it opened, I saw it contained a small refrigerator. The refrigerator too was locked and she took her time unlocking it. I edged away from the fan towards her, looking back at the others. They didn't appear surprised to see a refrigerator locked in a wooden cupboard and weren't paying any attention. Goddamn, deception lurked always in ambush. I would have to learn to look beneath the surface, expect the unexpected. The refrigerator door swung open and from a stack of cans, Coke, Pepsi, Fanta, she extracted a cold Heineken.

I laughed with delight and then couldn't help it. 'You wouldn't have a Bud would you?' Not that I drank Bud, I preferred Rolling Rock.

The Heineken was returned to the refrigerator, the door began to close.

'Hey, I was kidding, just kidding. I'll take it.'

She shut and locked the refrigerator, then shut and locked the cupboard, before turning back to me and placing the cold, frosted can on her desk.

'One hundred and eighty rupees,' she said, allowing it to perspire temptingly onto the blotter.

I felt embarrassed. Like a good poker player she'd called my bluff and wanted to see my hand. My mouth was so dry I couldn't even salivate over the can.

'I have dollars only.'

She held out her hand. I mentally calculated the exchange rate and took out a five-dollar bill. She took it, opened her purse and returned the correct change in rupees. Only now, when the transaction was completed, did she hand me the beer. It froze my hand.

'Thanks. Excuse me ma'am, could you tell me why your door has two numbers?'

'Old number, new number,' was as clear as she could make it.

She returned to her magazine, hunched over, now ticking the little boxes and checking the points she had scored. I popped the can. The beer slid down my throat, sweet as honey, burning with the chill. I hadn't heard the intercom or even seen her move but she suddenly announced, 'The detective will see you now.' I figured she must be telepathic too.

The door she'd indicated with the slight inclination of her head had 'Detective M.K. Balraj, Deputy Comm. of Police, Crime Branch (Retd.)' painted on the door in a Cyrillic flourish. I entered what seemed at first a small cave. Cold air embraced me, drying my shirt in seconds. I was grateful for the air conditioner, and then worried I'd catch a cold, or worse, pneumonia. This was as bad as New York in summer.

The only light in the room was an anglepoise lamp, slanted over a desk at the far end. It took a moment or two for my eyes to adjust and catch the movement behind the desk. The person was distinctly female, a telephone clamped to her ear. She half rose, smiled and jangled an arm of bangles at me, inviting me to sit. The door had clearly committed me to meet Detective M.K. Balraj, male.

'Where's Mr Balraj?' I tried to keep the surprise out of my voice, but it slipped through. I had been deceived yet again. I wanted male expertise, not a flounce of bangles.

She murmured 'unavailable' and returned to her conversation, speaking swiftly in Tamil, I think. I stretched and openly surveyed the room. It wasn't large but warmer, the walls were terracotta, relieved by modern art—bold and distinct slashes of yellows, greens, red and beautifully composed. The artist had even used the blinds as canvas. One had the impressionistic view of a city skyline, the other an impressionistic animal on prowl—a big cat (a leopard, a tiger?) quickly, briefly sketched in red. The desk was an antique, teak or mahogany with carved legs. Apart from the two phones and a couple of files, there was a silver frame turned towards her, draped with a short strand of fresh, white flowers, no doubt a family photograph. The flowers released a subtle perfume into the chilled air. A circular pipe rack, holding five pipes of different shapes, stood precisely beside the silver frame. Behind the woman was a four-foot-high Ganesha with a faded red body, giving it a century-old air. Reluctantly I admitted the occupant had good taste. I turned my back to the woman and examined the photographs on the wall. They were all black and white portraits of men, framed and arranged in rows. They had posed for the snaps, chests out, tummies in, dark faces above pristine white jibas and dhotis composed into artful smiles. I expected to see her in one or two of these self-important pictures but they were all of men. Maybe one was Detective Balraj, though a single face didn't appear in all as a connecting theme. The photographs jarred, there was little aesthetically pleasing about them. Impulsively, I straightened a crooked one. Apart from the photographs, the pipe rack and a man's hat hanging by the door there was very little evidence of Detective Balraj in this room. He had been gone a long time.

apu

Iyoooo, iyoooo enh thalanoovadhu. At times I felt I was living in an upside down world in which everything was wrong. I shouldn't be alive; I had no right to be. This feeling became more intense in unexpected situations, and now here it was again. He walked into my office, his eyes flicking around for Balraj, disappointed to find only me, and I was back at the beginning. Unbidden, memory awoke. I never remembered the precise day; was it a Monday, a Wednesday? It was in my diary but I never wanted to look at that day again.

It had been Madras-hot, hovering around forty degrees, the height of summer. Bathed in perspiration, steam-cooked alive, choking on foul air, I wobbled on my Bajaj scooter through dense traffic to the appointment. As I climbed those interminable stairs to the office of the Continental Op Detective Agency, I felt like Alice in Wonderland, not tumbling down a hole but up into it. I had tried to tumble back down but kept falling inexorably, up and up, feeling furtive yet adventurous, like my life was about to change. This upward hole was an escape from the dreary classrooms, the dusty chalkboards, the blur of faces, like me, marking time in their lives, waiting for something inevitable, like marriage, to rescue them. I walked in, trying to be bold. The receptionist waved me through like a traffic constable into another office, to a man sitting in the shadows. I heard a kindly voice, roughened by smoking, some whisky in the tone, asking me why I had come. I was answering your advertisement, I told him, and it seemed an interesting position. I didn't tell him I wanted to escape the destiny which awaited me and wanted to take a diversion before it claimed me for life. He seemed to read my thoughts, possibly catching the despondency in my voice. He asked why I thought I would make a good detective, and I replied spiritedly, 'Because I've always been a nosy parker.' He had laughed and hired me on the spot.

'Where's Mr Balraj?' were the first words the American said, sharp and quick. At least I think that's what he said, his accent was alien then.

'Unavailable,' I replied, still on the phone to Coimbatore, trying to trace a missing boy who had failed his tenth standard exams and run away from school in undeserved shame.

I knew little about this American, four hours late for his appointment, prowling my office. He had called Valli from New York and made the appointment. A New York attorney had referred the agency after we'd found a missing New Jersey girl. I had tracked her down to the Aurobindo Ashram in Pondicherry, immersed in her new-found sainthood. Who was he looking for? A woman? I noticed him rubbing the third finger on his left hand with his thumb; something was recently missing from it. He walked straight-backed, like a military man, and there was lightness in his movements even though he was restless with impatience. He had trained to project himself through body language and looked in good condition. There was a faint break in the middle of his nose, though I couldn't see a scar. He had a couple of days' growth: either he was fashionable or he hadn't shaved on the plane. His clothes were crumpled from his journey. Valli told me he had come straight from the airport, full of apologies. I smiled to myself when I caught the flicker of his approval for the room. I had personally selected the paintings and decided on the decor, though not the pipe rack on my desk or the tan coloured fedora by the door. Some things need to remain as reminders of the past. He glanced towards me. Beneath the impatience I sensed an urgency. He'd flown all the way for something that was very personal, to be revealed only to Mr Balraj. Of course, he wasn't here. Now, he could either confide in me or return to America. The young man my mother was busy arranging for me to meet in the hope I would accept him as a groom was also from America. Would they know each other? I had heard that Indians in America congregated together like filings on a magnet. I finished my call and waited for him to tell me his problem, hoping I could help him.

'The cab driver stole my suitcase just now,' he said with a resigned sigh.

'I am sorry. You should report it to the cops. Not that they'll find it.'

Surprisingly, he took this in good humour and smiled. He had the beautiful, white, straight-as-a-ruler teeth that all Americans possessed. 'Cops never do, even in New York. My attorney, Tony Pearson, recommended Mr Balraj.' He emphasized the 'Mr', wanting me to know he still needed to be convinced.

I laughed. 'How is Tony? I haven't seen him in years. He's such a typical New Yorker; drinks dry martinis and has fast hands around women. Is he still divorced?'

He smiled. 'Tony's always divorced.'

I gave him my visiting card with the phone numbers for office and home. I was expecting his but remembered that foreigners didn't follow the same customs about cards as we did. Everyone has a card here, even a bus driver. The little piece of paper reassures us that we exist and can prove it to strangers.

I glanced down at my notepad. 'Figgs isn't an Indian name.'

'It's Fig-gis.'

I waited. His corrected pronunciation didn't enlighten me on how he had that foreign-sounding name. He wasn't about to explain further. A true Indian would have given me his life history to explain how he had acquired his name. He could be a Parsi, maybe a Sardar. They changed their names to suit the climate. Figg-is could have been the anglicized form of Fateh Singh. My cultural curiosity, more than the investigative one, got the better of me.

'Where's your father from?' I asked, so I could pinpoint his town or village, his ancestry and even his social standing.

'Connecticut,' he said blandly, not adding another word, cutting me off from that line of curiosity. It would have meant something in America—an easterner, not a Texan or a Californian, but had no meaning here.

'And Nicky?'

'It's Nikhil. In school it changed to Nicky or Nick, sometimes to Nickel, that's a five-cent coin, and I'd even get called Five C. Life's easier if you have an English sounding name in America.'

Nikhil, I wrote, and added, north Indian? Punjabi?

He sat across the desk in one of the two chairs facing me, placing his still cooling beer can down on the polished desktop. An instant later he removed it and rubbed away the damp ring with his shirt sleeve. I smiled, at least he was house-trained, and slid over a coaster. He opened his shoulder bag, yet still hesitated. I read his thoughts in the frown lines so easily, saw his mind flicking through the possibilities in that hesitation. Was I the right person? Would I be any good? Was this going to be a waste of his time and money? I waited for him to decide. I wouldn't push. He removed a book from his bag, clutched it tightly, then handed it across as if he were saying farewell to a baby.

'This is an old novel,' he said. 'I'm looking for the writer.'

Georgetown by S.K. Naidu. I made a mental note, quite reflexively: Naidu a Telugu name, not Tamilian. The Telugus had come from Andhra in the early nineteenth century to trade with the British and had first settled in Georgetown. They'd flourished as traders, then landowners and had spread out across the growing city. They had contributed schools, colleges and hospitals to the city. The book was old, there was no dust jacket and the cloth binding had faded to a dull green. The edges of the pages had taken on a sickly jaundiced tinge. I opened the book to the imprint page: J.M. Dent & Co., London, had published it thirty years ago; only one edition. The next page had the simple dedication 'To my parents', a first novel then. I flicked through the pages, nothing much else about the author though someone, I presumed Mr Figgis, had made notes in the margins and underlined sentences and paragraphs.

'Why do you think S.K. Naidu's from here?'

'Georgetown's in Madras and Naidu's an Indian name.'

'There are Indians in Kenya, South Africa, the West Indies, Fiji. Salman Rushdie and Naipaul live in New York and London and write on India. And there are other Georgetowns in the world. Guyana has one too.'

'In fact, there are twenty-eight Georgetowns in the world. Seventeen of them are in the US, two in Canada, two in Australia and the other seven scattered around the old British colonies.' He had a good voice, with a slight rasp of exhaustion, except he spoke too quickly. I still strained to understand his clipped American accent.

'I thought the US, Canada and Australia were also old British colonies.'

A smile touched his eyes and lingered. Some people could smile without smiling. 'You're right. Except, he describes this city and the fort by the sea.'

'Have you asked his publisher?'

'I have. They don't know where he is. They've been taken over so many times they don't even know where they are or who they are.'

I began to read the first page: 'She was born in a large house with an interior courtyard on a side street in Georgetown.'

'Tony said Mr Balraj was good,' he said deliberately.

'So am I,' I smiled at his challenge, remembering to be courteous to customers even if they thought I was incompetent. I closed the book. 'Why do you want to find him?'

'I'm a theatre director. I adapted the novel for the stage and the New Haven Theatre wants to mount it. But I have to get his permission, it's called a release.' He took, almost snatched, the book back from me. 'Have you read him?'

He sounded innocent, yet I sensed he was really saying: I bet you haven't read him or even heard of him.

'In high school,' I said, as innocently. 'I think he's dead.'

'He can't be,' he burst out.

His panic surprised me. It was as if I'd wounded him in some way by using the word 'dead'. Yet, why should he care? If S.K. Naidu was dead and had left no heirs he could stage the play. Or mount it, or whatever.

He saw my reaction and added quickly to cover the panic, 'I mean he couldn't be that old. If the book's thirty years old and he wrote it in his mid-twenties, he'd be in his fifties. Or even say he was in his early thirties, now he'll be in his sixties.' He hadn't dispelled my doubt; my stare was unblinking, trying to decipher his intentions. 'Are you sure he's dead?'

I made a call, still watching him. He held the book tenderly in his long, slim fingers and I was reminded of Sarada's description of Ramesh's hands. She had told me he played her body as if it were a sitar. I didn't think Mr Figgis would make much of a musician—his fingers were restless and fidgety, more of a tabla player's than a sitarist's.

'Raj,' I said into the phone when the *Hindu*'s literary editor came on the line. 'I'm looking for the writer, S.K. Naidu. You've heard of him? Good, tell me if he's still alive and where I can find him.'

I waited on the line, listening to Raj's computer keys clicking in the background. When he came back on the line and spoke his few words I hid my disappointment. He had always been a useless mutaal, ever since school. 'He hasn't heard of S.K. Naidu since that book was published and has no idea whether he's alive or dead, or where he could be,' I told the American.

He had an I-knew-you'd-not-find-him look on his face. Doubts swirled like storm clouds in his eyes. Should he wait for M.K. Balraj, a fine detective according to Tony Pearson, or go with me?

'I'll find him, alive or dead.' Although I hoped I sounded quite determined I didn't feel it. We women do have to try harder than men to prove we are equal.

'How much?'

I hid my grin; he was half convinced, and I'd prove I was good. Once he'd decided, I knew this would be his next question. He was American, his shoulder bag, though slightly worn, looked expensive, he had on a Breitling watch, his jacket was linen, and that could be costly even in India. It wasn't that I was greedy but my other clients in the waiting room could afford only my lowest fees.

'Five thousand a day, plus daily bata,' I spoke quickly, the way Balraj had instructed. Don't give them enough time, never hesitate. Figgis blinked at 'bata' and I explained, 'Expenses.' Would he bargain me down? That would prove without doubt that despite his name and accent he was Indian. Everyone who walked into my office demanded a discount, whined, pleaded, cajoled and wept for it. I always gave it, only because I'd already hiked the price in anticipation. Now, with him, I would settle for half that. No, I'd drop a thousand, in two hundred and fifty rupee stages. I saw him mentally calculating the exchange rate. I could have told him it worked out to one hundred and eleven dollars a day, excessively expensive, if he accepted.

'What does the . . . bata . . . include?'

'Petrol, snacks, bribes. Mostly bribes. Everyone in this city and country has to be bribed.'

'Yeah, I'd heard,' he allowed a little contempt to leak into his voice. 'Do they give receipts? Research is tax deductible with the IRS.' A look from me was enough. No receipts. 'You take traveller's cheques?'

'Yes, but ten thousand in advance.'

He pulled out a book of cheques and signed two, one hundred dollars each. As he signed, resting his cheque book on the table, head down, I noticed again the indentation on the third finger of his left hand, the finger he'd been rubbing. Obviously he'd just, within the last day or two, removed his ring. Wedding? Signet? Wedding, I guessed. Men didn't hide signet rings. He tore out the cheques and passed them over.

'Your passport, please.'

I took it and opened it to the first page. It was a bit worn, bent slightly to fit carelessly into a back pocket. He was Nikhil Figgis, born in New York City on 2 August 1974. I would have liked to flick through the other pages to see where he'd been over the last few years, but after noting the number, I returned the passport and pulled out a clunky calculator from the drawer for his sake. Calculators assure people there's no hanky-panky. I calculated the exchange rate and wrote out a receipt for nine thousand rupees. I opened the right-hand desk drawer and lifting the .32 automatic which I used as a paperweight to hold down the loose cash, dropped the cheques on the pile of hundred- and fifty-rupee notes. Then I shut and locked the drawer.

'First thing tomorrow . . .' I began.

'No, now,' he said, and added politely, 'I think my two hundred dollars entitles me to ask you to start the search today.'

I sighed loudly though I understood his impatience and his value-for-money attitude. I wished I could start the next day. I called Ramakrishna and Chandra, they would have to take over my clients. One was an adultery case, the other a fraud. Neither would pay much. I finished the call, picked up the telephone directory and flicked through the pages. It was always the best place to start.

'I checked international inquiries, checked the web, checked everything I could check. He isn't anywhere, he's vanished.'

I ignored him, determined to do it my way and in my own time. He was right. There were hundreds of Naidus in the pages but no 'S.K.'

'Listen, he'll be old and broke, like most writers. You got any other ideas apart from the telephone?'

I wasn't about to admit he was right. Where would I start looking for an old man who had disappeared thirty years ago? What would Balraj have done? What had he taught me? Check births and deaths to start with. I looked at the time, 5.10 p.m., the offices would have closed, the babus long gone. Valli came in carrying a tray with two cups of sweet tea and a plate of Marie biscuits. She handed Mr Figgis his tea, then gave me mine, leaving the biscuits precisely between us. I pulled out my notepad and began to make notes of what I knew about S.K. Naidu: one old novel, one old man, wrote in English, familiar with Georgetown, read him. I stopped when I noticed Mr Figgis had taken a small, plastic box out of his bag and was concentrating on laying out four pills in a neat row on the desk. He popped the first into his mouth and swallowed it with beer. Then he noticed me watching him.

'Anti-malaria,' he said, and popped another. 'Anti-dysentery,' pop, 'anti-typhoid,' pop, ' anti-. . .' He shrugged, not caring, and popped that too. 'I was told not to drink anything, eat anything or breathe the Indian air. I'd fall ill instantly and die.'

'Who told you that?'

'My mom . . . mother.'

I added another word after I'd written 'Figgis'—'hypochondriac?'. He was watching me, his tea untouched, waiting. An instinct told me that S.K. Naidu wasn't phoneless. When I'd spoken to Raj, he'd said S.K. Naidu had been well-off. It meant he had money, and if he had money he was sure to have a phone. So, why wasn't he listed? Who'd know? I rose abruptly.

'Why don't you check into your hotel while I go out and talk to someone who might know something?'

'I'll come with you,' he said. He hitched the strap onto his shoulder and stood up. 'It's sort of urgent. I have two weeks in which to get his permission or I lose the slot.'

'New Haven's an important theatre?'

'Kinda like off-Broadway, though it's not in Manhattan. It's an important launching pad for Broadway.'

'You must be tired,' I insisted. 'And probably I won't get the lead tonight.'

'I don't mind, it's better than sitting in a hotel room, waiting for you to call.' He strolled over to the door, pausing to look at the black and white photographs. 'These movie stars?'

'Some politicians, some crooks,' I said, stuck with him now, wishing he'd go to his hotel. I didn't add that the photographs were Balraj's rogues' gallery of the powerful and corrupt who had once been his friends. They were just other pieces of memory for me.

'How do you tell them apart?'

'You don't.'

nicky/nikhil

Well, if Detective Balraj wasn't to be found, despite the appointment I had specifically made with him, I decided she'd have to do. I had a mistrust of beauty. Renee had been beautiful. Beauty was a coin for stardom in the theatre and film business, plain looks only cast you in character roles. Both men and women preserved beauty like misers and it made them selfish. This woman had an ancient yet modern beauty, like the faded wall paintings of Ellora I'd found in a book. I had been surprised to see her behind that desk. I wasn't aware India had female private detectives. It had female cops, even chiefs of cops. I'd heard of Kiran Bedi, who had single-handedly reformed the notorious Tihar jail in Delhi into a model prison. Go with her, I said to myself. She looked a ballsy woman; Indian women were, look at Indira Gandhi. She knew how to kick ass.

But Detective Apu was expensive. I calculated that at just over a hundred bucks a day, she wasn't as cheap as I'd hoped. How long would it take her to find S.K. Naidu? A day, two days? At her rate, the maximum I could afford would be about five days. And for two hundred bucks, I wanted S.K. Naidu found yesterday. In Mexico it was mañana, in Europe tomorrow, in America time was hard, definite, the numbers meant what they stood for—10.05 was 10.05, not 10.30, 11.15 was 11.15, not 12.00. But, as I left America, numbers had lost this hard definition, this precise science which ruled our American lives. Digits seemed to dissolve and lose their shape and meaning. In Asia, they just melted away to vague parameters when certain things could or could not occur. I saw the flush of anger, a dark coppery tone in her cheeks, but I wasn't about to move until she started the search.

She picked up her handbag and as she came around the desk I noticed she was taller than I had expected, around five-foot-eight or nine. Her blue salwar was so crisply starched that it surrounded her like an armour and thoroughly camouflaged her figure. She flung the dupatta around her shoulders with the flourish of a man tossing his scarf around his neck on a cold winter's day. Her hair was shoulder-length and glistened like black ink spilled on a page. She paused, took a step back and scooped up the strand of jasmine hanging on the silver-framed photograph to fix it in her hair. But first she touched the flowers to her eyes superstitiously as a blessing. I noticed she avoided looking at the photograph. Her perfume trailed behind her, out of the room.

I stopped at the open door. 'Before we go on, I'd like to file a complaint with the cops about my stolen suitcase. Hope you don't mind.'

I had hoped for an air-conditioned car, not an open air antique jeep. Despite dusk having descended and a smoky orange sun sinking below the stubby skyline, the heat hadn't abated. I was soaked again and the air stung my eyes and lungs. The jeep turned onto Nungumbakkam High Road, the way I'd come, and took a U-turn at the Taj Coromandel hotel. It was a fifties-style building, as imaginative as a matchbox standing on end. The traffic too was still pumping out poison. I tied a handkerchief to cover my nose and mouth, like a bandit in a hold-up. I glanced at Apu. Her profile was stubborn, staring ahead, not wanting conversation, so I didn't ask why she wasn't yet dead from this air.

The jeep wound and bumped along Nungumbakkam High Road and turned onto a narrower road in worse condition. According to the faded yellow signboard we were on Village Road. It may have been a village once but now shops crowded in on either side. There was just room for one lane between the double parked cycles and motorcycles. Buses missed them by millimetres. She pulled up at a pretty, red building, white paint neatly delineating every brick, looking as harmless as a ginger bread house. It stood in a compound shaded by a generous rain tree. A sign arched over the gate—Nungambakkam Police Station—with Coca-Cola logos at either end like quotation marks. A bored cop with an ancient rifle stood guard, not questioning our presence. In the small entrance hall, a sergeant sat at a low desk facing us. On either side were doors to the inspector of police and to an office, behind him through an arch were a couple of cells. They were unoccupied.

'I have to make a couple of calls,' she said, pulling out her mobile and already punching in numbers as she went out. 'File your complaint with Sergeant Sait. He understands English.'

I saw her palm a hundred to Sergeant Sait but it didn't make him any friendlier. He seemed to be in a bad mood. I was distracted by his hair. It stuck up straight like the bristles of a toilet brush and was pale orange. Around the sides of his head and in his well-trimmed moustache the hair was grey. I had seen orange hair before, normally on very fair-skinned people, but not on brown ones with sad, weary eyes. I was curious about the unusual colour but I sensed Sergeant Sait wasn't in the right mood for any such inquiry. He was poised with a tired ball pen over his report.

'Tell me.'

I was giving him a description of the taxi driver and the three numbers of the license plate that I remembered when two constables strolled in with a handcuffed man between them. They dropped him in a corner like a sack of potatoes and went into the station. I glanced at the man who was small and very dark, with unruly hair and a broad flat nose. He wore a grubby dhoti and an equally grubby T-shirt with a crimson 'Harvard' imprinted on the front. Somewhere between the telling and the interruption Sergeant Sait misunderstood my tale.

'You steal someone's suitcase and you want to return it to taxi driver who steal it first?' he was writing as he spoke before I could reply.

'Yes . . . no. For chrissake, I just told you, the taxi driver stole my suitcase.'

'Speak slow . . . speak slow. I don't understand. You don't speak English proper.' His pen was poised to make a correction but didn't. 'Why you let him steal it? You shouldn't such things do.'

I thought Apu had exaggerated when she said the sergeant spoke English. Instead, he played with the language, shifting the emphasis in pronunciation, changing the meanings. I spoke slowly, dropping each word like pebbles down a deep well of incomprehension, watching as the sergeant wrote each word. 'I get out of taxi and he drives off with another passenger, a woman.'

Sergeant Sait perked up. 'This woe-man, she is your friend?'

'For chrissake, I never saw her before in my life. And if I did I'd wring her neck off.'

I don't know whether Sergeant Sait believed me. He pored over the report and wrote furiously for a while before lifting his head.

'You make mish-take, you must not get out of the taxi.'

'I guess I should've spent the rest of my life in it.' I can be real sarcastic when I want to but I don't think it worked on Sergeant Sait. It never worked on the bullies in the schoolyard either; dumbshits couldn't tell sarcasm from a hole in their heads.

'Then you and suitcase will be together, not lost,' he said triumphantly.

The handcuffed man looked as if he'd fallen asleep. He was

snoring gently but he stirred when the typist woman I had seen on my way to Apu's office hurried in to interrupt briefly. She carried a neatly beribboned rattan package which she left on the sergeant's desk. I recognized her and felt a slight bond of familiarity, so I smiled up at her, hoping she'd heard my earlier apology. She returned a small ripple of a smile and left as hurriedly as she'd entered.

'Rani, you know?' the sergeant asked casually.

I shrugged her off but the sergeant wrote again, probably adding that I knew this Rani. He looked up. 'I can't promise we'll find case.'

Unfortunately, my mind was still mired in sarcasm. 'You would if there was a bomb in it.'

The sergeant made a note and smiled at me sweetly, revealing a Himalayan skyline of teeth. 'When it blows up we'll find the rascal or what's left of him.' He signed the report and turned it around for me to sign it. 'Sign please.'

I glanced at the FIR and realized I didn't understand a single word written down. 'It's not in English.'

'Why should it be? This is not England or America. Sign please.'

I signed with a flourish, believing all it contained was my complaint about a stolen suitcase with my manuscript and a few clean clothes in it. I rose, but the sad man in the corner bothered me. I wanted to know more about him.

'Who is he? What's he done?'

The sergeant glanced, a quick cut of contempt in the man's direction, and pronounced 'jungley', as if it were a curse. He shrugged at the second question. Then he gathered his report and hurried into the sub-inspector's room with Rani's package.

I stepped out of the police station back onto the noisy street to find Apu leaning against the jeep. She didn't see me immediately and I watched her for a moment. She seemed cocooned in unhappy memories. I passed my hand across her sightless stare. She started, then smiled too quickly, and we climbed into the jeep.

'What's jungley mean?'

She thought a moment. 'Uncouth.'

I laughed and she glanced questioningly. I shook my head. I was delighted that she'd said 'uncouth'. It had been one of my mom's favourite words until I taught her 'hoosier'. Mom could never wholly escape India, it would sneak up on her when she least expected it and embarrass her.

susie/sushima

I don't remember any more the street on which my house was. It wasn't on Armenian Street—yes, Armenians did live there once and even built their own church—but one of the narrower ones leading off it. You entered through a large door which opened straight out into the street. There are no sidewalks in Georgetown, darling, just the streets. The door had an intricately carved frame all around. With what? I don't remember, gods probably. India has gods everywhere and you're constantly tripping over them if you're not careful. Anyway, there was a passage and then you entered an open courtyard. Of course, all houses have courtyards, yes like haciendas, and even in crowded Georgetown our house had its own inner courtyard. That's where I flew when I dreamed I was a bird.

I told you about my dream, didn't I? It was always the same, night after night, and it came to me as I lay in my cot, sorry, bed, at the midnight hour. Sometimes these old words like cot just pop out of my mouth even though I think I've forgotten them. Of course, I knew it was midnight, at least it felt like that in my soul. I don't care what the clock said. And most of them didn't work anyway. I dreamed I had become this bird, not an ordinary one but something fabulous. I had a hooked beak, like an eagle's, made of gold, and silvery, melancholy eyes. Why shouldn't birds have melancholy eyes? They can't all be as happy as larks. I was about two feet high and you should've seen my plumage. My feathers were of a thousand bright silken colours, all snipped from many, many saris. Every colour of the rainbow was on my body, and then some more. But when I looked down I still had a child's feet and I remember how strange it felt to have such boring feet when I would have preferred talons, sharp as razors. I opened my wings and they filled the whole room, from wall to wall; folded, you wouldn't have thought that I had such a span. With one flap I was airborne, flying above my cot, round and round, and then I flew out of the door into the courtyard. In the courtyard when I looked up, the stars and the moon beckoned to me to fly up to meet them. But when I tried I found that the courtyard was covered with fine wire netting to prevent crows and pigeons from entering. But now I couldn't leave either because I kept bumping into the netting each time I tried to fly up to the stars. Every damn night it was the same dream, and the same problem. I flew up and bounced back down again. Each night, I circled and circled, searching for a hole in the netting. If I had talons I could've ripped open the netting but I only had a child's feet for my beautiful body. On the first night I slept in New York, I had the dream again. But this time, as I flew towards the netting, I saw a gap and stuck my head through, and then my body, and I flew away up to the stars. I never dreamed that dream ever again and even now when I try to remember it, it doesn't come back so clearly. I do miss the bird very much, though I doubt it would fit into a New York apartment and there isn't a courtyard for it to fly around in. What kind of sound did the bird make? It never made a sound; it was a very silent bird.

apu

Although Mr Figgis only mentioned his 'mom' twice there was a deep affection in the use of that simplified word for mother. I knew when he said it he immediately thought of her, and his eyes reflected an inner smile. Yet, for a moment, a fraction of a second, it was veiled with sadness. But it was gone in an instant and I thought I had imagined it. He wasn't a confiding type of man. Ask him where his father's from and he replies 'Connecticut'. Anyone else would've said Ludhiana or Katpadi or Pune or any one of our million places. So I couldn't ask about his mother. He was probably third or fourth generation Indian American.

On our way down from the office he had trailed me like a desperate wraith seeking solace, a real thalanoovoo. Shyam, Prasad and Rani were loading up their scooters and motorbikes with their products packaged in rattan baskets, tied with red ribbons and costing a hundred and seventy-five rupees each. He suddenly called out to them: 'I'm sorry', and when I looked at him in surprise, he said they'd understand what he meant. They didn't acknowledge his mysterious apology as they wobbled away with their loads. They were my tenants on the landing below. I didn't chitchat with them much, apart from a daily greeting, and only knew a little about their background. They'd grown up together as orphans in the Vincent Orphanage which I discovered when Rani asked me to investigate thefts happening in it. I had sent Bhuna, an eager young girl, to work as a maid at the orphanage and she found the matron siphoning off provisions and selling them on the street. I believe it was Prasad, always the dominant one in the triad, who had dreamed up the idea of making and packaging sexual aids and pornographic material to sell in this overheated city. And so here they were, in their shops the size of PCO booths, pretending to carry on a business they didn't do.

I was tired despite the crisp appearance of my salwar and the smile on my face. Deep inside I felt I was disintegrating. Like all foreigners Mr Figgis had been nervous of our traffic, holding white-knuckle-tight on to the sides of the jeep all along the way to the Nungumbakkam police station with a handkerchief across his face, bandit-like, to protect his pristine lungs from our dark pollution. I had introduced him to Sergeant Sait, with his startling orange hair and, slipping in a one hundred rupee moolah to take the FIR, had left them to it as I called my mother to tell her I'd be home late and listen to her complaints about my gadding-about-at-all-hours. Yelumani wolay varangai, amma.

When Mr Figgis emerged unscathed from the police station he asked me, 'What's a jungley?' My reply, 'uncouth', brought a broad, delighted smile to his face as if I had made a witty remark. He didn't elaborate on what had amused him so much; it was a private joke. Well, if there wasn't a laugh track on American sitcoms I wouldn't know when to laugh at those jokes either. I'm probably deficient of humour in moods like this.

'You shop at Nalli's?' he interrupted my thoughts as we passed the most famous sari shop in the city.

I replied, 'Not often. You should buy a couple of saris for your wife before you go home.'

'I may,' he said, worrying away at the indent on his marriage finger. I preferred men who lied outright; they always forgot later which lie they'd told. His ambiguous 'I may' allowed him leeway to embroider the truth or lie later. I turned left after Panagal Park, drove a half mile and pulled up outside Jeeva Park, another smudge of greenery in this crowded city that greedily gobbled up parks and gardens. The historian, S. Muthiah, had called this city 'gracious' in a book; obviously, he'd known it in a previous incarnation. I wish I'd lived then, fading into those old sepia photographs that were proof of its gentle past. I was a member of INTACH, a heritage organization, and fought to preserve this past, though it had increasingly turned into a losing battle as greed eroded this 'gracious' place.

He followed me into the park, docile as a village woman treading in her husband's footsteps. A cricket ball rolled towards me. I fielded it neatly and threw it back to the panting boy. I had played cricket for WCC and Tamil Nadu but never made the test team. Pale blue bowls of light dimly illuminated the park. There was barely any light to see, the boys played by instinct. Under the glowing bowls, men read their newspapers, a couple played chess, four boys were absorbed in carroms. At least they treasured this little island and enjoyed the space. Mohan sat at his usual desk under the old peepul tree, its crown a perfectly shaped umbrella outlined against the night sky. The ground was a carpet of crisp leaves. A cable ran down from a branch to the telephone on his desk. A plastic PCO board was propped on the rickety desk, underneath it in shaky handwriting was a declaration: Local Calls Only. Mohan was ancient, thin as a stick, with an owl's eyes, solemn and watchful and proud as the bird's. He bobbed his head at Mr Figgis when I announced his name with a flourish. 'Ask him,' I said to Mr Figgis who remained puzzled. I told him that Mohan had memorized every telephone number in the city directory over the last five years. Mohan corrected me—'eight'—in his high, thin voice.

S.K. Naidu's name was spoken out loud and Mohan bowed his head in reverence. 'The great writer,' he murmured, and when Mr Figgis asked if he'd read him Mohan shook his head. 'I have only heard of his genius.'

'But he only wrote one novel, I think. Are there others?'

'One is enough for any man,' Mohan said conclusively.

He closed his eyes so slowly that it reminded me of the moon sinking away at dawn. I yawned and stretched, as it would take him time to scan his memory nodules, or whatever, for the number. Mr Figgis wasn't impressed. He whispered that he'd read a piece in the Metropolitan section of the *New York Times* about an Indian woman who could add, subtract, divide, multiply and find the square root of the most complex numbers faster than a computer. It was a memory trick, he guessed, or an aberration in the brain.

'8-5-2-3-7-4-1,' Mohan spoke out of his dreaming.

I dialled the number. Mohan's eyes opened slowly with a beatific look as if he'd just performed a life-saving miracle. An automated message informed me that the telephone was no longer working.

I knew I shouldn't doubt him but I asked, 'It is the right number?'

'One hundred and ten per cent right number,' Mohan said indignantly. He opened a small silver box on his table, took a pinch of snuff in irritation at being doubted and stuffed the brown powder up each nostril. 'The telephone was disconnected five years ago over a bill dispute with Madras Telephones.'

'Now what?'

'At least we know he had a phone.'

'So, now what?' he countered. 'Trek around to the telephone exchanges?'

I ignored his sarcasm and smiled down at Mohan. 'We know the answer to that "now what", don't we Mohan?'

He laughed, more a witch's cackle. 'Yes, yes, yes. No more "now what".'

I delved into my handbag, slid a quick glance at Mr Figgis, and handed a hundred-rupee note to Mohan. He would've accepted a fifty but all this was bata and I made a note in my book for Mr Figgis' benefit. Every paisa would be accounted for at the time of reckoning.

'Why do you waste your time memorizing telephone numbers? You can get a computer.'

'It's my genius,' Mohan explained patiently. 'Every person has something of a genius in him or her. I have found my genius. Have you found yours yet?'

'I'm searching,' he said, humbled by the logic and optimism.

'Is that why we came all this way?' he asked as we left the park. 'You could've phoned him from your office and got that disconnected number.'

I allowed him to wonder until I climbed into the jeep, before answering, 'Mr Figgis, you heard him. He's a genius and, as such, we must respect him for that knowledge. He doesn't take phone calls, only by seeing the person before him is he inspired to recall the telephone number. He also likes meeting people and having a chitchat.'

He grinned, teasing. 'So I inspired him?'

'No, I did.' I didn't mean to snap but I was indignant that he should be so arrogant to believe he could inspire anyone.

'Listen,' he said above the din of car engines, horns, cycle bells. 'I'm sorry. Sometimes, I do get carried away. I've always been impatient, it's an incurable bad habit.'

I forgave him with a quick smile. 'I don't blame you. Here, unfortunately, everything takes time, without patience you'll go mad.'

As I backtracked the way we'd come and drove under the Gemini flyover, passing the US consulate with its bored cop resting his sten gun casually on the pile of sandbags and then the Cathedral silhouetted against the evening sky, I could feel the curiosity on the tip of his tongue. He wanted me to point out the passing sights, but there was nothing of interest to point out on the route. Instead I thought about Sarada's case. She was my best friend, we had gone to Good Shepherd together, then to WCC. After that she had left for Bombay to work in the hotel industry. She'd fallen in love with Ramesh but the problem with falling-in-love is that love doesn't give us an insight into a man's past, his character, his honesty. At least in an arranged marriage the family is known, firmly anchored to relatives and friends as references, if not to the bad habits of the possible groom; the good habits are invariably discovered too late in life when despair has settled heavily into the soul. Apart from Ramesh's sitarist's hands as a lover, Sarada knew little about him and I was supposed to unravel his past. Sarada could be useless at times. All she'd given me were his photographs, taken lovingly by her, and the address of his rented fly-by-night flat.

We were at the traffic lights on the Marina, and Mr Figgis was looking at the long, low colonial building at the corner, with its pillars and a veranda running along it's whole breadth. Armed cops stood guard at the gate.

'That's the inspector general of police's office. They were going to knock it down and put up a modern monstrosity. We fought them to preserve it and won. I think the police are proud of it now.'

'I'm glad you won. It's a beautiful building.'

At least he had an aesthetic eye. 'This is the Marina, and all along you'll find the old buildings the British left us. It's a kind of museum. Some are still preserved, but most are neglected. You should take a drive along it during the day. There's the Ice House where they stored ice from America when it came in on sailing ships, the Senate Building, the Nawab of Carnatica's palace and, about two miles up the road, is Fort St. George. It was . . .'

'Built in 1640. And I will take that drive, maybe tomorrow. Georgetown should be on the other side of the fort?'

'Yes, but between Georgetown and the fort is the high court. That building's worth a look at as well. We don't have as many dramatic monuments as Delhi or Agra or Jaipur for the tourists.'

I drove down to the beach avoiding boys and men playing cricket in near darkness. In the distance, we could see the winking lights of ships in anchor waiting to enter the harbour. We walked barefoot; the sand was fine and warm. The beach looked magnificent, it seemed to stretch for miles, and we claimed it was the second longest beach in the world. Once it was a health hazard, dirty with tons of rubbish, but now with some imported American machine the sand looked as if it had been scrubbed, washed and laid out to dry. The cooling sea breeze with its clean breath blew across the beach and into the city. A lighthouse swept its beam across the sea and the city. The beach, after dusk, was always teeming with life. Madrasis crowded the beach as far as the eye could see, sitting in groups, laughing, talking, picnicking. Kids rode ponies or flew kites. Countless lovers, discrete distances apart, all facing the sea, embraced or kissed, whispering endearments to each other, and the breeze carried their love and passion, preserving their secrets, across the city.

I didn't want to look at them. I had once been among them too. Even then I remember wondering how love could be nourished on such ungiving soil. These lovers, like us once, would have arrived separately, met by the Mahatma Gandhi statue and walked down to the sand before clutching hands. In the secrecy of this place I foresaw the complexities of their love and the dangerous boundaries that contained them: Brahmin/Mudaliar, Nadar/Chettiar, Sikh/Christian, Muslim/Hindu, Tamil/Gujarati, rich/poor. Only the brave, the bold, the heady-in-love-with-love pushing against the fierce winds of tradition, married for love. Men and women throughout history, and in movies and plays and tragic *Anna Karenina*-like novels, died bravely for love. In villages, dark Romeos and dusky Juliets were lynched or stoned or hacked to death because they fell wrongly in love. To love was a form of rebellion, an insurgency against the set order of planned destinies. Love upset the elders, set loose their juices of envy as they had probably not experienced such passion in their dry lives. I wondered, as I passed them, head averted, memory suppressed, whether America too planted such volatile minefields for love to cross.

'Quite a lovers' trysting place,' Mr Figgis said softly, surprise in his tone. 'I didn't think they would be allowed.'

'They're not, that's why they hide out here in the darkness. Sometimes the cops raid the beach and the parks.'

Catamarans, looking frail as matchsticks, were beached on the sand. Nylon nets lay coiled beside them. Hawkers with rattan baskets pestered us to buy peanuts, sweets, spicy snacks.

'I haven't eaten since the flight. I'm famished. What can I eat?'

I studied the passing array—patanis, verakadalay, bhajjis, samosas, bondas, jalebis—then smiled with genuine pleasure. 'Nothing. You'll fall sick and die immediately.'

He laughed. 'My stomach's a lot tougher than you think. It was raised on all-American junk food, and I bet that has more chemicals than these snacks. Pick something.'

I picked a newspaper cone of verakadalay, still warm from roasting, paid and opened it, spilling them into his hand. 'Verakadalay.'

'Peanuts back home, and they come vacuum-packed in cans.' He cracked the shell open, popped the nut into his mouth and chewed. 'Tastier than the canned ones.'

We walked to the sea, sharing the peanuts. The surf was gentle, low waves rolled in, licking the sand, the feet, ankles and waists of the waders. Women in saris laughed as if tickled by the water, not caring for the stains the water spread up to their knees. He didn't ask me why we were here as I walked with a purpose along the shoreline, letting the sea caress my ankles. He spotted my purpose at the same time I did—a man at a desk with a PCO plaque on it. The telephone line ran under the sand to his phone. He was round and dark, with a fringe of white hair around his scalp, enjoying the companionship of passing strangers.

'This is Muthu,' I announced with the same formality as I had used with Mohan. 'He is Mohan's younger brother.'

'And how is Mohan?' Muthu said, enjoying the joke.

'He always says that when I see him. They live together, both are bachelors.' Then with a snap, 'And they don't speak to each other but write stupid notes which their mother passes between them.'

'Why's that?' he asked Muthu.

'What else but a woman. Both of us loved her, she loved another. Now I'm a bachelor only because Apu refuses to marry me.' He turned to Mr Figgis, eyeing him expertly with a future in-law's calculation. 'Such a beautiful woman and still unmarried. I swear the world is full of fools.'

I laughed. 'Ah, if only I'd met you when you were younger.'

'I'm still young,' he said indignantly. 'You can test me out whenever you want. Just say the word.'

'You'd be too strong a bull for me.'

Muthu laughed uproariously, wobbling on his frail chair which sank an inch deeper into the sand. Mr Figgis looked surprised at my bold frankness, he had thought I would blush and flush. And he probably thought I was a virgin too.

Muthu held out his hand. 'Give it to me.' I handed him S.K. Naidu's telephone number. He studied it and then, like Mohan, seemed to enter a trance.

'Muthu memorizes the addresses,' I whispered.

'This is division of labour. In New York, all you do is call directory inquiry. Admittedly, if the person is unlisted you get zilch.'

We waited, the surf rhythmically soothing and comforting. There was something so patient, so ancient in its ebb and flow, a few million years of wearing down the shores, licking away the sands.

'149 Royapettah High Road dash 14,' Muthu's murmur was just above the surf's. I wrote it down and dropped another hundred-rupee note on the table.

'What if he isn't there?' the American said, doubting this genius as well.

Muthu shrugged and pointed a finger to the sky. 'In heaven then.'

Royapettah High Road wasn't a high road or a low road but a narrow, crowded road. There weren't enough lanes for traffic, which squeezed into every available bit of space and inched forward.

'Which one's 149?' He peered anxiously, eyes flicking left and right. 'Is it the old or the new 149? Muthu didn't say.'

'Must be the old one because he was remembering a five-year-old telephone book,' I said calmly. 'We'll find it.' I was concerned about him. He was tense, straining to be there, to meet this S.K. Naidu. Was it that important, the man's permission for the play? Art, no doubt, made its own demands. I preferred movies to the theatre, only because there was little theatre in the city. But at the moment I couldn't think of any other reason why Mr Figgis was so anxious. At one point I thought he'd get out and walk because it would be faster than the jeep nudging through the molasses. We were getting there—145, 147 . . . 151.

'You've missed it,' he said in exasperation.

'I couldn't have. The numbers jumped.' I stopped, traffic behind concertinaed, piling up like a crash, honking and yelling. I remained unperturbed, looking back. There was a narrow lane between 147 and 151. 'It must be down that lane.' I shoved the jeep into gear and looked back.

'This is incredible, insane, you're going to reverse.'

'Why not?'

He bit his tongue, probably thinking of jumping out and backtracking to the door number, leaving me to sort out the jeep. Like an engine shunting reluctant wagons, I did manage to edge back, quite recklessly, snarling traffic further. I grinned at him, reading his thoughts, then swung the wheel and edged through the oncoming traffic into the lane. God, everyone on Royappettah High Road hated me at the moment; I could hear the curses crashing against us.

'What are they saying?'

'The usual things about women drivers,' I smiled. 'Bad words, you don't want to know.'

'I can imagine them.'

The jeep shot down the lane empty of traffic. It was a dark alley, about a hundred yards, and ended at a towering gate. The gate was all black and a doorway had been cut out in one half of it. The faint number on the left pillar, white within a black circle, was 149-stroke-85. There was no name board, and no light. I switched off the engine. We sat a moment in what seemed like total silence. The chaotic noise of the traffic was muted here; it almost felt like a haven.

'See, I told you I was a good detective.'

'It says 85,' he said.

'And 1-4-9,' I smiled at him impishly. 'You're a pessimist, aren't you? You believe in the worst.' I took out a comb and ran it quickly through my hair. I never bothered about make-up. 'I thought all Americans were optimists.'

'We are, in America; we lose our optimism as we travel eastwards.'

We climbed out to confront the gate. It was a formidable sentinel, at least eight feet high. There was no bell to ring either, people were certainly not welcome. I pushed the door, it was locked, and then banged on it.

'Maybe there's no one on the other side.'

'There will be, there always is.' I banged again, harder. The gate vibrated, and made enough noise to awaken any sleeping dog for miles. We heard a distant bark. When I banged again, the bark came nearer, racing towards the gate, until it was right on the other side. It sounded like a large dog, a Doberman or a German Shepherd; it also sounded hungry.

'Do you like dogs?'

'From a distance,' he said. 'It's not going to open the gate either.'

I smiled in triumph as we heard the small gate being unlocked from inside and a man shouting at the dog to be quiet. The door creaked open and a barely visible face peered out. The man carried a coil of rope in his hand.

'Are you from the telephone department?' he asked in Tamil.

'No,' I said.

'Pity,' he said, ignoring me and only addressing Mr Figgis, as if he had replied. 'I had instructions to hang them from the nearest telephone pole. Now, go away.' He shook the coil of rope at us.

'Ask him if this is S.K. Naidu's house,' Mr Figgis cut sharply through the exchange.

The man began to close the gate when I took a step forward to peer closer at his face. His voice had seemed familiar.

'Shyam! It's you?' I couldn't hide the shock and, above all, the chagrin at knowing that the answer to my search was my own tenant, just half a flight down from the office.

It was indeed Shyam, who now recognized me. 'Yes madam. Now, please, go away.'

'Is S.K. Naidu alive?' Mr Figgis asked in concern, nearer panic as if this Naidu would deliberately die on him now.

Shyam understood and snapped in English, 'I'm only the watchman, not his doctor.'

'We want to see Mr S.K. Naidu.'

'I have very strict instructions. He won't see anyone. Go away.'

'Not even me?' I smiled flirtatiously.

'Not even you, madam,' Shyam held the gate half-closed, the key ready to slide back into the lock.

I sighed dramatically. 'Pity, I'll have to raise all your rents then, maybe even double what it is now. And anyway, the lease will be over soon.'

Shyam had always believed life was unfair. An orphanage didn't give one much optimism in life. You always expected the worst, to be abandoned and betrayed constantly by life. He never expected me to be so mean and he gave me a withering, wounded look as he stepped away from the gate.

'I have to go to the toilet.'

'And take the dog with you.'

The door remained invitingly half-open and I stepped towards it.

'I don't need you any more,' Mr Figgis stopped me. 'We've found S.K. Naidu.'

'Not yet.' I had to be a witness to this meeting to find out what he really wanted with S.K. Naidu. I stepped through into the compound, letting him make up his mind.

nicky/nikhil

It had been totally weird, way out, travelling half way across the city to talk to some old guy sitting under a tree with his telephone and his photographic memory.

And boy, Apu didn't have a sense of humour. I wanted her to warm to me, chill out, but I kept saying the wrong things. My tongue was New York sharp but it was also my American impatience; I wanted a result yesterday, that's what I'd paid for. I had noticed the hundred-rupee tip added to her bata. I was jet-lagged, exhausted and hungry but pumped up with adrenaline. My chase was about to end. We'd find S.K. Naidu, he was somewhere in this city, sitting beside a dead telephone. Probably he hadn't been able to afford the bills. What would he be like: tall, short, dark, fair, friendly, grouchy? I didn't care, as long as I found him. I'd figure it all out afterwards, wing it.

When we passed Nalli's again I imagined my mom shopping there, buying saris in the days when she wore them. I had wanted to ask Apu where we were heading and to point out the landmarks, but I figured she'd snap: I'm not a tour guide. Her silence was impenetrable. I knew she'd find S.K. Naidu if only to make me look like an ass. The road was wide and very straight, divided by a barrier, emptying out now and she picked up speed. We had passed under an overhead rail bridge, the road widening gradually, and then we were on the beach. Far out to sea there was a line of ships, twenty or thirty, winking their lights patiently as they waited for a berth. They were silhouetted against a clear, starry sky. She had parked opposite a low, magnificent old building. It was what I'd imagined in colonial Madras, colonnaded, in mellow pale colours, with verandas running the whole breadth. The board said it was the office of the inspector general of police. She noticed my interest and explained how she, 'we', had fought to preserve it and won. She didn't explain who the 'we' were. I thought if she took up a cause, she would break someone's balls. I noticed how she avoided looking at the lovers, sitting like Buddhas, facing the sea. I figured it was prim virginal disapproval that made her look right past them.

And now, finally, I was outside S.K. Naidu's gate. I couldn't believe it. The doorway would, like those portals in science-fiction movies—*Star Trek*, *Star Wars*, *Matrix*—lead to a discovery that had been haunting me for years. Yet, I couldn't move, my feet entangled in a skein of emotions. Was I afraid? There was some of that, fear of rejection, fear of the unknown, fear of disappointment. I expected too much. Sometimes, as mom had said, you should leave well enough alone. She had these sayings from childhood; they would pop up unexpectedly, though she tried to suppress them because they sounded Indian. I should've listened to her. Also, I would've preferred to meet S.K. Naidu alone. I wished Apu had left, instead she'd charged on ahead, earning her rupees, proving herself to me. How could I get rid of her? I didn't want a witness to what could happen.

I stepped over the low threshold of the gate into S.K. Naidu's home, knowing I was going against Mom's wishes. Leave well enough alone.

susie/sushima

If it wasn't for you, I do believe I would have died. I expected permanence in my life, I thought I had a right to it, but this is America and nothing is ever permanent. It's always shifting around: words come and go, buildings come and go, cars come and go, fashions come and go, people come and go. It's a revolving door for change. India never changes. No, no, I'm telling you Nicky, it never changes, not for a thousand years. I bet even today there'll still be two kinds of cars, Ambassador and Fiat. They won't have CD players or mobile phones. We were lucky even to have an ordinary phone which barely worked. And one television channel, just one, so you won't need your remote; it's only off and on. All the women will be wearing saris like the others in their community, tying them exactly the same way their great-grandmother did and they'll be with the same boring husbands they married.

Divorce never happens in India. I had that idea fixed in my mind. No one I knew among my relatives and friends divorced. I swear I didn't know Gary was having an affair with Monica. I mean, they met at *my* dinner party, not on the street or in the bar, but at my dining table. She's such a skinny, pale, pretentious bitch. I'm surprised something like a Pulitzer could've popped out of that tiny brain. It just shows these Pulitzer people have no idea how to judge talent. How could he have even noticed her against the glow of my presence at that table? Oh, men have made passes at me but I was brought up strictly to honour my marriage; I never looked at another man with temptation after I married Gary. I suppose when he took Charlie for his evening walks and came back with a wide grin on his face I should've realized he was getting it off with someone. I certainly didn't think it would be Monica. He had the opportunities; after all he's a famous television personality, a television pundit. I know you never watch him but that has nothing to do with it. Some people respect his thinking, even if you don't. And then he says to me at breakfast one morning 'I want a divorce', as if he's asking me to pass the sugar. I wanted to die. I immediately had a thalanoovo. What's that? It means I got a severe headache . . . Did I actually say that? Well, I had a migraine and took to bed. That's when I called you at school and told you to come home. I needed you desperately: you were the only permanence in my life when I knew Gary was going off to marry Monica. Yes, yes, I know she's twenty years younger than him. It's what all men want, a twenty-something's body all their lives, changing them for still younger ones as they grow older and can't get it up anymore. At least my divorce lawyer got us the house in Westchester, child maintenance and my alimony out of Gary. I do love America for that. In India I would've got zero and been dumped back in my father's house like a sack of garbage.

I'm just cautioning you with my tale of heartbreak. Americans believe in love, they truly do, but not constantly for the same person. I think Renee is a fine woman. Of course she's beautiful, an actress has to be beautiful and not an ugly duckling. But actresses don't know who they are. How can they when they have to keep playing different characters? It must be like entering a maze and not knowing how to find your way back to your real self. She'll make a fine wife; I do believe she adores you. But I wish you had become a lawyer and married another lawyer. Lawyers know all the loopholes in love.

apu

I stuck my head back out. 'Are you coming or are you going to stand there all night?'

'I'd like to see him alone.'

In the gloom, he looked so . . . tense? Why did he want to meet S.K. Naidu alone? I felt a frisson of unease and hoped there'd be no harm done. I'd seen *The Godfather* trilogy and realized Sicilians and Indians were similar. They both nursed vendettas for years, centuries. India had its own godfathers. I'd also seen the Kamal Hassan film, *Nayagan*, in which he played the gangster godfather in a Bombay chawl. Balraj had solved a murder once. A man had been hacked to death and there appeared to be no motive at first. Then, winding back into the man's past, Balraj had discovered the vendetta. Thirty years previously, in the man's native place, a village near Nagercoil, the dead man's father had insulted the killer's mother. He had waited all those years to take his revenge on the son of the man who had insulted her. Sometimes the vendettas were even nurtured abroad. They hired killers to assassinate. Mr Figgis didn't look like an assassin but who did? Balraj had always advised: in a murder look deep into the dead person's past, the motive lies there. I wasn't going to allow him to see the innocent S.K. Naidu alone. No way.

'I'd prefer to meet him by myself,' he said again.

'Not until I know he's S.K. Naidu.' I can be stubborn as a limpet. 'Come and see the surprise.'

Admittedly, I was quite astonished, just as he was when he passed through the gate. We were in a vast unkempt garden, a jungle of trees and entangled undergrowth on either side of a narrow dirt lane winding away. In this natural abode, the chirrup of crickets was louder than the traffic; I strained but couldn't hear even a car horn. There was no house in sight. By the gate was a small one-roomed building, the watchman's station.

'He doesn't look broke,' I whispered. I felt I'd entered a secret place, stepped through into some sort of a wonderland. I waved around, my mind working naturally. 'This property must be worth crores and crores.'

We began up the lane. There was a half moon, shiny as a new silver coin, but the light barely penetrated the thick canopy above us. It broke through in slashes and slivers, a patch here and there. A small animal slid through a patch, stopping Mr Figgis dead in his tracks as it paused to glance at us in surprise, then hurried on, whispering through the bushes.

'Mongoose,' I said, and sensed his question. 'Not dangerous.' Then added maliciously, 'There'll be snakes in the garden too, probably cobras, grass snakes, kraits.'

'I don't mind snakes. I had one as a kid, it choked on a rat.' The lane wound through the trees. 'Obviously, he can't afford a gardener.'

From deeper in the undergrowth, we heard a lonely and plaintive call: 'Mayur . . . mayur.'

'Peacock.'

We walked on cautiously. The lane was a trap of potholes and I stumbled a couple of times. I wished I'd brought my torch and my gun. Then, through the trees, we glimpsed the glow of a lone light bulb, yellow and welcoming as a lighthouse for a lost ship. It took another five minutes of winding back and forth to reach the bulb. We stepped from the chaos of the garden onto an island of order, a neatly trimmed lawn, bordered by rose beds on all sides, like fencing. The lane widened into a swept gravel drive. The bulb hung from a wire in the porch of a huge mansion. The porch was wide enough for two cars and jutted out like the square prow of a ship. Behind it was the mansion, cold and silvered with moonlight, with dark and gloomy wings on either side. Pillars, thick as tree trunks, supported the floor above. They were spaced about twenty feet apart, along the verandas on either side of the entrance. Slate eaves overhung the windows like exaggerated eyebrows. I couldn't tell any colours in this light.

Mr Figgis whispered, 'This is the kinda house that I had imagined would be in Madras, old and gracious, with its colonial heritage stamped in every line.'

We climbed four wide steps and crossed about twenty feet of chequered marble flooring to reach the high green doors with closed shutters. The mantle around the door was of a dark wood, intricately, elaborately carved with deities and entwined with creepers. Each deity had its own compartment; ladder-like they rose up, then across. The deity at the centre was Ganesha. Above us hung a large glass chandelier. There wasn't a light to be seen inside. Yet, the mansion didn't feel deserted or neglected, the paint looked fresh, the mantle spotless. We hadn't left dusty footprints on the marble. Again, there was no bell to summon anybody.

Mr Figgis rapped on the door. The rat-tat faded, absorbed by the empty room beyond. We waited in the silence, it seemed complete and serene. And then, quite faintly, we heard fast clicking sounds. The sounds were stationary, neither approaching nor receding. I edged towards the clicking down the long, deep veranda, past rattan chairs and marble-topped tables. Around the corner, a long veranda continued down towards the glow of a lit room. The clicking grew louder and faster. One half of the shutter was open to let in the evening breeze, and we pressed our faces against the slats to see what was making the sound. A woman sat in a small pool of light at a desk typing furiously on a mechanical typewriter. A clipboard was fixed at eye level and she didn't look down at the keys even for a second. The remainder of the room was in deep shadow. I knocked on the door. The typist didn't stop. I banged harder, rattled the shutters, and this time the woman paused, uncertain of what she'd heard. Her fingers were poised to continue when I struck again, quickly. The woman glanced towards us, her face half in shadow.

'It's Rani,' I said in surprise, though, having seen Shyam, I don't know why I was taken aback. They were always together, yet their presence here puzzled me. Why were they here, in this particular house? 'Rani,' I called out.

Rani heard me but she couldn't believe a stranger had slipped past Shyam. She glanced quickly and saw us as two shadowy outlines. We could be dacoits, except that I had called her name. She decided not to answer the summons. Her fingers flexed above the keys, itching to continue. She peered at us again, but before she could get back to her typing, I called out, 'It's me, Apu.' Rani crossed to us quickly like a commuter rushing for a train. She didn't unlock the door but looked at us warily through the slats.

'What do you want?'

'I want to see Mr S.K. Naidu,' Mr Figgis said impatiently.

'What are you and Shyam doing here?' I demanded.

'Sir educated us and gave us the money to start our business, so we work part-time for him as repayment,' she rattled it off as if it were the most natural reason for their presence.

For me, it was a satisfactory explanation: India intertwined human strands not always visible to the naked eye. People connected, diverged and reconnected, their relationships subtle and hidden like the veins flowing through a body. I didn't believe in coincidence, it was only the conjunction of predestined lives and events. I was a believer in karma—things happened because they were meant to and for no other reason.

'S.K. Naidu,' he spoke urgently, feeling he was going to be prevented by this determined woman.

'You can't see him.'

'He's alive?'

'I haven't seen him in a year.'

'Is he in?'

'He maybe in, he maybe out.'

'Which?' Nikhil screamed.

'I'm only the typist,' Rani said and began to retreat from the threat in his voice.

'Please let us in to see him,' I said, sweet as honey, enticing her back.

'I can't. He never sees anyone.'

'We have to see him,' I said, then with the same sweetness. 'Or I'll just have to tell the kind people at the orphanage what you're really doing. And they're so proud of you too.'

Rani's sullen venom failed to penetrate my sweet smile. She

knew she'd made a big mistake by suggesting my firm investigate those thefts in her orphanage. It had allowed me to know her past. Rani had close ties to the two ladies who ran it, Madam Valli and Madam Surekha. They were proud of her success and she wouldn't want me tittle-tattling tales to them about her 'other' job. She stomped to her desk and brought back a key large enough to open a bank vault. The well-oiled lock opened with a click and she swung the door open.

'He'll be very angry with me,' she sulked, closing but not re-locking the door.

'I'll tell him I blackmailed you,' I said truthfully. 'What are you typing?'

'I don't know,' Rani replied evasively. 'And I don't know where he is.' She returned to her work, her fingers more furious in their clicking.

nicky/nikhil

If Rani hadn't opened the door I would have either broken in—the shutters looked fragile enough—or climbed up to the terrace above the porch. It looked easy to get to, and then in. I was ahead of Apu. I couldn't believe I was in S.K. Naidu's house. The feeling was unreal, surreal, not as I'd imagined it would be. Unlike my one visit to Linda Lund's penthouse, which had been featured in *Town and Garden*, I couldn't have imagined this house and the garden, the blackness in the rooms, the sense of intense privacy that enveloped us. There was no welcome here, just hostile reluctance from those who served the man. I should've waited for daylight, for the warming sun to light my passage through this coming encounter. How many more locked doors would we have to jig past, and who held the keys? I had rehearsed my opening line: Sir, I'm Nikhil. Should I add Figgis? I had mulled over that for months. Would Figgis mean anything to S.K. Naidu? Where would that get me with a private man about to be disturbed by two strangers, his tranquillity shattered? I couldn't think further than that, let S.K. Naidu take it from there.

We were in a large room which, apart from a desk and a chair, was bare. The marble floor was covered with a large Kashmiri carpet. Another unlit chandelier hung from the ceiling here. Two doors led out from the room, one past Rani, the other behind her leading into the mansion. I pushed at the door. It stuck a moment and I thought it locked. Another push and it yawned open into pitch blackness. We stood aside to let the weak light from Rani's desk fall into the room. It barely reached across the threshold, the blackness inside too severe.

'Do you smoke?' Apu asked.

'No, it's bad for health. Why?'

'Then you'd have a lighter or a matchbox.'

She edged in ahead of me, her hands running blindly down the sides of the wall to her left, then to her right till her fingers hit the light switch. We flinched, blinded by the chandelier throwing off megawatts. It must have had twenty bulbs nestled in crystal bowls surrounded by egg-sized drops of glass and crystals hanging like cold icicles. The hall was cavernous; a large circular marble table stood below the chandeliers. Surprisingly, a bunch of roses, still fresh, stood in a large crystal bowl of water. That was a woman's touch. I panicked, I'd not calculated for a woman. I had assumed S.K. Naidu to be single; only single men would live such severed lives. Were there children? It wasn't possible, there were no signs of the untidy passage of kids, they always left a trail of toys, clothes and games behind them. Of course, they could have grown up by now, lurking in other rooms as part of his joint family.

Apu instinctively crossed to smell the roses. Women always do that, the way they 'koochi-kooo' a stranger's baby. The roses were as fat as a man's fist, a purpley red. They sweetened the still air in the room. I thought she would steal one to put in her hair but she resisted. I noted the heavy lock on the front door leading out to the porch and the iron bars on the shuttered windows. Another heavy lock, open and with the key inserted, hung on the door we'd just stepped through. It was waiting to be locked. S.K. Naidu's home felt like a prison, its inmates in control of all the keys.

Gilt chairs with velvet cushions were scattered around, placed against the wall. Two old paintings hung on the walls, large and dominating. Apu whispered 'Ravi Varmas' and crossed to them too, one of a woman with a lamp, the glow delicate as in a Rembrandt, the other of a young man looking across a garden. She peered at the signature, nodding to me—they were the real thing, no doubt a family heirloom. But he was the only artist she recognized. The other paintings were modern abstracts, the kind I liked, but larger, filling up the wall space. Four were of nudes in erotic poses, not European women but Indian. One gazed at us through sleepy, post-coital eyes. The pale green sari covering her nudity was as fine and transparent as a spider's web.

I scanned the hall, barely noting the other objects. There was a glass-paned door at the other end. Just beside it, was a large easel but whatever lay beneath it was hidden with a black silk cloth. I crossed to the door, edged it open and called, 'Mr Naidu!' No answer. So I went on in, feeling bold. The room was a treasure house of silver bric-a-brac in glass cupboards. There was another, smaller chandelier above a settee and two facing chairs, a marble coffee table between them; all in all a more intimate reception room. The room led to another door beyond, filled with more cupboards and statuettes. A large television set dominated here, a couch and a couple of easy chairs facing it. At least S.K. Naidu kept up with the times; he allowed the world to selectively intrude into his solitude. A further shuttered door was locked. I faintly saw the outlines of a desk and filing cabinets, the office room of the occupant, I presumed. I backtracked the way I'd come just as Apu was about to lift the black cloth on the easel.

'Still no sign of him,' I said, opening the door that led deeper into the centre of the house. Apu followed reluctantly. She had wanted to see what was hidden under the cloth.

We passed through a ballroom with a parquet floor. Large gilt-framed mirrors reflected our passage to the raised bandstand. Instead of a band, there was an expensive Sony audio system with rock-band type speakers. On either side of the bandstand were toilets for men and ladies with clean towels and fresh soap in the dishes. The ghostly presence of S.K. Naidu unsettled me. Who did he dance with? Did he host balls? Soirees? I almost heard the music, waltzes and foxtrots and imagined elegant couples floating across the floor, laughing and flirting. There were wide doors on either side of the ballroom. I opened a shutter—that way led out to a terrace and down to the lawn at the side of the house. I crossed, the other door led to the interior courtyard. All the doors were locked.

We started when we heard music. It had happened suddenly, someone had turned on a switch. Apu cocked her head. 'Upstairs.'

We trailed back the way we'd come, and found the stairs. They were of white marble, wide enough for a dozen people to climb together, and the banisters too were of the same marble. A small, tired bulb illuminated the landing above the stairs. We climbed together as quietly as possible and reached a landing, the stairs continuing on either side. On the landing's wall was a strange ink drawing, quite large. It was of a man's head, more a skull, with brooding eyes. He wore a collar and his tie was a woman's naked legs. There was calligraphy writing beneath and we read: 'For S.K. to hang in his home if he wishes, Armand de Wet.'

We stopped at the top of the stairs. Closed doors loomed on all sides. 'Which way?' I whispered. I didn't know why we were whispering. Who was there to hear us? But somehow this strange house demanded respect.

'It's coming from the front,' Apu whispered. She listened a moment, the music more distinct. 'It's an Urdu ghazal, a love song about a man mourning the loss of his loved one. She left him for a warrior. . .'

Her sigh was almost a cry of sadness, the song probably a reminder of her own life. I knew what she felt with that sigh. I wished music, even those melodies that once enchanted us and had happy memories, wouldn't evoke such melancholy in our lives.

I was envious she knew this piece of music. I couldn't recognize it. I could tell Brahms from Beethoven, the Bee Gees from the Dead. They were part of my cultural immersion, but not this sad ghazal. Of course I had CDs of Ravi Shankar, Ustad Ali Khan, even A.R. Rahman but I couldn't fix them in my memory or imagination. I couldn't belong to them in the way this ghazal belonged to her and the unseen listener. A door was slightly ajar and we went through into a spacious billiard room. The table was covered with a dust sheet and on all four sides were raised benches cushioned in faded green velvet, for spectators.

'Well, we know he likes dancing, music and snooker,' Apu said.

I wasn't listening. Across the room was a door, wide open for a change, and I saw a glow of light. I edged to a side to get a clearer view. A fan spun above a chaise longue. A lampstand at its head threw some light down on it. Beside it was a table with books and magazines and a glass. I stood a long time, framing the scene in my mind, wanting to remember it in case I would never return. I just knew S.K. Naidu lay on that chaise longue.

'I've found him,' I whispered, not looking at Apu.

'It could be the servant drinking his master's scotch.' She went ahead of me quickly, protectively, as if ready for anything.

We were on the terrace, open to the sky, looking out at the choppy sea of trees that protected the mansion from the distant road. The trees were high enough to catch the city's glow, the stars dipped down to the treetops. The moon threw sharp, black shadows. A puff of smoke rose from the chaise longue and drifted slowly towards us. It had the rich, satisfying odour of an expensive cigar. I noticed Apu wrinkle her nose appreciatively, possibly remembering those pipes on her desk. We approached but still couldn't see the man. When we were five feet away, I glimpsed his bare feet. A white dhoti hid his ankles. The cigar waved in the air, conducting the music, the glowing tip leaving a trace of its passage like an orange firefly flirting with the night.

I watched the dark hand waving the cigar like a baton. It kept to the rhythm and the beats gracefully, revealing S.K. Naidu's knowledge of the music being played. I was sure it wasn't the housekeeper, it had to be him. Once I confirmed it, I would get rid of Apu.

I cleared my throat softly, but the hand didn't miss a beat.

'Mr Naidu?' My voice sounded unnaturally loud after all the whispering. The hand froze mid-air, surprised by human intrusion. The fingers tightened their grip on the cigar. The ghazal faded away as he pressed the remote. The silence was disturbed by the faint tinkle of Apu's bangles as she moved aside.

s.k. naidu

'Get out of here, get out of here, whoever you are. Now. Get out.'

My heart had skipped a beat, two beats, almost stopped, at the sound of an intruder's voice. Never, ever, through the decades, had my seclusion ever been disturbed at this sacred hour. I reserved this time to listen to my music, drink my two pegs of Black Label (with ice and soda), smoke my Havana cigar and ruminate with the heavens. This was the night I played ghazals and immersed myself in the melancholy lyrics. I was so disciplined in my regime. Tomorrow night I would play Carnatic music, the day after only ragas, Hindi classical the next, Bengali on another. I reserved Sundays for European classical. I savoured this solitude, cherished it in this chaotic world that prowled outside my gates. I seldom, if ever, left this house and compound. Servants did my bidding—the bank, the bills, the provisions. Years ago, Madras Telephones had presented me with an enormous bill of calls made to America, England, France, Germany as if I were the centre of a financial empire. I refused to pay the bill and they disconnected me. I never missed the damn thing; it was an irritant with its shrill summons. I had few needs. I ate sparingly, thrice a day, the simplest of foods—saadham, sambar, dal, kheera, thayresaadham, whatever Ethiraj prepared, depending on his culinary whims. My dress was modest—white jiba, white dhoti—though I was neither modest nor humble. I chose my friends as carefully as a woman would a piece of jewellery from the glittering arrays available. They believed I was lonely because I did not need their constant company. I had my mind and my books, far better companions and never false. No one, not even Rani, approached me in this hallowed place. I had threatened to hang her by her toes if she ever did. Admittedly, I'd not seen her for years, we communicated through the notes I left beside her typewriter. But this wasn't Rani's voice, or Shyam's or Prasad's. It was an alien's voice; a total stranger had penetrated my privacy. It wasn't an Indian voice either—the 'Mr Naidu' had an American nasal tone. My lines of defence, the locked gate, Shyam, Prasad, Rani and the locked and barred doors, had been breached. I had been invaded.

'Don't you understand the English language? Get out of here. Immediately, or I'll call the police.'

'Mr Naidu,' the voice repeated.

'Are you an imbecile that you don't understand the simplest command which even a dog would comprehend? Out, out, out. How did you get past my centurions?'

'Conned them,' the man said. 'Mr Naidu . . .'

'Con them on your way out. Now get out.' I pressed the remote, expecting obedience, and returned to my conducting.

'Mr Naidu, my name is . . .'

'I don't care if your name's Julius Caesar. Get out.'

But then I held up my hand. I took a deep exploratory breath, testing the air around me. A tendril of perfume, like a lone long hair on the morning pillow, scented the warm air. Yes, there was another person with the man.

'I heard bangles and now I smell perfume. You're not a fruit are you?'

A woman laughed. 'It's me.'

Her laughter gave me pleasure, it freshened the violated air. 'I hope you're as beautiful as you smell,' I spoke in the gentler tones of seduction. 'Perfumes are deceptive. They make us fall in love with the scents of a female.'

'Animals mate by smell.'

'Hah!' I was triumphant. The woman amused me. 'That's why they haven't evolved. They spend their time sniffing each other instead of discussing the nature of love and sexual attraction.' I took a puff on my cigar, enjoying the conversation with the unseen woman. It was always more pleasurable to be seduced by women's voices than by their presence: it gave room for fantasies. 'Are you the man's wife?'

'No. I'm a private detective and I found you.'

I gave a loud mocking laugh. 'Found! I was never lost.' She sounded young too, and it had been years since I'd seen a young woman in this house. It was time to test her further and amuse myself. 'So, if you're not his wife you may consider becoming my mistress. I assure you it will be a life of erotic leisure.'

She laughed again, quite delighted with the boldness of an old man. Young men hesitate to make such open propositions; they don't want to risk the rejection. An older man doesn't care much. Besides, she sensed I was just teasing her, which was what I wanted, to lull her into a false security.

'May I think about it?' She was teasing me too.

'I never allow women to think about erotic proposals. When a man meets a woman, he must decide immediately what he wants of her. Does he want her as a lover? A mother? A friend? And I never mention marriage. It spoils women, they constantly expect proposals.'

'How do you know what you want from me? I could just be the friend type.'

'Not from your voice, it simmers with sexuality.' I waved my cigar in her direction. 'Let me look at you.' I hoped I wouldn't be disappointed.

'Mr Naidu . . .' the man was taking a step forward too.

'Wait until you're summoned, young man,' I said sternly. 'I want to see her first.'

She edged around like a schoolgirl in front of the headmistress so I could see her. She didn't disappoint me, though I could not make out her shape under those voluminous clothes. Her eyes were bright with mischief and humour and many possibilities, I thought. She had the indolent eyelids of a courtesan. 'Perfect mistress material, shapely I presume, sensual, with a sense of humour. Sex without the humour is pointless in my opinion. Don't you think so?'

'It depends on the man,' she said. 'Men take sex too seriously, it's a labour for them to perform and they forget with whom they're performing.'

'Exactly. Maintaining the erection can be a hazardous duty for us men,' I was enjoying her company. She didn't titter with embarrassment as most of the insipid women I met would have if we spoke of erections and penetrations. 'We'll just have to see, won't we?' I took a sip of whisky, my eyes steady on her above the rim of the glass. She didn't feel threatened by me; this was only flirtation which I'd push to the limit. 'Do you play poker?'

The question was unexpected and it threw her off her complacent balance. I loved to prowl around women verbally, stroke them, make them purr, and then slide in from another direction.

'Badly,' she said.

Which meant she didn't play at all. 'Excellent. I love women who play poker badly. You can come and play strip poker with us on Friday night, around eight o'clock.'

She couldn't help laughing at my boldness. She looked across to the man still standing behind me. 'I'll bring him.'

'And his money, if you must. You can leave now.'

The man jumped in quickly. 'Mr Naidu, I've come to discuss a proposal about adapting your brilliant novel for a stage play and . . .'

'Oh god, you're not another one of them. I had some film fellow pursuing me relentlessly. He made half-cocked films about the damned Brits in India. He sent me a tape of one, it was pretentious and boring as hell. Now please go away. But you can leave her.'

'I think you should listen to him,' she said.

I smiled, revealing all my perfect teeth. I was delighted that I'd set the trap and she'd walked into it. 'If I do, will you go to bed with me?' Always reveal your motives to a woman when she's distracted by the travails of another man as she will often succumb to seduction to help him.

'Of course not,' she said, indignant at being out-manoeuvred. A minor setback. I knew she'd been worrying about the man, wanting him included in our conversation. I had noticed the determination and the quick glances she threw at him.

I feigned disappointment at her rejection. She was quick-witted and chagrined I'd outwitted her. Who was this man? She'd said she was a private detective. The man was her client, a boring one, pursuing me about a novel I wanted to forget.

'Then why should I listen to his drivel?'

'Because he's an extremely talented director and the play will be performed on Broadway in New York.'

'I know where Broadway is.'

'She means off-Broadway,' the man said quickly, in case I thought it would be staged in a major theatre where they performed mindless musicals for the masses.

The woman was looking at me with pleading eyes. They were large, expressive, a pale brown it seemed from this distance. She would be a woman with passion, if she was with the right man. I weighed her eyes against the hovering presence of the man behind me. I sensed the impatience but made him wait. I could refuse her but then the man would return. The man sounded the persistent type, like that filmmaker. They were of a different age and sensibility to me, I would have accepted the refusal—pride was all-important—and exited stage left graciously. How would I get rid of them now? I wasn't a physical man, too slim, and wise, to grab them by the scruffs of their necks and lead them out. Besides, they were younger and stronger. Should I call Prasad and Shyam? A scuffle would take place, spoiling my tranquillity with small violence. I sighed: how on earth had he come across such an obscure and forgotten novel?

'I suppose you've come all the way from that country to harass me until I capitulate? I don't like America or Americans so don't expect any favours from me. Well, let's see who you are.'

'Thank you, sir.'

He was tall, fairly good looking, with pathetically eager-to-please eyes, I thought, like a puppy dog wagging its tail for a biscuit. He took a step forward and offered his hand. 'Mr Naidu I'm . . .'

'I have no curiosity about you, young man, absolutely none.'

I ignored the hand; it faltered and fell back to the young man's side. I had been deliberate in my rudeness. It was the best way to deter pests. The man was young enough, vulnerable enough to flush both with embarrassment and a flicker of anger at this rejection. Yet, he didn't move. He disturbed me in a different way. He stood in silence, studying me. No, not studying; rather devouring me with those sharp eyes. I felt myself being photographed—snap, snap, snap—to be remembered later on and examined further with minute intensity. At least those eyes had some innocence in their curiosity, unlike that film-man who had a cheater's eyes and a round corrupt face.

'Neither do I have any curiosity about your career, young man, but if you want my advice why don't you do an American play? O'Neill, Williams, Miller, Simon, Albee? Why would an American audience want to see a play set in the past in a remote country they've never heard of? Besides, you look too young to have even heard of me,' I added, mockingly. 'So don't flatter me by saying you've actually read me.'

'I have,' he said and took out the book with the reverence of an autograph hunter. He held it up as proof and thrust it towards me. But I didn't take it; I stared at it with the alertness of a tiger sensing danger. I had expected to see a typescript of his play, like the film-man thrusting a film script at me, not the actual book. He took a step forward, believing the book was out of my reach and I too lazy to raise my hand a few inches. I had no choice then but to take the book, holding it with the delicacy of a piece of offal.

I glanced at the spine. It was wrinkled; the book had been well read. The gilt lettering was faint and cracked. An unread book's spine would have been pristine, the lettering still bold. That would dismay a writer, he'd know the book had been opened, a few pages read and then set aside for eternity. I smiled thinly. 'The one and only edition, and rare as a penny black.' I put it down on the table beside me, not caring to examine it further, believing it had been found in some second- or third- or fourth-hand bookstore.

'You'll love the play,' he said enthusiastically and with genuine passion. 'But if you do have problems, which I doubt, I thought we could work that through together while I'm here. I did bring it with me but unfortunately it was in my suitcase and the taxi driver drove off with the case. I've a floppy in my bag and I can print up a copy tomorrow.'

'Think no such thoughts, young man,' I said. 'I've no desire to see my work mangled by you or anyone else. Now, you can leave. Goodbye.'

She couldn't help herself. 'Are you always so rude?'

I smiled. 'Always. Rudeness flushes out the emotional system, politeness only constipates it.'

I waved my cigar at both of them, waving them away as if smoke, and turned up the music. The music rose, the singer's voice calling out to the stars and heavens to return her lover to her, but they would always remain deaf to the pleas of unrequited love. I should know, and so did the detective for I heard her sigh and saw her close her eyes to shut out memories. She made a move towards the stairs. To her surprise and mine, the man lowered himself to the floor and sat cross-legged.

'What are you doing?'

'Performing a satyagraha, sir.'

'You're not Indian, so it doesn't apply. Leave at once.'

He smiled. 'I'm as Indian as you.'

'That brown skin masks a true-blue American. Besides, I'm in a more comfortable position than you and can outlast you.'

I turned the music to full volume. The sitar, the flute, the tabla flooded the treetops and rose up to the stars. Of course, the nearest neighbour was a couple of hundred yards away but the startled birds stirred, squawked, chirruped, cawed in protest at such a rude awakening. My wild garden was not only a haven for serpents, mongoose, squirrels, iguanas but also a paradise for birds. Crows, mynahs, woodpeckers, sparrows, koels, peacocks and migrant egrets feasted on mangoes, tamarinds, bananas, guavas and papayas. In May, while the city stank in the summer heat, the garden air would be sweetened with the smell of ripe fruit. The woman clamped her hands over her ears and sank down gracefully into a yogic pose, her spine straight for the energy to flow between her brain and her kundalini. The floor vibrated to the tablas. I remained composed, and closed my eyes, as if immersed in silence. But their presence was an irritant, even with eyes shut tight I was aware of them even though they were silent. I lowered the volume.

He spoke softly, hurriedly, before I turned up the volume again. 'I was really moved by your writing,' he said urgently, wanting to seduce me swiftly. 'In just a few lines you've evoked the whole sense of a person's character and the period. After I read it, it haunted me for a long time and then I saw it as a powerful stage play. I worked on it for a whole year to capture and distil the essence of what you wrote about.'

He was interrupted by Prasad emerging from the shadows, soft as a cat. He carried a silver tray with glasses and an open bottle of soda. I noticed the woman trying to catch his eye but Prasad avoided contact as he handed her a glass of water. Did they know each other? Had Prasad let her in? Did I see betrayal in front of me? He took the other glass to the man who refused, still intent on looking at me. Prasad moved to the side table, poured me two fingers of Black Label and filled it with ice and soda. He avoided eye-contact with me knowing he'd be looking down into fury, and drifted back into the shadow.

'Have you directed Shakespeare?' I asked abruptly, desperate to be rid of the American.

'*Macbeth, Richard III, Taming of . . .*'

'An overrated writer,' I sneered, having got him to commit to an opinion. 'If he'd written in Bulgarian he would've died in well-deserved obscurity. I believe Sam Beckett was a greater playwright. We were friends in Paris. How I miss him!'

He still did not move. I sighed, looked at the book, then gently picked it up, weighing it as if testing the quality of what lay inside. I had never wanted to see this book again; I had neither the original manuscript nor a copy. I had burned them, along with other things, years ago. Now it had risen from the ashes and lay searing my hand. What else was going to rise from those ashes? I opened it warily. It was unsigned, and I reread the dedication to my parents. I flicked through the pages mechanically, avoiding the printed words. This was for their benefit, a show of interest to be rid of the man. I stopped, chilled. I knew the ashes were stirring the memories. The handwriting crawled like worms in the margins of the text. I turned to other pages quickly, unbelieving. More worms, serpents of writing writhing across the bottom of the pages too.

I looked up praying I was wrong, and whispered with controlled fury. 'Did you desecrate these sacred pages with your puerile scribbling?'

He smiled, happy at my recognition, misreading my tone. 'It was my mother. I found the book in an old suitcase of hers.'

'What did you say your name was?'

'You didn't give me a chance. It's Nikhil Figgis, sir.'

I hurled the book at Nikhil Figgis, missing him. It fell and slid on the floor, the railing stopped it from falling off. I knew it, I knew it. The dead lived, they came back from the fires.

'Get out, get out, get out immediately.' I rose in rage, looking down at the startled face and across to the woman who was staring at me in surprise. Neither moved and I knew I would have to leave, lock myself away from them. I took a quick step, then turned and spat that unmentionable name that hadn't sullied my tongue for many, many years. 'Did Sushima send you?'

'No, I . . .'

I raged on, 'All these years I never heard from her and now you dare to come here under false pretences to hoodwink me?'

He jumped up, angry at such a wild accusation. 'What false pretences? I do want to stage this play, I do believe you wrote a great novel. I want to be proud of you.'

'Get out. I'll never give you permission.'

I turned and hurried, almost ran from the terrace, losing my kolhapuri slippers, to enter the blackness of my room. I bolted and locked my bedroom door. I knew it was a futile gesture, the damage had been done, I had been violated by the past. She had sent this Nikhil to mock me, to show me what I had missed out in life, an only son, the fruit of my loins she had stolen away so long ago. I groaned at the thought that even at this moment the boy was reporting to Sushima that he had met his father, old as a vulture, decrepit and corrupted in his small empire. How they must be laughing at me! Damn her, damn him. There could be no forgiveness for such cruelty. I wanted to remain calm, to return to my sense of stillness, so I performed pranayam, taking deep breaths through one nostril and letting them out of the other. But that didn't stop my agitation. I unlocked the door and rushed back to the terrace to confront him.

'And you can tell your mother . . .' I started to shout and found the terrace deserted. They had gone. It was also that damned woman detective's fault for finding me. My whole purpose had been not to be found, to avoid all contact with people, except those of my choosing. A half-finished drink remained and I poured another peg of Black Label into it and knocked it back. It wasn't good for me. My doctor had advised two pegs a day and I had been strict in my obedience, which was against my nature. Today was an exception; Dr P.C. Cherian could forgive me if anything unfortunate happened. I swigged yet another peg, then paused, listening. I thought I heard a man shouting something but it was too indistinct, muffled by the trees. Cautiously, I made my way around the perimeter of the terrace, peering down, ready to spring back should they be on the lawns looking up towards me. There was no one in sight. Equally cautiously, I made my way down the stairs. I didn't need any light; I could make my way around blindfolded. The door leading into the side room was open. It had been closed earlier in the evening. I looked in. There was no one there. Rani had left her typed sheets on the table. I locked the door leading out to the veranda, and then, paranoid, I wondered whether I had locked the rude intruders in. I took a circuit of the rooms, opening and locking each door once I knew they were empty.

I returned wearily to the terrace; eyeing the empty glass, the half-full bottle. No, she wouldn't get me to kill myself, she had killed me many, many years ago though I walked, breathed, slept, ate, defecated. I clung to this human shell tenaciously in defiance against her. The book lay on the floor and I let it lie. In the morning it would be swept away by a servant, consigned to the rubbish.

I retreated to my room, the final refuge, bolted and locked the door, although ghosts could slip in through the cracks. Moonlight threw long shadows of my barred window across the teak floor. My bedroom was austere: a narrow four-poster bed, a bedside table with a reading light and a pile of books, a durrie on either side of the bed, an almirah for my simple clothes and a dresser for my silver-backed brush and comb. Above it was an oval gilt-framed mirror. I stared at my reflection, looking for any similarity with this son. The boy had been in shadow, while I had been exposed to light. We had the same thick shock of hair except mine was white, and maybe the same shape of our chins. Otherwise, there was absolutely no resemblance. I moved away, not wanting to remember any further. I had caught a glimpse of Sushima in my son's features.

Nikhil Figgis was a stranger, and never my son but hers. I felt too emotionally drained to change into my pyjamas and lay back on the bed, one hand clasping the other on my chest, as if laid out in a funeral room. I had to control my mind: that was man's weakest link, it flew away into corners I didn't want to explore. I remembered her clearly, after all these years, as she resurrected herself out of my hidden memory. Of course, she was still young; twenty-eight years had not passed. Her breath, soft and perfumed, tickled my ear. Even then it had been poisonous, but I hadn't known it, thinking she breathed love into my mind. I sat up abruptly, the pain hadn't lessened, it was sharp, suffocating me, and I cried out as I had done so long ago. I knew I couldn't allow this to happen again. I had to sleep and prayed I wouldn't dream. In the morning, she would be gone, consigned to being the forgotten. I took two Calmpose tablets from the bedside table and swallowed the sedative with a glass of water.

nicky/nikhil

I stood a couple of feet behind, I didn't want to cross the threshold of the man's patience entirely. My mom was right—he had a full head of white hair, not even a coin of baldness, neatly combed with a fifties' quiff. His cotton jiba was also the same white. The dhoti had a narrow green and gold border. Despite my intense study of the back of his head, I failed to distract him from Apu. She was looking down on him and smiling flirtatiously. Was she attracted to him? She did have an impudent appeal. I hadn't thought of her in any other way and, even now, I saw her only as an impediment to my plans. What did she see? Was he sensual? Handsome? Ugly? Magnetic? She hadn't lifted her eyes to even give me a hint of reassurance. His English was impeccable, it had to be, he'd written a fine novel, though he spoke with that faint singsong Indian accent. Someone had told me that Indians spoke English like the Welsh did. I'd never been to Wales and couldn't confirm that opinion. I couldn't believe it. They were exchanging views about sex like practised lovers. They'd forgotten my presence. I was the one who'd brought them together and I felt like a high school kid watching his best friend steal away the prom queen from under his nose. Not that Apu would have made a prom queen; she didn't look the type who'd want to be that popular with a bunch of zombies.

'I suppose you've come all the way from that country to harass me until I capitulate?' he spoke to me over his shoulder. 'I don't like America or Americans, so don't expect any favours from me. Well, let's see who you are.'

'Thank you, sir.'

I took a few steps to face him. This was the moment I'd been waiting for for so many years. Though I had the advantage of looking down at the supine man, indolent in his confidence, I felt I was at a disadvantage. His eyes were a dark brown, bordering on black, and they weren't welcoming. There was none of the 'fury' in them that Mom had described, but they sparkled like the bright embers of a banked fire. The contrast between the snowy whiteness of his hair and the dark, narrow face gave him a satanic air. I understood Apu's attraction to him. The face had strength, yet it was tranquil; it needed nothing from the world outside this house and garden. I was trembling inside with anticipation as we talked. I had expected him to recognize Mom's handwriting, look up and smile warmly. But then . . .

'Get out, get out, get out immediately. Did Sushima send you?'

'No, I . . .'

He cut me off, still yelling. 'All these years I never heard from her and now you dare to come here under false pretences to hoodwink me.'

I jumped up, angry at such a wild accusation. 'What false pretences? I do want to stage this play; I do believe you wrote a great novel. I want to be proud of you.'

'Get out. I'll never give you permission.'

I hadn't expected such rage. I had believed in my heart and mind that there would be a welcoming embrace, had dreamed of it ever since I discovered he was still alive and hadn't died in a car crash on the road to Bangalore.

Self-deception, I thought bitterly, how it blinds us to reality.

The book lay on the floor. I thought of picking it up, then left it where it lay and moved towards the stairs.

Apu caught up with me, the slow-moving zombie. 'What was that about?'

My voice was bitter with the rejection. 'He's my father.'

'Why didn't you tell me?'

'You didn't need to know.'

I was seventeen when I discovered that my natural father had written a novel. I had just finished high school with A grades and had been accepted by the Yale Drama School. Our new home in Westchester was another Hampton-like Gulag, only, without the sea, and I didn't have my buddy Mike for companionship. This wasn't a two-week exile from New York City, but a life sentence. There were no sidewalks: nobody walked anywhere, even to cross the street. At night everyone died for eight hours.

At the time, I had been smoking a joint in the attic. The attic was safer than the bathroom, my own room or the basement because, despite liberal spraying of my Boss aftershave, the smell of pot lingered. My parents had noses sharper than a Customs sniffer dog's; they could track a joint down the main street in midday traffic. Well, not so much Mom—she tolerated my many shortcomings—but Gary, who had a reputation to protect and didn't want his 'son' busted for possession. The attic contained the history of passing fashion in my family—discarded dresses and hats, Afghan overcoats, two-button suits, Nintendo games, LPs of forgotten rock groups. I had been lying down, studying my magnificent toes, when my gaze lifted half an inch and fell on a small suitcase half hidden by a faded shawl. I crawled across the attic and pulled the case out of its hiding place. It was larger than a briefcase and made of animal skin, brown hide with large spots of white. I had never seen it before. There was a faded Air India sticker by the handle with my mother's name and a Brooklyn address I had heard of, written in her hand. It was locked. Locks guarded precious possessions and I wondered what was so valuable to Mom that she had hidden it away. I foraged around and found a long, rusty screwdriver. The locks were as cheap as the suitcase and sprang open at barely a touch.

There was a parcel in it, wrapped in yellowing newspaper so brittle with age that it disintegrated the moment I picked it up. I found myself holding a neatly folded silk sari. It was a deep red, redder than blood, with a heavy, very wide border embroidered with stiff gold thread. It felt soft and sensual and cool. I smelt my mother in its folds. I had never seen her wear a sari of any colour, let alone this special one. Something hard and oblong seemed to be hidden within its folds. I opened it up quickly and found a book nestling in its silk bed, like a jewel. Coiled on top of the book was a long dead serpent of dried flowers and a small gold cylinder attached to a red string. I couldn't guess the original colour of the flowers; they were pea-sized now and as fragile as the paper, fragmenting into dust as I slid them gently off the book. I didn't pick it up immediately: may be it was something special, not meant for my eyes. Why else would it have been hidden away for so many years? It didn't have a dust jacket and the cover was a dull red. But it still had a new feel as if it were straight from a bookstore. I wondered why the dust jacket had been removed and wiped my hands on my shirt front before turning it around to see the spine. I shivered. *Georgetown* by S.K. Naidu, the father I had never known. Without a moment's hesitation, hungry for any morsel of my father, I began to read the novel. Mom had written her comments in the margins: 'not true', 'this is made up', 'good description', 'my mother fooled you too', but only my father's tale interested me . . .

Remembering that time, I hurried down the stairs, running away now from such humiliation to hide in the grim shadows. Apu was a few steps behind me, holding onto the banister. She caught up with me at the bottom of the stairs as I hesitated: right or left or straight ahead, which was the way out? She led me out the way we'd come in. Rani had gone, though the pool of light remained above the desk. The typewriter was covered with a cloth. Beside it was a slim stack of typed pages.

Apu's hand resting lightly on my arm comforted me. I hadn't wanted her to witness this rejection, although I had prayed for the embrace of acknowledgement from my father. What was the terrible sin that both Mom and he were incapable of forgiving? How can a child understand if he's not told what caused such implacable hatred of each other? I felt Apu vibrating too with her questions, but she remained silent and I was grateful.

'My mother told me he was dead,' I said finally, answering her unspoken questions. 'Then, when I was twelve years old, she told me my father was alive and, if I wanted, I could go and see him. I was shattered by her confession. I couldn't understand why she and Gary, my stepfather—more she—had lied to me. For the first time, I rowed with Mom. She said she had done it to protect me; she didn't want me yearning to return to India when we had such a good life in America. And, yeah, she'd divorced my father and married Gary. They had met in the Taj hotel, that was true she swore. But I couldn't come to India without hurting her. She had said it in that tone of hers, near to tears, begging me not to leave her. I know she sounds manipulative, but I was the only one she had and she didn't want me to leave her side.'

'What happened?'

'I don't know. She wouldn't tell me the details. Parents will always remain a mystery to us, they'll tell us only what they believe we should know. They create their own mythology to hide their failings and to fool us deliberately. They're our original censors, rewriting their history, even as nations rewrite theirs. Sometimes, it's pure fiction. All she'd say was "we didn't get on", and that covers a multitude of sins. But I know now why she left him.' I couldn't contain myself any longer and hit back at my father. I turned and screamed at the house. 'You're an arrogant, pretentious, cantankerous old man. You've got the manners of a pig and I'm glad I never had you as my father.' I felt better, though I knew it was childish.

Apu spoke with a put-on American accent, 'I don't mind if you don't like my manners, I don't like 'em myself. They're pretty bad. I grieve over 'em on long winter evenings.' She laughed when she finished, wanting to lighten the mood. I looked at her as if she had gone nuts.

'Phillip Marlowe in *The Big Sleep*,' she explained. 'I've read all of Raymond Chandler's novels.'

I smiled wanly, momentarily lightened. 'And memorized them too.'

We remained silent on the drive to my hotel. The night air was somewhat cooler, though not by much, and the traffic had thinned considerably. I felt her glances on me quite often, sympathetic and curious, but I stared ahead, not wanting to open myself up to her any further, desperate to escape into the cool, anonymity of a hotel room. How would she understand the wretched turmoil inside me, the shame of being rejected so brutally by my own father?

The entrance to the Lagoon Hotel was on a steep incline. She stopped, waiting for me to climb out. I woke from a daze, surprised to find myself under the bright lights of the porch. Then, impulsively, Apu stroked my cheek with her fingers, the gesture a compassionate farewell; it felt soft and delicate, like a lover's caress. The car jockeys waited for her to get out but she remained as I tiredly climbed out.

'I won't be needing you any more. And many thanks.'

She grinned. 'I told you I was good.'

'The best,' I agreed with little humour.

'I'll settle our accounts tomorrow and refund the money.'

I waved her and the refund away, not expecting to see her again, the only witness to my pain.

The Lagoon was a funky hotel, very elegant, with high ceilings and movie and news clips playing on a giant screen. Young guys milled around, clutching mobile phones and whisky glasses. I only wanted silence and privacy for my breakdown. The room was cool, decorated with movie posters. I hooked the 'Do Not Disturb' sign on the knob outside, locked the door, slipped the chain across and drew the curtains open. The city was flat as a pancake. It didn't have the awe of the Manhattan skyline or the historical landmarks of Paris or London. Comfortingly featureless, it demanded nothing further from me. I needed a drink to revive me, chilled Chablis, a whole bottle to myself. I doubted the hotel would have a bottle of Napa Valley Chablis. Though I'd not eaten all day, apart from a handful of peanuts, I wasn't hungry; exhaustion and disappointment had shrunk my appetite. The minibar only had miniatures of whisky, brandy, gin and vodka, with unfamiliar Indian brandnames. I risked the whisky and poured myself two of the miniatures. Once I drank this, I would move to the brandy, gin and vodka, obliterating all memory of recent events.

I switched off the light, drew up a chair and looked out at the expanding night sky. I saw Nikhil Figgis, né Naidu, a lost and damaged soul, reflected back at me. Was there any similarity between father and son? Our hair was similar, thick and heavy, but apart from that one feature, I did not recognize any others. My nose was smaller, slightly upturned, like Mom's, my mouth as well-shaped and sensual as hers. My father had a straight nose, and firm compressed lips, cruel I thought. That mouth could snap shut like a bear trap. I did not want to compare any more and my eyes turned away towards a city I didn't really see. What would I do now? I was heavy with the lassitude of disappointment and depression. I couldn't move or think through any plans. I had none. What would have happened if I had been greeted joyously, like a prodigal? Why, then I would still be at the house, talking, laughing, and telling my new found real father all about myself. We would be having dinner somewhere in that house . . .

'Oh for chrissake,' I shouted. 'Give it up, it's never going to happen. He hates you, hates the thought of you. You remind him of Sushima.' I understood why in the ancient times, men chastised themselves to be rid of sin and evil. I needed to chastise all hope out of myself, return to New York, get on with my career, direct Albee, Williams and make a name, not brood about a lonely man haunting his huge house.

The door buzzer startled me as I emptied the vodka into the glass. It intruded into my sad introspection, cracked the frozen layer of self-pity. Who could it be? Room service? I hadn't ordered anything. The maid? She could fuck off. I took my glass to the window again but the buzzer followed me. Couldn't they read a 'Do Not Disturb' sign? I sat stubbornly, in silence, but the buzzer persisted. I knocked back the vodka which only fuelled my outrage, and crossed to open the door.

'For chrissake, can't you read?' I yelled at the empty corridor, standing a good foot inside my room, ready to slam the door shut.

Then I looked down.

My Samsonite suitcase rested just by the threshold, squarely placed, so I wouldn't miss it.

Seeing it filled me with optimism for the world at large. It reminded me that miracles could happen when all hope was lost, and if India could conjure up my lost suitcase, it contradicted all Mom's pessimism about her old country. Lost-and-found here worked better than the New York transit system. I was overflowing with goodwill and, asking forgiveness, withdrew all the invectives I had rained down on the orange-haired cop. He had found my case and sent it up, not even requiring a tip or a bribe for his efficient diligence in tracking it down! I promised myself I would drop into the Nungumbakkam police station the next day and give the man a couple of hundred rupees.

I took a step forward to pick up my suitcase. As I took hold of the handle firmly, a hand appeared from the right side of the doorway and, before I knew what was happening, one bracelet of a handcuff clicked shut on my wrist. A hand remained holding the other end. I stared disbelievingly at the handcuff. What had just happened?

The hand was followed by the rest of the body: polished brown shoes, khaki trousers with knife-sharp creases, a polished brown leather belt with a brass buckle embossed with a red temple, a polished leather holster with a khaki cord lanyard running up past a perfectly pressed khaki shirt with epaulettes on the shoulders and, above the tabbed collar, a triumphant, cold face. There was a peaked cap with a polished leather visor on top of the face. The orange-haired Sergeant Sait appeared from the other side of the door where he had been waiting, pressed against the wall like a gecko, and behind him were two constables armed with ancient rifles.

'I am Assistant Commissioner of Police (Crime), A.C. Manian (IPS), Chengelpetta Range, and you admit this suitcase belongs to you?' The officer spoke slowly and clearly, as if I didn't understand

English. 'In the FIR, you called yourself Nikhil Figgis, no doubt this is an alias to confuse us. What's your real name? And you said you were from New York. Or is it Peshawar?'

He had a lean and hungry face which reminded me of Cassius. The cop would be perfect for the part; most American actors were a bit too heavy and well-fed to play that role. He also had a wolf's grin, baring its teeth at the kill. Why in such moments of stress and panic did reason go haywire? Why was I thinking Shakespeare? But I saw ambition in that face, he was on the fast track to a promotion and to success. The sergeant was also grinning and nodding, seeing himself rise up the cop ladder to cop heaven. I looked down, not at the suitcase, but at the handcuff. The steel was cold and hard around my wrist. Should I deny ownership? My name was on the airline sticker, with my NYC address, the old Riverside one.

I smiled placatingly. 'Yes, but . . .'

'You are under arrest for manufacturing and transporting bombs,' Manian said in triumph.

'Bombs! What bombs?' I yelled, and then groaned. I'd forgotten my childish, sarcastic crack at Sergeant Sait. It had been a glancing remark, a joke, thrown away and deleted since the meeting with my father. 'Are you crazy? I've never made bombs in my life. I don't know how to light a match, for chrissake. It was a dumb crack I made.'

My righteous anger failed to dent Manian's conviction that I was a terrorist. Every criminal denied his deed, even on his way to the gallows. Imperiously he held out his hand to Sergeant Sait who passed the FIR to him under my nose.

Manian skimmed the report. 'You confessed to Sergeant Sait that you had a bomb in your suitcase.' He handed it back to Sait. 'Make it easy for yourself. Which protest movement do you belong to?'

'None, I was . . .'

'You must belong to some organization,' Manian spoke with a kindly voice, wanting to confide his superior knowledge. 'Every protest movement makes bombs. This country's bomb-crazy. If they don't like the telephone, they bomb it. If they don't like the bus service, they bomb it. If they don't like a politician, they bomb him.' He paused, seeming to consider the last well deserved. 'Bomb-making is a small-scale industry here.'

I had had enough. I glared at Manian, then at the Judas, Sait. 'For chrissake, I was just joking. Tell him I was joking,' I pleaded.

I knew even as I said it that Sergeant Sait was certainly not going to admit to any such mistake in front of the assistant commissioner of police. It wasn't worth his pension to admit he'd goofed and dragged this important cop out of bed. Sait remained silent.

'Listen,' I demanded. 'Why would I admit there's a bomb in my suitcase to the cops?'

'Why not? Dumb cops go rushing to find the suitcase, open it and booooom we're blown to bits and pieces. If you see American films, always dumb cops get blown up by bombs in suitcases, cars, vans, telephones and what else.'

I admitted I had seen some of these movies. The logic, in my weary mind, seemed impeccable. I tried again. 'I was just joking.'

'Who makes jokes about bombs? You tell me. I've never heard of any bomb jokes. I only know lawyer jokes.' Manian patted me on the head as if I were a safely chained German Shepherd. 'What do you do when you see three lawyers buried upto their necks in sand?'

'Buy more sand?' I wondered where this was leading to. Was he trying to prove my guilt by telling jokes and seeing how I responded?

Manian frowned. 'Sand? Why sand? Buy cement.' He laughed in thorough enjoyment of his joke, as did Sergeant Sait and the two constables. They did not understand the humour but since the big man laughed, they did too. He cut them off abruptly. 'I hate lawyers. Open the case.'

I dug into my pocket and found the single key to the case. I bent to insert it.

'Not near me, you fool,' Manian shouted. 'In there . . .'

I shrugged and wheeled the suitcase into the room, leaving tracks in the carpet. I looked back and saw the heads of Manian and Sait peering past the door. I heaved the case onto the bed, unlocked it and stood back.

'Remove each item very slowly and place it on the floor,' Manian commanded from the door.

At least this was a distraction from my emotional turbulence, however weird it may be. I had to think fast, somehow convince this mad cop I had nothing to do with terrorists, bombs or movements. I prayed they hadn't planted something in my suitcase that would blow me to bits, my scattered body parts proof that they'd found a terrorist. Suitcase locks could be opened with a paper clip. I opened the case warily, flinching from the possible explosion. The surface looked untouched, as best as I could remember. Cautiously, I removed my shirts, trousers, boxer shorts, books, the precious manuscript, now worthless, and my shoes, and dropped them on the floor. I lifted the empty case to show the cops. Manian entered warily, eyeing the scattered items, waving me to move back towards the window. I watched him toe through the clothes and check the shoes. They looked worn and normal, the heels not filled with explosives. Sait edged into the room once he was certain nothing would go bang.

He was bitterly disappointed at Manian finding nothing. 'We beat up three taxi drivers for nothing.'

Manian was dismissive. 'So we'll do three new ones next time. They deserved it anyway.' He snapped his fingers, pointing to the manuscript and Sait picked it up gingerly. Manian riffled the pages cautiously, then read the title page aloud. 'Georgetown, a play by Nikhil Fig-gis, adapted from the novel by S.K. Naidu.' He held the manuscript as tenderly as Moses had held the tablets. 'S.K. Naidu is a great writer. He should be a Nobel prizer, a Pulitzer prizer, a Booker prizer.'

Though relieved at such heady recognition of my father, I was puzzled that one novel should have brought out such flattery. Manian was obviously a fan of the book. 'It's been out of print for years. When did you read it?'

'I've only heard about him,' he confessed, slightly embarrassed. 'My teacher at my Madurai high school spoke most highly of S.K. Naidu.' Manian weighed the manuscript, watching me, trying to make a decision whether to take this investigation further or not. 'So, you're a writer too?'

'I'm a hyphenated,' I said. 'Director hyphen writer.'

'Good, good,' Manian enthused. 'Do you like poetry?' and before I could respond, Manian closed his eyes and recited:

Your mind and you are our Sargasso Sea,
London has swept about you this score years
And bright ships left you this or that in fee:
Ideas, old gossip, oddments of all things,
Strange spars of knowledge and dimmed wares of price.

'You know the poet?' Manian opened his eyes, challenging me: Prove to me, he was saying, that you are who you say you are.

'Ezra Pound's "Portrait D'Une Femme".'

'He is a great poet, my favourite, along with Thomas Stearns

Eliot. I write poetry too, but not as good. But one day . . .' Manian sighed, not only for his longing but, I thought wryly, also with the realization that I was who I claimed to be and not a terrorist. 'One day I must read you my poems. I would like your opinion.' Manian's tone was warmer as he confided. The ferocity of a Cassius had softened to a loveable Puck, wanting to entertain and be liked.

'I'd like that,' I said and partly meant it, though I had said it mainly to placate the authority. I wondered whether an American cop would admit to writing poetry. I imagined one of them, beer-bellied, belt dragging down below the gut, reciting poetry as he walked up Fifth Avenue. No, it didn't work. Cops wrote novels when they retired, never poetry.

He gently handed me the manuscript. Then, in a manner of apology, put an arm around my shoulder. 'No more bomb jokes. Stick to lawyer jokes. Promise?'

'Promise,' I swore with huge relief, as if I had just stepped out of the shadow of the gallows. I had not even been read my Miranda. Did India have that? Sergeant Sait beamed the best he could, seeing his promotion vanish with such camaraderie from his chief towards the once-suspect. 'May I ask one question?'

'A million, my friend, writer hyphen director.'

'Why is his hair orange?'

Manian appeared to notice this for the first time, and then said curtly. 'Black hair dye. He wants to look younger for the women. But it turns orange—bad chemicals.'

He strolled to the door, carefully stepping past my clothes. He would have stepped out of the room and out of my life, if I hadn't held up my right hand. The handcuff was still attached. Manian tapped his pockets, then Sergeant Sait checked his. Finally the constables did the same.

Manian smiled an apology, 'Tomorrow, first thing, and I'll bring my poems.' They walked out of the room, apologetically closing the door, leaving me half handcuffed.

'I don't fuckin' believe it.' I surveyed the mess around me and decided to re-pack my suitcase, in preparation for my departure the next day. I had somehow, during this chaotic interlude, reached a decision. It had been a major mistake, at the age of twenty-eight, to look for a father I had never known. It was the divorce that had pushed me to make this journey. It gave me an excuse to escape. Renee had kept the apartment on Riverside Drive; I had moved out with my few sticks of furniture, my books and dumped them in storage. When I returned I would find an apartment, probably in Staten Island, depending on my finances. The thought depressed me, as did the pain of separation. I loved her still, despite all that had happened. I remembered I'd wake in the middle of the night to watch her sleep in the muted light of the street lamp outside our second floor apartment window. She always lay on her right side, facing me, as if the last sight before sleep seduced her should be me. When Renee and I were dating and during the first year of our marriage, we listened to each other intently. Language is only our thoughts spoken aloud. We revelled in sharing our thoughts with each other, but then we used the same language as a camouflage for our thoughts. Then, one day, we stopped talking or listening to each other and there was never a more terrible silence. I wasn't given to confiding in others, partly because I was constantly confused by the lack of a defined identity. Mom was to blame for this: she denied her own identity and had me stranded in this limbo. So the less I said about my marriage to Renee, the better. However, Indians whether in America or here, are an inquisitive race. They probed constantly for confessions, sometimes subtly, as Apu had. Divorce wasn't something I wanted to be boastful about. Failed marriages only meant failed and faded love. Subconsciously, I rubbed my ring finger, feeling the indent. What had happened? I still didn't know. I had loved continually but, at some point, her love had drained away, like Gary's for Mom. It was as if I, and my love, had become superfluous to Renee.

I dropped the packed suitcase on the floor. The bed looked inviting; sleep would heal me. I knocked back the interrupted shot of vodka and went into the bathroom to take a pre-sleep leak.

I was quick to leap back out, slamming the door shut, and stood in the middle of the room. India was definitely ganging up on me. I called reception and demanded to see the manager, and no one else.

Almost a quarter of an hour later, the buzzer rang. I opened the door to find a woman dressed in a high-cut yellow choli and a green cotton sari with a silver border of mangoes, smiling warmly as if we were long lost friends. She wore the sari low on her hips, revealing a smooth, tight belly, obviously to distract irate guests. She had a helmet of tight curly hair, a sensual mouth pouted for seduction and was sensually perfumed and powdered.

'I'm Sarada Menon, the front office manager.' She had a bright cheerful voice which would sound the same even at two in the morning. 'How can I help you?'

I didn't return her smile, merely crooked a finger as I backed into the room.

She hesitated, the smile faded. I bet she suspected I'd jump on her bones the moment she was in the room.

'Maybe you could explain your problem, sir,' she remained in the corridor. Her eyes dropped down to the handcuff dangling from my wrist and panic flashed in them. I could be an escaped convict, rapist, serial killer, I read in her face.

'You have to see it for yourself,' I backed in. 'And you can leave that door wide open.'

She took my suggestion and stepped in. I pointed to the closed bathroom door and stood beside her as she cautiously opened it. The bathroom looked empty and she gave me a 'so-what's-the-problem' look.

'Try the shower curtain,' I said, remaining where I was, protected by the door.

I was smiling, not with any humour, but defying her to step beyond. She bit her pretty lips, wondering whether to risk it, and pulled the curtain aside.

She jumped back as the jaws of the crocodile snapped wide open, revealing rows of wicked, serrated teeth. Surprisingly, she didn't scream or faint; it seemed as if she'd expected to see a croc in the bathtub.

'It's only a baby, three or four years old,' she said calmly, not backing further from those beady eyes that had scared the shit out of me. 'I'm sorry sir. We don't allow pets in the hotel.'

'I didn't think you did,' I replied with controlled calm. 'It must've come out of the toilet. In New York we believe there are giant crocs, flushed down as babies, which roam the deep intestines of the city. They wander in the blackness like creatures lost from a Jurassic age. Why should India be any different? Except, it's not mine. Maid service must have overlooked it when they were cleaning the room.'

'This is your room?'

'Yeah, I just checked in.'

'Then it's your pet.'

'Give me another room,' I asked reasonably. 'I'm really beat and just want to get some sleep.' She shook her head. 'Then give it another room. Or move it into the lobby.'

'I'm sorry, sir. We don't have another room vacant in the hotel. Besides, it needs water and we don't have that in our lobby.' The crocodile's jaws were still open, like a huge, hungry bird's. 'I prefer snakes, they're easier to carry.'

'So do I.'

She pointed down. 'Kindly remove it immediately.'

I stared at her, unbelieving, then tried another tack. 'You wouldn't object to it if it were a handbag. It's got a pretty hide.'

'I'd buy it, if it were,' she said. 'I must have at least a hundred, but not one croc skin. They're banned.' She glanced at my hand and noticed the slight indentation of a ring, paler than the rest of my finger or my hand. 'Maybe your wife would like it?'

'Ex,' I snapped, ready to murder the woman.

She instantly lost interest in the crocodile, looked at me speculatively, no longer the irate hotel guest, and took off on an unexpected tangent.

'You're experienced in these matters of love and consequences, most Americans are; they're always divorcing and marrying again. You understand love better than anyone else does because you've experienced the joy and failure of being in love more frequently than people of other cultures. I need your advice. Did you marry for love?'

She threw me with that curve ball out of nowhere. She waited for my reply, her warm, sensual eyes brimming with expectation.

'I did.' I found myself saying. 'We don't have any alternatives in America. You either fall in love and marry, or remain single.'

'There are lots of Indians in America, at least two million. Your parents could have arranged your marriage.'

'I didn't want one. My mom had always disparaged the institution. She made it sound like she'd been sold into slavery. She told me to fall in love and find my own wife. Then if the marriage gets screwed up it's all our fault and not our parents'.'

'Why did your marriage break up?' She was eager as an acolyte for my wisdom on love and failed marriages.

This dialogue was driving me nuts. All I wanted to do was to get to sleep, forget everything. 'The usual reasons. One person falls out of love, as banal as that, a story told a million times. Now could we sort this problem out?'

But she gushed on. 'I'm marrying for love. I don't believe in arranged marriages. I mean, I couldn't face screwing a stranger I'd just met.'

'Yeah. I know what you mean. A one night stand's okay, I'd hate it to last a lifetime. The croc,' I reminded her again, and stopped the discussion.

She backed towards the open door. 'We had a guest once who brought his own cobra, placed it in the tub and then demanded he be moved to a suite and given a free stay. Otherwise, he would inform the press. He had remained in the suite a whole week and ran up an astronomical bill. We realized it was his snake only when he checked out and asked for its return. By then it had been shipped off to the Guindy Snake Park. I'm sorry, but you'll have to get rid of your pet.'

'If this were America, I could sue the hotel for a million dollars.'

'This isn't America and it would take you three generations to get a final judgement out of our courts. Just make sure it vacates first thing tomorrow morning,' she said and closed the door.

I didn't fucking believe it. I slammed my fist into the bathroom door, the sharp pain a stab of reality in this lunatic world I had fallen into. I had to crash out, croc or no croc. I peered into the tub, the crocodile had its jaws shut. Its eyes were closed. It had either fallen asleep or, for all I cared, died of boredom. I washed and brushed my teeth and gently closed the door, locking it firmly.

apu

I was woken from my recurring dream by a man's kiss. Gilchrist nuzzled my ear and the tip of my nose, awakening me gently. I lay, eyes closed, my mind clouded by a sense of foreboding looming in the day ahead. I had slept restlessly, and now tried to remember the dream that, like the shadow figure that always hovered in the periphery of my vision, was just an illusion. I had been present in the dream, dishevelled from a ride, stepping into a chilled room, perspiration drying to form another layer of skin. I had carried in the odours of the city and I was embarrassed. A man—he didn't reveal himself—was present only as a voice, asking me why I had come, offering me tea, sitting me down, waiting for my reply. I stuttered, 'It sounds interesting,' and he laughed, not at me but at my innocence. There was kindness in that laughter, encouraging me to continue. He never showed himself in these dreams, but he never went away.

I put an arm around Gilchrist, gave him a kiss and pushed him off the bed. He was supposed to sleep on the floor but invariably slipped onto the bed when he knew I had fallen asleep. He was an Indian prairie dog with a dash of Labrador blood. I had found him as a pup, starving and scared on Gilchrist Avenue in Chetput and brought him home. Gilchrist was glossy black except for the white diamond patch on his chest and white socks on his feet. His heart and soul belonged to me. He comforted me with his adoration.

I sat up, thinking of Mr Figgis, feeling sad for him. I felt inordinately pleased with myself now, having found S.K. Naidu through my own skills. Admittedly, there were always unforeseen consequences when you found someone or something. Downstairs, in that mansion, I had seen Mr Figgis' face clearly as he skirted the light. It was set in grief, a dream had died and he couldn't come to terms with that. I wanted to comfort him, yet I knew an 'I'm sorry' would be inadequate. Instead, I had taken his arm to steady him and pull him back out of his misery.

In Naidu's presence I had felt a large, indolent jungle cat watching me. His eyes were arrogant like a zamindar's studying a village girl to be taken. But humour glinted at the edges. He was slim, without the familiar paunch of older men who indulged in good food and whisky, though the whisky was there on the side table. His eyebrows curved in a fine arc. They were expressive too as he could raise one half an inch when he asked a question. When Nikhil and his father were in profile, I noticed that the shape of their chins was similar. There was a small indent in both, as if a child's finger had pushed in the flesh where the chin curved outwards. No doubt after we left, Naidu had locked himself in with his many locks. He had tried his best to protect himself from just such an intrusion. The locks, the bars, the walls weren't meant for protection against thieves and robbers; they were there to seal him off from the past. There were so many questions I wanted to ask: What had happened between Naidu and Sushima? Why didn't you keep in touch with your father? Why didn't you return earlier? Why didn't you, why didn't you? Was it Naidu's fault that the marriage had melted down many years ago? I knew Mr Figgis needed comforting by someone whom he loved enough to trust. His mother? His wife? A best friend? They were so far away in America. I wasn't that person; mine would only be a genuine, though finally shallow, compassion. I knew little about him and didn't expect to learn much more. It was his life; his father had rejected him. He would return to America, replacing the wedding ring on his finger as the plane landed in New York.

The sense of foreboding returned. Who had amma found for me today? Sons were fortunate; they need never leave their home. Daughters were temporary occupants, like tenants, to one day move into their husband's home. My life was in this room. The desk at which I had studied many years, through school and college. My books of knowledge on the shelves, alongside novels, history, art. One wall, covered with corkboard, recorded my journey: photographs of school, college, excursions, a train ticket of the Grand Trunk Express, school and college diplomas, gold medals, a pressed flower from a Himalayan slope, a man's pipe hanging from a red ribbon and an eight by ten colour photograph of me when I was twelve in my Bharatanatyam costume, striking a classical pose, taken in the G.K. Vale studio. When I looked at that young innocent girl, I could hear him keeping the beat on his naked thigh as I danced for him. It was a special performance for one man in that barely furnished flat. I was naked, apart from the silver anklets, the bangles on my arms and flowers in my hair. He sat on the bed, while I danced to his beat—thuk, thuk, thukathal, thukathal, thuk, thuk. My feet stamped to the familiar rhythm, my body shining with sweat, devoured by his eyes alone. I had often danced naked in my locked bedroom, always alone, always fantasizing of dancing in front of that audience of one. I turned away. One day I'd have to hide that photograph, it was a constant reminder. This room was my shelter, the familiar shell where I could retreat. I could carry these memories with me, packed in cases, but not the room's warmth and nurturing.

I got up, shaking off the sad thoughts, and crossed to open the French doors. My balcony faced the sea. I sat cross-legged, watching the sunrise, red as a wedding sari. The air was cool and tangy, the sea gentle and deceptive as a lover's caress. I knew its moods, my life was entangled with it. It had the capacity for terrifying violence some nights, the waves guttural with rage. Catamarans, bobbing like leaves in the distance, approached the shore with their night's catch. On the horizon were dots of ships moving north towards Madras Harbour. The beach was deserted. In half an hour the sun would be blinding. I began my exercises, performing the suryanamaskar facing the sun as it rose in the heavens.

After my morning bath, in my dressing gown, my wet hair wrapped in a towel, I went down to join my parents for breakfast out on the patio. The house was quiet and calm, the shadows reluctant to leave their shelter, the red Chettinad tiles always cool underfoot. I made an effort to notice such familiarity. The pattern of the Kashmir silk carpets, how they caught the light as I crossed, the deities, frozen in gold and silver leaf, in the Tanjore paintings, the sofa on which I had lounged many, many evenings. I ran my hand over its back, as if it were a living thing and would warm to my touch.

The doors leading to the patio were wide open, the sea breeze ruffling the table flowers and Appa's newspaper. Beyond the patio was a lawn. It circled the swimming pool and stretched to the far wall. The wall was high and blocked our view of the sea, except for the narrow, locked wicket gate. It was our defence against the men who gathered in the night to brew their illicit liquor on the clean sand. The breeze picked up the bitter stench and doused us with it. They were not brewing arrack or toddy but an evil stew of kerosene and chemicals that killed the drinkers. My parents didn't complain to the police, who took their cut, because those dark huddles of men could take their revenge.

My mother, Parvathi, was waiting, a cat for the mouse, with the bait ready on the breakfast table. Amma and I could have been sisters, except for her greying hair and comfortable, plump body.

She wore a bright blue chiffon sari, decorated with small silvery motifs of a chakra and a light silvery border. Her blouse was a dark grey. In the centre of her forehead was a perfectly formed large red botu, about the size of a bullet hole. She was already dressed for work, and had been waiting for me. Amma owned a pricey interior design store on TTK Road, near the music academy. I dodged towards Appa, flicking through the *Hindu*, more out of habit, as there was little hard news to read apart from the endless ramblings of politicians. I dropped a quick kiss on the greying head of this slim man whom I thought graceful and handsome. He was dressed casually in an open-necked shirt and slacks, which fitted him perfectly. He smiled at me and took my hand to kiss, as courtly as a courtier. What I loved about him was that he laughed easily, and his laughter had long lightened my life. I believed I too laughed like him.

'You were pretty late last night, princess,' he said, as I moved to the side table. I drank fresh papaya juice, helped myself to a spoonful of uppumau with coconut chutney and sat at the far end of the table from Amma.

'I had this case,' I said and gave him every detail of how I'd tracked down S.K. Naidu and all that happened after we'd found him. Appa listened attentively, interested, my amma impatiently, wanting my full attention before she launched herself.

'Poor guy,' Appa said. 'I had a friend in college who didn't know his mother. She'd left when he was ten, just vanished into thin air, and it took him years to finally find her.'

'Where was she?' I asked, ignoring Amma pushing a pack of something towards me. 'She ran off with another man?'

'Something like that. The man was a guru, his ashram was in Rishikesh.'

'And I bet her marriage had been arranged.'

'He didn't tell me that.' He had noticed Parvathi's growing agitation and the sliding pack. 'I believe your mother's lined up a new sucker for you.'

Amma spoke indignantly. 'Is that the way you support my efforts to get your daughter married?'

'Isn't this the twelfth one? I believe the detective should catch her own man.' He smiled conspiratorially at me. 'Or should the word be "entrap"?'

'Trap, entrap, catch, I don't care which word you use. We're not talking crossword puzzles here. It's her *life*. She's not being one little bit cooperative. In one breath she says she wants an arranged marriage, but she won't accept the arrangements I make for her. That one's too thin, this one's too fat, that one smells, this one doesn't smell. Look, look for yourself.'

The packet was now directly beneath my nose. Amma had pushed my plate of uppumau aside before I had even had a taste. I accepted my fate. 'Which one is this?'

'You remember my college friend, Auntie Nala? Well, she's living in Washington now and is a friend of this family. He's perfect for you. He's rich, he's an American passport holder—not just a green card—he's of our caste and he was born and raised in this city before the family moved to the States,' she finished triumphantly.

'And as he's an American passport holder, no doubt his parents will demand a huge dowry for the privilege of marrying my daughter,' Appa said dryly. 'Those American families are as greedy as our people here.'

I was still not paying any attention. In fact, I was intent on avoiding the pack of snaps under my nose. Amma rose in irritation, sighing aloud, and came and stood behind me, trapping me in my chair. She snatched up the photographs and snapped them down on the table under my nose as if she were dealing out playing cards.

'See what he has. That's the front of his house, isn't it beautiful?' I looked down dutifully; the house was a picture postcard of an antebellum mansion I had seen in the movies. I was impressed, if he owned that mansion, he was rich. She snapped down another photograph. 'That's his BMW, it only cost him forty-five thousand US dollars. I checked with Prakash Mehta, he's an expert on cars.' Another snap. 'And that's his all-weather tennis court. They say it's at the side of the house but we can't tell from this picture. And that's the fountain,' snap, snap, 'and the kitchen. Only Americans can design kitchens to look like spaceships. God, if only I had a kitchen like that.'

'Why?' Appa teased. 'You seldom go into ours.'

'I'd happily to go into this one,' Amma retorted and snapped down another one. 'That's his swimming pool and . . .'

I picked up the snap of the swimming pool. It was Olympic-sized and the water was a sleek, clear blue. I could see the patterned floor tiles. I peered closer.

'What's that?' I asked sweetly.

'The swimming pool. What does it look like? The Bay of Bengal?'

'No, I mean, *that*,' I pointed towards a shadow that fell across the diving board. 'It's definitely a woman's shadow.' I passed it to Appa for confirmation. He glanced and nodded.

'It must be his ayah,' Amma dismissed my observation. She was not about to be side-tracked with such minor details.

'They don't have ayahs in America. It's either his wife or his mistress.' I knew too many tales of NRIs returning to India for an arranged marriage to a sweet traditional girl and for the girl to discover that he a) was already married, b) had a girlfriend he had promised to marry, c) was gay. The Indian bride was meant to cook, clean, and wait obediently at home for her lord and master.

'You always find something wrong,' she scolded. She too knew these horror stories but her college chum Nala had guaranteed the respectability of the family. However, she would have to override my nit-picking. 'So what if it's his mistress? He wants to marry you. You'll go and live in America and give up all this detective nonsense of yours.' She turned to Appa to confide in him as if he were a stranger. 'She does her Masters in Art History and ends up sniffing into other people's love affairs and their dirty lives. Talk to her, Vasu.'

He grinned at me. 'You could end up with the FBI.'

'No, it would have to be Pinkertons. Dashiell Hammett worked for them.'

'I thought it was Raymond Chandler,' he said in mock seriousness, knowing Parvathi was about to explode. He was to blame. He was a Chandler fan and had given me all those novels to read when I was a teenager. I became hooked on Chandler and Hammett. He still read them. If he had a long flight to Europe or America, he would take one of their works to reread; he disliked buying anything by a new writer fearing that he would discover, half an hour after take-off, that he hated the writing. He was a man of well-defined tastes.

'What are you two talking about?' Amma shouted. 'Once she's married, she'll never have to work again in her whole life if she doesn't want. She can go horse-riding all day if she wants to.'

'I can't ride,' I said.

'So learn.'

'Where's his photo then? Or am I marrying his house, car and swimming pool, along with his mistress?'

'God, she can be sarcastic,' Amma said. She had kept the best for the last and now conjured the photograph from the folds of her sari like a magician. 'Here,' and she sighed romantically in the hope that it would convince me. 'Isn't he handsome?'

I did not look at it, but took it anyway. I had heard the same sighing line from Sarada and had replied, 'But is he good in bed?' Despite their liberalism, I knew my parents would not appreciate such carnal queries from their sweet and only child.

'He'll be here with his parents at six this evening. Americans are very punctual so please be home by then.'

'I'll try,' I said, feeling a slight resentment that I would have to rush back so early. Amma had given them a time without even talking to me.

As I walked away, I heard her say, 'What should we do with her?'

Appa laughed. 'I know what we can do with each other.' I caught Amma smiling as she walked into her husband's open arms.

I retreated to my sanctuary. Once I had thought I would be as lucky as they were with love but it wasn't meant to be. I dropped the photo, face down, on my desk. I wasn't prepared to face him yet, not until I was dressed anyway. On the wall above the computer was the film poster of Raj Kapoor's *Awara*. It showed the legendary Nargis with Raj Kapoor behind her, wearing a white dinner jacket, kissing her bare shoulder. She wore an off-the-shoulder dress and was half turned to him. The two simmered with suppressed sensuality. It was a collector's item. I'd found it in the 'new' Moore Market by the central railway station; the old one, an architectural jewel, had burned down mysteriously. It had been on railway property and the railways had been quick to build a monstrosity in its place. Reluctantly, responding to the agitation of the old traders, the government had built a new Moore Market down the road. It was a poor imitation of the original but at least the traders had a home and they still traded in old books and memorabilia.

While I listened to A.R. Rehman's music for *Dil Se*, a favourite to lift my spirits, I filed my nails, glancing occasionally at the face-down photograph. I was pushing the age envelope. By twenty or twenty-two, all my girl friends, apart from Sarada, were married; I was nearing twenty-six, a withering hag. Each year pushed the possible groom's year up further, and there were fewer unmarried men by the age of thirty. Or else they were divorcees, like Mr Figgis. I could marry someone younger and mother him to maturity. But that didn't appeal to me. I had told Sarada I wanted only an arranged marriage and then, when the arranged men showed up, waving their BMWs and swimming pools, I balked. Amma believed I was teasing her with this insistence for an arrangement. I did feel for her, she was making every effort to find the right match. But, just like it would be if I were falling in love, who knew which man was the right match for me? God, some people were brave, they leapt into love or an arranged marriage like jihadis charging massed guns. Many were surprised that they broke through to the other side unscathed. My parents were the survivors. They met in college, dropped instantly into love and had remained in love.

The phone rang just as I was about to leave. Mr Figgis surprised me. I thought he'd be on his way to the airport by now.

'You awake?'

'Of course I am. So, tell me.'

'I have a crocodile in my bathtub and I have to get it out to some place called crocodile bank. Can you help me?'

'How big is it?'

'I don't have a measuring tape.' There was a long pause. 'And you don't sound surprised. Does every hotel room come with its own crocodile?'

I laughed. 'I'll be over.'

Uncertain whether he was joking or not, I called Sarada. Sarada told me the whole story and was disappointed that Mr Figgis wasn't the con man she had suspected him to be. And she was teary about his father's rejection of him when I told her that story. But, she said firmly, the croc would have to vacate. Where it was vacated to wasn't her business. I hung up and called Raj again at the *Hindu*.

'Read me S.K. Naidu's obituary.'

It was not a long one. S.K. Naidu had been born in Madras, son of S.V. Naidu, the landowner and prominent advocate, educated at Lovedale in Ooty, and graduated from Loyola College, Madras, with a first in English. He had done his Masters in English at NYU. His novel, *Georgetown*, had been published in London by J.M. Dent, and Graham Greene had written a good review. I waited, Raj had fallen silent.

'Is that all?'

'That's all we have.'

'He was married to a Sushima, there's no mention of her at all?'

'No. Who's she?'

'God, you're useless,' I slammed the phone down. My eyes fell on the photograph again and I flipped it over like a playing card. I didn't swoon. He was fair (was it touched up for my discerning eye?), with a square face. I liked the arc of his thick eyebrows. His mouth had a slightly feminine pout. Maybe he was gay. Indian men went to America and burst out of the closets like Superman from a telephone booth. I checked that thought. My appa had a feminine lilt to his mouth but he was straight. I searched for humour in the man's eyes. While his mouth curled into a stiff smile, his eyes were expressionless. I would have liked to marry someone like my father who always laughed. Before I left my room, I dug out a wide leather belt from among my accessories. The leather was supple and strong.

Our house in Neelankari, a southern suburb along the East Coast Road, was an hour's drive from the city. I remembered we had been one of the first to move out of the city sixteen years ago to that deserted beach. At the time, Neelankari was a small, friendly village on the main highway. Then, as if we had opened the sluice gates, the city had flooded the road in a tidal wave of apartment blocks, houses, stores, hotels and hospitals; and the neat, pretty village had become an urban slum. As always, I found the traffic a horror. To make it worse, being the main road south to Pondicherry and other towns, it was crowded with lorries and buses, jostling for space on the three lanes. Unlike the city, where the traffic flowed at the steady pace of lava, the East Coast Road traffic moved in bursts of speed where the road widened, then crawled where it narrowed. All the fatalities occurred on the wide stretches.

I knew my antique jeep was an affectation. I always felt dramatic when I drove it. I kept it for sentimental reasons too; it had been Detective Balraj's car. He had looked like a hunter with his safari suit, his pipe at an angle and fedora worn on a slant. I had to purge my memory and buy a Maruti or a Tata Zip, small, fast and air-conditioned. It took me half an hour to make the turn at the Tidel Park IT centre. It was an amazing mountain of glass and steel, an island implanted from Silicon Valley, meant to impress upon Americans and Europeans that Chennai was a modern, twenty-first-century city. Unfortunately, it was now mired in ancient, broken roads that contradicted the dream. It took me another twenty minutes to reach the hotel.

In the lift, I was suddenly glad that Mr Figgis had called me to help him out with this crocodile. I had snipped him out of my life, imagining him winging back to America to nurse his wounds.

nicky/nikhil

The morning sun didn't heal the jagged wounds in my heart. I was still depressed, sullen too, angry with my father. And that damned crocodile had made it impossible for me to take my morning shower.

Where was Apu? Now I understood Renee's impatience as she waited for the call back after an audition. When it never came, she would weep and I would comfort her, cursing the producers for not recognizing her great talent. One day they will, I would console her, the whole world will know you. That day came and she flew out of my life like a wild bird set free to soar in her fame-to-be. I checked the time and wondered where she would be now. Hollywood? On location? In LA, at dinner or at a party?

When Apu rang the buzzer, I opened the door immediately, as if I'd been lurking by it. At least I looked a bit more presentable. I'd shaved and changed into a safari shirt and khaki slacks. I looked as well as I could, except probably for the stain of melancholy I had noticed in the corners of my eyes.

'How are you feeling?'

'Don't ask, I swear this country's a lunatic asylum,' then added when I saw the sympathy fade at my snapped answer. 'Terrible. I wiped out the stock of miniatures in the bar and have a bad hangover. That's for starters.'

She saw the handcuffs then and I spilled out my grievances. I was so relieved to see her. She was the only familiar person in my life now, and it struck me how quickly we become dependent on strangers. She sat by the wide window, silhouetted against the harsh blue sky. I sat on the bed. She was a good listener, not interrupting my tale of woe until I flopped back on the bed in despair.

'Mr Figgis . . .'

'Nikhil, Nicky or Nick.'

'Nikhil, don't they teach you in America never to sign anything unless you understand every word in the document? If I know our cops, they'd have you confessing to JFK's assassination.'

'Bit late for that.'

'You should've called me when you saw it was written in Tamil. It's my fault, I thought he'd write in English. I was just outside the station.'

'Yeah, well, I figured you were busy tracking Naidu and I just wanted to find my father and not waste any more time. You know this Assistant Commissioner Manian?'

'He's new. I know some of the city cops. It's hard to keep track of them; they're shuffled around like playing cards.'

'One day he'll come back to read me his poems,' I sat up as she laughed. 'Now, I have to check this croc out today. How are we going to move it?'

She sat beside me on the bed and opened her purse. 'First things first,' she said, and took out a slim wallet. She opened it out on the bed. In it were four or five shiny steel picks, not more than six inches long, with hooks at the ends. Quite casually, she took my right hand and laid it on her lap. She took out two of the picks and began to work on the handcuff's lock as if it were the most natural thing to do. I felt the heat of her thigh under my hand but she didn't seem to notice the intimacy. Her hair fell by my face and smelled freshly shampooed. I didn't recognize her perfume, it was subtle. I sniffed as softly as I could and held my breath to analyse it. Cinnamon, slightly peppery beneath. My father had smelled it, his nose as sharp as his temper, but I couldn't remember any smell last night, apart from the smell of her flowers. I had been too preoccupied. Renee used Shalimar, she bathed in it. I noticed Apu didn't have flowers in her hair this morning. It was a seductive decoration in a woman. Mom never wore flowers, though she admitted that when she was much younger, before she married, her mother would insist she wear a strand of jasmine. She would buy the flowers from her regular door-to-door flower-seller and either she or a maidservant would string them together with strips of plantain bark. Mom had rebelled against this evening ritual. She thought it too quaint in America and substituted hats for flowers—fedoras, trilbies, straw hats or taffeta confections with artificial flowers or even baseball hats for casual wear. She could wear a paper plate on her head and still look stylish.

'There,' Apu interrupted. The cuff came off and she dropped it in the wastebasket. My hand remained on her lap and when she stood, it fell away in disappointment. 'Now for the croc.'

'Where did you learn that trick?'

'Around.'

She left me suddenly, and the room seemed to lose its light. I suppressed a moment's panic that she had abandoned me and wandered around the room, as if seeing it for the first time. My wrist felt free. I'd woken twice with the handcuff dragging at my hand or pressed against my face. I had twisted and turned the entire night, my mind in a whirl. I didn't know where this croc farm was; I didn't know what to do about my father either. Overnight, with a little healing sleep, I had decided not to leave yet. I had to make another effort. Maybe that ogre too, having slept, would be more forgiving. Who could I talk to? There was Mike, but it was night in New York. He'd either be asleep or getting laid in some woman's apartment. We had both decided on Yale, where we had roomed together and been laid together. No, that wasn't true. Mike was on a roll after Linda Lund, while I was on hold. That was the advantage of being white; freshmen wanted to be laid by a familiar race and not by an Indian American. Mike had scored in the first semester, it had taken me two semesters before I'd been seduced by Karen Nicoletti, a tall Italian American girl, who could pass for an Indian if she spent an hour or two in the sun. The affair had lasted two semesters before she had moved to major in journalism at Columbia. We had remained friends though. Karen would be asleep too.

There was a light tap on the door. Apu entered grinning, pushing a room service trolley ahead of her. She wheeled it into the bathroom, parked it carefully. Then she took a belt from her handbag and gave it to me.

'Now, it's quite simple,' she said softly, not wanting to disturb the crocodile if it was asleep. 'Crocs have weak jaw muscles in one way. If you hold their jaws shut, they can't open them. But once they clamp onto something it's impossible to open their jaws. So we have to get it when its jaws are shut.'

'Who's holding the jaws shut, for chrissake?'

'I am. What you have to do is quickly tie the belt around the lower portion of its snout. Not too tight, but firmly enough to hold the jaws shut. Understand?'

'Jesus, is this one of your courses in detective school? How to capture a crocodile?'

'Rom, taught me,' she said as if I knew 'Rom' as intimately as she did.

I didn't like the sound of what we were about to do. I could handle snakes, grab them around the neck. But then, my pet snake had only been a foot long and non-poisonous. This croc was three or four feet from shout to tail and, I assumed, wouldn't take this as calmly as Apu appeared to be.

'It's only a baby,' she whispered, and it had its eyes closed. 'No doubt it's frightened and bewildered. Don't worry, I did a week's course at the Croc Bank.'

'When? Last week?'

'Ten years ago,' she said matter-of-factly. 'That was on a school excursion. I have a good memory for these things. My squeamish school friends had shrieked at the Irula tribesmen handling snakes as if they were harmless coils of rope and catching crocodiles. The creatures didn't bother me. I was the first to volunteer to hold a snake and stroke a crocodile. I'm not being brave. It's safe as long as you move fast and I clamp the jaw down firmly. It's a piece of cake, as you'd say. You'll have to come closer to the tub; you can't do it from the door. Ready?'

She rolled up her sleeves and carefully removed her bangles. She wasn't wearing a wedding ring, nor was she wearing a marriage thali. I glanced quickly down to her feet, no silver toerings either. I had picked up some knowledge on the web.

'Hold it. Once we've done this tying up, what next?'

'We lift it onto the trolley, the lower half would be better, and wheel it out.' She moved quietly towards the tub. 'Oh,' she whispered, 'and don't tie it too tight. I don't want to hurt the poor thing.'

'Yeah, I know, they bruise easily.' I held the belt stretched out. I had come all this way to meet my father and now I was about to wrestle with a crocodile. I had seen those crazies doing it on National Geographic and figured there were a thousand better ways to earn a living.

'I think room service or the maid service should be doing this,' I whispered. Her glance withered me.

Apu crouched by the tub and cautiously peeped around the curtain.

'Don't you think we should choreograph and rehearse our . . .'

Her hands had shot out past the curtain and grabbed the croc. 'Quick,' she said.

'Oh shit.' I ripped the curtain aside. Her hands were holding down the top jaw. The crocodile wasn't taking it quietly either. Its body struck out, its legs scrambling for a foothold on the porcelain. The nails scarred the white surface.

'Hurry,' she said.

I hurried. It wasn't easy. She was arched over and I had to manoeuvre my way between her and the croc. I slipped the end of the belt under its jaw. The tail flicked back and forth like a scythe. God, the skin was warm and rough as sandpaper. Its front leg struck for my arm and I jerked away. Apu was holding on. I grabbed one end of the belt, jerked it up hurriedly, slipped it into the other end and yanked them together. The belt tightened around the jaws.

'Not too tight, just firmly, so it won't come loose.'

I knotted the belt firmly, not too tight, though I had no idea what she meant. The two ends dangled from the clamped jaws. Apu let go and sat back on her haunches. The croc eyed us maliciously, thinking only evil.

She stroked its head as if it were a cat. 'There, there,' she crooned. 'We're not trying to hurt you. We're just going to take you to your people living in the Croc Bank.' It seemed to like the sound of her soothing voice. It quietened but the malice in its eyes didn't quite fade away. She stood up, 'It'll be okay now. You get the tail and I'll take the head. Watch it's feet, those claws can rip your arm.'

'Gee, thanks.'

She confidently slipped her arm under the croc's neck and waited while I did the same under its waist. We lifted it together and manoeuvred around the bathroom to place it on the trolley.

She took a moment to study it carefully.

'It's a *Crocodylus palustris*, a mugger. Its habitat is India.'

'No kidding. How big will it grow?'

'They can grow up to twenty-three feet. This one's about four years old. They grow a foot for each year from their birth. Help me move it to the lower shelf.'

We wheeled out the trolley with the crocodile on the lower shelf. Its snout stuck out like the prow of a sleek yacht. Maids, guests and busboys saw us coming and jammed against the walls as tightly as they could. Another guest stepped out of his room, saw us and jumped back in, slamming the door shut.

'I bet Phillip Marlowe would never have done this,' Apu said, ignoring the cringing people as we strolled past.

'I'm sure he would've.' I hadn't read all the novels, only *The Big Sleep* and *Farewell My Lovely*. 'He was tough but he had a soft corner for strange situations and stranger women.' India, I was beginning to grasp, could be surreal. Here I was strolling as if in a park, wheeling a crocodile like a baby in its carriage, discussing a long dead American writer. It wasn't as safe and predictable as the US, the unexpected was bound to happen and you had to be light and quick on your feet.

'I think I would've made a good Chandler character. Don't you think so? I prefer them to Ruth Rendell's. They're prim and so British.'

'Is that what made you a detective? Reading those novels?'

She shook her head, not revealing any secrets, and recited, 'Down these mean streets a man must go.'

'And are there mean streets in this city?'

'Lots,' she said. We waited for the elevator, leaning against the railing and looking down at the foyer. She sighed romantically. 'I suppose Bogart must have slept with the Mary Astor character in *The Maltese Falcon*. I mean he loved her, yet he turned her over to the cops for murder. That always makes me cry. He should've let her escape.'

'He was a tough cookie.'

'Have you slept with many women?' she inquired politely as if asking me the time of the day.

I jerked around, trying to figure out the question and the intent behind it. She wasn't smiling but watching me gravely, reminding me of a child awaiting the answer to the meaning of the universe. Was it a pass? Why did she want to know?

'Not many,' I finally said cautiously, trying to figure what would come next.

'Are you gay then?' She was needling me.

'Not yet.' Did I look gay? 'Are you?'

'Oh no,' she said as the elevator came. Two passengers, seeing the crocodile, immediately edged out as she pushed the trolley in, unconcerned by their panic-stricken eyes. Apu remained grave and then smiled.

'Don't worry, I wasn't making a pass. I was just trying to prod you out of your stupor, you still look like a zombie. Anyway, I never sleep with my clients. Then they would demand a discount on their fees.'

I stepped in with her, the door closed, and we turned to look down at the foyer together. She hummed to herself as the elevator descended. I couldn't figure her out. After Renee, all I wanted was a monogamous, celibate existence. I would join an ashram and lead a life contemplating my navel. By the time I stepped out into the foyer, I had decided I would keep her at arm's length. We strolled through the lobby, people skirting us widely, and out to her parked jeep. We carefully carried the croc and placed it in the rear of the jeep. There was just enough space for it.

'If you don't mind,' I said as we climbed in, 'I'd like to see my father. The least I can do is say goodbye to *that* crocodile.' It had slipped out inadvertently but I thought it an apt simile to describe my father.

The high gates were still locked. The mansion still looked as impregnable as a castle. We banged and hammered on the metal but no one came to open it or inquire who wanted to be allowed in. The wall was too high and I didn't think it seemly to climb over.

'He'll accuse us of trespassing,' Apu said, following my eyes.

'What should I do? Should I apologize for springing myself on him? I did try to introduce myself but he stopped me.' For chrissake, why was I justifying myself? I had done nothing wrong to this man.

'Write him a letter,' she said and pointed to the rectangular slot cut into the gate.

'Saying what? Dear Dad . . . What's dad in your language?

'Appa. Didn't your mother teach you your mother tongue?'

'Sure, I know my English. And they didn't have Tamil as the second language in school either.'

'What about Telugu then? It's "nayana" in Telugu,' she smiled sweetly.

I ignored her mocking tone. I was slightly irritated. She had this edge over me where India was concerned—just because I was an Indian who didn't know his mother tongue, in fact, knew just fuck-all about this country except for what I had learned from books and the web. That would always be a sorry substitute for experience. I took a pad from my shoulder bag and rested it on the hood. Of course I had composed a hundred letters to my father over the years, pouring out my longing to see him, but I had no idea where to send them and the pages remained in my old notebooks. I had said a lot in those pages: how I'd celebrated my twelfth birthday sailing off Cape Cod, my first kiss with Linda (though not what followed the kiss), my 'A' grades in school, growing up with a stepfather and my estranged-from-India mother, and how I longed to meet him. But now, nursing my rejection and exiled outside the gate, all my creative juices had dried up. What should I say to get the gate, and my father's arms, to open?

I was staring at the high wall when I noticed two small hands appear from the other side. They gripped the top of the wall and then a head and finally a face appeared over it. It was a young girl. She looked familiar, almost like the one I had given away my wedding ring to. But I couldn't be sure, she looked like so many other urchins on the street and I'd only seen that one briefly. She had on a clean and neatly pressed school uniform—a red skirt, white shirt and a tie—and she wasn't carrying a dirty rag. She jumped down from the wall and moved with a cheeky grace. When she stuck her hand out to Apu she was given a few coins. Apu talked to her and received brief replies, a shrug and the only word I understood, a name—Ruth.

She turned her attention to me, 'Sar . . . sar . . .' I dug into my pockets, found a ten-rupee note, considered it awhile as if calculating its worth and, to her delight, passed it over. She skipped away, singing a song in Tamil.

'What were you talking to her about?'

'Who she was and how we could get in. Her name's Ruth. She said this is the only entrance and it will only be opened when the watchman's around. At the moment, he isn't. Not that I believed her. There must be another entrance but she wasn't saying.'

I returned to my letter. 'Dear Nayana, I'm sorry about the shock

I gave you last night. I had wanted to meet you for years and be embraced as your son. I guess, you hadn't given much thought to my existence and wouldn't want me in your life after what happened between you and my mother. I admit I used your book as an excuse to meet you. It seemed a good introduction as we would then have something in common to discuss. After all, we are total strangers. I wasn't hoodwinking you. I really think it's a wonderful book. I've adapted it for a play and would like your permission to mount it. As I shan't be . . .'

'Christ, what am I doing? Have I come all this way just to stand at the gate and write him a letter? No way.' I tore it up. 'He must come out at some time.'

'Well, you can't stand vigil day and night, can you?'

'My mom warned me that he was a very difficult man, that I shouldn't come here to meet him.'

'She could've kept in touch for your sake,' Apu said. 'Or did she want to forget everything?'

I bristled at her critical tone. 'It's hard to cling to the past when you've made your home somewhere else. It can be very confusing.'

'And you're confused?'

'You bet. I'm a "brown" American. I feel American as long as I'm with my friends. But the moment I leave the circle and move out, some red-neck shouts an obscenity and I'm reminded I'm not a white American. It's become worse since 9/11. It's like being kicked in the balls for something you haven't done.'

'And you've had lots of kicks in the balls.'

'Literally as well as metaphorically.' I threw the balled paper at the gate, not caring about littering the city which seemed one big trash can anyway. 'But this is the worst kick in the balls yet.'

She climbed into the jeep, checked whether the croc was still comfortable and started up the engine.

'You'll just have to wait for Friday,' she said.

'What's happening on Friday?'

'You must have missed the invitation. He invited us to play poker. The gate will have to open then. He can't play poker all by himself, it's not exactly Patience.'

'Today's Tuesday. What do I do by until then?'

'Sightsee. Lie around by the pool and get a tan. That's what most foreigners do.'

s.k. naidu

I sat slumped in the shade of the veranda in a foul mood. The Calmpose pills I had taken the night before had knocked me out for longer than I had wanted. I had woken an hour back feeling dull and nauseous. I had a hangover, something I'd not experienced for many years; rather, I hoped it was one and that I wasn't ill. That man, Nikhil, had haunted my sleep. He had materialized out of the walls, tables, ceilings and floors, a ghost haunting and mocking me. It was not possible to acknowledge a readymade man for a son. A son was a baby first, then a small human who eventually grew to his full height and breadth. I had never witnessed this miracle, and my mind and heart rejected Nikhil.

I hoped he had caught his flight back to America, back to that cursed woman, and I would never have to see him again. My life had to return to its placid, disciplined routine. I had lived all these years in such a strict regimen and he had come and upset all that. Now I was hung-over and feeling wretched. A sense of depression also fogged my mind, making it impossible to work. The pages Rani had typed the night before lay on the worktable. My early morning ritual was to read them, make the corrections with my fountain pen and then spend a few hours composing more pages for her to type. This daily exercise kept my mind occupied and gave Rani something to do. I didn't have the energy to read or to write. I sipped my coffee. It was cold.

Yes, our marriage had been arranged from my side. I saw her at my cousin's wedding. She was fourteen and so spirited in the way she played and laughed with the other children. I was all of twenty-six, an old man, but I was mesmerized by this girl. I couldn't take my eyes off her throughout that whole day and the following one too. She wore a purple silk padava and a matching blouse the first day, a green silk outfit on the second. I remembered the details so clearly. I spoke to her but she treated me with the courtesy of a child towards a friendly adult, calling me 'uncle', and returned to her companions. I didn't realize that love could be so instant, a bullet into my heart, and I couldn't escape its pain and its ecstasy. I twisted and turned like a bird trapped in netting but couldn't free myself of my thoughts and feelings for her. I was obsessed, a frightening feeling, and helpless. Of course, my parents were looking for a bride for me, I was nearing that age. My mother had someone else in mind for me, a nice plump partridge, the daughter of a Supreme Court judge, willing to pay a fat dowry for my body and soul. I told my mother that night that I had chosen my wife but that we would need to be patient for she had to reach a marriageable age. Her father was a prosperous merchant but socially a rung or two lower than our family. My father was a landowner and a successful lawyer. He was resistant to the union, but finally they met and discussed the arrangement. I would demand no dowry, instead I would pay one. I didn't want to see her maturing because I wouldn't have been able to keep my hands off her. When she was eighteen we met formally. I had returned from New York and was working on my first novel. I exulted at my good luck. She didn't remember me at all. In fact, I think there was fear in her eyes. Her mother was a most forceful and determined woman, she knew the advantages of her daughter marrying me. When you fall in love, you pray the other person will love you eventually with the same ferocity. She never did.

'Ethiraj,' I shouted and rang the small temple bell on the table in case the old man couldn't hear from the depths of the house.

Ethiraj popped out of the door where, he said, he had been waiting for the past half hour. I saw his concern for his 'aiyer', having heard about the rude intrusion the night before from Prasad. I hadn't come down for breakfast at 7.05 a.m. This being Tuesday, Ethiraj had prepared idli sambar. It lay congealed and cold on the dining table.

'Coffee,' I said curtly. 'And bring my notepad.'

'Yes, aiyer,' Ethiraj cleared away the cold coffee. 'First which?'

'The pad.'

He trudged slowly, back through the rooms into the vast kitchen. He was short, dark, and not a very attractive man, with a full head of white hair. Sometimes, it turned orange but never for too long as the white rose back in triumph. He had worked for me for thirty years and knew the cause of all my suffering. Ethiraj ran the household, along with his wife Mary. They had eight children, all named after biblical figures. Solomon, the eldest, worked for an oil company, the youngest was Ruth. While Ethiraj cooked and served, Mary, along with three maid-servants, cleaned and swept the house. Four gardeners were also employed by him to maintain the immediate garden. As I never communicated with any of my staff apart from Ethiraj, he and Mary only employed those who pleased them by paying back a small percentage of their salary in gratitude. He also had a small sideline, raising free-range chickens in the garden.

In the old days, this house used to have twenty or thirty people living in it, with distant cousins and friends dropping in at all times. The kitchen had enough space for a dozen cooks and helpers. Now, it was only he and Mary. Ethiraj was also a stickler for etiquette. His parameters of movement were the kitchen, the dining room and the veranda, he never ventured beyond or upstairs. That was Mary's domain. They looked more like brother and sister both in height and in their features. She didn't possess his sense of vanity; her hair was gracefully white, her body as thick as a teak tree, having borne so many children.

I pretended not to notice her, so she placed the notebook on the table, beside the typing. She was surprised by my appearance. I hadn't shaved or bathed and I had slept in my clothes. My dhoti and jiba were crumpled. She shuffled away quietly.

Of course, it was the wrong notebook. I found a blank page and uncapped my fountain pen. I was going to write Mr Nikhil Figgis a letter. The pen hovered, touched the paper, but did not flow. What should I say to the son I had never known? I was surprised to find I didn't know. Here I was, a fluent writer of the English language who could compose biting and sarcastic letters to the telephone company, the water and sewerage works and to Madras Corporation's lethargic babus, but not a word flowed out of my magic pen now. Although the news and editorials in the newspapers also enraged me, I never wrote to the press. I had no wish to see my name in print, no wish to be thought alive and well by distant acquaintances.

I had thought my one published work would have long been consigned to oblivion. But it refused to remain there. It kept being resurrected. Nikhil had found his mother's copy. It surprised me that she had kept it all these years; surely, she would have burned it. I had wanted to sign in the flyleaf: 'With all my love', but she hadn't wanted it as I had dedicated the book to my parents. Dedicate your next book to me, she had said. There hadn't been a 'next' book. I should have realized then—she hadn't wanted my love at all.

Think of Nikhil as a corporation official, I thought, and compose a letter dripping with acid thoughts. Dear Mr Figgis, I began, and paused. That had the right tone of formality and distance, addressing him as a stranger. I wrote 'please' and scored it out. I wouldn't be polite; it was not in my nature, son or no son. Don't visit me again, I wrote. That was simple and direct. Mr Figgis would get the message and leave me alone for the rest of my life. I stared at the line a long time. Is that what I really desired? A son . . . wasn't that what all men wanted? A son granted them immortality, they lived on for another seventy or eighty years, and they walked the earth again, bathed in sunlight, vicariously through his body. Daughters diluted a man's genes, they abandoned his name. Yet, I would have loved a daughter; I had always enjoyed the company of women. I smiled; that detective had a good turn of wit and presumably a good figure under that shroud.

I looked around at the estate. I was in the veranda downstairs, opposite to Rani's side of the house. Nearby was an ancient wood apple tree. A creeper with large waxy leaves snaked its way up the trunk and along the branches. I admired the symbiosis between them. Which was the wife, which the husband, which the father, which the son in this relationship that had lasted as long as I had lived? They had chosen to live together in harmony; separation would only come when the tree died. I had allowed them to exist in a smaller, peaceful jungle of shrubs, scrub grass and weeds. Beyond the shade of the tree was the well kept lawn that ran to the edge of the chaos. In my last will and testament I had stipulated that this wood apple tree should never be cut. The whole property and this house had been bequeathed to a school for below-the-poverty-line children in the neighbourhood. The trust had enough money to support my tree and the school. Of course, when I had drawn up the will, I hadn't known of my son. Being cynical and aware of the inner machinations of the people around me, I wondered whether Nikhil had returned to claim the property. Who knew? I tore up the unfinished letter and went to bathe, just as Ethiraj returned with my hot coffee.

susie/sushima

I swear I wasn't lying, darling. We were divorced. Your father was dead in my heart, he was dead in my soul, dead in my mind. So when you asked me about him, the 'He's dead' just popped out of my mouth. And once it had popped out I couldn't take it back, could I? It had been heard by you, it had entered your mind and it was too late to turn around and say, 'He's alive but I don't ever want to see him again.' I didn't want to confuse you. I wanted you to be one hundred per cent American and not keep thinking about India and your dad. You would've wanted to see him, so half your mind would be back there. I told Gary what I'd done and he too thought it was for the best. My dad had been a friend of Naidu's family. I wouldn't say friend exactly, they thought themselves superior to us—his father was a lawyer while my father was a cement merchant. Well, we certainly weren't broke. I think we were quite wealthy, in fact, but my father was cautious in his spending habits. Your father drove me insane with his so-called superiority, especially as he had done his masters at New York University. I'd gone to Church Park School on Mount Road—it took a good half hour in one of those old Indian cars—and I'd been to college too, Queen Mary's on the Marina, about a mile up the road from Georgetown, and it was nearer than my school. Before I could even catch my breath I was in my third and final year for my degree and my parents married me off. My mother was insistent, hammering away at me day and night as if I was a stubborn walnut. She said he was a very good match and wasn't asking for a dime in dowry. I finally capitulated. Your father said he'd seen me at a cousin's wedding when I was just a child. I didn't remember ever having seen him and if I had I would've run a mile. I went and prayed, not in the temple but in the Armenian Church on Armenian Street. It was a place of such solace for me whenever I was depressed. I was so depressed before I married your father. He was much older than me—ancient, I thought, when I sat next to him at my marriage ceremony. I was so embarrassed by the pitying looks my school and college pals gave me when they came to bless the marriage. He wasn't fat or ugly, he was quite fit, he played cricket and squash. Yes, he let me finish my degree but I felt as if I was under police escort—the driver always waited for me outside the lecture halls and I would never lose sight of him unless I went to the ladies' room. And, of course, he reported everything I did back to your father. Your father was unbearable at times. No, he never ever laid a hand on me except to shower me with gold and diamonds. He used his voice and wit, a more damaging weapon than his fists. Inarticulate men raise their fists to a woman's face or sadistically target her breasts, knowing a woman's beauty lies in both. But your father had worshipped me in his peculiar way. He elevated me to a deity incarcerated in a temple for eternity. I was suffocating.

That's why I love America. I can breathe freely here. No one's watching you all the time. And now I'm even free of Gary, may he and Monica rot in hell. They deserve each other. I know my horoscope didn't foretell my divorce, although it hinted there would be a change in my life. It didn't predict your divorce either; but then, it didn't even predict your marriage to an American actress. I can tell you now I didn't think Renee could act at all, apart from taking off her clothes in front of the camera. Her tits had more expression than her face. Ava Gardner, Katharine Hepburn and Audrey Hepburn didn't have to strip to prove they could act, darling. They had talent, Renee had none. And my horoscope also predicted I'd be very successful. I'm going to become very rich with the travel agency Julia and I have started. Did you know one per cent of the Americans own forty per cent of the wealth? That's the travel market we're aiming at, that niche, with Luxury Travels Inc. Luxury, luxury, luxury, that's my style.

nicky/nikhil

The drive along the East Coast Road to Crocodile Bank, Apu had said, would take over an hour, depending on the traffic. The road was chaotic with lorries, buses, bullock carts, wobbling cyclists, pedestrians, goats and cars. Apu skilfully threaded the jeep through the confusion. At one point, I aroused myself from my stupor to remark that there was a rhythm to the traffic. She agreed that there was a subconscious one—a road raga—you had to be attuned to. When a cycle swerved left, all the traffic, as if watching a conductor's baton, swerved in rhythm to the left. But past the village she pointed out as Uthandi, a small miracle occurred: the road widened to accommodate six toll-booths. They looked no different from the ones at the Triboro Bridge. Beyond them, the two-lane road was as sleek as an American freeway.

'This new road runs all the way down to Pondicherry,' she said with tourist-guide pride as she paid the toll.

A mile beyond the toll booths, she slowed for a Disney-type theme park pumping out high-decibel noise. Next door, a signpost pointed to 'Dakshinachitra'.

'If you want to know more about your roots, you should spend a day at Dakshinachitra,' Apu said. 'It's a heritage museum of the four southern states. They have your own state too, Andhra, where your father's family originally came from. Typical old houses from each state have been dismantled from their original location and re-constructed here. An American woman, Debbie, created this place. They have pottery and silk weaving classes, puppet shows, dance performances, music recitals, and historical artefacts. You could learn everything about south India here, without travelling around the four states.'

'I'm not sure I want to learn much more,' I said, still sulking. 'I'm confused enough.'

Apu shrugged, driving on. I was being a difficult companion.

The air smelled of the sea and the pine of the conifer trees. The quiet hum of the tyres made me feel more forgiving. To my right now, there were distant hamlets hidden behind coconut and mango glades and paddy fields, and I thought they looked peaceful, detached from this racing highway. Would they edge closer to join modern India, leaving behind their serenity to become like those slummy villages we'd passed? On the left, the ground sloped down to the beach and the sea. In this harsh light, it looked passive and lethargic, a flat plain of glittering blue stretching as far as we could see. Here and there we lost sight of the sea as estates blocked our view. Apu's hair was blowing back in the slipstream. She didn't seem bothered that she would look a mess. Renee had always tied a scarf so her hairstyle wouldn't be mussed by something as natural as breeze.

I wanted to snap out of my mood. Apu was trying to be friendly and I had been curt and rude. I looked around as if noticing the landscape for the first time. 'You know, when Christopher Isherwood first visited China he said it reminded him of Surrey, in England.'

She looked too and squinted back at me. 'Does this look like Surrey too?'

'More like Ohio, except for the palm trees, rice fields, the sea and the beach.'

We held each other's eye for a moment longer and then burst out laughing.

'You must have been to the States?'

'Never.'

'I thought every Indian's ambition was to immigrate there and die happily ever after. It's the Mecca of materialism.'

'I'm not every Indian. My father visits the States quite frequently. I've been to Malaysia and Thailand.'

'What's he do?'

'He owns a software company.'

Apart from this admittance, she kept the conversation friendly but impersonal. I was a client, not a friend. When I asked what all I could see while waiting for the Friday poker game, she suggested Fort St. George, the museum, the art gallery, Dakshinachitra and, of course, Georgetown. I could also hire a car and visit the eleventh-century temple and see the rock carvings at Mammalapuram, further down the road we were travelling now. I kept her chatting, though I already knew of these sites from the web. I would have four days at least to cover them comfortably.

A few cars and a bus were parked outside Crocodile Bank. Apu drove to the gate and chatted to the guard. I recognized the name 'Rom', dropped frequently. It worked, the gate swung open and we drove along a sandy track into a large shady grove. The track, which led to a distant gate, was a tunnel of shade. The sun was barely visible, merely a glow somewhere overhead, dropping shards of light through the foliage. She parked and climbed out. Visitors were wandering around, peering over low walls. A couple with three children had spread out a picnic lunch in the sand under one tree, as if they were on the beach. I too peered over a wall. The earth sloped steeply down to a still pool of fresh water. There, lying almost stacked one on another were hundreds of crocodiles of all ages, small, medium, large. A notice board warned: Do not put hand over wall. The crocodiles barely moved. They all looked like my *Crocodylus palustris*, and I was delighted I could rid myself of it among the hundreds below. There were a dozen other similar enclosures, each with different species of crocodiles. They barely smelled or maybe the sea breeze was blowing their odours out across India.

Apu called out as a European in an open-necked shirt, khaki drills and sandals strolled towards her. They embraced and kissed with the warmth and affection of old friends. So this was Rom. He was quite tall, his long hair in a ponytail. He had the relaxed air of a man accustomed to living close to nature. His face was narrow and his easy smile touched his grey eyes as he shook hands with me. He leaned over the side of the jeep and inspected the crocodile. It inspected him in turn, beady eyes following his every move.

'It's definitely not one of ours,' Rom spoke with more of an Indian accent than a European one.

'But you'll take it,' I said with the enthusiasm of a used car salesman. I moved to open the tailgate.

'No problem,' Rom laughed and helped me swing it open. The croc edged towards the yawning gap. 'Just give me the permit.' Rom held out his hand with the confidence of an immigration official demanding a passport.

'What permit?' I turned to Apu for support. I didn't like the sound of the word nor the sight of Rom closing the tailgate before the croc slipped onto his territory.

'The permit from the conservator of forests to trap and transport a live crocodile. It's a highly protected species.'

'I don't have it.'

'I can't take your crocodile then,' Rom clicked the tailgate firmly shut a half inch from the croc's snout. 'If I can't account for this mugger, I'm in deep shit with the government. I'm aiding and abetting poaching which carries a three-year prison sentence. I've no wish to share a jail cell with you. No insult intended, but I don't know you.' He grinned at Apu. 'I'd do it with you.'

She smiled back and I felt I was somehow out of the loop. I saw the opening and leapt in. 'It's not *my* crocodile. It was in my hotel bathroom when I checked in.'

'How did it get there?'

'It used its American Express card,' but Rom missed the joke and looked puzzled. He had not watched American Express commercials. 'C'mon, you've got thousands of crocs here. You can sneak this one. I mean just throw it into that enclosure.'

'Sorry,' Rom said sincerely, and explained, 'if it was an American, Australian, South American, Egyptian or Chinese crocodile, it could join the others over there. No problem. But this is an Indian one, and it must have the permit. In England, you have the Queen's stags or the Queen's swans. All wildlife there belongs to the State. This crocodile is the property of the Government of India.'

I had lost the plot, and fought back. 'Well, I'll just dump it in a paddy then and the government can find it.'

'You can't do that to the poor thing,' Apu broke in.

'You take it then, since you're so concerned about the poor thing.'

'I can't. It'll eat Gilchrist.' When we both frowned, she added, 'My dog.'

'Then she'll be aiding and abetting poaching,' Rom said. 'Once you get the permit, no problem.'

We leaned against the jeep looking down at the insoluble problem lying between us. It looked back at each of us, as if trying to decide which would make a tastier snack. I believed in my ability to bullshit myself out of any problem, but here I was hitting a brick wall. If Apu hadn't been present I would've dumped it in the paddy.

'I don't believe this is happening,' I screamed up at the trees.

My anguish failed to move Rom. 'I suggest you apply for the permit to trap and transport the croc. And I would like you to leave with it as soon as possible. If a forest official walks in and sees it, we're done for. They're constantly monitoring this place. It's their job.'

'How long does it take to get this permit?'

Rom rocked back on his heels as he considered. 'I'd say three or four months.'

'Months! I'm only here until Friday.'

'Ahh, that is a problem.'

'Maybe if you wrote a letter commissioning Mr Figgis to catch you a croc, it wouldn't take that long,' Apu said quietly. 'He's an American and he could be from some zoological American society who wants to study crocs and if he should trap one you'll take it.'

'No problem,' Rom said, then added. 'Oh, and don't let the cops see the croc either. They'll jump on you with both feet because they have nothing better to do.' He strolled back to the office, hidden behind the trees.

I felt exhausted, broken and beaten by this silent crocodile that was turning my life into a nightmare.

'It took me six months to get my divorce and that was a nightmare,' I spoke almost to myself, being reminded of Renee.

'Was your wife white?'

'Yes.'

'What happened?'

'Women change, we all change in a marriage. The heat of love is lowered to a simmer and a daily routine of living together. We expect too much from each other and when we don't deliver, the disappointment makes us bitter.' I wished people wouldn't keep reminding me of Renee, although I had invoked our divorce this time, as each question eroded the protective shell around my heart.

A peon came trotting out of the office bearing an envelope. I opened it, the letter was brief and addressed to the conservator of forests, requesting him to give Mr Figgis, of the San Diego Zoological Society, permission to trap and study a *Crocodylus palustris*. Crocodile

Bank would be happy to accept it as a gift once the study was completed.

'Okay, let's go and see this Conservator guy and hope this gets me the permit to dump the croc here.'

'I can't come with you,' Apu said as we climbed into the jeep. She checked the time and panicked. 'Oh god, I have to hurry. A potential groom's coming to see me.'

I was surprised. I hadn't expected her to enter into an arranged marriage. She was too independent, too adventurous for such a traditional commitment.

'A total stranger?'

'Of course not. His parents are friends of friends.'

'And if he's all right you'll marry him? You're crazy. You're leaving it to your parents to make a decision about your life, for a lifetime. How can you tell he'll be Mr Right? Don't you want to make your own decision about who you wish to marry? Arranged marriages sound like such snap decisions.'

Apu started the jeep, angry at my brief lecture on how she should conduct her life. 'You made a snap decision when you married, didn't you?'

'It wasn't a snap decision. We'd dated for over a year. She was my independent choice.'

'And look what happened.' She slammed into gear, and couldn't hide the triumphant note in her voice.

We drove back to the city, compartmentalized in our irritation with each other. I wanted to ask her a very personal question: What happens on the wedding night? You're two strangers jumping into bed for the first time. What happens if he can't make it, never gets it up? Do you know what to do, how to guide him into you? What about foreplay? What'll you do if he likes S&M? Adapt? At least,

I had learned Renee's sexual predilections and she mine. Apu gave the impression of being a prude and yet, at times, I glimpsed a wise sexuality in her eyes and in her conversation. At least, Karen had been bold and experienced enough to guide me. She wasn't a virgin, she'd acquired her sexual knowledge back in Chicago where she had deliberately allowed herself to be seduced by an older, experienced man to learn about sex. Although Karen and I had been the same age, nearly nineteen, she instructed me with the wisdom of a far older woman. After we'd broken up, I had met Renee. She was from Georgia and had the same ambition for fame and fortune as any aspiring actor. Renee was blonde and I leaned towards blondes like a sapling towards the sun. I had overlooked the hungry determination in her. The gold hair seduced me, reminding me of Linda Lund. I convinced myself Renee had loved me in the beginning. It was a natural liaison, the director and the actor. But then, pulled down by the endless round of casting calls and rejections, she had started to become bitter towards me. I couldn't help her up that golden ladder. She was lucky to have found Tom Bodnik the quirky filmmaker, an off-beat role and the discovery by the *Village Voice* film critic. I was now a footnote in her filmography.

Apu parked at the side entrance to the hotel. While I waited, she went to fetch a room service trolley. I looked back at the crocodile; it appeared asleep or bored in its small, shaky enclosure. Did it wonder what was happening to it? Did it know it was endangered? Did it know its body and soul belonged to the government? Did it worry it was dislocated from its natural environment? Did it puzzle over its karma? Did it long for other crocs to nuzzle? It was now my companion, until I could get the permit to leave it in Crocodile Bank.

'You can't be nameless,' I said to it. 'Everything is given a name and your real one's too long for me to pronounce. I hereby baptise you Renee, after the woman I love. If you're male, tough. She wouldn't appreciate that. She's a very beautiful woman with the most luminous blue eyes you've ever seen in your life. The camera fell in love with her, her close-ups made your dick stand up and salute. I doubt the camera will ever love you and your eyes certainly don't enchant me. They'd probably be sexy to another crocodile.'

Apu overheard this discourse and looked down at Renee with a new understanding. 'Was she that bad a woman?'

I considered for a moment. 'No,' I said, too abruptly.

'You're still in love with her, aren't you?'

'Shit, no. You kidding?' But from her glance, I knew that she thought this a lie. She was right too.

I climbed out, opened the tailgate and lifted Renee onto the trolley. The trolley had a white cloth over it and we covered Renee with it, before wheeling her in through the staff entrance. We thought we had got away with it when we stepped into the empty service elevator and punched my floor. The elevator stopped at the lobby and Sarada shot in.

'I told you, you cannot keep this . . . this . . . thing in your room. Pets aren't allowed. Please take it out immediately.'

I punched the button, closing the elevator and, as it rose, said fiercely, 'Miss Menon, I am in a very murderous mood at the moment and I doubt anything worse can happen to me should I strangle you.'

Sarada glanced at Apu, at least she would save her should I try.

Apu smiled at her. 'He's tried to dump it in Croc Bank but there's a slight hitch.'

'What hitch?' she panicked. 'It's a croc and should be with other crocs and not lounging in my hotel's bathtub. Or dump it in the river down the road.'

'Great idea.' I should have thought of that first. I could slip it down the bank and it would paddle away into eternity.

'We can't do that to the poor thing,' Apu said with such finality that my hopes were dashed. 'The rivers in the city are absolutely filthy and polluted. They were happy rivers once, a long time ago, clean and silvery flowing along the banks. But the people had resented such joyfulness and dumped their envy, sadness, disillusion, and despair into the waters to teach the rivers a lesson that they learned too well. They are now sullen and mean. Their serpentine bodies, sickly vomit-green, twitch occasionally, as they drag themselves out to sea.'

'That's very poetic and moving but I'd still like to put it in the river. It'll survive.'

She ignored me and turned to Sarada. 'He has to get a permit before they'll take it.'

Sarada closed her eyes. 'Oh my god. A permit! That means government and they hate giving out permits for anything, unless they're well bribed. This croc could die of old age, languishing in our bathtub, waiting for its permit. How long will this permit take?'

'Not long,' Apu said cheerfully.

The door opened and I pushed the trolley out and moved down the corridor back to my room and the bathtub. I wondered where Apu had acquired such optimism. I looked back. Sarada was watching me grimly.

'It's called Renee,' I said. 'But don't charge me for a double room. Or why don't you find a single room for it because I can't take a shower.'

'The hotel's chock-a-block,' Sarada was resigned. 'Anyway, as long as you don't take it for walks.'

Apu started to follow but Sarada stopped her to talk. I looked back, they were still talking when I let myself into my room. I'd been abandoned. I knew why. She was late for this husband-to-be. I wondered what he'd be like.

'Okay, we're home, kid,' I said to Renee. 'But first I have to shower, and then you can slip into the tub for a good soak. How's that sound?' I knew I was going nuts, chatting to a croc with its mouth tied up. If only I could zip up some people's mouths as easily.

I showered, and then meticulously washed the tub clean of soap and shampoo. I didn't want to kill Renee with polluted water. It was a welcome distraction, like looking after E.T., my pet snake. I gently pulled Renee out from the trolley and carried her to the tub, staggering under her weight. I lowered her in gently. I opened the cold shower and let the water run over her. The water seemed to please her, she closed her eyes as if she were having an orgasm. Then I plugged the bathtub so she could lie in half an inch of water. Very cautiously, I undid the knot on the belt and when it came free, I jumped back. Renee didn't seem upset or angry. Her jaws remained shut.

'Okay, I'm beat and you're beat, so why don't we order room service and call it a day?' I checked the menu for Renee. Being an Indian croc, would she go for curries? I'd play it safe. I called room service. 'One rice, a butter masala chicken, a salad and two large raw steaks.'

'You mean rare, sir.'

'Raw, like in uncooked.'

I switched on the television, expecting one channel, but mine had a hundred and five. Mom had got one prediction about India wrong.

apu

I was about to follow Nikhil but Sarada stopped me. 'Well, what have you found out about Ramesh?'

'Nothing yet. You asked me to investigate Ramesh just yesterday. Give me some time.'

'It's urgent. Aren't I paying you enough?'

'You're not paying me at all.'

'I didn't expect my best friend to be that mercenary,' she said, missing the humour in her anxiety. 'We'll discuss that later. I have to know whether he loves me truly. And whether he'll be kind and gentle and treat me well.'

'I'd have to marry him to find that out.' I turned to see Nikhil nearing his room. 'Who had Mr Figgis's room before he took it?'

'I'll check the computer.' Not to be distracted, she continued, 'All I want to know is whether Ramesh loves me. And if he's straightforward. It's as simple as that and you're making a big song and dance about it. He's coming to meet my mother tonight.'

'What time?'

'Around 7.30 p.m. Isn't it exciting?'

I checked the time. It was 4.45 p.m. 'Oh god, I'm late.' Nikhil would have to unload Renee himself. I jumped into the closing elevator, along with Sarada.

Racing back home, I let my thoughts wander back on the day. I had been aware of the warmth of Nikhil's hand on my thigh when I unlocked the cuff, his eyes on my hair, the slight dilation of his nostrils to smell my perfume. I had wanted to shake him out of the melancholy, out of his wounded mood. How much longer would he mope about a father he hadn't met before? Even the crocodile didn't seem to disturb his inner turmoil.

I wondered what it was like to be a stranger in this country, looking like you belonged but dislocated from the language, the people, and the customs. If I went to America with this possible husband-to-be, would I feel the same? It could be an exciting adventure to discover a new aspect of myself. In America, I could be a different person. I could be anyone I wanted to, not Vasu and Parvathi's daughter, the granddaughter of Gopal, great-granddaughter of Venu . . . Here, I was pinioned and defined by my ancestors, there was no escape. Then, I felt unsure, unnerved by the fear of entering a marriage with stranger and living in a strange land. The house, the car and the pool had looked unreal, a travel brochure to America. And whose shadow was that by the pool? The woman wore a swimsuit; the shadow hadn't shown the contours of a sari or a dress.

I was still irritated with Nikhil over his lecturing about arranged marriages. Love was hardly a guarantee for the longevity of a marriage. I had instinctively read the ripple of thought in his mind. How would I deal with sex the first night? He wouldn't understand that sex was only a minor part of a marriage. The union was complex enough without making sex the criteria for everlasting happiness. Whoever it was, I would grow to love my husband, accept him with his virtues and vices, and not compare him to others I had known. I wouldn't fall in love, it was too painful when it ended. I had dated during my college days, but not in the American way. A bunch of girls and boys got together and went to movies, picnics and hung out in coffee shops. A couple of my friends in the bunch had fallen in love with the guys and married them. The first special guy in my life was Harish, studying for his degree in computers at IIT. He was tall and slim, like my father, and seemed to have a sense of humour. We went to the movies together, held hands and experimented with our kisses. But I'd not let it go further. His first and only love was the computer. When he began to e-mail me every joke on the web, I withdrew. He was destined for a life in America, and he had planned for it. He had e-mailed a few times from San Francisco but I hadn't replied. I heard he had married.

A tourist taxi was parked in the drive when I arrived home at 5.20 p.m., having raced through the traffic. I sneaked in through the kitchen. Our cook, Andal, smiled knowingly and gestured to the patio—the future in-laws and their son were waiting. Of course, Gilchrist barked a welcome. I flitted through the living room, hearing a murmur of voices and ran up the stairs to my bedroom, chased by Gilchrist. I showered and then dressed; the man would just have to wait my pleasure if he wanted to meet me. Amma had laid out a black choli with a gold border around the sleeve edges, and a black sari with a heavier gold border. She knew I looked sexy in black and she was determined to make me look as desirable as possible. An arranged marriage was all about the right packaging. The twelfth! I could barely remember the others, a parade of young polite men who had spoken of their lives as if they were applying for employment. They were all successful, came from good families and were of my caste. Three hadn't followed up their suit, nine, I hadn't.

Amma hustled in in a state of panic. She held a strand of jasmine.

'I told you 5.00 pee. m. They're American and they turned up on the dot. Now they're getting impatient and won't wait forever for her highness to show herself.'

'Let them wait. I was busy.'

'Poking your nose in someone's life, undoubtedly.'

I sat at my dressing table to touch up my lips lightly and dab on perfume. Amma and Gilchrist watched intently. When I was done, she pinned the flowers into my hair and frowned when I took out a simple strand of pearls.

'You should wear the diamonds.'

'I don't want to blind him yet.' I leaned forward to stick a silvery tilak, shaped as a diamond, on my forehead. I wore the diamond earrings to please Amma and caught her approving smile in the mirror. Gilchrist looked concerned at my preparations and, suspecting mischief, barked.

'What's he like?'

'I like him.'

'You'll like anyone who wears trousers and is eligible enough for me. You even liked that creep who pinched my bottom within two minutes of our meeting.'

'At least he had good taste.' She kissed my head tenderly. 'If I were a man, I'd do the same. Now hurry.' She bustled out.

I found it nerve-racking to meet these suitors. How would I decide? From his looks, the way he talks, the way he behaves? But it's all show, isn't it, the way I'm being shown? Dressed up to act demure and placid, so he will like me. At least over there in America they can date a few times, not go to bed mind you, without harming their reputations. Here if I'm seen alone with a man more than twice, it means I'm soiled for others, even if we've never held hands or kissed. We Indians are big nosy parkers and bigger gossips. I know I'm partly at fault, I can't make up my mind. Maybe I don't want to make such an important decision. Maybe I want to remain a spinster all my life. It's the safest, isn't it? To remain undecided for life. I mean, look at Nikhil. He dated for a year, married, and then divorced. You have to wonder about him and I suppose about Renee too. They could commit and uncommit so easily. We can't do that here, we're stuck. No, that's not quite true. I can divorce him, it is an option now, more women are considering divorce, which only means more women are beginning to believe love is difficult to find.

My thoughts were interrupted by a soft tap on the door. 'Come in,' I called, knowing it was Appa. Amma always breezed in, without a by-your-leave.

He was smiling as he entered. I went into his arms, comforted by the strength of his embrace and his familiar smell. He stood back, holding me at arm's length. 'When you're all dressed up like this you remind me of your mother when we first met. You're a beautiful woman. I feel terrible thinking you could leave home at any moment. If only you could remain my baby forever.'

'You were both so lucky. You fell in love at first sight. You never had any doubts did you?'

'Never, not for a moment,' then he laughed. 'Except when I met the Playmate of the Month at a cocktail party in New York. She was gorgeous, but unfortunately, she hated Indian food. It would never have worked.'

I had heard the story before but still laughed. He told it to tease my amma. 'But falling in love doesn't happen to everyone, unfortunately.' I slipped on two gold bangles. I was as ready as I would ever be. 'What's he like?'

'It's hard to tell with these foreign people,' he said soberly. 'They're different from us, yet not quite. You know what I mean. They come flaunting their material success as if it is the only virtue. I wonder if that's the only lesson America teaches them.'

'Maybe twelve will be my lucky number,' I linked my arm with Appa's as we went out together, followed by Gilchrist. 'It will make Amma happy.'

He stopped, and said sternly. 'Don't marry to make your mother happy. It will only make your life miserable. Understand?' He kissed me on the head.

I could never decide whom I should study first when I entered the room. The suitor I could end up spending my life with? But he was only the tip of the iceberg, the cherry on the cake. When I married, I would leave my home to enter my husband's house, forever. I would be passed from father to husband, like a chattel. There was no return for some brides; their lives hit a dead end, sometimes death. The parents, my future in-laws, were the reefs beneath. They could rip my life to shreds if the man were too weak to control them. There were a million stories of in-laws harassing brides to their death. The cops called them 'dowry deaths' for convenience. Even the families swollen with American riches harassed brides, demanding bigger dowries, demanding obedience, demanding, demanding, demanding.

This time, as if in a game, I chose to leave the man to the last. A glanced around quickly as I entered—he was sitting apart from the others on a two-seater sofa. They were in the informal sitting room that looked out across the patio to the pool and the lawn. The light was fading to a soft pearly glow as the day breathed its last. Amma hovered in front of his parents, offering them bondas and samosas from a silver platter. The back of the father's head was greying and fringed the large bald pate, his neck thick set. He would be a bulky man when he stood up. The mother's hair, tied in a kondai, was decorated with flowers. The back of her neck still had a trace of powder, and two heavy gold chains left their marks in it. We edged around the chairs to face the parents. The father rose. He was stocky, with a broad strong face, a blunt nose, clean-shaven. A gold medallion nestled in his chest hair. He wore a shiny black shirt and fawn wool slacks. There was a heavy signet ring on the first finger of his left hand. The mother remained seated. I had the impression of a slim woman, smiling attractively up at me. She wore a bright green sari, heavily bordered with square patterns woven in gold threads. Her gold bangles were thick and heavy, worth any amount more than mine. I did a demure namaste and sat by Amma. Mrs Chakravarthy, in profile, had a sharp triangular nose, and a firm sweep of the jaw.

Finally, I looked at Arun Chakravarthy. He remained standing, tall, about six-foot I guessed, weighing eighty kilos, and appeared relaxed. His smile wasn't strained, he seemed pleased to see me. He was draped in success. If I checked his shirt collar, turned over that paisley silk tie and peered at the inner jacket pocket, I would read expensive brand names. He wore polished loafers with tassels.

He came over—'Hi, I'm Arun'—and wanted to shake hands, but I did namaste. He had a neatly clipped moustache, deep-set eyes and tight curly hair. I liked his voice, soft and deep. He returned to his seat and crossed a leg over a knee, revealing black silk socks. Amma bustled around with more food, mysorepak, jalebi and vadai. She took comfort in filling up her guests. Good food mellowed guests as much as good liquor. Appa sat by Mr Chakravarthy. I heard them talking softly, probing each other. Appa describing his software company, Mr Chakravarthy saying he was VP of DuPont. He had studied business management in Bombay before joining Sunderam Finance in Madras. Arun had been born and raised in Madras. He had studied in Don Bosco and then, when he was ten, Mr Chakravarthy had immigrated to the States. He had first worked for Josephenthal in their finance department in New York and then been headhunted by DuPont. They were visiting Madras only for three weeks. The city had changed. It was dirty, crowded, polluted, smelly. They had been ill with a stomach bug for the first three days. He could never live here. In his voice I recognized a longing to return to his American sanctuary and shake off the Indian dust and grime. Amma and Mrs Chakravarthy were discussing cooking and clothes. It was so easy to get all the Indian spices in America. Mrs Chakravarthy could just e-mail the Taj Mahal spice store with her list and the UPS would deliver it the next day. She even made rasam and sambar. It tasted better there than the sambar she had eaten here. Shopping here was such a hassle and then you'd find your rice, lentils, chilly powder, sugar adulterated with something or the other. Even the milk was adulterated with god-knows-what water. American milk was pure, she announced with finality.

'Do you cook?' she turned to me.

'Yes. I can make sambar and rasam too. This sea air gives it a special taste. But I don't cook meat.'

'Why not? We're not vegetarians. American meat is first class, not scrawny and stringy like the meat here.'

'I'm vegetarian.'

'She became vegetarian when she was sixteen,' Amma said quickly. 'Until then she was as non-veg as we are.'

'Why don't you and Arun take a stroll in the garden?' Appa interrupted before I faced a further barrage of American superiority.

I had been waiting for this part of the ritual. First the getting-to-know-each-other as parents, then free the youngsters to make their initial acquaintance.

I led him out, along with Gilchrist. I looked back and knew amma had probably crossed her fingers of both hands tightly. We walked towards our small pool and I waited for him to boast that his pool was twice the size. If he did, I would ask about the shadow.

'I'm not like my mom and dad, you know,' he said gently. 'Mom' and 'dad' were spoken with the American inflection, while his other words were in a more familiar Indian accent. 'I love India and I miss it. It has so much colour and life. I mean in Atlanta, after six in the evening, you don't see anyone on the streets. We retreat behind the locked and barred gates of our houses.' He pronounced Atlanta as Allaana.

'You seem to have done well there.'

'Pretty well. America gives you the breaks if you work hard. I went to Boston U and took my bachelors in economics, then my masters at Wharton. That's a great school. After a few years with Amex, I'd had enough of corporate life. So I moved to Allaana and started my own business with a buddy. 'We're into export and import, tying up with companies here. We have a turnover of five million annually.'

'What kind?'

'Any and everything that will make a buck. I hear you have your own business too?'

'Research,' I said, shading the truth. 'I head the company now and we have a turnover of . . . oh . . . one crore a year,' I exaggerated, not to be intimidated by American dollars.

We strolled around and around the pool, like bullocks tethered to thresh wheat underfoot. He played tennis in the weekend, had barbecues with his friends, travelled to LA, Seattle, Chicago on business, went to the movies. There was a big Indian community around Allaana. Every Sunday they met up at the Liberty movie house to catch the latest Bollywood hits. I didn't go to movies much, I didn't have the time, and preferred dance or classical concerts. I told him I was thinking of doing my doctorate in art history. My thesis would be on my favourite painter, Thota, also a top movie art director, and on whether art and cinema were compatible.

Arun laughed easily and told a couple of amusing stories of his misadventures while discovering America. He wanted to know whether I had thought of living in America. I confessed I hadn't. But most young women today left to live in America with their husbands. Would America allow Gilchrist in? Arun was sure they would but maybe it would be better to leave the dog with my parents. He wasn't fond of dogs or cats or horses.

We were skimming the surface of each other's lives as swiftly as ghee sliding down the sides of a hot pan, neither wanting to delve deeper just yet. We kept our emotions, quirks, longings, flaws, well hidden. Those would surface much later and not before we were married. Marriage would be a journey through the labyrinths of each others thoughts and emotions, that's if we reached that point of total trust.

Appa turned on the garden lights. They threw small yellow patches, leaving huge gaps of blackness. The sea breeze ruffled the pool and cooled the water. We had fallen silent, having exhausted the preliminaries. I wondered whether on an American first date, the couple fell silent too. Or did they fall into bed, their bodies continuing the conversation and exploration? Was the woman's orgasm proof of their compatibility?

I checked the time. 6.30 p.m. If I was going to catch Ramesh at Sarada's I would have to hurry. I looked towards the house and thankfully saw the parents rising and signalling for our return. We went in, chatting like old friends again, to show our parents we were indeed getting on.

'You're so smart,' Arun whispered. 'When I saw you I could hardly breathe. I think Indian women are the most beautiful and sexy on earth.'

'I thought American women were.'

'No way. You'll really be a great hit in Allaana. I made up my mind as we walked around the pool. I felt relaxed with you, you spoke well, you have style. I had dated a few American girls in Wharton and in New York but I sure didn't want to marry them. I wanted a traditional Indian girl, someone who would relate culturally and socially with me. We'd have children naturally and their cultural roots would continue. One day we could even return to live in India. An American girl would find that adjustment impossible.' He leaned towards me. 'I love that perfume you're wearing. It's unusual and very sensual.'

'It's blended specially for me by Muneer Mirza. His shop's on the street of perfumes, behind Rattan Bazaar.' I remembered S.K. Naidu's remark and Nikhil's breath on me.

I accompanied my parents out to their tourist taxi and waved to the vanishing tail lights, then picked up the hem of my sari and ran into the house. Amma, startled, hurried after me and shouted up the stairs.

'Where are you going?'

'Out on work,' I shouted down and shut the bedroom door. I was pulling on my jeans and tucking in the tails of a dark blue cotton shirt when she barged in.

'You can't go out at this time of the night.'

'It's only 6.30, so it's not night. I'll take Gilchrist with me.'

'As if he can use your cell phone and call for help if anything should happen.' She took up the black sari and began to refold it neatly along the ironed lines. When I continued getting ready, she couldn't contain herself any longer. 'Well?'

'Well what?'

'What do mean "well what"? You know what I mean. What do

you think of him? Did you get on? What did you talk about?'

'This and that,' I stopped when I saw Amma's anxiety. 'He's okay.'

'Just okay?'

'No,' I gave myself up. 'I am interested.' I hurried to the door with Amma and Gilchrist at my heels.

'What should I do then? You have to tell me.'

'Check whether our horoscopes match. I won't think about it further until we know for sure we'll be compatible.'

'What kind of person do you think I am?' Amma demanded from the landing. 'I'd never let you marry without checking the horoscopes. This is the first time we've moved from square one to checking the horoscope. I'll ask Vasu to find out how much dowry they'll be demanding'.

Gilchrist sat beside me, the wind flapping his ears like pennants. It was cooler, the air cleaner, and the traffic had thinned out.

'What have I done?' I asked Gilchrist. At least a dog responded with frowns, a slant of the head, moist appealing eyes. It was better than talking to a croc, even if it was called Renee. They were as expressive as logs in the water. 'I've started the wheels turning, put the juggernaut into gear. Horoscopes are going to fly back and forth, purohits will be consulted to cast joint horoscopes to plot our rosy future. How many children will I bear? Will they be sons? Will the sons be successful? Arun's okay. I mean, I didn't go weak in the knees when I saw him. But that would be lust, wouldn't it? That's what Sarada meant. We're confused by all these separate pressure points in our bodies. Lust-love, love-lust, liking, loving, hating, tolerating. You liked him, didn't you, Gil? At least you didn't snarl at him like you did at that guy from Delhi. You took an instant dislike there. But he doesn't want you to come with us . . . that's *if* we decide to marry. I couldn't leave you behind. You're more precious to me than a future husband, even if he does have an Olympic-size swimming pool. What should I do? Set into reverse? Or just let it be and see where it goes?' I fell silent. 'I'm going to let it be.'

It was a decision to be indecisive and that calmed me down. I was going to lie back and let my karma river float me down to my destiny. It could sail into the rosy sunset or it could sink long before it even took the bend in the river.

Sarada lived with her mother in the Regency Towers apartments on Cenotaph Road. It was a pale grey block with white balconies, surrounded by parked cars. I pulled up half a block away at 7.28 p.m. to watch and wait for Ramesh. Gilchrist settled on his haunches, sniffing the air. He was used to my mysterious errands where we sat and waited for hours. At least, Ramesh was punctual. At 7.32 p.m., a silver Honda pulled up outside the Regency and Ramesh climbed out. He carried a bouquet of flowers. The driver hurried around to open the already opened door. Ramesh ran a brush through his hair to reveal the broad sweep of his impressive forehead and combed it back deliberately. He was tall and lanky, though he could do with more muscle around his shoulders and chest, and he had a beak of a nose. I'd say he was passably handsome. Sarada screamed 'Ramesh' from her flat window, reminding me of a teenager getting a glimpse of her favourite pop star.

I could imagine his surprise when he stepped into her home. He would stop and stare, like everyone who first entered the flat did. They would expect three-star hotel décor, the arbitrator of taste for the middle classes. Instead, like Sabu in *The Thief of Baghdad*, they would be carried on a magic carpet far from the city, across hills, plains and rivers to be set down gently in a village nestled in a grove of mangoes and coconuts, surrounded by green rice fields.

The room they would enter would be of such rural simplicity that it would remind them of their grandparents' home in their ancestral villages. The walls were bare of paintings and mish-mashed photographs of places visited. Instead, surrounding the guest, like a panoramic cinemascope, not in Technicolor but in black and white, was the entire Ramayana drawn in intricate detail. Like a comic strip. A quick scan of the panels replenished everyone's memory—Vishwamitra in Dasaratha's court demanding Rama's services, Rama defeating the demon, Rama breaking the great bow in Mithila and winning his Sita, Kaikeyi dripping her poisonous plans into Sumitra's ears, Rama, Lakshman and Sita in exile, Ravana capturing Sita, Jatayu battling Ravana and dying, Hanuman finding Sita's jewels, Hanuman setting fire to Lanka, the battle between Rama and Ravana, Sita's trial by fire, their triumphant return to Ayodhya.

Sarada's mother, Lakshmi, held court there, as if she were the queen of Ayodhya. With her quiet sense of humour she was quite unlike Sarada, a passionate scatterbrain. Lakshmi's hair was straight and always tied in such a severe kondai that it lifted her brows and corners of her eyes which were dark and watchful. There was the faint zig of a scar on the left side of her forehead. She'd been in a car crash not worth mentioning among the thousands that occurred daily. Also, she was taller and slimmer than Sarada and moved with the supple ease of a dancer. I had never met Sarada's father. She described him often as 'slick as ghee'. He was a pilot with Air India and, back then, Lakshmi was a deputy station manager in Madras airport. They had met, married and split in a record time of two years. They weren't divorced—Lakshmi refused to give the wretch that. He had dumped her with two kids to pursue an airhostess in British Airways. I wondered whether she believed in marriage any more, arranged or the fall-in-love ones.

The driver gave Ramesh a once over, and straightened his tie. That indicated there was a familiarity between servant and master. The driver would know Ramesh well enough to discuss him.

Balraj had advised, 'Always talk to the servants first. What they don't know about the family they serve isn't worth knowing. Servants gossip about what's served for breakfast, lunch and dinner, how much jewellery their mistress owns, where it's kept, how much they quarrel, how many times they go to the toilet. It's their form of entertainment, and cheaper than the cinema.'

I was poised to climb out of the jeep to talk to the driver as soon as Ramesh entered the building. But the driver hurried back to the car and drove away fast. I followed. I had to talk to him.

I followed the Honda over Kotturpuram Bridge, past the Chettiar estate, and left down a side road. It turned into a closed petrol bunk with a garage beside it. Pulling up a few yards behind it, I slipped my hand into my purse and took out the Swedish knife Balraj had given me. The shiny, flat, six-inch steel blade was sharp enough to split an atom. I walked softly with Gilchrist beside me. He had been trained to play a role on my order. The car had been parked in a pool of weak light. The driver opened the tank and as I neared I saw him slipping in a tube to siphon the petrol into the plastic can beside him. Great. A thief was easier to deal with. Besides, I had the edge of surprise—he was too absorbed in his theft. I judged him at about five foot five and around fifty kilos. He jumped as I slid my left arm swiftly around his neck and touched the edge of the knife to his cheek just enough to serve as a warning. To be certain he would not fight back, I snapped down to Gilchrist.

'Snarl.'

Gilchrist snarled, not the well-fed, pedigreed snarl of a Labrador, but one that drew deeply on his dangerous ancestor the dhole, which frightened even the tiger in the jungle. The driver froze in my arms. He smelled of beedis, cheap cologne and coconut hair oil.

'Shall I hand you over to the police?' I whispered in Tamil into his ear. I felt him relax: I was only a woman. 'The dog will kill you if you make a move.'

'No, I beg you. I hate dogs and they hate me. I was just borrowing this petrol to pay the moneylender, or else he'll cut off my fingers. On my pay day, I will be repaying it.'

'I'll tell Ramesh.'

He shrugged. 'So tell him. It won't make any difference to me.'

'Don't you work for him?'

'I work for Mr Suresh Agarwal,' he tried to turn but I tightened my grip. 'Don't you know Mr Agarwal? He's the son of Mr Brijesh Agarwal, the plantain baron. You can't eat a plantain in this city without Mr Agarwal getting a cut. His father was . . .'

'I don't want a family history. But you know Ramesh well?'

'Since he was a boy. He and Mr Suresh were in Don Bosco together and then they were both in Madras Christian College. He's like Mr Suresh's brother.'

'Tell me about Ramesh then.'

He stiffened, sensing my purpose now. 'Never,' he said, trying to sound brave.

'How would you like it if I cut off your balls?'

'What difference would that make?' he said mournfully. 'My wife won't fuck me anyway.' He turned his face slightly into the light, his eyes strained to get a better look. 'Maybe I should get a second wife. What do you think?'

'If the first one won't why will the second?'

'She'll be younger.'

I laughed. 'Then when she stops you'll be back where you started, and stuck with two wives on top of that.'

'You're right.' He straightened as best he could and spoke firmly. 'Go ahead and cut my balls off. I won't say a word about Mr Ramesh.'

I let go of him and stepped back. He turned, a narrow ferret-face with darting eyes, calculating his chances. I snapped my fingers. Gilchrist snarled, showing all his teeth. I dug out a fifty-rupee note from the pocket of my jeans. Each pocket had a note tucked in it. If I pulled out a wad of notes they would go for it and I couldn't bargain. I held it up like a biscuit, just out of reach.

'Mr Ramesh is going to marry some poor woman soon. He had started an export-import company with his partner from Um-rika but they lost the product they were going to export to Um-rika. So he's in money trouble now. He's also wearing Mr Suresh's suit and I was instructed to make sure it wasn't damaged. He's already married, his wife's in Bombay. He used to work for a petrochemical company in Bombay, in marketing, before he was sacked and he returned to Madras.' He was out of breath, his gaze steady on the note. 'Why didn't you offer the money first, instead of frightening me like that? It's not nice.'

I gave him the note. 'I've always wanted to cut off a man's balls and I thought I'd start with you.' I backed away a few steps, then turned and walked to my jeep.

The driver called out. 'You wouldn't want to be my second wife?'

'I would've liked to be your first wife,' I laughed. 'But you already have one. Bad luck.'

I didn't drive away immediately. I sat in the car, an arm around Gilchrist, feeling down and bitter. How could I tell Sarada that

Ramesh was already married? That was the problem with love. You fell in love with strangers who happened to brush past by chance. I thought of Arun's remark—'I want a traditional Indian girl.' It seemed so long ago now. Was I that traditional girl?

We had gone to Bangalore together on a divorce case. We had taken separate rooms at the Comfort Inn and spent the day working together. That first evening, it was over dinner, our hands touched and held involuntarily. I hadn't understood my own feelings for him until that touch, and until that moment I'd been unaware I'd wanted his touch for months. After that I wanted him to touch me all over. We spent the night making love. He was experienced and gentle; I began the shy virgin and, by dawn, had become the insatiable lover. Each night we made love after our day's work. My own boldness surprised me; I was exhilarated to reveal myself naked to this man. And when we returned to Madras I was enchanted by my love. We both were. I rented a small flat in Cressourt Apartments in Besant Nager. I had found it in the rental classified section and signed the agreement, paying the deposit and rents in cash. Cash kept secrets.

That was our chinnawheedu, a physical shelter for our hearts. It overlooked the sea from the tenth floor. I furnished it simply, tastefully—a divan with a hand-woven bedspread and low tables. For curtains, I draped old saris on the windows. The harsh light muted to pinks, green and blue, enchanting the room with subtle colouring. I bought a second-hand refrigerator for the cold drinks and the food, a hot plate to cook, as it took too much paperwork and proof of identity to get gas canisters. We had a CD player too as we both loved music. He had a wonderful voice. On weekends, I cooked, spending hours on my chicken kormas and pilaus that tasted even more delicious in our secret retreat. Our needs were stripped down to the barest of necessities, our bodies and love. I told my parents I was hanging out with my pals and could always be reached on my cell. Then one day, I shut the door and threw away the key, never returning to that chinnawheedu.

'Ram, Ram, Ram,' I cried, 'how can the pain still be so unbearable?'

nicky/nikhil

I was really pissed off with Apu. I called her home and someone said she had left for the office. The office receptionist interrupted her study of *Cosmo* to state she hadn't seen 'Madam'. It's urgent, I have to speak to her, I insisted. Of course, she'd have Madam call me the moment she arrived, any moment now. Could I please state my good name and where from? I replied 'America', after my good name.

The glare outside my window was intimidating and I could see the lava stream of traffic seeping along the road. I prowled the room, impatient to be out of it. Nearly half the morning was gone. What was she doing? All I wanted was a quick call back with a time and place.

Apu came on the line, talking briskly. 'Sorry, I didn't return your call, Nikhil. So tell me.'

'The crocodile.'

'What about it?'

Did she suffer from amnesia? 'I have to get that permit, remember.' Apu kept silent.

'I need your help to get it.'

'I can't today, I'm sorry. I'm very busy. Definitely tomorrow.'

'Tomorrow! I wanted to get rid of it yesterday.'

'It won't be hard,' she said. 'You have Rom's note, take it over to the chief conservator's office and they'll issue the permit. It's on Jeevans Road, that's in Saidapet. It's not far from your hotel.'

'You okay? You sound kinda down.'

'I'm fine,' she said, too quickly, and disconnected.

I couldn't blame her. She had found my father, that was her assignment, and then she had trekked over to Crocodile Bank. She couldn't hold my hand twenty-four hours of the day. I would've liked to see her though. I wondered whether the husband-to-be arrangement had worked out. I should've asked her, how did it go last night? Did you like the guy? How can you tell he'll remain the way he is now after a year or two of marriage? Will you jump into bed with him on your wedding night? It was crazy, marrying someone because the horoscopes matched or because he came from the right family. Hell, some 'right' families had axe-murderers, psychopaths, kleptomaniacs, pyromaniacs among them. If you were lucky, you uncovered the crazies after a couple of dates and bailed out. Here, you married them first.

I wished my father had paid his telephone bill and remained connected to the world. I could've called him, suggested we meet on neutral ground like combatants in a war, or a truce. A restaurant. A bar. The Marina beach. Dakshinachitra. Crocodile Bank. That huge empty mansion gave me the creeps. I imagined hearing eerie dance music in that ballroom, the click of snooker balls ricocheting around the table, the television flickering to an empty room. Why hadn't he remarried, or moved out to an apartment? Surely, he would want to escape memories. If I returned to that house I would hear Mom's soft laughter and her footsteps drifting through the rooms. I resolved to be patient and wait for the Friday night poker game, wondering whether Apu would play strip poker.

I stuck my head in the bathroom. 'Well, wish me luck,' I said to Renee, 'I'm going to get your permit so you can join your relations in the pond. I bet you don't have kleptomaniacs or pyromaniacs in your family. Probably a cannibal or two when you guys get hungry, but that's to be understood.'

The conservator's office was a fifteen-minute ride in an auto-rickshaw. I wore my bandit mask on the trip. The office was nondescript, not a preserved relic, and showed signs of neglect. Grey-green fungus crept down the once white walls. Dust eddied around the verandas. The building was set back in a compound, shaded by tamarind trees. A few people milled around aimlessly. There were signboards, stuck out like railway signals above the doors. I wandered down a corridor until I found a board announcing 'Mr Y.S. Gaitonde (IFS), Chief Conservator of Forests'. The door was closed. A man in a white shirt and trousers sat on a stool outside it reading a Tamil newspaper. He didn't look up.

I opened the door. The room was empty except for a cleared desk. There were two telephones on a low table beside it, one blue, the other black. Behind the desk was a straight-backed chair with a small towel hanging over the armrest. On one wall was a large map of the state, the forest areas painted a vivid mango-green. On another were photographs of tigers, elephants, deer, crocodiles, flamingos, panthers, monkeys and bison.

'On tour,' the man said without looking up.

'When will he return?'

He looked up surprised at hearing an Indian speak in an American accent. 'Next week, longer.' He folded the paper. 'What do you want?'

'Next week! Who's the number two? An assistant conservator?

Can I see him?'

'What do you want?' he repeated and stood up.

'A permit,' I said, edging along the corridor, looking for the next signboard. It was the office of the revenue officer. I didn't want to waste time with this low-level security guard.

'Wait, wait. What kind of permit?'

'A permit,' I snapped, recklessly dismissing the man's capabilities. 'It's as simple as that, and not your business.'

'If you want a permit to shoot a cheetal or a tiger, you will not get one. Impossible.' He paused. 'You will have to apply to Delhi and pay heavy bribe.'

'I don't want to kill anything.'

'So tell me,' he said, sounding like Apu on the phone. Then he announced formally, 'My name is Natarajan.'

I took out Rom's letter and watched as Natarajan read it. He didn't comment on it and instead asked, 'Which country you are from? You are Indian?'

'America, yes.' I took the letter back, cursing Natarajan for wasting my time.

'I'd like to go to Um-rika,' Natarajan said as he held up his hand to stall me from sliding away and popped into his boss's office. He came out with a foolscap size cardboard with red tapes attached to it on either side. He took Rom's letter, placed it on the cardboard and tied the tapes together so the paper was held in place. I had thought 'red tape' was a colloquialism.

Natarajan also had two sheets of blank foolscap paper. He fetched another stool of the same height and patted it, indicating that I should sit.

'You must write a letter requesting this permission to the conservator. You have your card?'

'No. I don't carry cards.'

Natarajan was disappointed. 'They are very important, then people know who you are.' He unclipped the pen from his shirt pocket and passed it to me, along with the sheets of paper and the file.

'Write,' Natarajan ordered, then closed his eyes to compose his masterpiece for this naïve Um-rikan. 'From Mr Nikhil Figgis of San Diego Zoo Society, USA. To Shri Y.S. Gaitonde, bracket IFS bracket, Chief Conservator Forests, TN. Dear Sir, RE: Study of *Crocodylus palustris*.' I looked up, surprised. 'I know technical names of all forest creatures. Write. I am doing doctorate on the above mentioned *Crocodylus palustris* in its natural habitat. As such, I request permission to therefore capture the said *Crocodylus palustris* for intense study. On completion of this study, I request permission to donate the said *Crocodylus palustris* to the Crocodile Bank. I remain, yours most faithfully, Mr Nikhil Figgis.' Natarajan's face broke into a beautiful smile of accomplishment. It lit his eyes, dark and friendly, and his moustache wrinkled up.

'Write a copy. This is for your file.' I copied out the letter though I hadn't planned to keep a file.

From the window ledge behind him Natarajan materialized an inkpad and a seal. He adjusted the date on the seal, stamped it in the inkpad, then stamped both Rom's letter and mine. They were now officially 'Received'. Reverentially, he gave me my copy.

'Will this work?'

'Most certainly. I will get the permission.'

'How long?'

'How much can you pay?' Natarajan countered, and then added, 'Tea money for the officers.'

Recklessly I took out a bundle of hundred-rupee notes. Natarajan was impressed with such largess. He plucked the bundle from my hand, counted out a thousand and carefully returned the rest.

'Advance,' he said, and slipped the letter into the file, below the red tape. He rose and walked down the corridor. When I didn't follow, he beckoned. We went to the far door and Natarajan entered with me following a step behind. We were in the main office and my heart sank. It was about half the size of a tennis court and crammed with desks. The desks were piled with files and along the walls open wooden shelves sagged under the weight of hundreds more. The edges of the papers were brown and curly, the air fine with the dust of ages. Natarajan approached the head clerk, whispered something, then pushed across eight hundred rupees and the file. I waited as the head clerk, an elderly man, with a solemn well-fed face, many years in service and very experienced in matters of permits read and reread my letter and then Rom's. He then examined me and the money, and slid it into a drawer in his desk as swiftly as a cardsharp palming a card. A blank sheet of paper made its appearance. The head clerk picked up a large plastic board, leaned back in his chair, rested the sheet and my file on the board and composed his own 'note'. I noticed that no one in the office hunched over his or her desk. They all used these large boards so they could sit back and work. I didn't see what was being written but Natarajan now stamped it with a different seal. The head clerk signed it and slipped it into the file. He handed the file to Natarajan who took one step past the head clerk to place it on the desk of the assistant head clerk. This one, a young woman with spectacles, had been discussing something animatedly with a colleague and was cross at being interrupted. Natarajan's smile mollified her. He told her something in a low voice. She looked at me, then read the file. She read it thrice. Then she composed a further note. Natarajan stamped this note too, she signed, and he added it to the file. He leaned past the woman to place the file on her colleague's desk. I was excited and elated—at this pace I would have the permit in no time at all. Natarajan was a magician. By the end of an hour, the file had moved a whole row, fattened by each clerk. But then, it hit a vacant desk. Natarajan conferred with the next clerk who insisted that the vacant desk should examine the file first before he could add his note. He left the file on the vacant desk.

'Tomorrow, come tomorrow,' Natarajan said, leading me out. 'Permit definite.'

I had expected a miracle but wasn't too disappointed. He was confident he would deliver it 'tomorrow'. Renee would remain in the bathroom for just another day. I had a day ahead of me and had planned to take an auto-rickshaw to Georgetown to find Mom's old home. While we searched for an auto, Natarajan gave me the lowdown on his job and himself.

The peons are the corpuscles of the administration. Without peons, the department, the entire functioning of the Indian government, would come to a grinding halt, not a file would move from one desk to another. He carried the files from his boss down to the lower echelons then back up, and read them on the way. Natarajan was a compassionate young man of twenty-four. He had been working in the Forest Department since the age of sixteen. Only two months ago, he had been made 'permanent', which meant this job was his for life, plus a pension on retirement. He had a glowing future as a peon. In turn, this 'permanent' had increased his dowry from twenty thousand rupees to ninety-five thousand rupees plus cooking utensils, a motorcycle and a colour television set, twenty-one-inch. As a member of the backward class, a Vanniyar, he was a resounding success and in great demand among the parents of many eligible girls of his caste. His father, Rangarajan, also worked for the Forest Department but out at the

Vandalur Zoo on the outskirts of Madras/Chennai, beyond the airport. Rangarajan was an illiterate watchman who had had Natarajan educated till the tenth standard. Through his father's twenty years and his own eight years in service, Natarajan knew how to manipulate the machinery. He knew how much money was spent on feeding elephants in the zoo and how much money vanished in transit to the Mudumalai Tiger Reserve. Also, the government encouraged nepotism. An auto-rickshaw stopped and he bargained the fare for me as the driver claimed his meter didn't work.

Blacktown was the city's lung, my father had written. It inhaled the poor from distant villages who came to trade with the granite fort, then breathed them out a generation later, rich and learned. Out of those lanes and by-ways, out of the steaming foetid heat of once mud and thatch, they spread out, slow as lava, fertilizing the plains to the west, jungles and villages, with hospitals and grand homes, universities and hotels, palaces and private clubs, shops and garages. They grew along the roads, which were once the pathways to distant battlefields. The roads were the umbilical cords of memory for the people who had left Blacktown, never to return, even when the city, ashamed of such a slur, renamed it Georgetown in honour of the foreign monarch who ruled the country.

Apu had said Georgetown was like a casbah. A casbah evoked low buildings, snaking along a maze of mysterious streets. Georgetown's southern skyline was jagged like bad teeth, evoking not mystery but confusion. One tooth was an Athenaeum-like temple with six pillars holding aloft the triangular crown. It was perched on a nondescript low building, as if it were an afterthought. Another tooth was a church spire stuck skywards like an implanted incisor. Rows of molars, plastered with signboards, were broken up by higher buildings, some modern, some over a century old and neglected. The Esplanade was wide enough to warrant the grand name but as dangerous to cross as a minefield. Buses careened through it like loose canons. When I faced Georgetown, I had the high court to my back. It was a deep shade of red, with minarets and domes, and resembled a Mughal palace or a mosque. To my right, on the corner, was a pristine art deco building announcing itself as 'Parrys'. When I had seen the signboards to Parrys, I'd assumed it was a suburb and not a company's name. The road adjacent to it, Rajaji Salai, ran parallel to the sea and the harbour and was the eastern boundary of Georgetown. The western boundary blurred Georgetown into Flower Bazaar and Rattan Bazaar seamlessly as a quilt.

I crossed the Esplanade with a herd of pedestrians, pursued by buses, and entered Mom's old neighbourhood. I wished my father had included a map in the novel. I didn't remember a Thambu Chetty Street. It wasn't in the novel and that should have warned me as I moved down it in search of names that were more familiar. Georgetown was a simple grid—the longer blocks ran north to south, the shorter, east to west. Like Manhattan, except these streets were narrow, blacktop lanes. There were no sidewalks, and I mostly navigated sideways, just as Mom had said, past handcarts, bullock carts, cycle rickshaws, auto-rickshaws, motor cycles, cars, even trucks, and zillions of pedestrians. I paused at a corner, watching the confusion, and realized this was deceptive too. They all had a purpose, the cart man with his cart for hire, the small boys weaving through with their metal teacups, the shoppers with their wads of cash. The edges of these lanes were wrinkled with litter, plastic bags, balls of paper, and the dust swept out of shops. Mongrels mooched through, in search of morsels. Although I was rank and dank with sweat and dust, I was surprised to find that I felt contented. I was drifting invisibly down the street, part of the flow and chaos; no one would single me out as a stranger as long as I didn't open my American mouth. In that heat, I had melted into Georgetown, Madras/Chennai, India. This was what I had wished for, to feel at home in a world I hadn't known. I breathed the same air Mom once had, saw what she had seen, heard the same frenzied sounds of commerce, though not through her disillusioned heart. Soon, I believed, I would stand exactly in front of her old home, like a soldier returning home after a long war. This was enough for me. Yet surely, she couldn't have lived in this confusion. She told me she had lived in a large house with an elaborate, carved entrance door and a huge inner courtyard. She had said it was off Armenian Street, though with Mom that could have meant a few miles away, and it was near a temple. In his novel, father had called it Rosemount Street. I figured it had to be somewhere.

I walked down a street full of lawyers and remembered Manian's joke. Their shingles, Advocate Raman, Advocate Krishnan, cluttered every inch of the narrow buildings on either side. In small cubby-holes, men and women were industriously hammering out litigations, appeals, summonses on upright typewriters. As I criss-crossed, working my way north, I noticed that each street had an identity. There were bathroom fixtures streets, pump streets, hardware streets, electrical fittings streets, steel rod streets. And inside, men sat behind glass counters under fans, waiting patiently for their customers. There was a confusion of eras here too, the old and new, hidden behind a chaos of signboards, large, small, insignificant. The second floors had barred verandas.

I revealed myself to ask for directions to Rosemount Street. They heard me, and knew I was not one of them. They conferred, discussed, scratched their heads and finally shook them. They had not heard of any such street in Georgetown. It had to be elsewhere in the city. 'Near a temple,' I added, and was told there were many temples in Georgetown. But I wouldn't give up. As I worked my way north, the streets became residential. The houses were old, with two floors, the front doors and their frames elaborately carved, lovingly polished. Mom's house had to be one of these, but which one? I paced up and down three of the streets, the mystery hidden safely behind those carved doors. On both sides of the doors were barred verandas and I could look through a dark passage to the sunlit glow of an inner courtyard. At least father's description of the house was accurate. But where were D'Souza Street, Da Gama Street, Bentinck Street? No one knew them; they were the figment of a writer's imagination. I thought I should knock and ask an inmate, 'Did you know my mother, Sushima? Her father was a wealthy cement merchant, like his father before him. The family had lived here for over a hundred and fifty years. They hadn't betrayed their roots and moved to fashionable Kotturpuram or Adyar.' That was in the novel too. Well, I had come this far and I possessed American confidence. The knockers were heavy brass rings, elaborately inlaid with designs. I banged it down. A woman appeared finally, nervous and wary, not to open the door but to peer at me through the bars. 'Did you know a Sushima and her family? Cement merchant,' I asked. The woman shook her head and retreated. I wondered whether she understood English. I tried other houses at random then, dropping those brass rings down heavily. No, they didn't know a Sushima or a cement merchant. These people weren't rude, they were polite, they wanted to be helpful but they couldn't give me the answers I wanted—a nod of the head and a pointing finger. Only my father could help me, if he wanted to. I retreated. In the novel, there was a church, an ancient one, over three hundred years old. I was surprised to find both rainbow-coloured temples and staid churches crammed between buildings. I wandered into one with a sandy compound surrounding it. It was a low, long building with rain-stained walls and rain-stained crosses. All the doors were locked but a plaque informed me this was the Church of Assumption, built in 1640. I discovered a couple of new Baptist churches, crouched in corners. Then, as I made my depressed way out of Georgetown towards the Esplanade along Armenian Street, I came across a high wall with a heavy door. I climbed four steps and entered an oasis. This was the church in my father's novel: the Armenian Church built in 1772. It was exactly as he had described it. It had high walls surrounding it, the heavy entrance door, and the spacious compound with the old neglected church dominating the garden to one side. The walls were yellowed with age and massive pillars supported the ceiling of the main building. Standing apart was the belfry tower. Both buildings held aloft crosses, mounted on gazebos. There was a graveyard in the shady garden and I wandered to read the headstones, the lettering long faded by centuries of rain and sun. I sat down, tired. Although the Esplanade was just beyond the wall, I barely heard the traffic. The silence was tranquil and it calmed my dislocated spirit, even as it had Mom's so long ago when she felt really low, and I now felt a sense of continuity as if she were sitting beside me.

s.k. naidu

I remembered my invitation to the woman detective, given in the spirit of flirtation and seduction. I had spent these days wondering whether she would accept it and if she would bring Nikhil with her. I had granted permission before I had known his identity.

The past few days had been trying for me. Confusion and disarray had plagued my well-ordered life. A vengeful army couldn't have caused more disruption. It had taken me two whole days to wrench my life back to my daily regimen. Even then, I would find myself adrift, wrestling with thoughts I didn't wish to remember. I had lost my spare appetite too; food had grown as distasteful as my thoughts. Ethiraj tried to seduce me with my favourites, a coimbu from Kerela, a vegetable biryani from Hyderabad, a poriyal from Chettinad. I picked at his offerings and pushed them aside. Books, I had always found, were the best distraction. I could wrap myself up in the coverlet of fiction or philosophy or history and hide from the world. However, even in those pages, a word, a sentence, a thought impinged into the present. I had enjoyed my solitary walks, up and down to the gate with long elastic strides. My doctor had advised me to walk for an hour daily. Despite my iron discipline, my little jungle failed to distract me. I didn't notice the mynahs or the parrots or the rainbowed woodpeckers, the squirrels and the mongoose escaped my attention. My eyes became unseeing, retreating inwards. What should I do? Should I avoid this son? Wear him out by hiding behind the high walls? In uncharacteristic indecision, I finally allowed fate to take control. I could have locked the gates, ordered my staff to prevent them from entering on Friday. But, if Sushima's son had the temerity to return, so be it. I would bow to the inevitable that I would have to speak to him. But nothing beyond that. I would force politeness and courtesy from my lips: How are you? How many plays have you directed? Are you married? These were the inconsequential questions spoken between strangers. Around a poker table, there was little room for any intimacy. I would not ever inquire after her. By avoiding her existence, I would avoid any discussion about myself. No doubt she had poisoned Nikhil against me with her lies. She had had a monopoly of his ear and his mind for all these years; there was no room for my justifiable antidote.

Yet, Nikhil had come here for a reason. I dismissed the tale about my novel and the adaptation of a play. I would never give that permission. That was a fabrication to invade my small world. I had smelled New York on him, sensed the hope and optimism of that city on his skin. I had spoken ill of his country but that had only been my warped sense of humour to deflect his attention. I had lived on Spring Street, south of NYU, in a tiny studio apartment. It was in the basement and I would emerge daily like a mole seeking the sunlight. On the floor above me, in an apartment exactly the same size as mine, lived a dancer. Tap-tap-tap, thump-thump-thump—the music seeped through my ceiling, waking me up every morning and, at night, disturbing my sleep. I complained, naturally, which is how we met. She was a Brazilian and I was surprised that a South American had long blonde hair and smoky, grey eyes. She insisted I learn to dance as she was a teacher too. I learned to tango, waltz, foxtrot, twist, dance whatever was popular. Our relationship began in friendship, turned into an affair and broke up when I refused her offer of marriage and an apartment in Rio. I had told her I planned to marry an Indian woman and live in my hometown and, hopefully, die there too. I do think of Celia often, especially when I dance. I drank beer in the Lion Pub and rubbed shoulders with Norman Mailer, Gay Talese and writers from the *Village Voice*. I had seen *Waiting for Godot* at the Village and written to Samuel Beckett a most intelligent letter on what I thought of the play. To my total surprise, I had received a reply and flown over to Paris to meet him. Beckett was a taciturn man but somehow I enchanted him and we talked for many evenings on, not about theatre, but the sorry state of mankind. I'd also met Leon Uris and Irwin Shaw in Paris. In those days, American writers had exiled themselves to that beautiful city, but they were the last writer exiles. Those were my happiest days.

nicky/nikhil

I stepped out of the elevator, exhausted. I carried a new pack of playing cards and a bottle of Indian whisky. The 'wine' stores in the city, I had discovered, never sold wine, only beer and hard liquor. I needed a couple of drinks, a shower—I'd have to stand on the bathtub ledges—and to crash out.

I stopped at the door at the sound of the murmur of a solitary voice murmuring something inside my room. It seemed to be singing. Cautiously, I opened the door and stood on the threshold. Before me were the two blights of my life, the cop, outlined against the window like an opera singer, and, lying on my bed, denting the pillow with her perfumed hair was the front desk manager, Ms Sarada Menon. They were enchanted with each other and didn't notice me. Assistant Commissioner Manian was reciting some poetry.

> Move on her lips
> The tip of your tongue;
> Do not scare her
> By biting hard.
> Place on her cheeks
> A gentle kiss;

Do not scratch with your sharp nails.
Hold her nipple
With your fingertips;
Do not scare her by squeezing it tight.
Make love
Gradually;
Do not scare her by being aggressive.
I am a fool to
Tell you all these.
When you meet her
And wage your war of love
Would you care to recall
My 'dos' and 'don'ts'.

Manian stopped mid-flow as I strolled in, crossed to the dresser, opened the bottle of whisky and poured myself a drink as if they weren't there at all. I pulled up a chair and sat looking at them. The spell was broken. Sarada shot upright, patted her hair and adjusted the folds of her sari though they weren't disarranged.

'I was reciting poetry to this beautiful woman,' Manian said.

'He recites so movingly,' Sarada stood up.

'See,' Manian said jovially. 'You heard a few lines. Can you guess the poet Mr Director hyphen writer?'

'It didn't sound like T.S. Eliot.'

'See!' Manian said triumphant. 'She's one of our poets from the eighteenth century, Nagaratnamma. She had more passion than the T.S. Eliots.'

'I like it,' I said, and then added maliciously to screw the assistant commissioner, 'you also told me you were married.' It was a wild shot, but Manian flushed.

'You said you were a bachelor,' Sarada snapped at him, the spell in pieces.

Manian would have been happy to toss me out of the window at that moment. He placated Sarada. 'I'm divorcing my wife any moment now. She doesn't understand me one bit. She believes I should spend my time more fruitfully conniving with politicians and making money instead of composing poetry.' He turned to me, brimming with hostility and his power as a cop, 'I am here to arrest you.'

'For chrissake, not again,' I said in disgust. I fixed another slug; the whisky made me reckless. 'I told you I was just joking about that bomb. And you never found one, did you? So why don't you leave me alone?'

Manian crossed to the bathroom and flung open the door. Rom's warning popped up in my mind like a flashing red light: 'Don't let the cops find it, they'll jump all over you.'

'Is this another joke?' Manian demanded from the bathroom door. 'I traced it to this hotel and Ms Sarada Menon was kind enough to pinpoint the exact room where it was hidden.'

My resentful glance was prettily deflected by Sarada's shrug. 'I'm sorry. He threatened to torture me if I didn't show him where it was.'

'Listening to him recite is the torture. What worse could he do to you? No, don't tell me.'

'Attend to me,' Manian commanded. 'You will come and stand beside me.'

'I told Chunky dear it was an avatar of your wife so that was why I let it stay and didn't report you.'

'Chunky dear!' I grinned at Manian and crossed over to stand beside him. He was pointing dramatically into the bathroom. Renee was there no doubt but so was a very dark man, his back to us.

He was leaning over the tub, caressing Renee and crooning softly. His poetry was more seductive than Manian's and Renee was humming too.

Manian shouted at the man and pointed an accusing finger at me.

When the man turned, I recognized him—the 'jungley' from the police station. In turn, he remembered me and though we had no common language we recognized instantly that we had one thing in common—an animosity towards Manian. He shook his head and returned to communing with Renee. Manian was bitterly disappointed that the jungley hadn't fingered me for the crime and I had once more slipped out his clutches. I returned to my chair and my whisky.

'I'm applying for a permit to move it to the Crocodile Bank.'

'That's moving vital evidence,' Manian said quickly. 'It must stay whereis-asis, until I find the persons who had this crocodile poached.'

'That could be forever,' I said.

'Maybe even longer,' Manian's voice was bland. 'And you cannot leave the country until I have established the truth in this matter.' He turned to Sarada and in a voice husky with longing said, 'I do have more poetry.'

'Recite it somewhere else,' I snapped, and went to the door, holding it as wide open as possible.

'You can recite on the roof terrace under the stars,' Sarada said, and went out. 'But don't you have some poetry about love?'

Manian would have followed her, eager as a puppy.

'Haven't you forgotten something again?' I said, pointing to the bathroom.

In his erotic euphoria, Manian had. He stalked into the bathroom and returned dragging the jungley by the handcuffs.

'What's his name?'

'Ganpathi. You call yourself a director hyphen writer and have no appreciation for beautiful poetry'

'It ain't theatre,' I retorted. Then I shut the door on them and returned to my chair and the bottle. I was turning into an alcoholic.

I yearned to talk to someone I knew well, to temporarily escape this land of strangers. Impulsively, I called Karen at home and her answering machine picked up. She would be in office now and I couldn't call her there, she would be busy.

apu

The family purohit, Ananthanarayan, believed that I was deliberately thwarting his predictions. It wasn't his fault, but mine.

'You're the one who predicted she'd be married by the age of twenty-one,' my amma scolded. 'I have it here, in black and white in your own handwriting. And then you predicted she would marry that boy from Sydney. You said it was a one hundred per cent guarantee, it was in her stars.'

'Amah, she is fighting her stars and the planets,' Ananthanarayan retorted. 'I am not to be blamed if she avoids her karma. She's doing full battle against the sun and the moon too. I have been absolutely correct in my calculations. See . . . ' He thrust the school notebook under her nose and then under mine. 'There, in black and white, you can see when she should have married. It was a most propitious time for her marriage and the boy from Sydney was the correct choice for her.'

'But he died in a car crash two months after marrying a girl from here,' I reminded him.

'That's not my fault,' Ananthanarayan argued with the skill of a lawyer. 'He had married the wrong girl and she brought him bad luck. If he'd married you, he would still be alive and well. Now, have you the horoscope of this new boy?'

'I don't trust other astrologers,' Amma said. 'Here's his date and time of birth. He was also born in Madras, so that should make it easy for you.'

'I can cast anybody's horoscope, even if they're born in Timbuktu.'

'That's why you have my horoscope all wrong,' I teased him. 'You've calculated my birth place as Timbuktu.'

Ananthanarayan didn't deign to answer this insult. His sulking delighted Amma. It was the first time someone had bettered the old goat in an argument. Although she bickered with him, she believed he was the best. He was the family purohit and had performed all the family ceremonies, including the bhoomi puja for this house so many years ago, even before the earth had been broken. The house was built according to vaastu. It faced west, the rear open to the east so the gods could look right through with a golden eye at dawn and sweeten the family's life with their sacred breath throughout the day and night. Their breath blew all the bad luck away and dumped it across the rest of India. Amma wasn't an overly superstitious woman, like some people we knew, but she was aware that you hedged your bets with pujas and prayers against the ill omens that life could spring on you. Like me not marrying at that propitious time.

Ananthanarayan was a wizened man, bent into the shape of a question mark by his years. He was thin as a stick too. As far back as I could remember he looked physically the same. His bare chest, crossed by his sacred thread, with sagging breasts, wasn't a pleasant sight. He was bald, with a sprig of fine white hair sprouting from the back of his head. Despite his age he had a fine memory and announced that this being the twelfth suitor the match had to be fortunate. He sat cross-legged on the floor of the patio with a school notebook and a fountain pen. Amma sat opposite, intent on the mystery he was about to reveal. Once more, he drew my horoscope quickly. A large square divided into four squares along each parameter. Then he drew a similar one for Arun and, checking on his date and exact time of birth, opened his reference book to find Arun's rasi. He cast his horoscopes according to the star sign at the time of birth and the angle of the moon. Only then would he start to match the two.

'As you know, compatibility varies from person to person,' he said, turning the pages. 'Does he want financial stability, social stability or love and affection from Apu? Her star is Mesha rasi and she loves beauty. The man, for best compatibility, should be born under Mithuna, Kanni or Makara rasi.' He looked up and hedged his bet with a wintry smile. 'But what is ordained by destiny cannot be changed.'

I'd had enough and stood up, heading for the door.

'Where are you going?'

'I have to meet my client, Mr Figgis.'

'At this time! It's 7.30 pee. m.' Then she noticed my outfit. 'You're looking plump. Are you wearing two salwars and a choli? Why?'

'It might get cold,' I said, and slipped a string of fresh jasmine around my wrist.

'Madras never gets cold. This isn't Delhi or Simla.'

'The air conditioning does. I'm taking your car.'

'Take Gilchrist with you for safety. And lock all the doors.'

'Stay,' I ordered Gilchrist. He had risen at his name. 'I'll be fine and I will lock all the doors and windows.'

'What's Mr Figgis like?' she called with a note of suspicion.

'Don't worry. He's not my type.'

'I wish I knew what your type was. It would make my life easier.'

Oh, I could've answered 'like Appa', but his type was rare.

From the hotel lobby, I watched Nikhil descend in the elevator. He waved to me from the third floor. I could barely recognize him. He wore a cream linen suit, a pale blue shirt and a dark blue patterned silk tie. He was tense.

'How do I look?'

'A gentleman,' I smiled. 'I didn't know you needed to dress up for a poker game.'

'It's to impress upon my father that I'm a respectable son, not a con man. I feel he belongs to the old school of impeccable attire.' He lost his buoyancy suddenly, punctured by despair. 'God, I'm nervous. Will he throw me out again? Is he going to curse my mother? He may not even let us in. He could've given that guy orders to lynch us if we show up again.'

'Don't worry so much. We'll see when we get there.' I plucked at my salwars. 'I came prepared for the game. It'll take them weeks to get all these layers off me.'

'You've played strip poker before?'

'I've never played poker. What are the rules?'

'You said . . .'

'I said I did because I thought that would stop him from throwing us out. Anyway, it got us the invitation. So how do you play poker?' I looked at him intently, as if waiting for him to unravel the mysteries of nuclear science in a few seconds.

He shut his eyes in despair at my ignorance, then said, 'Okay, here goes. I guess they'll be playing draw poker. The dealer deals out five cards, starting on his left. He puts up the money for the pot. The player on his left starts first. The cards run high to low, ace down to two, the deuce. The ace can also be used in a straight. That means in a hand of two, three, four, five, it can be any one of those numbers. A pair is two of a kind, two pairs four of a kind. A straight is a sequence in which not all cards are of the same suit. A flush is five of the same suit, but not in sequence. A straight flush is a sequence of five of the same suit. A royal flush is ten up to the ace of the same suit. There are variations of draw poker like the three-card and five-card but I hope they won't be playing it tonight. Got it?'

'I think so. How will I bet?

'Poker is also bluff. You keep a poker face when you only have a pair and con the other players that you have a royal flush. The other players will bet money against an item of your clothing.'

'That's what I thought. Raise you one rupee for two blouses and a bra.'

'Maybe it's not a good idea. I don't want you to end up in a bra and panties.'

'I doubt it. You're pretty good at poker?'

'I've played some. We used to have a weekly game in Yale. One evening I sat in on a game with some Chinese kids from Hong Kong. I cleaned up five grand that evening and blew it on a weekend in Paris.' He went around to open my door. 'I'd like to thank you before any shit hits the fan. I know this wasn't part of our deal. You found him for me and you don't have to play poker.'

I laughed. 'He invited me. You're my date. I bet he won't throw me out in the hope that I'll lose all my clothes.'

'What have you been doing since I last saw you?' we spoke in perfect unison as he climbed into my mother's Honda. We laughed.

'You first,' he said.

'You're the guest. How's Renee? How's Madras? Have you been to Georgetown yet?'

Balraj had taught me how to listen. I hadn't been listening before that; I'd been too preoccupied thinking of what to say once the speaker had finished. With Sarada, neither of us really listened as we talked simultaneously. When you listen, Balraj had said, look into the shadows of the other person's eyes and try to see what they're not saying. It's more important than the words coming out of their mouths. Words are deceitful and duplicitous; they're the means of seduction. But the shadows will reveal the truth. Be still, be silent. The longer you're silent, the more they will tell you. Silence is the vacuum that has to be filled with words. I looked into the shadows in Nikhil's eyes and heard the keen of a lost child searching for sanctuary.

'I've been back twice now to the conservator's office. The file moves up a desk or two, then slides back a desk or two. I get the privilege to pay for their tea. They drink tea as expensive as scotch. And then the file moves up another desk. Renee's file's as thick as a play manuscript, god knows what's in it. When you look at the office you have to figure that every tiger, elephant, buffalo, every wild animal must have its own file. I bet a tiger has to get a permit to kill a deer for lunch.' We laughed at the thought of every creature pushing paper around the jungle in this obsession for paperwork. 'I spent the rest of the day in Fort St. George and discovered that I do have a connection with its history. I went to Yale and there was this huge oil portrait of our founder Elihu Yale in the Fort museum. He must have cleaned up a fortune here to be that generous.'

'He married Catherine Hynmers in 1739 in St. Mary's Church,' I interrupted briefly. 'Did you go in there?'

'I did, after getting depressed in the museum. I mean they have original lithographs by the Daniels brothers that are crawling with fungus. The oil portraits are so badly lit you can go blind looking at them. And they have mould too. Doesn't anyone care that history is rotting away? And you can't even see all that original East India Company crockery in those dusty glass cabinets.' He fell silent; I could see he was struggling to keep his feelings under control. 'St. Mary's Church depressed me too but not because of any neglect. It's beautiful and it has to be the oldest Protestant church in Asia. But those plaques dating back to 1652 really got to me. All those Britishers died so young from malaria, cholera and god knows what else, most of them were just kids, and women.'

I knew what he was thinking in those silences. He didn't say them out loud, thinking they would offend me. I wanted to tell him, yes, the museum is neglected. We Indians don't care about our past the way other cultures do. We erase it. He was talking to distract himself from the meeting looming closer and closer. I didn't respond to his last remarks. I wanted to say that those Englishmen and women were brave to come to that old India and die, while his mother had fled this new one forever. Why hadn't she returned with him, eased the meeting with his father? Surely, after twenty-eight years, the two could meet in a civilized way.

S.K. Naidu's gate was wide open and inviting, almost like a trap. I drove past Shyam, still skulking by the gate with his rope, ready to hang anyone from Madras Telephones. There were five cars parked outside the house. Nikhil had been silent for too long now and was looking at the house with uncertainty. We climbed out and I straightened his tie though it didn't need straightening. I hoped my concern would comfort him.

'He did invite us to play poker tonight,' I reassured him again.

'But that was before he knew I was his son. He'll probably throw me out and let you in.'

'Don't worry so much. I'll distract him. I'll dance the dance of the seven veils around the poker table if need be. I have more than enough on to do that.'

At least I distracted him enough to get a smile. 'And I bet you can dance too.' He was teasing.

'I can. I learned classical dancing until I was ten. I still do some when my teacher Gayatri asks me to perform with her. Don't young girls in America learn ballet dancing or to play the piano?'

'You never cease to amaze.'

'That's why I exist, to amaze,' I laughed. 'Relax, think of something else.'

I gave him the opening. 'How was the potential husband?'

'Handsome and successful. We got on well. He's an American too. His name's Arun Chakravarthy. Do you know him?'

'No. And "getting on well" the first time you meet is enough?'

'What else? Isn't it the same on your American dates?'

'That takes longer to judge; two or three dates before we figure we're getting on well. Sometimes you think you're getting on well and she tells you to drop dead. When will you decide?'

'I sort of already have. My mother's matching the horoscopes and my father's discussing the dowry factor.'

I allowed him another long silence before taking his hand. It was damp. 'Is this a date?'

'No. It's a poker game.'

I held on to his hand, too late to release it, too late to dampen the expectation of my gesture. Men always read my signals wrong. He was strung tighter than a veena string and I had wanted to reassure him that he had my support. But he had got the wrong impression of an intimacy. If only I had obeyed Balraj's advice on silence. But that was in dealing with criminals, swindlers, using silence on the guilty for them to fill it. Nikhil needed the distraction now, I couldn't let him drown in my silence.

nicky/nikhil

I had been nervous all day, wondering whether he'd let us in, wondering how he'd receive me, wondering how I should talk to this man. His screams 'get out, get out' echoed still in my mind, they'd haunt me all my life, waking me out of sleep even when I became an old man trying to remember my father.

The hotel pressed the wrinkles out of my only suit and, descending in the elevator, I looked down on the waiting Apu. Her face looked like a small, dark rose above her voluminous clothes, her salwar bellowed around her like a balloon. I was sure she had a double layer on.

I couldn't believe it when she asked me how to play poker. It had taken me a couple of years to learn the game and I was supposed to teach her how to play it in a couple of minutes? I ran her through the rules, doubting she'd remember them.

As we climbed into the car, I felt I was on my first date again, hoping to grope the girl in a darkened movie theatre or in the dark corners of someone's apartment. I had been lucky with Linda

Lund, no teasing, no foreplay, a straight-forward lay, spoiling me for other girls. I read in *People* she'd married into her caste, East Coast money, either a Rockefeller or a Dupont.

I had wanted to ask Apu about the man she was planning to marry but that would have to wait. I had told her about Manian first, then my visit to Georgetown and she listened with the same silence as Renee had on our first date. Except, Apu's eyes darted to me occasionally, expressing sympathy, then laughing at my description. I liked the way she listened, alert to my nuances. It was always like that at the start, the intensity of paying attention and the desire to impress. Eye-contact was important, look deep and drown in each other's eyes. And as you listened, you thought which answer would be the best to manoeuvre her into bed, for the night or for the lifetime. The dross of daily living was highlighted to entertain, to amuse and interest the other.

When I told her about the museum, I had to control my anger at the wilful neglect. For god's sake, in America this museum would be air-conditioned, climate controlled, humidity controlled, fungus free and sterilized. In the States no human could have a healthier environment than a work of art. But I didn't say this out loud, knowing she would be resentful, although she knew I was being truthful. Of course I knew that India couldn't afford such American munificence and it made me melancholy. But even without such wealth they could preserve the past better if they cared enough.

I was surprised to see the gates wide open. I remembered that night, now seeming like so long ago. That gate had been the magic entrance to my father's heart. It had been shut then and we had forced it to open. Now that it was open, I felt it wasn't welcoming.

When she took my hand, the sudden intimacy threw me a curve

ball. Her hand was small and delicate like a bird's wing. It was cool and dry. I wanted to let go so that I could wipe my damp palm and take her hand again, but I kept a tight hold. This familiarity made the evening feel like a date, from the looks to the physical contact. Had she also held Arun's hand? I smiled thinking what was such a glancing physical contact in this culture almost always led to a sexual encounter in the States. I lifted her hand to my face and drew in the perfume of the flowers on her wrist. They were the same flowers she had worn on the day we had met in her office. I had barely noticed them then but now I lifted her hand up to the lights. The small buds were white and virginal and looked vaguely similar to that brittle coil on my father's book wrapped in that sari. Those had been black, and had fragmented at my touch. I wondered why Mom had preserved them, and that red cord, so carefully along with the sari.

The house was no longer dark and mysterious and bright lights reached out to welcome us. The chandelier at the entrance was on, sprinkling the chequered floor with the shadows of tinkling glass. The front door wasn't open but the shutters were. We looked through into that main hall and saw that the other doors were open and all the lights were on. But the house was still as silent as before. Rani wasn't typing tonight. I strained my ears, believing I could hear a waltz but that was my imagination. Apu released my hand and rapped on the door as I wiped my hand dry. I wanted it to be cool, even chilly, and firm when I shook hands with my father. This would be the very first touch with the man who'd sired me. How d'you do . . . Sir? Mr Naidu? Dad? No way. Apu knocked again and we finally saw Prasad emerge from way back and approach us slowly, like a materializing ghost. He was dressed immaculately in white.

When the door was finally opened, I said quickly, preferring to be thrown out now than be humiliated once more by my dad, 'I've come to play poker with my father.'

Prasad merely opened the door wider and stepped aside to allow us in. At least he hadn't been ordered to throw us out. The door closed and he led the way deeper into the house.

'What's his mood like?' I asked.

'You'll see.'

We followed him through rooms we hadn't seen before and down a passage that led onto a courtyard. It was open to the sky. Sloping red, tiled roofs covered the walkways all around. Black teak pillars, smooth as silk with elaborately carved bases and tops, supported the roofs. There was a raised well in the centre of the courtyard and beside it was a metal bucket attached to a coiled rope. At the far end, Prasad veered to his left and opened a door.

'The bald one cheats,' he whispered to us as we passed into the air-conditioned room.

The door closed behind us and I was pinned against it by my father's basilisk glare. He sat facing the door, five cards in hand, about to place a bet. A new cigar was stuck in his mouth. My father spoke no words of welcome hoping, probably, to dissuade me from coming in any further. No handshake, not even a friendly wave. I was reduced to the child facing a parent. The man was a stranger but undeniably my father and though we were only meeting for the second time in our lives, I couldn't stifle the sense of being the child. When I had been younger, mom's authority had ruled my life. Gary was only a surrogate authority. Mom might have been casual at times but I knew how far I could push those parameters even with her. Her eyes would take on an icy look of contempt if I came home with bad grades, if I was caught playing truant, if she smelled the pot, if I stayed out beyond the curfew. She believed in those television commercials: Do you know where your children are? She didn't want me to grow up with that American laxity towards their children. She held on to that part of her Indianness. A son was precious, raise him right and he would care for you in your old age, while a daughter skipped off to her husband's home. And now I was finally in my father's home, staring into those fierce eyes.

What had I done wrong? How could I dampen the anger that simmered there?

I knew my father was forcing me to retreat, to turn away and leave him alone so he wouldn't have to know me or learn anything about Mom. I vowed I wouldn't break this fragile connection between us by mentioning her name, Sushima. She was the sharp knife that could slash this possible bond.

Only when he asked me something would I reply. I moved cautiously towards the empty chair like I would if I was holding the gaze of a snarling dog.. There were others at the table but I didn't take my eyes away from my father's. I wanted him, and him alone, to forbid me to sit at the table. I made it to the vacant chair and sat directly opposite my father at the round, baize-topped table.

I sensed Apu slip into the chair beside me and let out her breath gently. We had made it across the minefield of rejection. My father had capitulated. His eyes dropped to his cards as I sat: permission to join the game had been granted. Only now I turned away to study the other players. There was a slim, regal woman sitting next to my father and they seemed suited for each other. I heard Apu's intake of breath even as the woman raised a finger to her lips and smiled.

'You know her?' I whispered.

'Lakshmi, Sarada's mother. I thought she only played bridge.'

My father too noticed the gesture and turned to Lakshmi and I sensed their intimacy as he smiled and Lakshmi smiled back a reassurance. The other three players were men around my father's age. He was still rude enough not to introduce us to them. Mentally, I named them Man One, thin and bald, the cheater; Man Two, overweight with vanity-slicked hair; Man Three, smaller and bespectacled, half bald. They folded and slid their cards across to Lakshmi. She shuffled expertly, then dealt to her left to my dad, and then to the others, including Apu and me. Apu watched me to learn how I behaved at the poker table. I placed a neat stack of one hundred-rupee notes in front of me on the table. Apu opened her purse and placed her money down too.

'Your money's no good at this table, young lady,' my father said. 'You were only invited to play strip. Are you going to play it, I wonder?'

Apu smiled and returned the money to her purse. 'I'll play it whichever way, Uncle.' She had deliberately used the respectful, and faintly intimate, term 'uncle'. Man One examined his cards and then slid a fifty-rupee note to the centre of the table. Man Two spoke a bit too loudly. 'See your fifty and raise you fifty.' He pushed his fifty onto the table and added one more. Man Three, after some hesitation, threw down his cards, rose and went to the bar in one corner of the wood-panelled room. Behind it was an array of bottles. Beside the bar was a table with covered chaffing dishes and a stack of plates with serviettes.

Apu removed her jasmine bangle and put it on the table. She showed me her hand, she had beginner's luck, a flush. 'See your one hundred and raise you fifty.'

'Hold it,' Man Two said. 'That's only a bunch of flowers worth a couple of rupees. This is real money. You've got to give up something more valuable like . . .' he had an unpleasant smile, '. . . your salwar. That's worth a hundred and fifty'.

'Since no one spelt out the value of my bets prior to the start of the game, I'll place what value I want on them. These flowers are very special. They came from my puja room.' Apu smiled at him, then at my father, the final arbitrator. 'This gold bangle, for instance, could be worth a couple of thousands. Or ten thousand.'

Man Two turned to my father to appeal. He had imagined an evening of delight as Apu lost all her clothes to him. He obviously believed he was the best poker player at this table.

'S.K., we had better make up her rules of play. Otherwise, it's going to take a year to get her down to her bra and panties.'

My father smiled. 'She has us there. We were so eager to see her beauty, we forgot to price it. And since we're not the brutal Kauravas, we can't unwrap her against her will. You'll have to gamble big to get her undressed, my friend.'

I had a pair. 'See your one hundred and fifty and raise you five hundred.' I slid over the money, figuring the boastful man a bad poker player, a show-off, who'd played penny ante all his life.

'Who's the chap with her?' Man Two demanded.

Neither my father nor I immediately answered his petulant query.

I placed my cards face down, waiting patiently for the game to continue, ignoring Man Two's demanding squint. My father was the host, he had to perform the introduction and I wondered how it would be done. Would I remain a stranger, Mr Nicky Figgis, just a visitor? I looked across and caught my father's eyes before they dropped to his cards. He smiled as if to say, 'Well, you tell them who you are.'

Both of us remained stubbornly silent. We looked at each other across the curious stares of the poker players.

Who would fold first? Who would be bluffed to reveal his hand? Who had a royal flush, who had only pairs?

'His name is Nikhil,' my father said, and gained their attention. Lakshmi took his hand, holding it tight. She smiled at him encouragingly. 'He's my son.'

There, the paternity had been confessed to his friends. It would ripple outwards to the others. I smiled in relief. Apu squeezed my hand, smiling too. Son and father had identified each other finally. Although I was staring at my father, I sensed three heads turning first towards me and then back to my father. The men were looking for similarity; we should be the mirror images of each other. That's why fathers had sons, to see their reflections in them.

'You don't have a son,' Man Two broke the astonished silence.

'He doesn't have any children,' Man Three said.

'None that he's acknowledged,' Man One giggled.

'I do now,' my father silenced them. 'He materialized out of thin air like the veritable genie from a bottle. I knew a child existed somewhere but I had hoped it would be a daughter. Instead, it's a son, a full-grown man, a blue-blooded American.'

'He looks Indian to me,' Man Three said, peering at me through his thick glasses.

'That's a clever deception,' my father said.

Man Two sat back to laugh at my father. 'Who's the mother? Or can't you remember?'

There was no retreat from down the slippery slope. A son implied a mother and they were demanding her name. My father could invent one, claim amnesia, but the proof sitting opposite him would deny his lie. I suspect my father had spoken the name out aloud only once in the last twenty-eight years. It would be rusty on his tongue, poisonous in his mind.

He said it aloud now with bitter venom, 'Sushima.'

I felt the sharp prick of Mom's name; it cut deep enough to bring blood to my face.

'I hope she isn't planning to join you in India,' my father continued to spit his venom at me. 'I have absolutely no intention of seeing her.'

'You won't have to,' I spoke bitterly, resenting my father's tone. 'She died on 9/11 . . .'

Her beauty, her love, her spirit, had vaporized in that conflagration. I had grieved and raged with the thousands of others. I had witnessed the moment of her death live on television. Yet hoping, praying she had escaped, I had searched the hospitals and streets for days.

I had believed this tragedy would delight my father; it would make him triumphant that he had outlived Sushima, that she had been consigned to an awesome pyre more dramatic than a pile of sandalwood and ghee. I expected him to rise and toast her death with gleeful pleasure. Instead, my father flinched from my announcement as if I had placed a curse on him. He clamped his hand to his mouth to prevent a mourning groan. Rising slowly, he turned and walked to the French doors behind him. Then he opened them and stepped out into the night.

I looked at Apu in shock, as if she had the answer to the puzzle. But she shook her head, not understanding either.

'Oh my god,' Lakshmi finally broke the silence. 'He still loves her.'

'He couldn't,' Man Two said. 'He's never once talked about her. He hates her, I know that.'

'You know nothing, you bloody fool. Nor did I.' She rose to go out to my dad.

'No,' Apu stopped her, and turned to me. 'He's your father.'

I listened to the swift exchange, unbelieving. I wanted to agree with that man. My father hated my mother and, I knew with certainty, Mom had hated my father. I had always believed this hatred was mutual and understandable. My father had shown such rage that night and even now had spoken her name with such vile passion. Yet, it was as if I had struck my father, the lashes of my words had marked his face and wounded his eyes. Lakshmi knew him better than I did. Better too than my mom had. She too waited for me to comfort my father, the stranger who had confused me now with revealed love. There was encouragement in the slant of her head towards the French doors leading to the silvered light. I wanted to wait to see if my father would return. I wanted to wait to give him time to absorb this long suppressed love. Surprisingly, we both loved the same dead woman now. She drew us closer together from out of the ashes.

I turned to Apu. 'How was I to know? He never gave that impression. I mean, I didn't mean to hit him like that.'

She smiled and stroked my cheek, the way she had the first night. 'You do spring things on him.'

'What should I say?' Women knew such things; they had an innate knowledge of how to comfort strangers and children. Most men, including me, had no command over the language of compassion.

'Tell him about her. He will want to know now.'

The others were waiting. They looked equally stricken for their old friend. I went out into the night to look for my father.

I heard one of the men say too loudly, 'Deal.'

The night was warm and moist, as a woman's tears. The half

moon was carved sharply out of the pure sky and the stars were pinpricks of shiny silver. In Manhattan, I never saw the moon or the stars, the sun was only light falling on a sidewalk. I wanted to gather my thoughts and emotions. How could love be sustained so long when my own for Renee had evaporated in a few years? What was the etiquette? Should I console my father? I had consoled the estranged Gary, and Gary me. We had embraced and held on to each other. What should I do with my real father? Would I be allowed an embrace?

Five steps led down to a small lawn. Beyond them rose the barricade of trees and shrubs. There was no immediate sign of him. I went down and saw a beaten path to my left leading through a tunnel of trees. I followed it, entering deep shadows, disturbing dozing creatures on both sides and overhead. Twenty yards in, I reached a clearing, a neatly cut circle, canopied by the branches. I smelt the cigar before seeing its pink glow. My father was sitting on a slatted wooden bench. He could have remained invisible if it hadn't been for the whiteness of his dhoti and jiba. I remained at the edge, wondering whether I had been seen and how I should break the melancholy silence.

s.k. naidu

I had not expected that reply. A bolt of unbelievable pain slipped through my heart, and it cracked and spilt out the secret I had hidden even from myself. My soul, my soul . . . shrivelled. I had spent these years convincing myself I hated her and, like the sad fool that I am, I forgot that hate is akin to love. They're both volcanic passions, impossible to contain. I must have risen and left the table, I needed my solitude to understand this terrible grief I felt for my wife of so long ago. I wasn't given much time. I heard his cautious approach; he was silhouetted against the faint light of the card room.

'Why did you come now?' my tone was not welcoming. 'It's too late in my life to acknowledge a son.'

'I wanted to come much earlier, when I was twelve and learnt you were alive.' He moved into the circle. 'I couldn't while she was alive.'

'So she'd killed me off and then resurrected me. How miraculous! If she hadn't died we'd never have met?'

'We would've.'

'What do you want from me?' I pleaded. 'There's nothing I can give you.'

'I want to know you.'

'Know!' I mocked him. 'How do you *know* anyone? Are we maps that you can read so easily? I've acknowledged you as my son, isn't that enough? I didn't *know* my father though I lived with him all my life. He remained a mystery. I knew the surface of him but not the interior maze we all live in. Parents are a mystery. We meet them too late in their lives and they don't yield up their secrets to inquisitive children.'

'All right,' he conceded. 'I needed to meet you then, learn who you are and to see where I could have belonged once.' I remained silent, not inviting him to sit down beside me. I didn't want his comforting. 'She seldom spoke about you and when she did it was not kindly. She had also detached herself from India; for her, it didn't exist. I had to discover it myself through books. She didn't even have a photograph of you, not even a wedding snapshot. So

I spent years imagining what you were like. Were you tall or short, thin or fat, funny or sour? Would you have loved me? When you don't know, you make-believe.'

I barely listened, remembering only Sushima and fate's tragedy. 'What was she doing at the World Trade Center?'

'She had a partnership in a travel agency. Luxury Inc., they called it. It was a good location, right there among the high-flyers wanting to take a break on a cruise ship, private islands, luxury hotels. She loved her work.'

'Sushima . . .' I sighed her name, not with a poisoned tongue, but soaking it with sadness. I sensed her in the glade now, young, beautiful, vivacious. 'Yes, I'm sure she died having enjoyed every moment of her life.' I watched him, half enviously. 'Did she love you?'

'Yes, very much.' He wanted to give me something more of her than her fortunate love for him. 'She was great fun to be with. She was kooky. She had no sense of direction, even in Manhattan, and she was constantly losing her keys. The doormen always had to open the doors for her, day or night. They didn't mind. She would smile at them and they'd have licked the floor for her to walk on. When she came to the PTA meetings at school—I went to the Academy in Manhattan—she would always rush in late and sweep everyone off their feet. She was always late and breathlessly apologetic. People always forgave her though. They even forgave me when they saw her. I was suspended from school for a week and she talked Mr Perkins into rescinding his decision.'

I savoured Nikhil's description, remembering her. 'Yes, even here she had that effect on everyone. She . . . she dazzled, is how I'd describe her in writing.' Now I made room without openly inviting him. Nikhil sat. 'You weren't an obedient boy?'

'I'm afraid not. I was suspended because they found pot on me. Anyone would think I was carrying a .25 automatic.'

'I was sent down for a whole term,' I boasted. 'I went to a boarding school near Ooty—Lovedale—but that was for staying out all night with a local girl.'

With these minor confessions of indiscretion we fell into a companionable conversation. He told me about his A grades, the first girl he kissed, a Linda, and how he'd met Renee and how they had parted. I listened, approvingly. I didn't want too studious a son, he would bore me. He did have a couple of my genes. In exchange, I told him of my days in New York and NYU. He appeared to listen but caught only the surface of my anecdotes. We fell silent, the cigar down to an inch or two, the air stained with its smoke. Although these were surface intimacies, which could have been exchanged between strangers, they uncovered the faint treads we were taking into each other's lives. 'Are my grandparents still alive?' Nikhil broke the silence.

'My parents are dead. Longevity isn't a strong suit in our family.'

'Any uncles or aunts? I'd love to know, I mean meet, them too.'

'An uncle, younger than me. Suresh is an important man. He's in the IAS and now secretary for finance in Delhi.'

'My mother's . . .?'

'Her mother, Kumari. I believe she still lives in Georgetown.'

'I went to look for the house.' Nikhil was excited. 'But I couldn't find it. You had made up the street names in your novel. I must meet her.'

'Yes, I had,' I said and waited a long time before continuing, 'I'm not sure she can meet you.'

'Is she ill?'

'I wouldn't know. Once a couple separates, the other family

falls into a forgotten abyss. I think her husband died about five or six years ago, without ever seeing his daughter again. His name was Nikhil. So she did keep a continuity of her past without telling you.'

'Yes. I didn't know that. I'd like to meet Kumari.'

'I'll try,' I said. 'I wrote her a letter of condolence when her husband died. Maybe I should have paid my respects personally but I couldn't bear the memory.'

Nikhil saw his chance. 'I know it's late in the day to ask the question. What happened? Why did she leave? Why did you let her go? What made her hate you so much? What . . .'

'In all your years she never explained?' I was amused.

'No,' he said, not wanting to rain her abuse on my head. 'Apart from saying that you were to blame.'

I felt exhausted, emptied out by this night of emotional upheaval. I stood up and tossed the dead cigar into the undergrowth. 'I think that's enough excitement for tonight.' Nikhil rose too and we walked back to the house. 'My vulnerability doesn't mean I'll give you permission to mangle my novel.'

'I may have improved it,' Nikhil smiled.

'Impossible.' We climbed the steps together to the French doors and the lights. I hesitated, then made up my mind: I had to unburden myself, purge the past and who better to do that with than a son. 'Why don't we meet some time tomorrow?'

'That's great. Any time. But I'd like to meet somewhere else, not here.'

I looked around, startled. 'Why? What's wrong with here?'

'Nothing,' he smiled, not threateningly, almost apologetically. 'Sort of a neutral place, without bad memories.'

'I haven't been out of the compound for years,' I said, shivering at the thought of leaving my sanctuary, my hermitage, to be contaminated by the crush of unwashed humanity out there. 'All right, for your sake. I'll send the car, but I choose the place.'

'Great.' He stood in front of me, hesitated and said softly. 'I'm sorry about Sushima.'

'Thank you, but it's twenty-eight years too late,' I said, and went in quickly. I passed from one world into another as I stepped into the card room. I'd forgotten the players, continuing with their lives and the card game. Apu looked up at us and first smiled then frowned down at her cards. She had hit a long losing streak—her bangles and two kurtas were divided between the three men like loot. Only her dupatta covered her low cut choli, brief as a bikini top with sleeves. The expanse of smooth amber skin sloped down from her shoulders to the rising curves of her breasts. A younger woman's body always reminded us old men of so many lost opportunities and the passage of time.

Deepak stared at her nakedness with greedy eyes. 'You'll have to bet your dupatta,' he cajoled and teased. No woman would remove her dupatta; it would have to be another item.

Nikhil looked irritated.

I broke the spell of sensual riches. 'I'm retiring for the night, so I'll be missing the rest of the entertainment, I'm afraid.'

Lakshmi threw down her cards. She took my hand, looked up into my face with affection, then smiled at Nikhil. We moved towards the door together, hand-in-hand.

'You want to stay and lose the rest of your clothes?' I heard Nikhil demand of Apu, the irritation more open. He scooped up his money.

Apu threw down her cards too, grateful for the interference, reached across the table, and scooped back her salwars, the bangles and the strand of jasmine.

'That's not fair,' my friends chorused. 'We want another shot at the choli.'

'You had your chance,' Apu laughed as we left the room.

I didn't lead Lakshmi up to the bedroom. I wanted her comfort still, though not in the bed. I mourned for Sushima as if her death had occurred that very day and not so long ago. The bed would be a betrayal to her memory, although I knew how foolish I was being.

'It was a shock,' I said.

'Love. You still harbour it for her.'

'Harbour's the right word, I suppose. I've kept a lantern in the darkness in case she would sail back one day. It couldn't be snuffed out like a wick, no matter how hard I tried. God, how I longed for amnesia or death, so I could forget her forever.'

We still held hands, like children afraid of being lost in the dark, and she knew where I was leading her. There were times when she was confident she knew me too well. But now, I know she found herself in the company of a stranger. We had been together for nearly twelve years. Appropriately, we had met at the poker table. It had been at a Diwali party thrown by Ishwar Bhagchand. Ishwar, a Punjabi, followed the north Indian custom of playing a card game on Diwali. She had learned poker from her rascal husband, as addicted to poker as he was to airhostesses. I had flirted with her boldly, testing her humour. She had sensed my loneliness beneath my wit. So, when I invited her to our weekly poker game, she had known my motives.

I didn't turn on the lights but left her in the middle of the dance floor and crossed to the audio system. I flicked through the stacks of CDs, peering in the faint moonlight, found what I wanted and slid it in. I was by her side before the tango started. We danced well together, I had taught her.

'Would you have contacted Nikhil if he hadn't come tonight?'

'I don't know the answer to that. I had hoped he would come, I hoped he'd bring her so I could see her again and her cruelty would cleanse me. Instead, she's left me with the lamp still alight. It will only be extinguished when I die.' We danced across the floor and back. I held her tightly. 'Does that disillusion you?'

'No,' she smiled, and I knew she was lying for my sake. 'It proves you have the capacity to love. And I never expected to marry you. I'm content with what we have together.'

apu

We hadn't spoken on the drive back until I parked under the hotel porch. I wanted to tell him it wasn't my fault that I'd lost my kurtas. After the first flush, I couldn't even dredge up a pair. I suspected the bald one, who was the dealer once Naidu left, had deliberately dealt me bad cards. I had hoped Lakshmi would protect me, but Lakshmi had left the table soon after Nikhil had followed his father out. When she had returned, a few minutes before Naidu had, her eyes were faintly red. She had been weeping in private somewhere.

'You mad at me or your father?' I said. He was sulking like a schoolboy over my nearly lost modesty.

'If you so enjoyed your strip poker you should have stayed on and played to the end.'

'I had bad cards.'

'You could've discarded.'

'You didn't tell me I could in your lesson. So you're mad at me for losing at the stupid game.' I laughed, teasing him further. 'Maybe I should've played on. It gave those old goats a cheap thrill.'

'I didn't expect that from you,' he said primly.

'What do you expect from me?' I was amused at his possessiveness. 'Don't you ever see American girls in those string bikinis on your beaches? They leave little to the imagination. I had a lot more covering me than they have. But you wouldn't see anything wrong with them, would you? You have this idea of me as a prim Indian girl.'

He changed the subject, speaking irritably. 'And he's still impossible. He wouldn't answer my questions.'

'Which questions?'

'About what happened between them.'

'God, you want your answers immediately. Give him time. He's been wounded badly, he needs to collect himself. And why should he tell you, when your mother wouldn't?'

'She gave her version. Two people have to share the blame. What about me? I've waited all these years to meet him.'

'You had her love. He was denied it. Or he lost it.'

'But he found another. They're obviously lovers.'

'You can't deny your father some pleasure. You have a strange idea about Indian women. We make good mistresses too, you know. Rich men keep theirs in chinnawheedus.'

'Chinnawheedus?'

'Small house, in Tamil. They buy it and install their mistresses in it so they can visit them. The women are also known as chinnawheedus, behind their backs of course.'

'Does the wife know?' he asked in surprise. 'In the States, men are far more discreet, especially the rich who don't want to lose their millions or billions in a divorce.'

'Unless she's deaf, dumb and blind. She doesn't care. She lives in the big house, her children are the heirs and she won't be pestered for sex. It's very civilized.' I wanted to talk about myself, not on and on about him. I wanted his reaction now, while he was vulnerable. 'It's an important night for me too.'

'Why?' he was half out of the car. He bent to look at me and said in a sarcastic tone, 'Because you nearly stripped?'

'My father and Arun's father are discussing my dowry,' I snapped and he slammed the door on me as I said a final goodbye.

I had wanted to dispel his image of me, I wanted to shock him and tell him I'd danced naked for my lover in our chinnawheedu. I had to tell someone, release the secret that was consuming me inside. I missed the caress of his hands over my body, the hard thrusts inside me. I wanted to weep again.

He tapped the window. He hadn't left and looked worried. 'Are you okay?'

'I'm fine,' I said and drove away quickly.

nikhil

Her face began to crumple like she was about to cry. I couldn't understand what I was feeling. Why should I care if she lost all her clothes at that table? And yet, seeing her so vulnerable had strangely disturbed me. Why had I got mad at her? Because she had flashed her shoulders and some part of her tits? That was her business. Admittedly, I was stuck with this image of an Indian girl, pure as driven snow. They weren't supposed to play poker and lose half their clothing. They were meant to be sweet innocent virgins, awaiting the marriage bed. But she meant nothing to me. I had paid her for her professional services and she had delivered. She had got into the poker game so I could meet my father again. Besides, she was going to be married soon to some Arun. She had made up her mind and was only waiting for the horoscopes to match and the dowry to be agreed upon. I had to stop thinking about her.

I was in the click-your-heels and dance/sing exhilaration of that late night movie *Singin' in the Rain* guy—I had been recognized by my father as 'Nikhil, my son'! We hadn't embraced or kissed, hadn't even touched yet, but his words were like a magic mantra—my father had acknowledged me. I was S.K. Naidu's son, I was now Nikhil Naidu, if I wished to be that. I loved the sound of it and said it out aloud, 'Nikhil Naidu.' It didn't have the conflicting feel of Nikhil Figgis, adopted by Gary and granted his name for legitimacy. Screw him now. An instant later, I felt deflated. I hadn't yet absorbed the shock of discovering that my father was still in love with my mom. I felt his pain, clinging onto that torch. She had snuffed hers out the minute she had walked out on him. 'He's dead,' she'd told me. My father and I were similar, both dislocated by the love we had for her. Mom had stolen me away in her womb to dislocate me from my father and India. One person always loved more, that was the gamble you took in life. At least my father was anchored firmly in that house; he was set in a concrete identity, S.K. Naidu of Madras. I was now afloat like a spore in the breeze. And yet, I felt a sense of unease, even foreboding. He had said something I'd missed, a word, a phrase, which was important to my understanding. What had he said? He had loved New York, he'd learned to dance from a girl, met Mailer, *Village Voice* guys, gone to Paris . . . in New York he had done his masters in . . . NYU. NYU! Gary had been at NYU too. Had they met? But then, a million students had been to NYU and never met or even crossed paths.

I swallowed my four daily pills, then checked on Renee. She

had eaten her steaks and seemed asleep. Unable to calm myself, I grabbed my swimsuit and went down to the hotel pool; I would swim until I was exhausted. The pool was about the size of a postage stamp. Three strokes would get me across. I figured I'd have it to myself but a woman was churning the waters. When I slid into the pool and she stopped, I saw it was Ms Sarada Menon, modest in a one-piece swimsuit. I hadn't wanted to talk to anyone in this mood but she paddled over to me.

'How are you and Renee, Mr Figgis?' she asked in her normal cheerful voice.

'Fine,' I said and swam away. I lapped the pool twenty times, scarcely drawing breath. I thought she would tire and leave. Each time I turned, sharp and quick as a shark, she remained in place. Her fine brown legs patiently kicked in the water. I remembered now that she knew Apu, they had talked by the elevator. And, I stopped a moment, her mother was my father's lover. But Lakshmi had raised a finger to her lips to protect her secret and I wouldn't mention it. Sarada also knew Indian women who were a mystery to me. I couldn't read them as I would an American girl.

I stopped beside her. 'Do Indian women believe in pre-marital sex?'

'Some do, most don't.' She wasn't surprised at the question, as if she were expecting it. 'Most of them leap into the marriage bed clutching how-to-screw textbooks in their hands.'

'The *Kamasutra*?'

'No. That's too advanced for beginners,' she smiled. 'Whom do you have in mind?'

'No one,' I said and swam away again. Or did I? I had wanted to touch Apu's smooth shoulders, let my hand drift down to her breasts. I smothered the image—I was to become a celibate sadhu—

and returned after ten laps. We were side-by-side, legs afloat, arms hooked over the edge. Delicate drops of water, sweet as perspiration, lingered on her face and bare shoulders. I didn't feel the urge to caress her shoulder, within a finger's reach. I was a romantic, not a seducer.

'More and more urban women are falling in love,' Sarada continued. 'Love can't be helped, it's like a contagion. But some, like Apu, want the traditional arranged marriage. I've no idea why. You should ask her.'

'I don't know her well enough.'

'You could. When I'm confused, I suffer from insomnia. Do you too? Talking to a total stranger always helps.'

'The insomnia or the confusion?'

'Both. When did you know you were in love with Renee? How did you know you were in love?'

'I guess when I found myself constantly thinking about her. I'd find myself rehearsing a new play and then, as if I were in a dream, I'd start awake to find myself thinking about Renee. When I was away from her, I felt I was in darkness. She brought the light in with her.'

'And other women didn't?'

'Not that I noticed.' I would've added that one other woman had, Karen. She had brought in the glow, and then when she had transferred to Columbia, taken it with her. I found I thought of her often. I missed her wit, her energy, her laughter.

'So you decided then you'd marry her?'

'Yeah, on such slim dreams we decide to marry. I didn't want her to carry the light away.' I felt quite relaxed talking about Renee now. 'Admittedly, she was reluctant. She had her career obsession but I thought I couldn't bear the loneliness without her. This dark chasm yawned in my life. I thought she would fill it. I convinced myself I was in love with her and I guess she convinced herself too.'

'Yes, I pray that love will dispel the loneliness. If it's true love, won't it?' She added hopefully.

'I wouldn't know. What I possessed for her was true love. I think now, she didn't feel that way for me. We came apart at the seams after a couple of years of life together.'

'I think of Ramesh a lot.'

'Ramesh? I thought the cop's name was Manian.'

'No, no.' Manian's a sort of test for me. I'm physically attracted to him but I know that after one night I'll get sick of his poetry. He's the apple in the tree, I mean. You know, Adam and Eve and the apple.'

'So who's the serpent?'

'My body,' she laughed. 'Our bodies are always the serpents that wind us up into knots. Our bodies are easily tempted by the curve of another body, the muscles on a man's shoulders, the imagination of locking loins together.' She paddled her legs, then said determinedly as if I'd convinced her with my silence. 'I'm going to marry Ramesh.'

'Does he bring light into your life?'

'God, yes. I can scarcely breathe when he's beside me. I guess that's love, isn't it? You must come to the wedding.'

'Can I bring Renee too?' I said as I helped her out of the pool.

She laughed. 'Only if you can keep her big mouth shut.'

apu

I watched the sea from my balcony. It stirred with anger; the silvery plain heaved and tossed. Far below in the deep I imagined the cauldron bubbling and boiling. Vishnu was stirring the oceans. The waters were confused, the waves crashed into each other, racing in and retreating. On monsoon nights, I would sit here and watch with joy the sea carrying the hard rain in on its broad back. The rain would lash my face, soak me in seconds, as it hurried on inland to nurture the earth. I wished for that now.

Why had Nikhil been angry with me? What had I done? He too had looked down on my expanse of skin, the brief choli. I'd not meant to tease those juiceless men, and I'd played poker only for Nikhil's sake. He had looked at me as if I was a cheap woman. I resented the cataloguing men did with their eyes over an inch of bare skin. You smiled, and they were already in bed with you. I never wanted to trust my heart or my body again, they were deceitful and devious. My mind had firmly chosen Arun. I lifted the strand of jasmine to my face, the way Nikhil had done, and inhaled the perfume. The scent was fading, soon it would die altogether.

I fell asleep on the balcony and was woken at dawn by Gilchrist's cold nose against my cheek. The fitful sleep hadn't purified me; the soiled feeling remained. I took a long shower, scrubbing hard. The water revived me.

Amma called: a man had come to buy the jeep. Why was I selling it, she wanted to know. I went down. He was a young man with a reckless air about him. He would wear a safari hat, slam in a CD audio system to pump out high-decibel American rock music and drive too fast. It was his second or third car. His family was rich. I felt sour and didn't return his wide, inviting smile. He left his red Toyota in our drive to test drive the jeep. When the man returned, we bickered over the price and settled for thirty thousand. He would return with the cash.

I joined my parents for breakfast on the patio. When I kissed the top of Appa's head, he looked up from his paper with a satisfied smile. Even Amma looked content. The trap had been sprung; I could read it in those looks.

'I would've told you last night but you came in a bit late,' he said, sitting back to recount every detail, making me laugh at times. 'I had dinner with Mr Chakravarthy and we finally agreed on the dowry. I fed him as much Black Label as I could to mellow him down but it was like haggling in the bazaar. I said, "I guess you new Americans won't be following all our old customs." And he quickly said, "You see it's difficult for us. Our son is our most precious possession. We live among other Indians and if we go home and say that we didn't get a dowry, they'll look down on us."

'I laughed and replied, "Why are you giving in to peer pressure? You're independent in independent America. As you've broken away from all things Indian, you should break away from such archaic customs." He replied, "Ahh, I wish we could. My sister lives in Chicago, you see, and the first question she'll ask is why I haven't followed our customs."

'I know how the Indians live in America. They claim to believe in American values, and live by them in their daily exterior life. I bet he commutes to work like other Americans, works hard, grabs a BLT at his desk, hangs out around the water cooler talking about last night's game and leers with the other guys at women in cocktail bars. A large Stars and Stripes flutters on his front lawn, which he mows on weekends and, on July Fourth, he throws a tandoori barbecue. However, once past his front door, he relaxes in a dhoti and jiba, feasts on the thali his wife has prepared and watches pirated videos of Bollywood films. I really thought America would have changed those dowry habits and told him, "Americans don't have the dowry system for their women. Or do they?" And he said "But they're a new people compared to us. Some of them do have what they call pre-nuptial agreements. Think of the dowry as a pre-nuptial."'

'How much?' I interrupted Appa, but he wasn't to be hurried.

'What's the hurry? I told him, "That's to save the very rich from being ripped off by the divorce courts." Then, get this, he tells me that his son is so rich that you'll live like an IAP.'

'What's that? It sounds like a disease.'

'Indian American Princess. You'll be a maharani in America, according to Mr Chakravarthy. I told him you and Arun like each other and we should consider these emotions as well. I wanted to add that when we become in-laws, we shouldn't be so insistent in our demands. We will be seeing each other, once a year at least, and when we go to the States to visit Apu like so many other parents visiting their far-flung children, we'll have to eat and drink and be polite with each other. And, of course, he reminds me again, Arun isn't a green card holder but one hundred per cent American passport holder, the magic pass into the land of plenty.'

'Are you going to tell me or not?' I asked again, and prayed it wasn't exorbitant. The Indira Gandhi government had banned dowry but it was a toothless piece of legislation. 'God, it's such an iniquitous system.'

'Thirty-five thousand,' he winced and added, laughing, 'dollars. I offered it in pesos or roubles but he doesn't have a sense of humour.'

'Thirty-five!' One of my friends, Vasanthi, had to pay twenty-five lakhs plus a Maruti car to the groom's family.

'And once we have the horoscopes, we must start the preparations for the wedding,' Amma said in her bustling, waiting-to-go voice. 'Mrs Chakravarthy, Nirmala, would like it done before they returned to America. That doesn't give us much time.' She spoke faster, panicked by each thought, excited too. 'We have to buy your wedding sari and saris for our relatives. I'll have to book a kalyana mandapam, find a good caterer and get the old goat Ananthanarayan to prepare for the ceremony. He'll be delighted—he's finally going to get you married. He said he had to perform it in his lifetime. We'll have the mehendi the day before the muhurtham. Then we have to get out all the invitations.' She turned to Appa. 'Should we hold the reception at the Taj Hotel?'

He had made me smile. As Amma had reeled out the programme, he had mimicked taking punches to his jaw. 'Why don't we have it here?' Appa said. 'We have enough space on our lawn and we don't have to invite the whole world. We can have the reception and the marriage ceremony on the same day.'

'That depends on them too. They may think we're being cheap. I'll talk to Nirmala. But these American families love a big show. When Padmini's daughter was married to that boy from San Francisco, his family insisted the reception be held at the Sheraton. And now that we've all picked up that north Indian habit, you'll have to have a bar at the reception. In my day no one drank at weddings, today they only come for the booze.'

In their excitement, they seemed to have forgotten I was listening to this juggernaut rolling on inexorably. 'Shouldn't we wait to see whether our horoscopes match?'

'Stop being so superstitious,' Amma said. 'Of course they'll match.'

'You're the one who's superstitious. You're the one who insisted on it.'

'No, you were the one.'

'All right, I was,' I said and rose from the table. 'But I'd still like to wait.'

I went upstairs to sit on the balcony. The sea was calmer today, as if it had had a good night's sleep and was just waking up. Appa knocked and came in. He pulled up a chair, sat and held my hand. I gripped it tightly, knowing I would lose it soon. He would no longer be there to wipe away my tears, pass on his strength. I would miss him, miss Amma, miss Gilchrist. Tears tingled in my eyes at such thoughts.

'What's it like?'

'America?'

'Yes. In the movies and on television everything looks so neat and clean and shiny. And everyone's rich, like Arun.'

'I did ask you to come with me but you never had the time. I don't know enough about America; I've only been to New York and Boston. That's only skimming a huge country. I love New York. What happened on 11 September to that city was ghastly.' We had watched it live on television, moment by moment, and saw the second plane hit the tower. We had stayed up all night, transfixed by the horror, silently weeping for those who had died in that violent collapse. I didn't know then that Nikhil's mother had been in that conflagration, and now it seemed so much more real. Back then, from our great distance, it had looked like another Hollywood special effect, and we knew we'd never be able to experience the same sense of tragedy as an American.

Appa sighed at the memory of that night. ' "The evil that men do lives after them; The good is oft interred with their bones". I wonder what good deeds those terrorists ever did.'

'Mr Figgis comes from New York. His mother was in the building when it happened.'

'I'm sorry,' he sighed. 'It's a great city. But there is a dark and dangerous underbelly in America you never see in films or television. There the poor are worse off than our poor because the gap is so much wider. They have as many beggars as we do, and they beg on street corners while huge limos glide by. The rich are too rich. Men like Bill Gates are richer than some nations and I believe that to be unjust. I call it the Midas country, if you have the luck. You know Midas, don't you? He was the King of Phrygia, a greedy man, who asked the gods for a boon. The god, Dionysus, granted him the power to turn into gold whatever he touched. Of course it was a double-edged boon: he could neither eat nor drink and when he embraced his daughter she too turned to gold. Dionysus took pity on Midas then and told him to bathe in the Pactolous river to wash away the boon. Sometimes America is like its food, golden but tasteless. I don't like what they're doing now in Iraq, Afghanistan, and around the world. The dichotomy of America is that, within, it struggles to be a fair and just society, but outside its shores it shows a cruel and indifferent face.' He sighed. 'It's a schizophrenic country. Let's say it's complex. For some people it's instant love, for others the opposite.'

'And you?'

'Wishy washy,' he laughed. 'I like it, yet it dismays me.'

'Will I like it?'

'I hope you will,' he tightened his hold. 'It will be your home soon, so you should prepare to like it. I don't know what Atlanta's like. I suspect it will be a conservative city, being in the deep south. They burned it to the ground in *Gone with the Wind.* You've not seen that movie, have you?' I shook my head. 'It's confederate country. We judge and see America so much by movies, you know, we form our opinion according to what Americans want us to think about them. There are a million and a half of us Indians there so I'm sure you'll meet them in Atlanta. They're everywhere.'

'I don't want to go all the way to America and just mix with Indians.'

'You will. From what they told us over dinner, they seem to know mostly Indians, just a smattering of white friends.'

'I'm going to miss you and Amma very much,' I whispered. 'God, when I want to talk to someone I love you'll both be ten thousand miles away. I'm going to miss everything; there's nothing I won't miss. I'll miss this city, all the people I know and grew up with. I'm going to miss this sea and it's smell, I'm going to miss the noise of our city, the confusion that isn't really confusion. I'm going to miss the food, especially Andal's cooking.' I drew a shuddering breath; the catalogue grew even as I spoke. 'Will I ever return?'

'Of course you will,' he whispered too. His face drawn, tired with these thoughts. 'You'll be back every year, like the others.'

'I think Mr Figgis's mother did the right thing. She left India and never returned. Why should I hold on and on? We should let go, cut the ties.'

He smiled, sadly. 'What about us? Don't you ever want to see us again?'

'Of course I do. That's the problem, that's why I'll be shuttling back and forth.' I didn't add that on each visit I would see changes as they grew older, more infirm. I could be far away when they died; it was a heartbreak looming in my future. 'But his mother never did want to see her parents or her husband or her friends again. She must have been a brave and very stubborn woman. I don't think Mr Figgis should have returned, she hadn't wanted him to. She knew that if you try to live in two places, you'll be lost.'

We fell silent, holding hands and watching the sea. There was no sea in Atlanta, and I would only stare at a pool of still and lonely water. After Appa left, I remained on the balcony; his words ebbed and flowed through my mind to the rhythm of the sea.

s.k. naidu

Nikhil showed me the invitation card to a dance recital he had found slipped under his door. It was for a classical dance performance called 'Chidambaram', and, at first, he didn't know why he had been invited. The lead dancer was a Gayatri Vishwanathan. Then, when he turned it over, he smiled. One of the female dancers accompanying her was Apu.

I examined the card with distrust. We were sitting in the stands, just the two of us, in the M.A. Chidambaram Stadium by coincidence. Since I had been forced to leave my sanctuary, I thought it best to return to one of my old haunts. I had spent many days playing cricket on this ground and I felt at ease in such familiar surroundings. The city had changed since my self-imposed exile. The traffic was sheer insanity, everyone on the roads deserved to die in my opinion, and return it to the safety and quiet of the old days. I had arrived by myself first, to acclimatize, and sent Shyam in the car to pick up my son.

'It's a temple town, about two hundred miles south of Madras,' I returned the card. 'Bah, humbug. It will be another Bharatanatyam recital. It used to be performed by Devadasis erotically in the temples once. They danced to seduce the gods, and the priests of course. And then it was rescued from such earthy decadence and now it's as respectable as *Swan Lake*. Our girls should learn belly-dancing; it's not as pretentious and a lot more erotic. I wish I had been old enough to watch Tahia Caroca dance. She had a spectacularly lithe body according to Edward Said. Her dance was subtle and sensual.'

Nikhil smiled, 'What kind of dances do you like, if any at all?'

'The Crazy Horse,' I said, deliberately.

'I think I could do with a heavy shot of culture. May I invite you as well?'

'Do I need culture? I doubt it. I'm cultured up to my neck. But let me consider it.'

The stadium was an ugly concrete bowl with a stubby roof sheltering the spectators. There were no seats, but ledges on which to sit. The sun was half way home and we were in the shade. Apart from us and Shyam, a deferential row behind, there were no other spectators. The cricket match was unfolding lethargically in the centre. I watched with keen interest.

'I used to play for the team once,' I said. 'I follow their fortunes, though mostly in the sports pages. I gave it up years ago. It's a soothing game, it gives us time to dream and philosophize, which is why we Indians have taken to it. It's the subtle deceits in the game that we love too. Apart from that, it suits the tempo of our climate. Have you ever seen the game played?'

'Once. I was directing *Medea* in Boston. The actor who played Jason had an English background. His father had worked in London and my Jason had gone to school there. He had learned to play cricket too. He thought since I was Indian I knew the game. He talked a blue streak about test matches and some guy called Tendulkar. When he discovered I knew nothing about cricket, he took me to a game on a Sunday, our day off.'

'What did you think? I love watching it.'

'I fell asleep. We'd been rehearsing for three weeks and I was exhausted. It's a good sport to sleep through. Nothing much has happened when you wake up an hour or two later.'

I was disappointed. I had mistakenly thought we would have cricket in common, another tiny link in our long separated lives. How else could I talk to this stranger? What about?

'What games did your stepfather take you to?'

'Baseball. He was a Mets fan.' He waited a moment then added. 'They had divorced, you know.'

'Now how would I know that?' I said with some asperity.

'It was just an expression, the "you know".'

'What happened? If that marriage also failed, maybe I'm not entirely to blame for the failure of ours.'

'He found someone else. Monica's a minor writer—a couple of short stories in the *New Yorker*. She's also a white American. I believe he did love my mother but she didn't want another child. He wanted a white kid of his own. I wasn't his idea of immortality.'

'I didn't think Gary was racist.'

I turned, startled. 'I didn't say his name.'

'Did he ever say mine?'

'No. Well, he certainly knew Mom had been married to you. But he never spoke as if he knew you.' He was waiting, looking at me with such fixed intent, holding his breath. 'I know he went to NYU too.'

I watched the game, considering what I had just said. Should I explain? I allowed the game to carry me along time, clapping politely to a ball struck for a boundary. Nikhil didn't clap, he watched unseeing, attuned only to me, waiting for my version of the events that had changed his life and mine so radically and painfully.

'He knew me,' I spoke finally, not taking my eyes away from the game, maybe even trying not to remember, but Nikhil had the right to know. 'We were in NYU together. He was majoring in journalism, while I was doing literature. We came across each other in our very first semester playing squash. I was pretty good, so was he; except, you Americans play with a harder ball. It's a deliberate attempt to be different from the rest of us. We played for NYU and over that semester got to hang out together, as you say, after a match. He was curious about India, curious about the world. I'd say unusual for an American, but he wanted to become a great journalist. I spent a Thanksgiving at his home. His parents lived in Connecticut, Fairfield. They still live there?'

'They moved to Florida. You knew him quite well then. He never gave me that impression.'

'Gary wanted to join the *New York Times*,' I continued, mesmerized by the past, not even aware of the interruption. 'But he didn't get the job. He ended up with *Newsweek* magazine. They sent him on an assignment to India and, of course, he came south to Madras. He was a good friend and I couldn't allow him to stay in a hotel. I insisted he stay with us. I had been married to Sushima two years then.'

The game below ended suddenly. I checked the time. The players, as if hearing a silent signal, trailed away to a distant pavilion. The stadium's shadow cut across the field, masking most of it. Yet, it was still early evening.

'Did your mother tell you I knew Gary?'

'No,' he said. 'They kept it secret; they knew I'd never forgive them if I knew such a truth.'

'And what is the truth?' I mocked in a bitter voice. 'I want no pity from you. I was to blame for my own foolish actions. We can't dictate our destinies; our karma descends upon us like a firestorm. We burn in our own actions. Gary was a handsome man, very

WASP. Is he still like that?'

'He's greyed a bit, but yes, he's always well-groomed, some women think him beautiful. Mom did. They were like two sides of a gold coin, one dark, the other white, and both beautiful.'

'I saw it happening,' I said, as the light began to fade more swiftly.

What did I see happening? How could I recount every detail that was etched in my implacable memory? God, how I hate memory. I could suppress it, but never erase it. It scuttled like a mouse to hide in the deeper recesses of my mind. I had been delighted to see Gary after four years. Gary had brought the excitement of New York to placid Madras, in his manners, his speech, his quick wit, his elegance. I had met Gary at the airport and driven him home. We had laughed and talked, old friends meeting again, exchanging reminiscences, remembering mutual acquaintances. And Gary saying no, he'd not married. He didn't need marriage, he was laid easily. Even during our student days, Gary always had a chick hovering lustfully beside him. God, if only I had crashed on that dangerous highway between the airport and home and murdered us both so I would never have to see the future.

Sushima had been out when we had arrived at the house. She was 'out' frequently, shopping, playing tennis at the club, seeing friends. Yet, when she returned home at dusk, she carried no packages, no gossip of whom she had met. Just the silence of her return. Gary had been impressed with the size of the manicured garden, lovingly nurtured from end to end. He loved the old house too and he had a large airy room facing west. In NYC, he had no idea I lived in such style back home. Hell, I only had a studio the size of a shoebox. We played snooker as we used to once on winter evenings in New York and drank good scotch. In those old days, we drank Buds or Coors. We had sat down for dinner, later than usual. Neither of us mentioned Sushima's absence, although I yearned to show her off, this prized possession I loved, to Gary. I wanted Gary's envy, no woman in New York could match Sushima's beauty. She was a true apsara with those high cheekbones, sensually curved lips, eyes alight with fire, the pale coppery skin that scorched my hands. Which woman had such perfect, firm breasts with hard nipples? And then she entered the dining room, carrying in the bright lamp of her beauty and her smile. Gary rose from the table; she remained at the door, still with that smile.

I returned to the present, looking at the empty field. 'I made the introductions casually, "Gary, Sushima, my wife. Sushima, Gary, my old college pal".'

I remembered those fatal words, although neither of them heard me. In that microsecond, I was frighteningly aware that I had ceased to exist. They were two naked people across a dining room. I had risen then in dread, thrusting myself physically to break that contact. They turned to me, still smiling, yet not including me in their thoughts or their hearts. I couldn't articulate those dreadful moments to Nikhil.

'They lusted for each other, they were drawn to each other like magnets,' I said simply, breaking a long silence as we walked across the deserted cricket field. 'I had a strange sensation, an unexpected emotion at that moment. I envied them. How often can it happen in life that two people, strangers from the far ends of the earth, should have the great good fortune to meet and fall instantly in love and in lust? It can happen from one to another, not both at the same moment.'

We were nearing the pavilion, Nikhil silent by my side, head down. Then he hesitantly touched my arm. I didn't like being touched by strangers but I allowed his hand to rest on my shoulder. Then, unexpectedly, before I could shake off his hand, he put an arm around my shoulder. It seemed to comfort him, and I sensed his compassion.

I sighed. 'You cannot talk someone out of love, or lust.'

I climbed into the car, breaking the contact gently. My son's compassion and my own acquiescence to that half embrace had surprised me. I had expected a defence of Sushima, instead I had the comfort of his arm. What was he comforting me for? A friend's betrayal or a wife's?

'Did they tell you how they met?' I said in the car as we turned onto the Marina. It was a splendid drive with the beach and the sea to the left, those grand monuments of British rule to our right. I thought they had enriched India intellectually, while raping her at the same time. That was the way with all relationships.

'Yes. They told me they'd met in Bombay. She was attending a dinner party at the Taj Hotel hosted by a cousin, and Gary happened to be staying there. He had just returned from meeting a politician. They would smile at each other, deeply in love, at such a coincidence in their lives. She'd vanished into the night then and Gary didn't know where to find her. He tracked her through the hotel, the cousin's party, friends of friends and finally found her staying with friends in Juhu. They had had tea together and walked along the beach. You know, when you ask how two people met, they always have different versions of that meeting. He'll say he met her walking down 6th Avenue on a bright summer's day and she was wearing red shoes. Then she'll laugh and say, no, we met at Christine's party, it was summer and I had on a pale blue dress and white shoes. Or something like that. But Mom's and Gary's versions matched, as if they'd rehearsed their act for their audience of one—me.'

'Was she married in their story?'

'Not yet. She said she was betrothed to you but not married. She didn't think she'd ever see Gary again. Yours was an arranged marriage that she didn't want at all but her mother forced her into it. You came from a good family and the match was very important for her family. Much later, Gary called her from New York and she realized she was in love with him and left you.'

It sounded a sorry tale to me, filled with inconsistencies that, as a child, Nikhil couldn't unravel. He hadn't put his mind to it. After all, why should parents lie to a child?

'Maybe her story's true. Maybe they had met earlier and when they met again at my house, which was an even greater coincidence, they were already in love.' I preferred this explanation—the gradual growth of a relationship, walks on beaches, phone calls, letters. Not that horrifying, irrational cohesion between two souls. Except, it was another deceit. Sushima had never been to Bombay.

I stopped the car near the Gandhi statue. We got out and began the long walk across the fine, warm sand to the beach. I was surprised how clean the beach was. Nikhil told me about how he'd met Muthu and first learned of my address. We looked around, the crowd hadn't abated, the lovers of years ago remained in position as if they hadn't moved, and we couldn't see the PCO desk. The sea had grown unpleasant. Waves, two and three feet high smashed down on the sand, clawing the earth. It drove back the paddlers.

'She did mention you were hell on earth to live with.'

'I was twenty-eight, and set in my ways. I had nurtured my bad habits. I am a difficult man, as you know now. I am intelligent, impatient, arrogant, rude and possessive. I doubt there are worse traits a man can have. To make it worse, I was also jealous. I knew I owned this beauty, this Rembrandt, this Faberge, and if I had been a medieval prince I would have locked her away in an ivory tower.' I looked out to sea, the distant ships waited patiently to reach port. 'When did they marry?'

'About seven months before I was born.'

I laughed out loud. 'She called me from New York, begging for a divorce. I had a phone then. She said she would return to India for that reason alone and confront me. I refused to give it. I wouldn't. I begged her to return and love me. Of course, she couldn't. As if love can be conjured out of someone who doesn't have it.'

'You mean she was still married to you when she married Gary?'

'Oh yes, your mother was a bigamist.' I turned to stroll back to the car, invigorated by the immense sea, which I hadn't seen for many years, and the relief of unburdening the painful memories to my son. I felt lighter suddenly, my footsteps buoyant.

'Did you know she was pregnant?'

'Not when she left. Possibly, she didn't know herself. On 16 May, the height of our wretched summer, she walked out of the house at 10 a.m. She carried only a small case. I watched her all the way from the rooftop, knowing I would never see her again.'

'You could've stopped her.'

'Yes, locked her away. Better still, strangled her, kept her in a grave so she would never ever leave me. No, I let her go.'

apu

I had to wrench out the past and start living in the present. I watched the pipe rack on my desk, as if it were a living organism.

Where could I hide it, so I would never find it again? I picked it up tenderly, held it at arm's length, opened my window and dropped it out. The fedora . . . He had bought it in a hat shop on Lexington Avenue, near 42nd Street. I didn't want to hide such tangible memories, only to find them unexpectedly when I'd forgotten where I'd hidden them. I sent the fedora sailing out into the blue, harsh sky. Too quickly, I slammed the window shut again, as if I'd fly out in pursuit to retrieve it. I took the silver frame and removed the photograph, not looking at it and, reluctant to burn it or tear it up, squirrelled it away in the lower drawer of my filing cabinet among forgotten files. Whatever else, it was the only image I had of Balraj and me together. I would have continued with my acts of erasure, but Sarada's call interrupted me.

'Well, what's happening? What have you found out?'

'I'm working on it,' I said defensively. What should I tell? What shouldn't I tell? Your mother's S.K. Naidu's lover, but I had been cautioned to keep silent. How long could a parent hide secrets from a child? Probably forever, if hidden deep in the vaults of deception. 'I spoke to the driver. He said Ramesh was financially shaky.' It was a polite, evasive word for 'broke'.

'Oh, I know that,' Sarada dismissed it airily. 'He's just starting this new business. Love doesn't depend on money you know.'

'But it does help.'

'I'm the modern woman. I work too. I'm not some frumpy housewife sitting at home making masala dosai for my husband. I need more intimate details, not a financial statement.'

'What kind of intimate details?' That he's married already, I thought, though I would have to confirm it before telling Sarada.

'The kind that will put out my love for good.'

'He could be a vampire.'

'Then we'll love through eternity.'

'Sarada,' I said exasperated. 'If you love him truly, what difference will it make what I uncover? It shouldn't affect your feelings.'

'Men lie. You know that. I mean is he married already with ten kids? That's what I want you to find out.'

'Ask him.'

'No, I can't. I don't have the guts.'

'Where is he now?'

'He's out of station on business.'

'What business?'

'How do I know? Business is business. You never ask a man his business.'

'When's he back?'

'Day after tomorrow, he said. Listen Apu . . .'

I cut her off gently. I had warned her. The phone rang again. This time it was Gayatri, reminding me that I had a rehearsal that evening. One of her chorus dancers had fallen ill and I had had to take the dancer's place. I hadn't wanted to. The last place I'd danced in was our chinnawheedu, and I didn't want any more memories. But Gayatri had been desperate. I had danced the tiny role before and I'd agreed. I spent the morning on my paperwork, writing up the reports on my company's investigation into a theft of industrial secrets, a man cheating on his wife in a chinnawheedu, uncovering a forged property document by finding the original. I discussed other cases with my colleagues and then went out to check further on Ramesh. When I married, I would miss my work. Maybe I could take Appa's advice and work for a private detective agency in America.

Ramesh had a flat in Buckingham Apartments on Taylors Road in Kilpauk. It was off Poonamalle High Road and not far from my office. Buckingham Apartments was a white three-storey building, already tarnished by the rains, with washing hanging over the balconies. The chowkidar was asleep and I strolled past him into the lobby. There was a power cut. The lift had shut down and I trudged up three flights of stairs, avoiding children leaping down. Ramesh's flat was on the third floor at the far end of the open corridor.

Out of the corner of my eye I glimpsed Balraj's familiar safari suit but with great will resisted jerking around, knowing one day I had to stop believing he would return. I knew it was an illusion, my mind was playing with my memory. I rang the bell and waited. When no one answered, not even a wife or mistress, I took the picks out of my wallet and worked on the lock. As I opened the door, his neighbour popped her head out. She was a dark, squat woman wearing a faded nightgown, loose as a punctured parachute, eating a banana. I smiled at her and slipped into Ramesh's flat.

I was astonished. I had expected to find skeletal furnishings. Instead, I found myself in an exotic and stiflingly hot garden. He seemed to be a frustrated horticulturist. The floor was a lawn, plastic, but the potted plants all around were real. They had been watered, nurtured, pruned; they were labelled too, with their Latin names. There were also bonsai trees in exquisite pots and blue gardenias and purple violets. Would this garden be the ground on which love would be vanquished? I took out my digital camera, focussed it for a wide angle, and shot the room. I pushed past the foliage to a door, opened it and was relieved to see it was a bedroom with no exotica. I started on the built-in cupboards. He didn't have a vast wardrobe, a few slacks, shirts, underwear. On top was a suitcase, empty. I opened his bedside drawers and found a pack of condoms, a stack of snaps and a framed photograph, face down. I turned it over.

It was a wedding picture of Ramesh wearing his marriage garland. Beside him was his garlanded wife, the pallu covering her head, dripping heavy jewellery.

I sighed and sat on the bed, weighed down by secrets. The woman was young, not very pretty, she stared back at me with solemn, nervous eyes. I sighed again, took a shot of it and returned it to the drawer, face down. I had no right to demolish one person's love for another. I felt angry that people probed into their loved ones' lives and then cremated that love using those unhappy discoveries. Men lied, yes, but sometimes to protect their love too. They kept their chinnawheedus but didn't abandon their wives.

I was shuffling through the snaps, not really seeing them, when I heard the front door open. It wouldn't be Ramesh, it could be the wife. I quickly slipped the bundle of snaps into my handbag and crept to the bedroom door. I peeped through the gap. It was Ramesh, hurrying through to the kitchen. I heard the refrigerator open and shut, a tap gush. He returned to his garden room, a can of Coke in one hand and a watering can in the other. While he drank, he lovingly watered his plants. Every now and then, he'd stop to prune a dead leaf, straighten a stem. These loving gestures moved me. If a man could love something with such intensity, he was capable of love for other things too. He finished tending the plants and took a last look around. The look on his face disturbed me. It seemed as if he were wishing his silent companions a final goodbye. He returned to the kitchen and came out quickly, veering towards the bedroom. I skipped back, and slipped into the bathroom. I stepped into the shower stall and drew the plastic curtain closed.

It was only when I turned to face the wall that I saw the six-foot high photograph of a mature, twenty-four-year-old *Crocodylus palustris* hanging on it. The photograph was water stained. The crocodile had been neatly dissected with a black marker pen. Squares and rectangles demarcated its back, its legs and its tail, like the territories of Europe. Arrows pointing to each area drew my eyes along them to end with printed suggestions: handbags, shoes, coats, belts, wallets. Ramesh had poached Renee and abandoned her in Nikhil's hotel room. Did Sarada know he was involved? I doubted it. He had probably borrowed her master key to dump Renee in the vacant room for collection later. Why hadn't he killed it? I didn't sigh, I wanted to scream and stamp out any flickering love between Ramesh and my friend Sarada.

Ramesh came into the bathroom to take a last piss. I peeped through the opening. He looked preoccupied and depressed. Then, accidentally, I pressed the camera button and the flash went off. Very cautiously, he drew back the curtain and saw me, a woman he had never seen before, looking back with furious eyes.

'Who are you?' Ramesh managed.

'How dare you poach an innocent crocodile? And why didn't you keep it here instead of dumping it in the hotel room?'

He wilted from my angry blast, scrambling to discover who I was. 'I am a very strict vegetarian. I cannot bring meat into my house to feed the crocodile.' He gathered his wits and zipped up. 'Anyway, who are you?'

'More importantly, who are you?'

He would have left me in the shower stall but I moved quickly and blocked his way. He feinted and ducked past me into his bedroom. I followed him even as he hauled out a trolley case and stuffed in a few shirts, two pants and his underwear.

'You're a scoundrel,' I said, standing over him but not stopping him from packing. 'That's who you are.'

'Fine, fine, I'm a scoundrel. Who are you?'

'I'm a private detective. Sarada hired me to find out about you. She thinks you love her.'

He stopped packing. 'A private detective! Why would she want one?'

'I just told you.'

'I'm not a scoundrel.' He sat on the bed to look up at me, spreading his hands persuasively. 'I have all these dreams to make money and they all go wrong through no fault of mine. If I were a true and proper scoundrel, I would have succeeded, wouldn't I? I would've cheated people of all their money and absconded.'

'Isn't that what you're doing now? Absconding?' I didn't want to acknowledge the pleading in his eyes.

'Yes, but this is only a temporary abscondment. I just need some time, that's all. I love Sarada very much and when we're married, I'm going to take her away to America. We'll go to Butte, in Montana, I have a cousin there and he's said . . .'

'But you're already married,' I snapped with the ferocity of a crocodile snapping up a dangling leg.

'I'm not married. Who told you that?'

I yanked open the bedside drawer and slammed the framed photograph of him and his innocent bride down on his bed. He flinched as if I'd hit him with it.

'Who are they then? That's you and that's . . .?'

'Vinodhia,' he said. 'I'm divorced and I can prove it.' He rushed to the other side of the bed, opened the drawer, scrambled through old bills, news clippings and rent receipts. He came up triumphantly with a document decorated with many signatures and seals. 'See.'

I scanned it quickly. I had seen enough of them. He had got divorced from Vinodhia over a year ago.

'What happened?' I asked in a gentler voice, returning the papers.

He put the papers away tenderly. 'Neither of us wanted to marry but our parents were very insistent. Vinodhia and I are cousins, you see, and both our parents had decided when we were still young that it would be an ideal match. We did try to make it work but then Vinodhia too thought I was a scoundrel as I had spent all the dowry money on investing in a water-to-petrol project. This man said certain natural herbs could turn water to petrol.'

'Yes,' I said wearily. 'I read about him in the papers.' I had skimmed the story that had run for a few weeks, surprisingly. A young man from Madurai claimed he had found herbs in the Ghat foothills which, when mixed with water, could perform this miracle.

'It wasn't my fault. Even the chief ministers and bigwig scientists from Delhi said it was possible. I thought we'd get very rich. I mean look at all the water we could get and turn into petrol and sell at twenty rupees a litre,' he said in a dreamy voice.

'How much was your dowry?

'Two lakhs. I have a marketing degree from Manipal University, so my parents thought me worth that much.' He returned to finish his tale of woe. 'And then suddenly all these scientists said it was impossible to turn water to petrol. I mean, hadn't they read the Bible? Jesus turned water into wine, so why couldn't we turn water to petrol? It's more profitable than wine.' He thrust his hand out to me, palm up. 'See my lifeline, and there's the fortune line. It proves I'm not a scoundrel and that one day soon I will make my fortune. But it will have to be in Butte, Montana.'

'I don't see Butte, Montana, written on your palm.'

'That's because you're not a palmist,' he chuckled. 'But it is there. And I'll take Sarada away from that sordid hotel job and buy her a Cadillac.' Ramesh stood and as he threw the divorce papers into the bag, said with great dignity and passion. 'I love Sarada very much. I will die if she doesn't marry me.'

I was in my sighing mood, it had been that kind of a day, and I was moved by this declaration. If I had been the object of it, I would've fallen into his arms and forgiven all his sins.

'Why did your marriage with Vinodhia fail?'

'I couldn't fall in love with her. My feelings were frozen at only the acceptance of her as my wife. I wanted more out of my marriage and so did she. She too couldn't fall in love with me. We're told it will happen with familiarity and with time but it didn't happen. We both had had enough of each other after a year. She stopped screwing me too, at least that was some compensation.'

'You didn't try hard enough,' I said defensively. I didn't want to hear more. Love would bloom between Arun and me, I was certain of that. Not in an instant but over time, love would come sliding into our lives like honey down our throats.

The doorbell rang once, rang again. He looked at me, was it for me? I shook my head. He tiptoed to the front door as the bell rang yet again, prolonged this time with impatience. He peered through the peephole and hurried back. The trolley case was packed, he zipped it shut and then clutched my hands in his. They were sweaty.

'Tell Sarada I love her very much. I will marry her and make her happy.'

He grabbed his case and hurried away, not to the front door but to the kitchen. When the bell rang again, I counted up to sixty before sauntering across to the kitchen. The kitchen opened onto a small balcony and the door was open to the warm breeze. I shut it and crossed to the front door.

From his epaulettes and the stars on his collar, I recognized an assistant commissioner of Tamil Nadu police. Behind him was a scruffy, wild-haired man wearing handcuffs and a very grubby Harvard T-shirt. And behind them was Ramesh's neighbour, munching on a kebab, along with three other women, all still in their long nightdresses.

'Mrs Ramesh,' he announced as he stepped in, dragging the tribal man with him and shutting the door on the curious neighbours. He didn't notice the exotic surroundings. 'I have an arrest warrant for your husband. He with one other poached a crocodile from . . .'

'I'm not Mrs Ramesh.'

'Then who are you?'

'I'm a private detective. I was looking for Ramesh and the door was open.' I swept an arm around. 'He's not here.'

'Why were you looking for Ramesh?'

'That's confidential.'

'Can I see your identification?'

I delved into my handbag and, as I pulled out the laminated ID card, Ramesh's snaps fell to the floor. Both of us ignored them. Manian checked the card and returned it to me, disappointed. He looked down at the snaps, stooped and picked them up. He began to flick impatiently through them and stopped at one.

Manian showed the photograph to the tribal who nodded. 'Yes, that's one of them. Mr Ramesh.'

Manian flicked through the others eagerly, then showed him another. Again the tribal nodded: 'That's the two of them.'

'Can I see it?'

I looked at the photograph. There were three men posing around Renee. One was the tribal, the other was Ramesh. I peered harder at the third. It was Arun. I handed back the photograph, my mind blank for the moment, yet strangely enough I wasn't surprised. I remembered him saying 'anything and everything that'll make a buck'.

I edged past Manian to the door. 'How did you track him down, sir?' Always flatter the high-up cops. 'That was clever work.'

'It took time,' he said proudly. 'This idiot,' he turned to the tribal and slapped him on the head as if it were a horse's rump, 'finally remembered that one of the men had given him a paper. This poaching business was to be an ongoing project and therefore they would need this idiot, Ganpathi, to be on call. The idiot had left the card in his hut. I sent a constable all the way to the jungle to find the card and bring it back. It was Mr Ramesh's card.'

'And the other man?'

'I'll find him. It won't take long now.'

I opened the door as Manian noticed his surroundings for the first time. There were now eight women outside, all in punctured-parachute nightdresses, bunched in the corridor, whispering and eating like busy locusts.

nikhil

Already I felt the dread of what was to come, the unveiling of a terrible betrayal. I listened not to his words but what lay beneath them and watched the clouds gather in his eyes. It had been part of my learning as a director to hear and see beyond the flat words of text on the page.

'They lusted for each other, they were drawn to each other like magnets,' my father had said, breaking a long silence as we walked across the grounds. His voice, now an old man's, quavered, shaken by the earthquakes of his memories as he tumbled down into the chasm they had opened up for him.

I wanted to enfold my father, so slim and frail, in my arms. Place a soft finger across those lips to stop up the pain that was in every word he had spoken. He wasn't by my side, but back there in that dining room watching his life disintegrate. I touched my father, hoping to break the chain that held him firmly to that past. Then I placed my arm tenderly around his shoulder, as I had done so many times with my mother. There was a momentary tension in the muscles, then he relaxed. I was surprised. I was taller by five or six inches. It had been a sleight of mind that I had thought myself smaller at our first meetings. I wanted to draw him tighter to drain the pain. It was a familiar pain, like Renee's betrayal. Hers had been a career move, she'd told me. Bodnik wasn't a friend or an acquaintance. Yet I too had been just as helpless.

I was embarrassed when I had to tell him my mother's version of how she had met Gary. It sounded so false now and I tried to justify it in retrospect. Who was the bigger betrayer? Mom, who left a husband she had never loved, or Gary, who stole her away from a friend in whose house he'd broken bread? Who else can betray, except those closest to you?

'I let her go,' he had said.

I remembered that small suitcase and imagined Mom walking along that drive in the heat and glare, never looking back, yet knowing she was watched. I admired her bravery; she had leaped from being the loveless housewife in Georgetown, Madras, to New York City to marry a man with whom she'd fallen instantly in love. That she was hurt later, betrayed by that love, was no fault of hers. She had granted Gary his divorce without a whisper of protest, maybe remembering her true husband. I couldn't blame her for the love, but I also couldn't forgive her for the story they had concocted together to deceive me. Probably, I would've done the same, so as not to earn a child's lifelong enmity.

I slept dreamlessly, afloat and suspended gently, deep in a warm, caressing sea. The light, soothing and gentle, enveloped me in a large, round halo. Crocodiles didn't scuttle out of the shadows, my father didn't snap and snarl, my mother lay still in her grave, the women vanished. It was a healing sleep, repairing the wounds in my heart. I was comatose, exhausted by the past events.

In this delicious state of inanimation, enclosed in the bauble of water and light, a sound rippled through me. It approached, jagged and nervous, disturbing the water and light, agitating them with its rude presence. I thought it was Renee, both of them, rushing at me, and thrashed away. I awoke, dismayed by the reality of the ringing telephone. It was 6.00 a.m. and the morning light was muted like the one in my sleep.

'Who is it?' I snapped.

'Nicky, it's me, Karen,' she sang out. Before I could reply, Karen being Karen, she rushed on faster than a lightning bolt. 'Boy, you sound grouchy as the Grinch. No, worse. You sound as if you're suffering from PMS. I was drinking a glass of chilled Chablis and waiting for the Chinese delivery guy when I thought about us. You've been hovering at the edge of my consciousness. So what the hell, I said, I'll call him and find out whether he's alive or whether India's swallowed him up and turned him into a sadhu. It is sadhu isn't it, am I pronouncing it right? Have you gone totally ethnic? Are you underground with your roots, all muddy from the Indian earth?'

'How did you find me?' I jumped in at her pause for breath or a sip of that Chablis in her hand. I imagined her long, graceful fingers twirling the stem of her wine glass.

Karen's laugh was a bubble of happiness that was always at the point of bursting. 'It's so good to hear your voice. I spent the day thinking about you being far away. I'm a journalist, didn't you know? Masters from CSJ in communications, a bonafide card-carrying member of the union too, a rising associate editor in the glossiest magazine in New York City being paid a pittance. Notice the word "associate" and not a mere "assistant", the promotion earned me a princely hundred bucks a month extra which the IRS will snap up like a piranha sensing blood in the waters. Hey, Nicky, you're not saying much. How about a congratulations?'

'Give me a chance,' I laughed, she heard it all the way in New York City. 'Congratulations. And I've been thinking about you too but every time I figure I'll call, it turns out to be late at night in New York.' We exchanged time zones quickly. 'You still haven't told me how you found me.'

'Oh, that. I called Mike. By the way, congratulations to you too. He told me the divorce had come through. You were a real dummy to have married her, Nicky. She's a walking condom, I swear. You can buy better flavours from a slot machine in the ladies' room. She'll drop Dicknik when she gets her claws into Tom Cruise, you watch.'

'C'mon, Karen,' I snapped. 'You don't have to be bitchy about her. She was good for me while it lasted.'

Karen 'meooowed' into the phone. 'Nicky, my sweet, you know I never liked her. I'm not going to be nice now that you've split. The couple of times you had me over for dinner, her beautiful face would squeeze into the shape of a dried prune. And I bet she made cracks about me to you, didn't she? C'mon, you can tell me now. What did she call me? Really, truly bad names?'

'A few.'

'Tell me, I can take it. Renee the Ripper wasn't bright enough to have a big vocabulary. I was always surprised she even knew enough English to act. I guess she depended on emoting, like charades, to express herself. I bet when you directed her you wrote out her dialogue on a blackboard and nailed her feet down to hit the right mark.'

'Hey, at least she knew a few more things than Hugh the Hound ever did. He thought David Lynch was a partner in Merrill Lynch and Francis Ford Coppola a new taste of coffee in Starbucks.' She laughed, loud and long. 'And how is Hugh? That guy was born in a straitjacket.'

'You sitting down?'

'Lying down.'

'He's floating down the river into the wide blue Atlantic. No, not really. He moved to LA, his bank made him a VP and thought he should be as far from HQ as possible. He wanted me to tag along as Mrs Hugh but can you imagine me in LA? I'd have to spell out every word if I wanted to talk to anyone in La-La land.'

'I'm sorry. When did it happen? Why didn't you tell me?'

'A month back. I needed time to figure out how I felt about losing Hugh to LA. I feel fine,' she paused either to sip wine or to blink back tears. 'I thought I was in love with him. Oh hell, I was, but I couldn't bear the thought of spending my life with him and living in Westwood with two and a half kids. Everyone says "I'm sorry" when you break up a love affair. You know it's what people also say in condolences, "I'm sorry", the English language at times is fucking inadequate.'

We laughed together. God, it felt good to talk to her; her humour buoyed me. I realized what I enjoyed most was talking American, it was my language. I understood her meanings and nuances, apart from her accent, and I felt homesick. Here, I had to focus to understand the spoken English; it was fractured and funny. 'America' became 'Um-rika', 'I am' became 'yam'. Karen spoke pure mid-western American.

Karen was still talking. 'I'd like my wedding present back. What did I give you?'

'A wine rack. And she's got it.'

'Hell, there goes my twenty bucks. So, Mike said you were in India, looking for roots, searching for an identity and trying to find your father. I didn't even know you had a real father, I always thought it was Gary. I mean I knew he was your stepdad but I thought your real dad was dead. You gave me that impression. You never talked about him, even to me.'

'He's very much alive. And I found him.'

'You did!' Her voice rose to a scream of delight. 'What's he like? Tell me. Did he embrace you with open arms and kill the fattened cow? No, you can't kill cows in India, can you? Wait, let me get a refill.' The telephone fell and I imagined her scrambling across the parquet floor to the kitchen that overlooked an airshaft. I wished then that I was with her in the living room. She'd curl her long legs under her on the sofa and rest her head on my shoulder. Although we had broken off the affair, we spoke two or three times a week on the telephone and saw each other at least twice a month for dinner. Either she picked up the tab or I did, then we'd stroll back to her apartment on 74th Street and West End and continue talking. We were wary about becoming lovers again though. I missed her, missed those fine summer evenings in Manhattan. But I didn't want to say this long distance. When she came back with her wine, I told her everything about the meeting and my new feelings for my father.

There was a long silence when I finished. 'You still there?'

'Yes,' she sniffled. 'I'm weeping for him. Poor guy, he still loved her. God, that's what I hate about falling in love. You fall in love and the guy doesn't even notice you. He just wants to get laid, period, and you're burning up inside.'

'Yeah, I know. And then last night we had a civilized dinner together. He didn't know where to eat as he'd not eaten out for years, so we ended up at a dhaba.'

'What's that?' She tasted the word. 'Dubba.'

'Dhaa-baa,' I laughed. 'It's a north Indian word. It's kinda like a truck stop joint and very, very spartan. They just have a few charpois for the drivers to sit on and serve the food on leaves. But this place did have plates, cutlery, chairs and tables. And you know what? I paid for the meal. My dad doesn't carry any money on him.'

'He sounds like a Rockefeller, they never carry money either,' Karen said. 'What's he like really? Is he a raja or a maharaja? Are you a prince-raja or whatever they call the sons of these guys? Your mom was a real princess, I thought. She always made me feel dowdy even if I wore a Christian Dior gown with a diamond tiara on my head.'

'No, he's not a raja or maharaja, just a solitary old man.'

'Well, he's got you now. He must be so excited, having his son with him,' she paused a long time. 'You gonna stay there?'

'No, not this time. I don't know. I don't want to push him yet and . . .'

'You're more American than I am, Nicky,' Karen said. 'Jesus, Nicky you can't even speak your own language. What is it? Hindu? And you're not even Hindu are you?'

'Hindi. And my language is Telugu. No, I don't speak it. I can learn it though.'

'Yeah, a linguaphone native. I speak Italian only because I grew up speaking it with my grandma. She refused to speak English with me. Your mom only spoke English, I never heard her say one word in the . . . what? Tulglue?'

'Tel-u-gu,' I repeated slowly. I couldn't admit I'd heard her speak a word either, not within my hearing. 'But they speak Tamil in Madras.'

'It's not called Madras anymore, don't you know? It's called . . . wait a moment . . . here I have it . . . Chennai. The operator told me that when I wanted your area code. Why did they change the name?'

'Escaping the past. Madras was a British name.'

'Hell, that's no excuse to confuse us all. My father used to wear bleeding Mad-ras shirts, now they'll be called bleeding Chennai. It doesn't sound as good. How would they like it if we called New York New Amsterdam or changed Los Angeles to Los Diablo? It would suit LA right and it would be more appropriate.' Karen stopped, her mind racing. Then coming back, the way women do, she said, 'Who's this detective? You called her Apu.'

'Oh, she's just the detective who found my father.'

'I don't trust men when they slide too quickly over a woman's name,' Karen didn't laugh this time. 'You're not in love with her, are you? No, they don't fall in love in India, do they? They have arranged marriages. They meet the day before the wedding, get hitched and jump into bed. Isn't that right? God, how do they do it? It would scare the hell out of me. Is this Apu beautiful? We have an Indian girl working in our accounts department. She's a stunner, the guys drool over her. She's as delicate as a butterfly, with burnt buttery skin. I feel like a rhino next to her, so I don't stand too close. She plans to go in for an arranged marriage as well, although she is pure American. What's with this arranged marriage? I couldn't see you doing that, even after Renee.' She paused long, waiting for me, then prompted. 'Well, what's she like?'

'Very beautiful, not burnt buttery skin, more pale coppery,' I waited too, and then added, smiling. 'And she's into arranged marriages too, she doesn't believe in falling in love.'

'She going to arrange one with you?' Karen said softly.

'She's arranged it with some guy in the States. His name's Arun.'

I thought she would laugh. Instead, she said, 'How long are you staying out there? Forever and forever? What about your work, you're supposed to be a stage director and I want to see you doing a play on Broadway.'

'Soon,' I soothed. 'I'm trying to get my father's permission to stage his novel. He's holding out.'

'But you are coming back?'

'Yes.'

I didn't want to say when, as I didn't know either, and had sensed the word 'alone' on the tip of her tongue. To change her sombre mood, I said, 'I found a crocodile in my bathroom.' I didn't add I'd christened it Renee.

'Crocodile,' she said, and didn't sound surprised. She was a New Yorker. One evening, after dinner, we had been strolling along Columbus and met a man walking with a llama. 'I thought they had snakes in India, and elephants. Just imagine you walk into your room and find an elephant in your bathroom. You call down to the reception and say "I've got an elephant in the shower", and the guy says, "It's not an elephant sir, it is your shower".' She broke into peals of laughter.

We talked some more about my father. Then, when we both heard the buzzer for the Chinese food delivery, we said 'goodbye, goodbye', wishing we could be across a table and add a kiss to our goodbyes, as we went our separate ways into the Manhattan night.

'I don't mind being called in the middle of a New York night,' she said before she hung up. 'Remember, we used to wake each other up in the middle of many nights.'

I thought about her a long time, lying in bed alone. She would be picking the food out of the cartons, not wanting to dirty a plate which she would have to wash. Then she would watch television, PBS usually, and read at the same time. While I was having breakfast, she'd be ready for bed. It was this confusion of time that increased my remembrance of her and the city. How long had we been lovers? Only two semesters, but they had been intense. We were both just eighteen and insatiable with the sexual virility of youth. We had made love every day, twice sometimes, lain and examined each other's bodies minutely and with wonder. I had been jealous of her experience, that other lover whom she never named. We had been too young then to have survived the long distance run of marriage. Now, ten years older, we were both bearing the wounds of other loves. She had been light about Hugh but I knew she ached. That was why she had called, of course, to announce the break up. It was passed over swiftly but had been meant to be lodged in my conscious mind. Hugh had been inappropriate for her but she had fallen in love. He was the ideal American husband, a good Catholic too, and ambitious for American values. When I had voiced my comment—'For chrissake, why him?'—she had replied, 'Women always want a good provider, we still have our Neanderthal genes demanding the hunter bring home the mammoth on a plate.' How did I compare against Hugh in the mammoth stakes? Brown, vaguely Hindu, and she would be lucky to eat a marmoset for dinner.

I picked up the invitation card from the bedside table. Chidambaram. A town and a stadium. I had looked it up after my father's terse explanation. The town was named after a temple, dedicated to the lord of dance, Nataraja. It was so old and re-built so many times, they could only date a part of it back to the thirteenth century. It had to be huge, it covered sixteen hectares, and one of its halls had a thousand pillars, another one hundred. There was also a Ganesha temple in the complex, the idol was the biggest in India. I wished I could visit Chidambaram. Was there a need to pray in a temple? I didn't know the rituals required for worship. There'd be no pews or sermons or a book of prayer. I had only been to a temple once, in Queens, out of curiosity and not any need for the sacrament. Mom had never taken me there. She dismissed it as American, of a few years antiquity, while she had visited Tirupati for Lord Balaji's darshan before she had married my father. Who would know? The dancer, Apu, if she was to dance for Lord Nataraja. She was Hindu, brown, versed in the rituals of worship, I was sure. Maybe, she could take me to a local temple in the city and show me how I should pray. For her it would be out of belief, for Karen out of curiosity only to observe an exotic act. And for me? I suspected it would be curiosity too as it sat uneasily with my upbringing. Mom had wanted me grounded in American reality and to forget India, as she had.

My ritual now was the daily visit to the conservator's office and a cup of tea with the peon Natarajan. I thought how circuitous India could be at times. Here I was with Natarajan, a name that had meant little to me before, and now that I was to view 'Chidambaram', I was in the company of the dance god himself. Surely, in this land of omens, this was a good one. The file moved another few desks, gorging paper on its languid journey. 'Be patient, be patient, we will succeed,' Natarajan the peon would console, extracting a few more hundreds out of his Um-rikan friend.

At 6 p.m. Prasad called from the lobby. He and Shyam were taking turns at serving aiyer in his new avatar as a socializer. My father wasn't alone; Lakshmi sat beside him in the rear seat. I wasn't disappointed, my father was gradually enfolding me into his life. I was surprised when the car, after edging down a narrow road beside a flyover, turned into the large compound. The museum theatre was a semicircular building of red sandstone with many arches. People were drifting up the wide steps, blown in by a gentle breeze.

'I never expected to find this here.'

'It was built back in the nineteenth century. The Brits would've taken it, they took everything else that wasn't nailed down,' my father said as we went up the steps. 'They brought their love of English theatre to us. Wherever they settled, they built a theatre for their entertainment. There's the Gaiety on the mall in Simla, another in Calcutta. Apart from their own amateur theatricals, I assume British theatre companies would tour the empire to entertain the colonizers. I think they enjoyed light comedies, nothing that would tax their intelligence.'

'It's beautiful.' The floor sloped down all around the semi-circle, and then flattened for the eight front rows. The proscenium stage was large and what I loved most was the massive mantle of wood that framed the stage like a curtain. It was carved and polished, the carvings not as intricate as those around the doors of the houses. 'I'd love to do a play here. What are the acoustics like?'

'Very good,' Lakshmi said. 'You can hear clearly, wherever you sit. There's just one problem: don't sit close to the sides. You can't see what's happening on stage left or right, depending on which side.'

'You know theatre?'

'Only amateur acting. My daughter used to love it, but she dropped it,' she said, unaware that I knew her daughter.

The air conditioning was freezing and Lakshmi, who had come prepared, wrapped herself in a shawl. We edged towards the front row seats and found three together. Five musicians came on stage to sit cross-legged to one side; they tuned their tabla, ghatam, violin, mridangam and moorsing. A delicate woman tested her small finger cymbals and whispered into the microphone before her.

'Why did you take up theatre?' my father asked. 'It's a fatherly concern, a strange sensation for me. There's no money in it, is there?'

'Was there in writing?'

'None. But I had the good fortune to be born wealthy. You should've taken up engineering or what do they call it? Dotcom.'

'Is that what you would have raised me to do?'

'Oh yes, Indian fathers always want their children to follow respectable, boring professions. I was a bitter disappointment to mine. Did your mother encourage you to take up theatre?'

'No, she behaved like an Indian father, but Gary encouraged me. She wanted me to become a lawyer. Or a doctor. But that was the way with the older generation in America. They came as doctors or engineers or dotcoms. The new generation, guys and girls of my age, has produced movie directors, playwrights, actors, painters, writers, comedians, singers. We've flown the coup of tradition. We've been given the freedom to choose and we don't have to follow our parents' dictates.'

apu

I stared at the mirror and thought it was someone else. For many days now, I had been this way. I didn't know who that person was staring back at me, and it left me unsettled. Until now, I had always known who I was. It wasn't the image that dislocated me, the exaggerated eye make-up, my face pale with powder, streaking in the green room's heat. It was something within me. Disappointment? Disenchantment? Relief?

This was a classical dance performance and I was wearing a blue silk sari with a gold border, specially stitched like pantaloons to give me the freedom to move while dancing, with the pallu thrown over my shoulder and tucked into my waistband. My choli was a pale blue silk. I wore nose studs, earrings, silver anklets with bells and gold bangles. The bells and bangles tinkled when I moved. My hair was knotted in a kondai, pulled back tight. I dabbed my face with a towel as I waited for my performance with Gayatri, who was dancing the lead. She had created 'Chidambaram'. We had performed the composition many times and had rehearsed for two evenings before this show. I had a small role, that of a handmaiden's. Behind me, handsome lithe men flexed and stretched their beautiful bodies. I knew my parents were in the audience; Arun's parents had made their excuses and Amma was angry. I knew why they hadn't come but didn't tell her. I had dropped an invitation off for Nikhil and wondered whether he would be there. I hadn't looked for him.

Sarada, casual and cool in a chiffon sari, smiled at me in the mirror. She had tried all day to reach me.

'I know about Vinodhia,' she was saying. 'Ramesh told me everything. It was a miserable marriage. He did tell you he loved me and he'd die if he didn't marry me?'

'Words to that effect, but he didn't mention dying.' I took Sarada's hand. 'You're lucky. You've fallen in love and he loves you, whatever his faults. And he does have quite a few. But you both do have a passion for each other and I hope you haven't confused it with love.'

'At least I reveal my passions. You're as controlled and cold as a . . . as a . . . crocodile.'

'How would you know what crocodiles do underwater?' I retorted, hurt by her accusation. 'They could fall in love with other crocodiles and have passionate affairs in the cool water. They just don't flaunt it the way you do. That's why men are always grabbing your bottom.'

Sarada smiled a cat's-got-the-milk smile I knew too well. 'I went swimming the other night with Nikhil. He has a great body, muscles in the right places and really sexy too. You should go swimming with him one day. I mean, before you marry this Arun.' She smiled. 'Just as a test.'

'You can't be lusting for him too,' I said crossly. I dabbed at my face again, trying to calm down. 'What happened after the swim?'

'Well, he is very experienced,' she watched me, probably hoping to make me jealous. 'I mean the guys over there have affairs with all those American chicks and know everything about sex. Our guys here just get into a hooker for a quickie. They're in an out before you can take a deep breath.'

'You slept with him?' I was angry, but not sure why. Sarada could do what she wanted. So could Nikhil.

'Did I say that?' Sarada smiled blandly back at me in the mirror.

'He won't make a good husband. He's just split from his wife but I think he's still in love with her. What can be worse than marrying a guy still in love with a woman who dumped him?'

'Who said anything about marrying him? I didn't. Were you thinking about doing that? Dumping Arun for Nikhil?'

'You have too vivid an imagination. He's more messed up than you are. He doesn't know whether he's brown or white, American or Indian, and that father of his is as randy as a goat.'

'So the crocodile isn't as cool as she wishes to be,' Sarada mocked.

I banged my anklets as I went out to dance. Sarada's chuckles echoed after me and I had to return. 'Manian's looking for your lover because he poached that crocodile with Arun. But I guess you know that.'

Sarada's chuckle faded. Then she asked with concern, 'Your Arun?'

'Yes.'

nikhil

Gayatri came on stage. She was a handsome woman with bright flashing eyes. Her chorus came in behind her, remaining upstage. Apu was one of them. The music started and the performers began the dance.

My father leaned over, whispering softly. 'The cosmic dance of Shiva symbolizes the movement of the planets. This opening scene shows five dancers who also represent the five elements . . .' They were using circular movements as they kept time with the tabla's beat. The section lasted around ten minutes, before Apu and two of the other dancers danced off the stage. 'In this second part the two saints Patanjali and Vyagrapada get a vision of Shiva's dance after years of penance. The place they have the vision is in Thillai or Chidambaram, that's why it is regarded as the centre of the universe, and an elaborate temple was built there by devotees and the king. The dancers are enacting the building of the temple. Those sculptors are chiselling the stones. Together they're building the mighty gopuram and paying homage to Nataraja, the god of dance, king of dance.' My father fell silent, listening to the woman singing, then continued. 'She's singing about the formlessness of Shiva while Gayatri dances the Ananda Tandavam, the dance of bliss. The esoteric concept of Shiva as a dancer signifies the cycle of creation and destruction, followed by re-creation. He is the absolute power of the universe. His dance is ultimately located in the heart of the devotee . . . the rhythm of life is the dance of Shiva.' My father too kept the taal, beating softly on his thigh. 'Now, in the second half, Gayatri portrays different devotees and their songs. One is the story of the untouchable Nandanar who longs to have a vision of Shiva's dance in Chidambaram. Another is about the female poet, the heroine, who is in love with Shiva. Now we have Gayatri as the nayika awaiting her beloved at her doorstep. The finale is the dance of the ego. Verses of Thayumanavar describe the oneness of the human soul with the ultimate Shiva. The saint sings that this is possible only with a complete negation of the individual self.'

I was the first on my feet to applaud when the performance ended. Otherwise, the audience's enthusiasm was muted. My father was quiet too and told me that for the aficionados this was a 'new' work; it would need a decade of digestion before they approved. This conservative city was unused to innovative dances.

I had enjoyed not so much the dance, but the choreography. It had been more theatre than dance as the story unfolded in Gayatri's dramatic gestures and movements. The lighting was static, I thought. It could have been better lit, with more shadow, a hint of colour, and movement.

'I'm going backstage to congratulate Apu.'

'Give her mine too,' my father said, then smiled. 'She danced well and tell her she'll make a wonderful belly-dancer.'

I climbed to the stage. In the wings, there was a crowd of well-wishers. This was the excitement of theatre: the emotional highs and lows immediate, the praise and damnation too. How often I'd stood in the wings to watch my actors, wishing each time that I had directed them better. It would come with time. There was no sign of Apu. I asked another dancer where she was and he said she'd gone.

I looked around. There were three flats on either side. The lighting rig consisted of just three poles suspended above the stage. I was used to a rig with thirty or forty lights, more if the play demanded it. The theatre was primitive but I savoured the familiarity. The backstage was clearing as the dancers and well-wishers wandered away.

I moved onto the stage. My father and Lakshmi were sitting in the empty auditorium waiting for me. The stage lights were dimmed but I couldn't help imagining how I would stage *Georgetown* and looked around.

'Why did you adapt his novel?' Lakshmi asked.

'It'll make a great play. It's set in that grand old house. I'd have a high window upstage centre with a faint light flowing down to the open courtyard centre stage.' I stopped. I was telling her about the set and how I'd direct it. Not why I had loved it. 'When I read it I wanted to belong to that house in Georgetown. I wanted to be related to those people, to take part in their quarrels and love affairs. They knew who they were, they had their places fixed in the family hierarchy and in their society like the name cards at a grand dining table. I envied them. I saw myself in the book; I was the son, Krishna . . .'

My father rose and spoke out aloud. 'Let them lie forgotten.'

But I couldn't. I had to be persuasive. 'Aren't you proud of the characters you've created? They've lain neglected for decades and I want to bring them to life. I want people to see your creations, feel for them the way I did.'

'Those characters don't deserve better,' my father said harshly, turning away, still unsettled by memory.

'Don't be a grouch. It'll make a wonderful play,' Lakshmi said.

'Have you read it?'

'Of course I have. I found it in the public library. I love it.

'You never told me,' he was surprised.

'I didn't tell you because you never mentioned it to me. Even if you don't want to give your permission, at least invite your son to stay with you. You're rattling around in that house like a lost ghost.'

He looked at me. 'Does he want to?'

'Why not?' I smiled. 'It may even get me the permission.'

'Don't count on that.'

'I'll have to bring the crocodile.'

'As long as it doesn't drink expensive scotch.'

Lakshmi linked her arm through my father's as we went up the steps to the exit. 'Don't mind him. But I must warn you he leads a regimented life. He wakes at five, works from 7.00 a.m. till noon, then has lunch, a nap, tea at 4.30, drinks at 7.30, dinner at 9.30 and lights out at 10.00 p.m.'

'You make it sound like a prison,' my father said.

'Well, isn't it?' she replied.

s.k. naidu

I had agreed to Lakshmi's proposal, and then worried whether it would work. What would it feel like to have my son under my roof? I had no idea. I was also nervous. Sushima, I said the name again, silently, had left me with a deep-seated pessimism about human relationships.

The house was big enough to avoid constant contact with Nikhil. I could hide away in my room, while he wandered around at will. It had been many, many years since I'd lived in close proximity with another. Lakshmi came and went, impermanent in my household, a fleeting guest. She shared my bed but not my daily life, though she knew my routine. I was always relieved when she left. I didn't consider my brother, making his occasional forays south like a mughal prince on a quick raid from the imperial capital, a guest.

Lakshmi had made my house sound like a prison. I hadn't thought of it like that. All the doors had locks, but the keys were on the inside. It was my fortress, protecting me against all invasions. But it's true that every fortress also becomes a prison, depending on one's point of view. Our history was littered with countless forts captured through treachery and betrayals from within. I ordered Ethiraj and Mary to open all the doors and windows to allow in the sunlight and the dust and warm breeze. Prasad welcomed Nikhil, took him to his room and revealed some of the secrets of my household.

nikhil

'Are you sure you'll be comfortable in my house?' my father had asked. 'It's not very modernized and we don't have the American appurtenances of your hotel.'

'Appurtenances?' He used the same ancient language as mom. 'I never knew such a word existed. I'll be fine, if you'll have me.'

'Then you're welcome.'

I saw the house in daylight for the first time, lit by the afternoon sun. The pale yellow walls rose like cliffs, punctuated by windows and slanted eaves. It didn't appear haunted as it did in moonlight, but cheerful in its sunny stateliness. The rooms were mellow with light too, and I followed Prasad and the suitcase, while Renee remained in the car for the second trip. My room was at the rear, overlooking the courtyard. I figured I was above the card room. The other windows faced west. I wondered whether this was the same room Gary had occupied so many years ago. Had he seduced Mom in this four-poster bed? I didn't want to think about it. There were also a large teak cupboard, a couple of easy chairs and an antique roll top desk with a circular chair. The bathroom was large but without a tub or a shower stall. There was an Indian and a western toilet, a plastic bucket with a mug hooked on the rim. The wash basin was large enough to bathe in but the mirror was speckled.

'I can't leave Renee in here. She'll have to be left loose. When I come to take a leak at night, she might snap off my dick. Don't you have a room with a bathtub?'

Prasad shrugged, not having ever seen a bathtub. 'Shower,' he pointed to an old, large showerhead, punctured with holes. A cylindrical geyser was fixed to the wall above it.

'I mean the crocodile needs the bathtub, not a shower. Maybe I can leave it outside.'

Prasad looked out at the huge garden and the tangle of undergrowth, so did I. Renee would be lost forever in that jungle.

'We'll lock her in another bathroom.'

Prasad led me to the next guest bedroom, the same as mine with the same bathroom. It looked a good enclosure for Renee.

'Do you have a dog chain, any chain, around?' I asked when we went down for Renee. 'I want to give her some fresh air; she's been in that toilet for days and must be sick of air conditioning.'

Prasad wandered away and returned finally with a long length of chain. We lifted Renee out and tied the chain around her neck. I undid her belt and we both stepped back. She wasn't perturbed; she blinked gratefully up at the warming sun. I walked her around the side of the house; it was a leisurely stroll as she waddled slowly. Her snout rotated like a gun turret, looking for a target. I found my father on the side veranda hunched over a desk and a sheaf of papers. He looked up annoyed, then remembered and smiled.

'Settled in?' He took in Renee too.

'Yes.'

'Wander around while I do some work. We'll have drinks on the terrace at . . .'

'7.30 p.m.,' I completed, wanting to ask what he was working on.

Before I turned away, my father added, 'Thomas Mann had written, "Solitude gives birth to the original in us, to beauty unfamiliar and perilous, to poetry. But it also gives birth to the opposite: to the perverse, the illicit, the absurd",' and returned to work.

I wandered with Renee, keeping a safe distance, until I found the bench my father and I had sat on that night in the clearing. I chained Renee to a sapling and lay down on the bench, the sun filtering through the leaves, dropping coins of golden light on me. Parakeets, plump as ripe mangoes, peered down at me past their blood-red beaks, as if trying to remember me for a future occasion. The solitude was also healing. I could think of Karen and Apu, my father and Mom, India and America. I felt them unwinding in my mind, disentangling slowly as the garden with its soft rustle of leaves, the sleepy cawing of crows and the scratching of hens in the undergrowth, lulled me to sleep. I woke at dusk, stiff from the hard bench, remembering where I was, and smiled to myself. I'm in my father's house, I thought. I rose and looked for Renee. She'd gone. There was no sign of the chain either. I felt relief at first—my albatross had flown—then panic.

'Oh Christ. Renee, Renee . . .' I called, as if she would respond to a name.

Then I noticed a trail of flattened grass and bush that snaked through the undergrowth. I followed it cautiously, expecting an ambush. Here and there, she had paused and changed direction. I found her a hundred yards into the jungle, still as a log. Scattered around her, and adrift on the bushes, were chicken feathers. They clung to her jaws as well.

I grabbed her chain. 'Why didn't you tell me you were hungry?' I scolded, tugging her away from the crime scene. No doubt they were my father's chickens; cheaper than the scotch, I hoped. I returned to the clearing and tied the chain in firm knots to a tree so she wouldn't be able to pull free.

s.k. naidu

I bathed, dressed, chose my cigars and went downstairs to choose my CDs for the evening. Nikhil stood in the reception hall, dressed in a cream kurta pyjama. He looked awkward in this ethnic costume, as if he were playing a role. I wished Sushima hadn't alienated him so much from India. Her hatred for me had encompassed the whole nation. But I appreciated Nikhil's effort to start the journey. If he remained here long enough, he would grow at ease with it. He was standing in front of the covered frame that I had deliberately left out as a reminder. I remained in the shadows, watching. The cloth was black silk. He picked on the edge, lifting it slowly, expecting a rare painting. Instead, he found only an elaborate gilt frame. The painting had been cut out crudely, leaving jagged edges of the canvas.

'It was of your mother,' I said, taking a step forward. Then I took the black silk cloth and carefully re-covered the frame. 'A friend painted it, just after we married. It was a birthday present. I burned it and kept the frame as a reminder.'

It was 7.30 when we went up the stairs together and out to the terrace where we had first met. The chaise longue was in the same position, with the scotch, ice, soda and the audio remote on a side table. There was now a second glass. Prasad had positioned a chair at an angle, half facing the chaise longue. I fixed Nikhil a drink without asking and poured myself one before settling back in my favourite position. Nikhil declined a cigar and watched me light mine.

'It's bad for health.'

'Ah, the American motto, like in "God we trust".' I blew the smoke deliberately in Nikhil's direction; the soft breeze carried it away across the treetops. I didn't want any further discussion for a while in this hour of tranquillity, and clicked on the remote. A woman's sweet voice floated across the trees.

'That is Kishori Amoṇkar singing. Listen, she has a wondrous voice. This alaap of Raga Alhaiya Bilaival is wonderfully inspirational. She is singing about the soul of a devotee seeking solace from the Almighty.'

'Did burning the painting give you solace?' Nikhil asked when the song ended and silence drifted in between us.

'Some. I burned everything that belonged to her. Some people are born with a limited capacity for love. I'm one of them. I loved your mother and couldn't summon the strength to love again. It takes courage to fall in love; I'm not brave enough to risk my soul.'

'Lakshmi?'

'We're friends. While your mother was alive, and as we weren't divorced, I could have an affair with a clear conscience—that was my excuse for not marrying again. I'm old and have the right to be embittered. You're too young. You must get married again.' I smiled. 'I suppose we have that much in common, we both lost the women we loved. But we're only two of the many millions throughout time to have loved and lost.'

'Maybe I want to grow up to become a divorced, arrogant, rude recluse,' he said and smiled.

I laughed. 'A laudable ambition, but you don't have the talent for it.' I studied my son. 'I believe that having you as a child growing up in my home would have made me more human. Would you agree?'

'Probably,' Nikhil smiled. 'Then again, you might have made me miserable.'

'I have a talent for that too,' I admitted, and sank back into my music, soothed by the song for a long while. He seemed relaxed too, legs outstretched, but I noticed he only sipped at his drink.

The girl emerging silently from the shadows on bare feet startled Nikhil. She came to stand beside me and I placed an arm affectionately around her shoulder, drawing her closer.

'My cook's daughter informs me that it's dinner time. I send her to the local school. One day she'll become a teacher, she says.'

'It's Ruth, isn't it?'

'How do you know that?' He told me then how he had stood outside the gate trying to write me a letter when Ruth jumped down from the wall. I didn't confess that I was in a wretched state of literary constipation in my efforts to write a letter to him probably around the same time.

Ruth turned shyly towards Nikhil and I noticed a ring hanging on a string around her neck. I reached out and held it. It looked like someone's wedding ring. I noticed Nikhil staring at it but when he put out his hand she drew away sharply.

'What's that she has around her neck?'

Ruth whispered into my ear and I smiled. 'She says a prince gave her the ring. She never saw him—he dropped it into her outstretched hand. She believes one day the prince will come on a great white horse and carry her away to his palace. And there she'll live happily ever after.'

I tousled her head. 'How I wish we could remain children and believe in ever-after love.' She tugged at my hand. I finished my second drink and rose to accompany her. She gestured to me to bend down and whispered into my ear. 'Ruth says you have a couple of visitors. This place is becoming like a train station now. You had better see them. It's my dinner time but take your time,

Ethiraj will keep your food warm. Ruth will show them up.'

I was pleasantly surprised to discover that I had enjoyed my son's company on the balcony. He had been respectful, silent when I wished and his presence had been reassuring. He hadn't imposed himself, taken command or disturbed my tranquillity. I ate my phulkas and subzi and when Ruth returned from her errand she told me that Nikhil's visitors were a policeman and a young woman. It was the same woman who had questioned her outside the gate, she said. Her innocent admission only confirmed she had been playing truant from school and I lectured her, severe as a headmaster, about the importance of education. I wanted her to be a professor and not a teacher and to dissuade her from dreaming of princes on white horses. They existed only in our mythology; the most she could hope for was a young man on a two-wheeler in this city.

I retreated to my bedroom, instinctively locking the doors but, after some thought, unlocked them. I didn't know why. I didn't expect my son, now a grown man, to seek me out and have me tell him bedtime stories. Would I have had the patience for a child? Although Nikhil had said I could've made his life miserable, I didn't believe I would have. I would've revelled in that experience, even as my mother had, telling us stories of Rama, Bhima, Hanuman, Tipu, and singing sweetly and softly as my brother and I fell asleep. I had missed this pleasure with my own child. I only had the comfort of my books and settled back to continue reading Marquez's *Living to Tell the Tale*. I had his entire oeuvre; his country and its characters were so similar to ours. I read half a dozen books simultaneously, gulping them down like a sleeping potion, including J.D. Salinger's biography by his daughter, reread others like Nehru's *Letters to his Daughter*, the original 1878 imprint of *the Madras Journal of Literature and Science*, Romila Thapar's *History of India*. I seldom read fiction. Before I slept, I always read a few slokas from the Gita, they comforted me for the night ahead.

nikhil

All my life had been spent in western clothes, and the flowing kurta, well below knee-level, and the narrow-legged pyjama was an outfit from the wardrobe department. I felt like a fake; I was playing a role. Was it this easy to claim an identity? I decided to remain in it one night, in the hope I would eventually feel comfortable. I waited in my room like a small boy banished in punishment till 7.30 p.m.

Downstairs, I had faced the easel and lifted the black cloth to see what lay beneath. My father had crept up to me, quiet as a cat. 'It was of your mother,' he said and stood beside me, both of us looking at the empty frame. 'A friend painted it, just after we married. It was a birthday present. I burned it. I kept the frame as a reminder.' I wondered why he had but couldn't ask just yet. We were still formal, like guest and host, despite him admitting that I was his son. It was a heavy, ornate gilt frame, more appropriate for Rembrandts, Botticellis and Goyas. Was it meant to represent a window into a vanished soul, a tunnel through which he viewed a happier past? I imagined him standing here gazing through the opening for hours on end as if it were a movie screen on which he could recreate my mother as he wanted her to be, but not really wanting to see her. Memory could be less painful than the real images, even a painting. He must have burned all the photographs too, as mom had, though I pretended to believe the lie that she had lost them.

I listened to his music. I believed now that I'd worn the correct clothing for the song. It seeped through the fabric, filtered through my skin, lodged inside me. I floated with that voice across the trees and to the sky.

I had thought of telling my father that it was my wedding ring on Ruth's neck, dropped into her palm just hours after my arrival. But then she had been playing truant as a beggar child and I didn't want to get her into trouble. I wished I could take it away—it hadn't brought me luck or happiness—but maybe her innocent dreams could transform it into her good luck charm.

I don't know why, but I stood respectfully as my father left the terrace with Ruth. I had never stood up when Gary left the room. I walked around possessively in this safe haven, looking up at the stars, across the trees and the lights of the city. If it had been possible I would've opened my arms wide and embraced them all. My glass was empty. I refilled it and went to my chair. Then I moved to the chaise longue like a child about to do something forbidden. I sat gently—it was still warm from his body—then lay back to see what my father saw. The trees weren't visible, only the stars and the moon. I understood why, with such company, my father treasured solitude.

Footsteps, quick and urgent, and the soft tinkle of bangles, disturbed my thoughts.

'Where's the great S.K. Naidu?' Manian's voice demanded.

'Gone,' I said, looking up, not at him but at Apu, who drifted by and stood near the railing and looked up at the stars.

'I wanted to read him my poetry. He would be a man of appreciative tastes, unlike you. Where is my evidence?'

'Chained in the garden,' I said, my eyes still on Apu. Her arms were tightly folded and she didn't seem aware of her surroundings.

'Why would anyone poach a baby croc?'

'It's a diabolical scheme. They export them as babies to America, grow them to twenty-seven feet and then they can get a hundred handbags from their skins.'

'Why not just send the skins?'

Apu turned halfway to look at me. She smiled.

'All wildlife skin exports, snake, tiger, deer, crocodile are banned,' he said. 'Live animals too.'

I wished Manian would leave and take Renee with him. 'Have you found who the "they" are?'

'Yes, one Ramesh and one Arun Chakravarthy, an American. I'll catch them. I wanted to check whether the evidence was safe.' He looked up and around and waited, hoping for an invitation to remain but I was watching Apu. She moved from the railing to the chair. I was happy she did that, it meant she planned to stay a while. We fell silent, ignoring Manian until, finally, he waved and left us alone together.

'Drink? There's only scotch.' She shook her head. 'You all right?

'Fine,' she tried to smile.

'Was that your Arun?'

She smiled wryly. 'Some detective! I should have investigated him.'

'It wasn't your fault. You said he was the friend of a good friend back in the States.' I was going to add tritely 'I'm sorry', but as I wasn't, I kept silent. I was actually quite elated, as if I'd been circling a high wall and had suddenly come upon an open wicket gate I'd not noticed before.

'Yes. But even friends can't guarantee a person's integrity or honesty. How can a father guarantee his son's good behaviour? He and Ramesh were in school together here and they cooked up this get-rich-quick scheme. Ramesh is like that but I didn't think Arun would be.'

'Where is he?'

'Skipped back to the States, I guess.'

'It could've happened to Philip Marlowe too,' I said gently, wanting to ease her pain.

'Probably. He always fell for the crooks. The women either shot him or he sent them to prison.'

We sat in comfortable silence. She shifted her chair so both of us faced the stars. Tendrils of her perfume and the smell of the jasmines in her hair drifted across. It reminded me of our first night here. My father had remarked on how a man had to make up his mind when he met a woman. A friend? A lover? A mother? How, if you began with one relationship, did you change midway to the other? Lover to friend? That was possible. Friend to lover? I was uncertain. Karen and I had gone easily from one to the other. I sensed Apu had come for a reason, apart from showing Manian where the croc was hiding out.

'What'll you do now?'

She laughed. 'Wait for my mother to find another boy. Man, I should say. She's getting desperate.'

'What about you? You won't find your own?' She shook her head and I continued recklessly. 'You're really afraid of falling in love, aren't you? You're afraid of making your own decision. You want to limit your emotional choice to the man you marry so you will have to love him. This cuts out all the risk. Falling in love is a risk and it hurts bad at times.' She remained silent. 'What happens if you never love the man you're married to? You ever think about that?'

'I will,' she said quietly. 'You first like the person, then when you're married, you give free rein to your emotions. It's hard explaining something like this to a westerner. Arranged marriages have worked for thousands of years.'

'So has falling in love.'

'If your father arranged a marriage for you today, would you accept the girl?'

'Of course not. I would need to know her a lot better before I committed myself to marriage.'

She smiled. 'You mean sleep with her first, don't you? That's usually what men mean when they want to know a woman better.' She stood and stretched. 'Any luck with your father giving you permission to do the play?'

'Not yet,' I rose too, reluctantly, wanting her to remain, to hold her hand. 'I'm running out of time. Whatever happens, I'll leave after meeting my grandmother.'

'And what about Renee?'

'God knows what's happening there. If she's still with me I'll take her back and feed her the pigeons in Central Park.'

We went down the stairs side by side, remembering the time we had climbed up in the dark in search of a man. I wished now I'd not committed myself to a time frame. How long would it take to get to know her better? I wasn't sure. We crossed the hall and went out. Her car was parked under the porch. I opened the door and we stood close together.

Apu put out her hand. 'In case I don't see you again, good luck with her and your father.'

I took her hand and drew her towards me. She didn't resist, watching me gravely. When I lowered my mouth to hers, she responded to my kiss. I had never felt such incredible softness. As her kiss lingered on, her eyes closed, and I sensed she was remembering another lover. Then she withdrew.

'I think I should tell you that even before I knew Arun was involved with the crocodile poaching, I'd decided not to marry him.' She touched my cheek quickly in parting.

'You did?'

'Yes. Our horoscopes didn't match.'

I laughed. 'You believe in that mumbo-jumbo?'

'Yes, I do. I have these beliefs in the same way that you have yours. Your mother must have believed in matching horoscopes too when she married.'

'Sure, she believed, and look where it got her.'

'Stars don't create love, they only point the way to it, like the North Star guiding ancient mariners across the sea.' She shut the door and started the car.

I watched the tail lights fade into the night. Having avoided Mom's attempts to convert me to astrology as a science of prediction, I wondered whether I should believe in it now. I had my birth date, the exact time, the exact place. So, would an astrologer match my stars with Apu's or discover that the heavens thought us incompatible? I looked up to the stars, wanting them to guide me through the shoals.

Too wide awake to sleep and not hungry at all, I knocked a few balls around in the billiard room, then opened another door leading into a darkened room. I found the switch for the light. It was the library. The room glowed. The floor was polished teak and against the walls were rosewood cabinets reaching the ceiling. They reminded me of the townhouses on the Upper East Side, between Lex and Third, with small and large arches of glass doors and windows set in the scrolled wood leading to the books. There were keys in the locks of the doors. I strolled past these silent houses, passing rows of leather-bound law books, my grandfather's, and rows of hardbacks of great writers. Balzac, Chaucer, Dickens, Eliot (George and T.S.), Faulkner, Grass, Hemingway. Zola would be at the end, in the basement. History and science, religion and philosophy, they were all in their well-ordered places reflecting an almost military mind for perfection. In my own limited library, Molière was next to Simon, Albee beside Mamet. There were great leather armchairs, well-worn with use, with footstools in front of them. Behind them, poised like inquisitive flamingos, were antique lamp stands with green glass shades angled for the light to fall on the reader's book. On a low table was a telephone. I picked it up and smiled at the silence. A shelf of manuscripts, neatly standing on end, caught my eye. I opened the door and counted twenty-seven of them, each neatly bound. I knew my father was their author. It was his life's work, typed out by Rani each night. Here were the keys to my father's mind and heart. I took one out. The first page had only the title *A Virtuous House*, no author. I took down another, *Urmila*, also authorless. I read the titles of all twenty-seven manuscripts. Not one had the author's name in it. 'Urmila'—the very simplicity intrigued me. I tucked it under my arm and went out.

I read myself asleep and awoke with Urmila on my mind. She reminded me of my mother. Not entirely, just fractured glimpses that stirred memory. I took the manuscript down with me and wandered through the rooms until I found the dining room. The polished mahogany table would have sat twenty, the chairs awaited them. A place was set only at one end, its back to the window and the lawn. Ethiraj was waiting beside the table. I asked for coffee and Ethiraj brought it, along with a plate of dosais. He watched and waited while I ate.

'Gone one chicken,' he announced. 'It ate.'

I wasn't thinking of chickens but Ethiraj waited for a response. 'How much?'

'Two hundred.'

I paid him for Renee's meal, a Kentucky Fried would have been cheaper. I tossed down another two hundred. 'And get some steaks for her, that chicken was pretty scrawny.'

I followed Ethiraj into the kitchen, drew a bucket of water and took it out to her. She was asleep and I left the water by her side. I lay back on the chair, recalling the softness of Apu's lips and, thinking about the kiss; there had been a hint of passion in her response. My kiss had reminded her of someone. Then I thought about Urmila, who had left her family for another man. The novel was poignant, beautifully written, the style more mature than in *Georgetow n*. I had just reached the start of her new life in Delhi with her lover when a hand suddenly grabbed the manuscript and jerked it out of my hand.

s.k. naidu

I awoke refreshed and wondered why I experienced a pleasurable sensation till I remembered that my son was with me in my house. It was still dark when I performed the suryanamaskar on the balcony. When surya finally rose and blessed me with his brilliance, I bathed and dressed. Mary knocked at the precise time. I knew she waited outside, always early, and brought in my morning coffee along with Rani's typed pages and the morning newspaper. It was a comforting routine that sustained me. As usual, she wandered around my spartan room, looking for enough space to set down the tray and, like always, she placed it on the dresser.

'Did Nikhil stay up late?'

'Late, dinner not,' she grumbled as she went out of the door. Their routine had been upset waiting up for my son to have his dinner before they locked up.

I read the paper and then moved to my study to work for an hour on Rani's pages. Despite all the years of working for me in the evenings, and no matter how much more I paid her, she remained sloppy and careless. I couldn't imagine how she managed to earn a living typing documents in her little booth. I went down at exactly 8.35 a.m. for breakfast and Ethiraj informed me that Nikhil had already eaten and was sitting in the garden. He was grumbling about a missing chicken and I hoped it had flown the coup. Beside my plate was a letter. I read it and took it along with me.

Nikhil sat in an easy chair in the deep shade of the wood apple tree. I thought of warning him that the fruits were as hard as cricket balls and he should move to a safer place. Beside him, chained to the tree, was his crocodile. I watched from afar, they seemed to be at peace with themselves and each other. The garden too was peaceful and quiet.

He was reading a manuscript and I presumed it was his play until I drew nearer. The initial shock soon turned to outrage when I recognized the familiar red cover of one of my manuscripts. I had been violated. I rushed down the last few steps and snatched it from his hands.

'How dare you enter my library and take this manuscript without my consent?' I shouted down at him, unable to control my temper. 'I didn't give you permission to sneak around the house.'

Nikhil sat up, shocked. He blinked, then stood up. He said mildly, 'Hey, I didn't sneak around and break down any doors. I was looking for something to read. A book is meant to be read, not hidden away.'

'I didn't give you permission, and you have no right. . .'

'God, permission, permission. You sound like a bureaucrat, for chrissake. This country's strangling in red tape. I didn't see any shitty forms to fill in triplicate, there was no peon guarding the door.'

'Don't you use such language in front of your father. Is that how that woman Sushima raised you?'

'And now you're my father?' Nikhil mocked. 'I didn't give you permission to claim that role. You're still a stranger to me and will probably remain one always.'

'Nothing would suit me better. Your presence has totally disrupted my routine and my thoughts. She sent you to haunt me, to remind me of her betrayal because she couldn't do it herself.'

'She's never left this house. You're still obsessed with her, you keep her alive in your thoughts. She's dead, she's been vaporized into ashes.' He grabbed Renee's chain, unknotted it. 'C'mon Renee, we're checking out of this asylum.'

He dragged Renee; she skidded along the grass, unable to keep pace, nearly strangling. I remained under the tree, clutching my manuscript. No one ever read my writing, apart from Rani.

'Your grandmother has given permission for you to visit her.'

'No doubt in triplicate,' Nikhil shouted back.

I sat on the chair abruptly, holding my novel. I glanced at the title—*Urmila*—written twenty-seven years back and barely remembered. It was the principle of privacy, I reasoned to myself. And mine had been violated. That was wrong, wrong. There were areas where children weren't permitted to enter their parents' lives—the past and the bedroom. My collection of manuscripts was my past. Those words were mined from the subsoil of my soul; no one had the right to sift through them while I lived, and without my permission. That was wrong. I had left instructions that all the manuscripts would accompany me to the funeral pyre. But then, who had I lost now? A son? I had barely known him, a whisper of a touch in the sixty-five years of my life. I hadn't had time to love him. Now there wasn't any more. At least we had something else in common—quick tempers.

I went into the house. I wouldn't stand out on the balcony and watch him walk away from the house the way I had watched his mother.

nikhil

I chained Renee to a chair in the front veranda and stomped upstairs to my bedroom. I had, 'fastidious' as Mom used to call me, hung my clothes up in the closet, put away shirts, socks and shorts in the drawers. I hauled my suitcase onto the bed and began packing again. I seemed to spend my days packing and unpacking. I picked up *Georgetown*, hefted it, wondering whether to hurl it into the rattan wastebasket by the desk. The thought reminded me of Renee, the time she really, really pissed me off. I could've even slapped her. We were at the end of our marriage, those periods of interminable silence; the only time we talked was when she wanted to communicate her anger or I my desperation to hold on. I had returned home late one evening. I can't remember what we began to argue over. I was at my desk when she stalked over and in cold rage swept all my papers—notes, essays, stage directions, my diary, letters—off the desk and, when they crashed on the floor, kicked at them. I had felt then that my thoughts and emotions in those papers were being trampled on, treated with contempt. How dare you do that to my work, I had screamed as she walked away. What had I done to my father but violate his thoughts and feelings? Those bound, unread, authorless manuscripts were his diaries and I had, however unthinkingly, read them. I stopped packing and sat a long while on the bed, working up the courage. I was afraid I had gone too far. I had searched and found my father, then screamed at him and wounded him. He had every right to be angry; I had no excuse, except my quick temper. I finished packing and went to look for him. He wasn't in the garden or anywhere in the house. I knocked on his bedroom door but no one answered. I remembered then that he had stood on the balcony watching Mom leave him, and made my way there. He was standing in the shade, hugging the manuscript, staring at the lane that lead out to the gate.

'I'm sorry,' I said, swallowing hard like the guilty child I was. 'I shouldn't have taken it without your permission. It was unthinking and disrespectful. I'm also sorry I lost my temper.'

It seemed he hadn't heard me, he remained still. I waited a long time, believing I'd stupidly blown it. We cannot help who we are and, as my mom had said, after the words have popped out you can't pop them back in again. They've lodged like pellets in our memory, never forgotten until we die.

When he turned, I sucked in air. He had grown gaunt and he looked feeble, a much older man, as if time had suddenly hurled him into the future. His stare remained unblinking. Then he walked towards me and I couldn't read his intentions until he put both arms around me and held on to me tightly.

'I believed I had lost you just when I found you because of my inherent bad temper. I shouldn't have shouted. You're not a child. Thank you for giving me another chance.'

s.k. naidu

I held the present in my arms. An old man, I would soon vanish, taking the past with me. In holding my son, I felt my own body of long ago—the sinewy muscles, the strong bones, the beating heart, the steely confidence of youth. I would live on another generation now and, for this, I was grateful my son had returned to me.

I whispered the Gita's sloka I had read the night before:

From anger comes bewilderment,
From that the wandering of the mind,
From this the destruction of the soul:
With soul destroyed the man is lost.

He whispered back, giving me his strength. 'For what it's worth, I thought your writing powerful and very moving. You must have written it just after Mom left.'

'All my best work has been written since she left,' I said wryly and freed him from my embrace. We stood apart, inches away.

'Why not publish it?'

I had to smile. 'I write, as Daphne du Maurier once said, to discover what I think and feel. I've no wish to bare my soul to grubby readers.' I paused. 'I accept your apology,' and then added.

'I apologize too for my outrage. I shouldn't have spoken so harshly. A father should treat his son with respect, even as the son must respect his father.'

'Does love enter the equation?'

'You cannot love someone you don't respect.'

'You respected my mother?'

'Despite her many flaws, yes. Otherwise, I couldn't have loved her. I respected my father too, but he was too remote for love.'

Nikhil dressed in his kurta pyjama for our visit to his grandmother Kumari. I had no affection for her, I'd never had, and made no special concession for her. He wanted to take her flowers and we stopped to buy a dozen red roses, the American symbols of love. I didn't dissuade him.

'I'm really excited I'll be seeing her,' he said, holding the roses. 'Mom didn't tell me much about her, except that Kumari had been angry with her for marrying Gary. In my fairy tale world as a child, I had imagined grandmothers to be warm and loving. Gary's mother, Grandma Barbara, hadn't been unkind to me but my four cousins, the children of Gary's brother and sister, were the ones bathed in all her affection and attention. They were, after all, golden-haired children. I was the dark one, out of place at the Thanksgiving and Christmas tables. Her eyes would slide away from my face like a rain drop off a window pane.'

We stopped at the conservator's office in pursuit of the permit for Renee. I waited in the car, allergic to bureaucracy, and thought of my son sitting at that table, still a child, yet perceptive enough to notice his grandmother's subtle dismissal of him. The image saddened me, he wouldn't have felt out of place at Diwali with me. I also felt a sense of growing unease about our visit to Kumari.

Nikhil returned, waving an envelope with the triumphant smile of a Chamberlin returning from Munich.

'I got it, I got it,' he said as we drove away with the prized possession. 'I can dump Renee in Crocodile Bank tomorrow, and it only cost me . . . ten thousand rupees.' He opened the envelope and looked puzzled. I took it from him, it was written in Tamil. 'It does say that, doesn't it?

I read it, then smiled. 'I'm afraid it doesn't quite say that.'

'But Natarajan said . . .'

I laughed and read out the fatal line. ' ". . . permit to return the *Crocodylus palustris* to its native place on completion of said research".'

'What the hell does that mean? Where's its native place?'

'Where it was born, and lived. We all belong to a native place, we call it our ancestral place. It's the place where our ancestors came from and where our families once lived. Renee has to be returned to her native place, the river from where she was poached.'

'And where's that river, for chrissake? She wouldn't know one river from another.' He slumped back in the seat and closed his eyes. 'How will I find it?'

'Ask your detective, Apu. I'll bet she knows how, she's a very enterprising young woman.'

He smiled, pleased at the thought of seeing her again. I was happy with my suggestion—at least they would meet again.

'Where are we going?' he looked out of the window, the car nudging along a narrow street towards the rear of Kilpauk.

'I have a duty to perform,' I said. 'I would never have done this if you hadn't disrupted my cloistered life. Though I must admit I'm quite enjoying it.'

The car stopped and Prasad got out to open the door. Nikhil followed. We were outside a small hall, painted in fairytale pink with green piping. It stood a few feet behind an open gate, in a garden compound shaded by rain trees. The doors were opened wide to pollute the air with raucous Tamil film music that made me wince. A thousand years of civilization reduced to such cacophony! Prasad hurried ahead of us, smiling to himself, like an usher. There were about thirty men and women in the hall, along with a dozen children, all in their best finery: the women in bright saris and cheap jewellery, the men in placid white, the female children in blouses and long skirts. The children played and shrieked and danced to the music even as their celluloid heroes and heroines danced on the big screens. The adults, separated by an aisle, with women on the left, men to the right, sat on metal folding chairs gossiping loudly. Customs hadn't changed in the years of my exile. They rose respectfully as I passed them, moving towards the dais at the end of the hall. Rani and Shyam, hung with rose garlands, sat on gilt chairs with red cushioning, glowing in each other's company and proud as royalty. Rani wore a rich red sari with a heavy gold border. Her hair was plaited with flowers, marigolds and jasmine, around her neck hung a mangalsutra, the symbol of a married woman. Painfully, she reminded me of the time when Sushima was beside me. I had glowed, though Sushima hadn't. Rani wore bangles of gold and jasmine on her wrists. Shyam wore a cotton dhoti and jiba but was otherwise unadorned, except for the coil of jasmine on his wrist.

They rose as I approached. When I stopped and smiled at them, they prostrated on the bare cement floor and placed their foreheads at my feet. I touched their heads with both hands, raised them up and embraced each in turn, shouting my blessings above the music. I handed them the thick envelope of money that was passed, quick as a baton-change, to a man sitting behind the couple with an open notebook on his lap. I nudged Nikhil forward to shake Shyam's hand and do namaste to a newly shy Rani. Then I stood beside Rani, and Nikhil beside Shyam, while the photographer flashed a dozen stills for their album. Prasad joined us for more photographs and then came other guests, including Mr and Mrs Ethiraj and Ruth, all wishing to be frozen in time with Mr S.K. Naidu and his foreign son.

We sat on folding chairs placed beside the wedding couple. Befitting his origin, they offered Nikhil a Coca-Cola, while I received sweetened tea. I politely declined the plates of bright yellow jalebis and dark brown gulab jamuns. Nikhil didn't have that privilege and both Rani and Shyam insisted he join their spare feast in celebration. We sat for ten minutes while the children continued to play and dance. I watched them intently, as if searching for Sushima again.

When we were in the precious silence of the car, Nikhil said, 'Mom had kept her wedding sari, along with your novel. There was also a coil of flowers. I think they were jasmine. They crumbled into dust when I lifted the book out.'

'I always wondered what she had carried away in that case,' I said. 'Why did she preserve that memory of us?'

'I don't know. I couldn't ask her. It was her secret; I wasn't meant to discover it.'

'Where did you marry Renee? In a church?'

'No, in City Hall, downtown Manhattan,' he said, and shrugged it away. 'It was a brief ceremony. We said "I do" to each other, there was no incense, no music, no sonorous slokas, no cascading colours, no children. Only a drab bureaucratic office. Renee had carried a bouquet of roses and worn a white, demure dress. I had worn a suit. It was a popular day, early spring, and there must have been another forty couples getting married too, kind of a nuptials assembly line. My mother and her mother were the witnesses.'

'Her father?'

'Her parents had divorced. He was somewhere in Texas with his new wife. My stepfather was in LA on business. After the wedding, we went back to the apartment for a big party. I remember more about the party than the actual wedding. We had our friends over, around thirty couples, and I think quite a few affairs either broke up or started that night.' He sighed happily.

nikhil

It felt so good to reveal pieces of my life to my father. He listened with such interest, and I knew he was greedy for much more. Admittedly, they were only small dabs on the canvas but over time I would fill it up so that he could see me more clearly.

The car passed the high court, the domes and minarets silhouetted against the dying light. The sky was a fading blue, wounded with great streaks of red and orange. We crossed the Esplanade and entered Georgetown along Armenian Street, edging through the thick congestion with the loud horn as a prow to clear a path.

'How should I address her?'

'As ava, that's grandmother,' my father said. 'By the way, I didn't tell her you're Sushima's son.'

'Why not?' I asked, although I suspected it was because I seemed to upset the past order.

'I thought it best to surprise her.'

'I bet she will be. Who did you say I was?'

'A relation wishing to pay his respects.'

'How long has it been since you saw her last?'

'Not since your mother left me.'

The car passed familiar sights, but as it moved further north, following turns according to the one-way signs, I was on unfamiliar lanes. I hadn't walked this far in my search. The streets remained as busy as ever, as if people had no time for sleep. The neon lights from the shops covered the streets in a blue haze. But soon the commerce gave way to quiet places of residence. Prasad made another turn onto Pedariyar Koil Street and into a deep silence. We passed a temple and stopped in front of a shuttered house with a massive teak front door. The walls were off-white and no light could be seen inside. There was a small circular porch before the door. The floor was covered with the leaves of a neem tree that grew out of the blacktopped street. My father climbed out and stood looking at the silent house for a long time.

'When I first came here with my parents to meet her parents, the whole house was ablaze with lights,' he said softly in a voice drenched with memories. 'The windows were wide open and all the relations were framed in them, looking down at us. The street was alive with people too. The door was wide open and her parents stood just inside the threshold, waiting to welcome us. Her mother carried a silver tray with bowls of kumkum and sandalwood paste and a string of jasmine. Out on the street as well as on the floor of the porch was an intricate, many-coloured kolam. I think the one on the street was of a peacock with its tail spread; the one under the small porch was a good luck swastika. I followed my parents around the kolams so as not to disturb their harmony and we went into the house.'

He held his breath then let it out, emptied of those memories. Two steps led up to the porch and another three to the door. There were no elaborate kolams now, just a vague faded pattern of white rice powder. He lifted the brass knocker and let it drop, once, twice, and we could hear the echo of an empty house. We waited for the shuffle of bare feet, then the bolts were drawn back and a servant girl opened the door.

She couldn't have been more than fourteen and spoke with some asperity to my father.

'S.K. Naidu,' he replied.

She stepped aside to let us enter a gloomy corridor, lit by a bare bulb. The doors on either side were closed. We followed her towards the light at the end and stepped out into the courtyard.

I stopped at the edge of an oasis. 'It's exactly the way you described it in your novel.'

I looked first at the flooring—it was a field of glazed flowers in natural earth colours. Above my head was the netting and the clear night sky. On all four sides, graceful columns of teak held up the arches that supported the red tiled roofs over the aisles. Above was another floor with similar pillars and arches, and wooden railings of a deep rich blue. In the centre of the courtyard, a marble fountain, shaped like a lotus, bubbled with water that flowed down through canals, cooling the air. Large terracotta pots with flowering plants, cannas, bougainvillea, and wide spreading palmyras gave the impression we were in a garden. I thought of Mom growing up here, there was enough space in this courtyard for a child to play many games. I wanted to see the room she had slept in, breathe the air and touch all the things once familiar to her touch. At the far end, rattan chairs with high curved backs were placed around a low table. The only intrusion into this tranquillity was the television blaring loudly. A woman sat facing the television, her back to us.

The servant girl led us towards the television and whispered to the woman. She replied and the girl left reluctantly. They had been watching *Bay watch*. I moved to stand behind my grandmother, and looked down at the perfectly white hair. It was tied in a neat bun, circled by a string of fresh jasmine. She wore a white cotton sari and a white choli, no jewellery, not even a bangle. I wondered whether she still strung the flowers herself, as Mom had said she did while giving me a glimpse into her family's routine. A commercial break broke the spell.

'I believe American women were genetically created for those swimsuits,' my grandmother spoke in a soft, accented voice. She gestured for us to step into her line of vision. Father went first, steeling himself it seemed. He looked at her, did namaste, then averted his face too quickly, before taking a seat. I followed him and understood why he had turned away. I was looking at my mother, many years older, and I too was suffocated with melancholy. Her image lay in the perfection of the face and dark deep-set eyes, the high cheekbones. My grandmother's coppery skin was barely wrinkled, but had loosened with age. She acknowledged my presence with a quick, perfunctory touch of her palms. Her eyes were on my father.

'I got your note. Why did you want to see me after all these years?'

'Him.'

She turned to examine me, taking in my clothes and the flowers before looking into my face. She blinked, as if trying to remember whether we had met before.

'What about you?'

'I'm Sushima's son,' I smiled and held out the bouquet. She ignored them.

Her eyes snapped to my father angrily. 'Why didn't you tell me?'

'I knew you would refuse to see him. He's come a long way.'

'I've no daughter by that name,' she said in a flat voice.

Oh shit, I thought, trying to control my anger at the venom in her voice. But I wouldn't stand for this shit from her, grandmother or not.

'I was mistaken. I thought you were my mother's mother.'

I wanted to get out of this house, as unwelcome here as I had been in my father's. Here too my mother had left behind her debris of destruction by falling in love.

'Sit,' she commanded. 'You're as impulsive as her.' And when I didn't obey, she continued. 'I'm an old woman, not used to such surprises and shocks.' She turned to glance quickly behind her. 'Where is she? I refuse to see her.'

'You won't have to. She's dead.'

If my father had been lashed by my announcement, Kumari's face remained as impassive as if I'd delivered a weather report. She acknowledged the death of her daughter with only a curt nod of her head. She couldn't lower it further in grief. There was no grief left; death was the final parting of her flesh and blood. She didn't ask how Mom had died, so young still, or how she had lived.

'I told you to sit.' She said. 'I thought you reminded me of someone.'

I smiled. 'You want me to do tricks as well?'

'You're the son of your mother, she would also answer back. She wasn't a good daughter, she showed no respect.' Her voice rose, suddenly giving voice to her buried anger. 'She disgraced and dishonoured our family with her cheap behaviour, running off with that foreigner.'

'That's history,' I reigned in my anger. Be cool, be patient, I told myself.

'Nothing is ever past; it remains in the present as long as we draw breath. She remains a wound, bleeding into my memory.'

'Hey, ma'am, so why am I to blame? I didn't cause the pain. Listen, I didn't even know you existed, she never talked about you.'

'Just like Sushima,' was all she could say and it sounded like an insult. She rose, 'Wait,' and left us to the television. The servant girl returned with a tray of tea and biscuits. We refused politely.

My grandmother's behaviour took away some of my disappointment. I wasn't going to be angry or dejected, though the shit was falling on my head. I looked up at the netting, remembering Mom's dream of that multi-coloured bird trying to escape this house. I couldn't blame her; I felt the walls closing in on me in the face of Kumari's hostility.

My father was speaking, rewinding memory. ' . . . and when the time came for me to meet Sushima, she emerged from that room, out of the shadow, wearing a wonderful pale lemon sari with a darker choli, the pallu drawn over her head. I believed then I was to marry a woman who would always perform her wifely duty to her husband.'

I looked over, my father's face was distant, still looking towards a long shut door to his left.

Kumari returned with a bag, opened it, and drew out four airmail envelopes. She passed them over to me.

'Your mother wrote to me after leaving with that man. You can have them.'

It was Mom's writing, probably only a single sheet each as the envelopes were thin. She was a talker, not a writer. I checked the stamped dates. The first one was probably written on her arrival in New York, the second announced her marriage to Gary, the third, seven months later, was about my birth, and the final one a year later. I figured it would have been her 'Drop Dead' letter. I turned them over, surprised. 'They've not been opened. Why didn't you open them?'

'I knew what they would contain,' Kumari said. 'I kept them to throw in her face when she returned. I couldn't forgive her for her weakness. She had succumbed to lust and love like a cheap woman. It was her duty to remain married, just as it was my duty to remain married. It's written in the Vedas, the Upanishads, the Sutras, that we must be bound by our duty. There can be no other consideration than duty.'

'You never told me she'd written,' my father said sharply.

'She deserved my silence and yours.'

'I could've made that decision myself,' he said, looking at the letters, possibly believing that in them there could have been reconciliation.

'She was *my* daughter, I made the decision.'

'But she had left your household for mine. *I* was her husband.'

Kumari ignored him. She drew out a large envelope. 'These are photographs of your mother, from her childhood to her marriage. Her life ended there for me.'

I didn't take the photographs. 'You envied her spirit and her free will. She wasn't about to be trapped by some archaic concept of duty and fall into the same ruins of your life. She fell in love and that's what you couldn't forgive. She didn't deserve a mother like you.'

'And I didn't deserve a child like her,' Kumari said spitefully.

'No wonder she escaped from you.' I held onto the letters, believing I felt my mother in them. I would've liked to read them but, again, they were history. 'I loved my mother deeply and have good memories of her. I don't need this, it only tells me how unhappy she was in this house.'

I dumped the letters on Kumari's lap as I passed her on my way out and found I was still holding the flowers. I dropped them in the marble fountain.

'You should've told me about her letters,' I heard my father say. 'I deserved that much respect.'

I turned to wait for him to join me and saw her brush the letters off her lap as if they were crumbs.

'Burn them,' she told the servant girl, 'at once.'

I remembered that, in the novel, my father had drawn Kumari as a strong yet warm character. He hadn't scratched down further because he was blinded by his love for mom. I also remembered mom's scribbled comment in the margin beside that description—'my mother fooled you too'.

'I better rewrite her character in the play,' I said, making it sound light, as if she were a typo, but feeling painfully depressed as we went out.

'That was bad judgement on my part,' he said gently. He put his arm around me. 'I'm sorry, truly sorry for her behaviour.'

'Hey, it's not your fault, Pop.'

'Pop! You'll Americanize me yet. I have something for you.' He slid a hand into the deep pocket of his jiba, drew out an envelope and gave it to me. 'I thought this would be a celebration.'

I opened the envelope. The letter was brief, it granted me all the rights to his novel *Georgetown*.

apu

I knew when he drew me near that he was going to kiss me. I could've pulled back, shaken his hand and climbed into the car, but

I wanted to feel a man's mouth again, to feel its passion and be reminded of Balraj. Nikhil's mouth was different, not pressing down hard with wanting and passion, but gentle and questioning. Could he go further? I felt confused then and pulled back, still savouring his kiss. I wasn't sure why I had accompanied Manian; may be to let Nikhil know that I too was disappointed. I was thankful the relationship with Arun hadn't had the time to flare into love. That would have been agony. The decision to break it off had been made before love took a stranglehold.

I had told Nikhil I decided not to marry Arun because our horoscopes didn't match. That was a lie, they had matched almost perfectly.

When Nikhil called to tell me about the mix up with the permit it felt as if the stars were shifting around so we could be with each other for a while longer. I picked him up at dawn and told him that Manian had been relieved to drop the case and clear the crocodile off his desk. He had released Ganesha in my custody and dropped the poaching charges as the letter from the conservator's office was justification enough.

I borrowed a Maruti Gypsy to accommodate Renee for her journey home to her ancestral place. Ganesha sat in the back, relieved to be out of the clutches of the police. The poor thing had been imagining spending his whole life in handcuffs and being cuffed by irate cops. He sat beside Renee, crooning, telling her she would soon be among family.

It was still cool and the traffic thin as I drove south along the highway. It was a comfortable silence until Nikhil spoke.

'I'm sorry about what I said to you a few days back. I thought you were just scared to fall in love. You were in love once, weren't you? And hurt pretty bad.'

I looked at him, then away at the road, thinking how transparent I had been. I would tell him everything when I was ready. We were clear of the city's clutter, moving south, passing rice fields and mango groves, sunflower and red chilly fields. We passed through a firework of bright colours. Neat children in school uniforms trailed along dirt lanes to join others on the main highway heading for their schools. Despite the car's speed, it grew warmer, more humid as the sun rose, blinding us.

'Yes, I was in love,' I said finally, many miles later. I'd never spoken of this to anyone before. It was hard to pry open my heart; it had closed long ago. I glanced at him. He was patient, waiting for my story.

'It wasn't meant to happen . . .'

'It never is.'

'I didn't expect it to happen and when it did, I didn't know how to deal with it. We think of love a lot, wanting it and dreaming of it, but never knowing how it'll happen and with whom. All your life you're standing in shadow and then you find yourself suddenly in sunlight. You think the tree has moved but it's the sun that's moved and found you. It warms you first, then burns you. I was twenty-two . . .' I told him how my parents weren't exactly overjoyed at my quitting the college teaching job to become a private detective. Of course, Amma blew her top. How could she tell prospective sons-in-law that their bride-to-be was a detective, sniffing into people's private lives? I had slid down the social ladder of respectability in her eyes.

'Of course, he was married.' Then added with spirit to justify what had happened. 'But they had no children.'

'Of course not,' I heard the cynicism in his tone but ignored it.

'We went to Bangalore on a divorce case . . .'

He was a good listener and I was emptying myself, even losing my breath at times. I poured out everything, even about our passion in our chinnawheedu.

I looked around when I finally stopped talking. We were on a Ghat road, on either side were thick, almost impenetrable jungles. Ganesha sniffed the familiar air, smiling happily, telling Renee she was near her home.

'Madam must turn there,' he interrupted and pointed to a clear grass patch off the road.

I turned off and followed a narrow grassy track. It was twilight in the jungle. Trees towered around us and shrubs pressed in on both sides, impatient to reclaim this opening into its heart. The air was glasshouse hot and still. Silvery langurs, harvesting fallen fruit, bounded up trees in fright and boomed out their warnings to other creatures. They looked down on us with angry wizened faces. A herd of grazing cheetal turned towards us, poised for flight, watching us with curiosity and fear. Wild pigs scuttled for cover, squealing their warnings. Birds shrieked from treetops, peacocks called their alarms. We had intruded into another world and upset its wary inhabitants, accustomed to different dangers.

'Tiger, one or two hours passed,' Ganesha pointed down to the soft ground as the Gypsy passed a curve. He had seen the fresh pugmarks, and looked around, lifting his head to smell. We passed elephant droppings, large as canon balls and disintegrating. The litter of their feeding, snapped branches and uprooted saplings, had cut a swathe through the jungle.

'Will we see it?' Nikhil asked, eager to see a tiger. Ganesha shrugged, waving to the dense undergrowth.

'It would be camouflaged by the stripes of sunlight and shadows. It could be sitting ten feet away and you wouldn't see it.'

We drove for half a mile, the jungle's alarms rippling around us.

'What happened then?' Nikhil asked. 'Why didn't you marry him? Couldn't he get a divorce?'

'He was working on that,' I said, surprised at my own calm. 'And I was planning to break the news to my parents that I was finally going to get married. It wasn't an arranged marriage but a love match.' I sighed, smiled wryly and tried to keep my voice as flat as the engraving on a tombstone worn down by grief. 'He was walking along Thambu Chetty Street in Georgetown—not on work, just shopping—when a stray bullet hit him. No one knew where it had come from. I imagined it circling and circling the world and then, in the dense crowd, it found him. It was meant for him, I wasn't.'

'Did you investigate his death?'

'No. I didn't have the strength for that. The cops did and they said it could've been an old enmity. Murder always comes out of the past.'

I stopped the Gypsy at the river's edge. Ganesha jumped out, his feet finally on familiar earth and not on the cold stone of the city. We sat in the car, staring at the water. The river was about forty feet across, and clear as a child's mind. It flowed swiftly on its journey down from the Ghats, bubbling with happiness, bouncing around the rocks, foaming with joy. The sun caressed the surface, turning it to gold in places and trees shaded it near the banks. On the opposite bank, among the rocks and in the shade, we spotted three or four of Renee's relations.

Nikhil brushed my cheek with a soft kiss. 'It's my turn, I'm sorry. When did it happen?'

'Five months ago.'

I thought I would cry again but there were no tears left. I felt I had woken finally and forever from a long illness into sunlight.

'When does grieving stop?' I pressed my face against his palm.

'I don't know. I think it just fades away to hide somewhere in our memory and then when we're reminded about something, it returns to us.'

'You won't tell anyone . . .'

'Like who?'

I smiled. 'The next possible husband? He'll have to know, I couldn't betray him. He's expecting a virgin on his wedding night. Would it bother you?'

'No, but I come from a different culture.'

'Yes, you do.'

We got out, looking at each other, smiling. Nikhil helped Ganesha lift Renee out of the back and carried her down to the water's edge. She had smelled the river long back, knowing she was returning home. They placed her down tenderly and Nikhil held onto her a moment longer.

'Well, Renee, this is where you were born, your native place,' he said gently. 'Did it make a hell of a difference that you spent a few days in a hotel bathroom? I doubt it. It didn't change you in any way. You know deep down inside that you are this creature we call a crocodile. No one can take what you are away from you. You think, you move, you behave, and maybe you love too, like a crocodile. You don't try to be anyone else, you don't worry whether you should be a tiger or a deer. You aren't confused with longings or dislocated by identity. You are who you are, always. Goodbye, my friend.'

Renee was already moving with certainty down the slope. She paused a moment, smelling the sweet river air, and then slid into the water with a child's glee, causing scarcely a ripple. We both took a step forward to see her under the clear water, kicking with joy as she went deeper and deeper into the shadows. Then she was lost to sight. We waited in silence, hoping to see her join her own kind on the other bank but she didn't surface. Ganesha had stolen away softly into his jungle.

On the drive back to Chennai, Nikhil didn't mention Balraj again. Neither did I. We were in silent agreement that he belonged to my past. He would live on only in my memory. I let Nikhil talk. He was excited about the permission for the play, he was already casting it and seeing it staged. He mentioned names, Aditya, Priyanka, for the main roles, fine Indian-American actors, his set designer, Frank, and the music he would choose. It would run a few weeks in New Haven if he were lucky with the *New York Times* review, the only one that counted. The *Times* could make or break him. Then he would take it on tour to a dozen American cities familiar to me from a geography book. After that, a new play by an American playwright, Betsy Someone. It would be ready in a few months and he was excited about that too. It was about a white American family, set in a suburb. I listened, and from his voice I knew he had already left India. His thoughts were the running-bounding leap of a Superman, but his ankles were trapped firmly in the Kryptonite of India. He was in Manhattan, talking to his actors, Karen, his friends. He was walking down Columbus Avenue, then Broadway, across to Houston. The city came to life in his excitement, and I was meant to see it through his eyes and his feelings. He was taking me there on a magic carpet of words.

Somewhere, I interrupted quietly, 'Tell me about Karen,' and he was surprised that I'd noticed her name. He hesitated, and I waited like he had for me. He told me then about the call, laughing about it, delighted with Karen's affection for him. I learnt about the affair, the friendship, the continuation of their feelings for each other, muted by his marriage to Renee and Karen's affair with Hugh. But both were over their distractions. Although he didn't say it, I knew he would call Karen first, probably from the airport, and they'd meet, hug and kiss. He would be home then, finally.

***

Sarada had come home for dinner. She was six months pregnant. Ramesh was out of station in Delhi. He had become respectable after marriage and worked for a foreign bank. I only hoped he wouldn't regress into one of his crazy schemes.

We went up to my bedroom and she saw the poster. Nikhil had sent it by FedEx, in a tube, without a note. I had unfurled it and pinned it up on my wall of memories, and then sat and watched it as if a film was playing before my eyes. I had acquired this habit as a child. I would watch stones, watch a piece of wood. Amma used to ask why I watched things that didn't move. I had said, when you watched them long enough they revealed their inner movements, you saw the secrets they held back from those who just looked at them. I liked the poster. The light in the background, a pale, washed out blue, suggested dusk. In the foreground, the faint outline of an Indian courtyard, a woman's face was framed in shadow. Her yellow pallu fell over her forehead and she had a faint smile, as if amused by what she saw through the golden bars caging her. She had a bird's body, its brightly coloured wings outstretched for flight. I watched the bird-woman, as if expecting her to fly, and wondered what she meant. Below the woman was the play's title. *Georgetown*, Adapted and Directed by Nikhil Naidu, From the novel by S.K. Naidu.

We went to the balcony and sat in the night. The sea was gentle at this late hour, preparing for sleep.

'Did he propose?' Sarada asked.

'I think he would have. He wanted to return with some piece of India. I was that memento. But I told him I didn't want to live in America. I didn't want the confusion of my friends who come and go annually, snatching at something here they remember only vaguely. They come for three weeks and take huge gulps of India and they hold on to it for the rest of the year while they live in America. They live there, far away, but their thoughts and feelings are back here, their lives fractured by their longing for home. When they go, they should never return but become a part of that American soil. And Nikhil's too American to live here. I'm sure I'll see him again, but as a friend. When we returned from the jungle, he stayed with his father for a week. It was a bit late to be father and son. I think they became friends too. He'll come to see his father once or twice but once his father's dead, he'll have no further reason to come.'

'You're a real mutaal,' Sarada scolded. 'Arre, you like him, I know that. You should've grabbed him with both hands. Now, you're going to be a spinster all your life.'

I laughed. 'I'm not that big a mutaal. We've been in touch on e-mail. He's coming here in a couple of weeks and wants to see me. He wants to talk.'

'About what?'

'We'll see,' I said, watching the silvered sea, the waves seductively caressing the shore, again and again.

nikhil naidu

It was good to be back home, good to be among old friends, good to embrace Karen again. She wanted me to move into her Upper

West Side apartment but I needed space. I had just divorced, I had just met my father, I had my work. She understood, though she was disappointed. We picked up the pattern of our old habits, a weekly dinner, walks along the streets, concerts and plays. *Georgetown* played for four weeks, not bad, and it would move to the Spring Street Theatre, off-Broadway, next fall. The reviews had been good, and encouraging enough for my name to get some recognition. It had given me immense satisfaction to tell my father's story. Yet I felt unsettled and displaced.

The sidewalk outside my window was slushy with newly fallen snow. I had found a small, one-bedroom apartment, rent regulated, on Montague Street, in Brooklyn Heights, above a Greek restaurant. The odours of mousakka and olive oil drifted up between the floorboards. I had furnished the apartment sparely, and I'd hung up a framed poster of *Georgetown* like the one I'd sent Apu. She had e-mailed to ask me what the bird meant. I said I'd tell her when I saw her next. I needed to talk some more to her. The kiss had lingered like an echo that wouldn't fade. Beside the poster was a framed photograph of my mom. I was just a block away from the Promenade and I went out to stand and look across the river at lower Manhattan. The wind chiselled my face. I was a long way from the co-op on the Upper Eastside and Westchester, a long way from my father and Apu, but not far from Mom who had vanished along with the twin towers. I could hear her voice still, and I smiled each time.

'That's why I'm telling you darling, you won't like India at all. Not one bit. You'll hate it. Why? Because you're an American, like me, and you're always so fastidious. India certainly is not that, not in the least. It can be a very deceitful place, and most confusing too. You have absolutely no idea how miserably hot it can get there. You won't just be blackened, you'll be burned to a crisp. Yes, like the burnt offerings I sometimes make for your dinner, if you have to joke about my opinion. I'm only telling you this for your own sake. If you love me—and you do, I know it—you won't even think of going there. Put them out of your mind, for my sake darling. There's nothing there for you.'